Red Bluff
of Tucson

Paul Cox

Llumina
Press

ISBN: 978-1-62500-450-0

Historical Characters Incorporated into Red Bluff of Tucson

Lieutenant Baldwin (Union)
Lieutenant Bascom (Union)
Captain Baylor (Confederate)
Captain Baylor (Texas Ranger)
Mr. Brown
Captain Calloway (Union)
General Carleton (Union)
Cochise
Mangas Colorado
Fritz Contenzen
General Crook (U.S.)
The Earps
Jesus Elias
Santiago Esquibel
Captain Fritz (Union)
James Gillett
Sergeant Holmes (Confederate)
Captain Sherod Hunter (Confederate)
Union scout Jones
Billy the Kid
George Lloyd
Captain McCleave (Union)
Captain McNelly (Texas Ranger)
Manuel Molina
Mr. Morton
Estevan Ochoa
William S. Oury
Palatine Robinson
General Sibley (Confederate)
Al Sieber
Marshal Stoudenmire

Lieutenant Jack Swilling (Confederate)
Lieutenant James Tevis (Confederate)
Soloman Warner
Colonel West (Union)
Ami White
Agent Tiffany
Tribolett
Mickey Free
Private Leonard (Union)
Captain Tom Ross (Arizona Ranger)
Romero
Sergeant Bill Todd (Arizona Ranger)
General Wilcox
Lieutenant Barrett (Union, still buried somewhere in Picacho Pass)

Chapter 1

FEBRUARY 28, 1862

A wind cold enough to burn skin hissed through needles of giant saguaro, around thorns of mesquite, and into the hunched backs of one hundred soldiers. For three weeks the sky had been a churning sea of steel gray clouds. Four days earlier, after emerging from a blizzard in Apache Pass, the snow turned to rain. Now, Company A, Texas Mounted Volunteers, lined both sides of the muddy Overland Stage Road. Bearded, dirty and wet, the handpicked riders sat in stoic silence. Their broad brimmed hats were tugged down tight against the cold. None of them, except Caleb Felton, expected such a winter so far south.

At the head of the column, Captain Sherod Hunter pulled a watch from his pocket and wiped the fog from its glass. One hour of daylight remained. Lieutenant Felton would return soon. Hunter could count on that. The lieutenant was neither Texan nor Arizona Ranger, so when he joined the company, he was only offered the rank of Third Lieutenant. Caleb Felton, whatever he might have been east of the Rio Grande, had proved to be one of the most able men in the outfit. He was certainly best qualified to reconnoiter Tucson.

Hunter's orders from General Sibley were to occupy Tucson, New Mexico Territory, and open communications with Southern California. He was to guard the mineral deposits and protect the citizens of the region as well. Should Hunter encounter Yankee forces he could not defeat, Sibley promised reinforcements from Mesilla under command of Colonel Baylor. However, Mesilla was three hundred desolate miles to the east.

Captain Hunter turned into the wind and glanced back at his small army. With a shotgun or Sharps rifle across every saddle, they sat at the ready. Around the waist of each man, a wide leather belt held a tomahawk, Bowie knife, and two Colt pistols. Most of the Texans had lariats and could entangle an enemy horse on a dead run.

These were seasoned fighters, calloused by life on an unforgiving frontier and used to its freedoms. They signed up as Confederates but at heart they were rebels. Without a gray uniform among them, they looked more like a band of pirates than a company of soldiers.

1

Hunter's men were well armed and on good mounts, but for the most part were guerilla fighters. They could annihilate any Yankee force twice their size in a running battle, yet wouldn't stand a chance if a large trained army was stationed in Tucson.

When Felton ducked into the tent in Mesilla and volunteered for the three-year enlistment, Hunter was skeptical. The Company was nearly full, and this was to be a crucial campaign. There was no room for fools or adventurers.

Hunter re-enlisted as many experienced men from Baylor's Mounted Riflemen and any Arizona Territorial Rangers he could find. Felton appeared to be more like a riverboat gambler and a womanizer. But when Felton, dressed in a suit fit for New Orleans, spoke, his words were those of an educated man. When he suddenly switched to Spanish, his accent was almost flawless. His skin was dark and his eyes brown. When questioned, Felton claimed he was not Spanish. His mother, he said, was the daughter of a Portuguese sea captain. Yet he had the look and mannerisms of a Spanish gentleman. That was enough for Hunter. There would be a need for spies the further west they went, spies that could blend into Mexican villages and towns. Most of Hunter's men had lived in New Mexico Territory, and would be easy to recognize.

When Hunter handed Felton the quill and asked for his full name on the enlistment papers, there was a moment of hesitation. After an explanation that the signature was one of the few regulations Sibley required, Felton signed Caleb Robespierre Felton.

Unfortunately, the Texans, joining one of the most formidable fighting forces since the Alamo, didn't take the dandy seriously. When the latecomer warned everyone to prepare for cold weather, they laughed. Felton smiled along with them. The Portuguese, he explained, had sailed the seas for centuries and could read the skies. His mother had taught him to do the same. It was going to be unusually cold. He said it only once, then quietly went about his business, which included the purchase of a full-length buffalo coat.

Captain Hunter turned out of the wind and looked back toward Tucson. He could see a black speck of movement outlined against a dingy ribbon of muddy road. It was a rider and he was coming fast. Placing the watch deep in his vest pocket, Hunter sat up straight. A minute later, he glanced at Second Lieutenant Jim Tevis next to him. "That's Felton. He can ride like the devil."

Tevis shrugged. "Who would've thought? The way he came into Mesilla, we took him for a tenderfoot. I wouldn't say it to his face, but sometimes I fancy he's part Comanche. He's nothing like what we all thought him to be. Nothing adds up to suit me. I heard some the boys say he can speak some French...and even knows his share of Greek."

Hunter nodded. "Know what you mean, Lieutenant. When he first signed up in Mesilla, he told me he was the son of a hellfire and brimstone Methodist preacher. But before he left, he spent half the days and all his nights in saloons."

"He wouldn't be the first black sheep son of a preacher I ever heard of, Captain. I've seen him enough times in the whiskey shacks to know he's strayed *way* off the straight and narrow. The women in those places stuck to him even if he didn't pay for what they were selling. He doesn't seem to have a care in the world. He's not poor either."

Watching the road intently, Hunter turned up his collar and blew into his cupped hands. "No Yankees dogging him."

An icy blast of wind sent a chill down Tevis's back. "It's cold as hell. You ever tell Felton about that posse that came in lickity-cut just after he signed up? The way they described the man they were chasing sounded mighty close to our Portagee Lieutenant."

The Captain leaned to one side and spit a brown stream of tobacco onto the trunk of a palo verde tree. "Matched a good many of our men, Lieutenant. Including you."

Felton was less than a mile out and closing fast. Tevis smiled. "Recon so, Captain. The men sure took to him. Except Jack Swilling. He's still sore at losing that shindig they had. That son of a preacher can fight like a son of a bitch. Jack's six feet and not easy to get the best of in a row. Never saw any man throw his fists like that. Felton never even tuckered out."

"Jack's a good man. He should have hobbled his tongue. The way I heard it, he was all right until he brought Felton's ma into it. That's when Jack stepped over the line. Sometimes he doesn't know when to stop."

"Sure enough. It was a good joke Jack had going. Even Caleb went along for a while. Grandson of a 'porch of geese captain.' Still a good joke I'd say."

Hunter snorted. "Well, it's Jack and the rest of us that're skinning rabbits to stay warm. I'd say Caleb Felton's been doing most of the laughing since the bottom dropped out of the thermometer."

"I never did see ice on the Rio Grande before. He was on the money there."

"He'll do," agreed Hunter. "He didn't turn a hair when I asked him to go into Tucson alone and scout it out."

"Yeah, I know. I told him I'd lived there a while and there weren't many women in town. He said he was volunteering just so's he could get first crack at what there was of them."

Mud was seen flying from the hooves of Felton's black stallion as he covered the last quarter mile. Sporting his buffalo coat, he rode into the wind with his head barely higher than that of his horse. Man and beast moved as one.

Tevis shook his head. "Damn if he's not part Comanche! Sure as the hinges of hell, rides like one."

In a matter of seconds, Felton was leaning back in his saddle as his horse slid to stop in front of Hunter and Tevis. His coat was covered in mud, as was the red scarf wrapped around his neck and face. Only his brown eyes were exposed to the weather.

Felton pulled the scarf down, revealing a freshly shaven face. He saluted with a smile. "Todos esta bien, Captian. Los Yankees han salido."

"Gone?" questioned Hunter. "Gone where?"

"They left seven months ago, Captain. Went east. Nobody knows where. Just before the soldiers shipped out, the Overland Stage got wind they were leaving, so they went too. The stage used to run through town twice a week, but the entire line shut down, lock, stock, and barrel. Last May they made one big caravan and took off for California.

"Used to have a newspaper called the *Arizonan*. It's gone now. Without the stage, there's no mail, no news. Tucson has been in total isolation. Bandits are coming up from Sonora. An Indian called Cochise and his Apaches have been murdering and stealing at will. There were over two thousand people around town before all this started. Now there's only about twenty whites and three hundred or so Mexicans. Those that are left would hire the Devil himself if he pranced in there and offered to fight the Apaches. The citizens want protection. They'll welcome any military force that offers it with open arms."

Captain Hunter glanced at Felton's smooth face and the scarf. "Where did you get your information, Lieutenant?"

4

"Found a barber," grinned Felton. "I told him I was some kind of fool up from Magdalena looking to file some mining claims and he seemed convinced enough. Nobody knows more about what's going on in a town than the barber, unless there's a barkeep. Getting a shave is less risky than going into a saloon. And barbers love to talk."

While Hunter considered his next move, Tevis' lips curled into a friendly smirk. "Where'd you get that pretty little scarf? You didn't have it when you left."

Felton shrugged and suppressed a smile of his own. "Well, I did meet a nice little señorita in front of the Shoo Fly cantina. When I told her I had to ride back up the stage road into that cold wind, she offered it up."

"Just like that?" asked Tevis, shaking his head. "You beat anything I ever saw."

"You say they'll welcome us," interrupted Hunter. "But we know there are several Union sympathizers in Tucson. Hughes, Contezen, Brady, Warner. Was there any mention of them?"

"No, sir. Right now, the Apaches are the problem. Since the Union soldiers pulled out, more than a dozen people have been murdered. Most of the ranches are in ruins. The stock has run off. Only a man named Pete Kitchen is holding out.

"The mines are mostly shut down. Hardly any supplies can get into town. Fact is, the majority of people feel betrayed by the Union government. The barber kept saying it was 'national neglect of the frontier.' I would say that under present circumstances, anyone voicing sentiment in favor of the Union would run the risk of being tarred and feathered."

"Were there any signs of new fortifications? Did the Army leave anything we can use?"

"No, sir. Except for two or three nice houses and a fair-size church, Tucson's not much more than an adobe windbreak if you asked me. From end to end, the whole town is no more than a quarter mile long and at best, half that wide. There's an old wall around the part of town where most of the people are living, but it's crumbling to pieces. They call what's inside the wall the Court Plaza. The plaza is less than five acres and you could put the entire town on a twenty-acre farm.

"All the adobes scattered around outside the plaza are abandoned. The only defense for the town that I could see were the dogs. The town's full of them."

5

Tevis spoke up. "Tucson was an old Spanish presidio. Most of the walls fell down ten or so years ago. The old timers still call it the Old Pueblo. Whites run most of the stores and such, but there's a few good Mexican families still living there. Those adobe houses don't look like much from the street, but you can bet your bottom dollar they're warm and dry inside."

Hunter nodded. He turned and signaled for his other officers. Three lieutenants and a sergeant galloped forward. One of the lieutenants had a bruise on his chin and a scab on his lower lip.

Hunter explained the situation and issued his orders. "You will inform the citizens that we are on a war footing. In addition to the several empty adobes that will be available to us, we will, with respect, take lodging wherever we find it. Oaths to the Confederacy will be required of anyone choosing to remain in Tucson. We will issue vouchers for what you need in the way of supplies.

"Extend every courtesy to the people including any Pimas, Papagos, or Maricopas you encounter. They may be needed for scouts. These Indians are friendly to whites and always have been. They're nothing like the Apaches and Comanches. I want no trouble with them. Any questions?"

Lieutenant Jack Swilling scowled at Felton and his scarf. "We best corral the horses in the plaza in front of the church, Captain, and post guards. The Mexicans call it the Plaza de la Mesilla. It's just a short walk from there to the plazas where everybody's took to livin'.

"The Apaches have been scoutin' us for days and these horses we're ridin' are the best in the Territory. Them red devils will surely come after 'em.

"And I know some of the men in town. Brady'll never take the oath. Neither will Fritz Contezen. Both of 'em is tough men. They was with the Texas Rangers and fought the Comanches. But they're for the Union. Best to arrest 'em and send 'em to jail or they'll be trouble."

Captain Hunter thought for a moment. He wasn't aware that the German had been a Ranger, but Contezen and his brother's heroic fight with thirty-five Apaches was well known throughout the Territory. Hunter also knew Brady lived near Tucson when the land was known as the Gadson Purchase. Sam Hughes, a respected businessman, would likely go Union. These were honorable men, brave, and resourceful like all those that dared live on the edge of civilization. The least the Confederacy could do was treat them as gentlemen.

6

"The horses in the front of the church, then. Lieutenant Swilling, assign guard duty for tonight to Sergeant Holmes. Have him pick men from your platoon to rotate through the first night. We will deal with the Unionists tomorrow. Make no mention of any oaths today. I will address the town in the main plaza at eight in the morning.

"Lieutenants Tevis, Swilling, and Felton, I want you to ride in ahead of the column. We will hold here a quarter hour. Spread the word who we are, and that we are coming in by a column of twos. I don't want them to think we're Sonoran bandits and panic. Inform them we'll be taking food and lodging where we can get it. Make it clear, that this is war. Tell every man they are required to be present in the plaza tomorrow."

After saluting, Tevis, Swilling, and Felton wheeled their horses and galloped three abreast toward Tucson. Riding in the middle, Tevis glanced first at Swilling, then at Felton. "I'll take the adobes. Jack, you take the saloons. Caleb, since you're so slicked up, you get the big fancy houses on the edge of town. If the street names they painted on the adobes are still readable, you'll find them on Calle del Arroya and Calle Real."

Felton laughed. He looked good-naturedly over to Swilling. "Want to trade, Jack? I'd rather have a drink than get the cold shoulder from a bunch of rich folks."

"No," grunted Swilling.

Still smiling, Felton tried again. "When I finish up, how about I buy you and Jim a round or two in the Shoo Fly Saloon?"

For several seconds there was no sound but the pounding of hooves. Swilling softened. "Deal. Then you can tell me where you learn't how to fight."

"Oh, now that's a long story. The short of it is, in my younger days, I did some prize fighting up and down the Mississippi. It didn't take me long to figure out it was too hard on my face. I gave it up after a few months."

Swilling seemed pleased. "You make any money at it?"

"Some. Not much."

"So, that'd make you a professional fighter. Now that explains ever'thing. That there is a horse of a different color."

Tevis glared at Felton. "Prize fighting. I declare!"

"How *the hell* old are you?" asked Swilling. "You musta been fighting as a wet-behind-the-ears kid."

7

Felton shook his head. "Boys, I'm going on thirty-four. I believe that makes me second oldest in the company."

"The hell you say," barked Swilling. "I'm thirty myself! You don't look no thirty-three."

"Well, I'm only twenty-six," agreed Tevis. "You don't even look old as me."

"Never gave it much thought," said Felton. "Maybe it's just the shave."

"More'n likely," said Tevis, trying to keep a straight face. "It's that...'porch of geese' blood."

When Caleb Felton chuckled, Tevis burst into a guffaw. Swilling joined him. When the three men galloped by the first adobe of Tucson they were laughing uncontrollably. They didn't sober up until reaching the outer wall of the church of San Augustine. They rode past several empty adobes then cut across Calle del Alegria and Calle del Arroya to enter Court Plaza.

As their horses slowed to a walk and splashed across pools of standing water, Tevis pointed out a hitching rail. "That's a cantina and as good a place as any for me and Jack to start. Caleb, you see those wood frame rooftops out yonder?"

Felton looked in the direction that Tevis indicated. "I see two."

Swilling and Tevis dismounted and sank ankle deep into mud. As they wrapped their reins around the rail, Tevis nodded toward the houses. "That's where the rich folk live. Since you're the dandy, those people are all yours. There's those two you see, and on around behind these adobes, you'll see one more. They're whites in the three big houses and a Mexican named Ochoa who lives in a long flat-roofed adobe. It sits between the wood houses, but out by itself a piece. He's Spanish stock and runs a freight outfit, or least used to. All those folks are big medicine in Tucson."

Reaching inside his coat, Felton retrieved a five-dollar gold piece. "Hey Jack," he said, flipping the coin to the lieutenant, who reached out and snatched it from the air. "If I'm not back by-and-by, you two start without me. Could be, I'll run into that señorita again."

Swilling opened his hand and glanced down. "Five dollars! Hell, you stay as long as you want, Felton. It won't affect my appetite none if you don't show up at all."

"You watch yourself," warned Tevis. "These Tucsonenses women are the marrying kind. If we sit out here in this desert long enough, you'll be gettin' mighty lonely."

Felton tipped his hat and started back across the boggy plaza. "Don't you worry, boys. Any woman that would take up with the likes of me wouldn't be worth marrying."

The dismal light of a cloud-covered day faded into twilight. A faint brush of crimson colored the western horizon. The north wind was calming, lazily shifting directions. Captain Sherod Hunter faced his men.

"Column of twos. On a walk."

CHAPTER 2

Several windows of a long flat-roofed adobe hacienda were already shimmering with the glow from oil lamps when Lieutenant Felton knocked on his first door. It was opened by a stoop-shouldered Mexican woman wrapped in a brightly colored *rebozo*. Her face was wrinkled and brown as boot leather.

"Yo soy Lieutenant Felton. Quiero hablar con el Señor de la casa, por favor."

The woman stared into the eyes of Felton for a moment. She slowly closed the door. A long minute passed before the door swung open with a jerk. A short man of slight build held a lamp close to his face. He wore fine Mexican-style clothes and a closely cropped beard. He squinted, his eyes roving skeptically over the stranger in front of him.

"You do not look like an officer, Señor," he said. His words were spoken clearly but his accent heavy. "What army are you with?"

"I am with the Confederate States of America, sir. A company of soldiers is on its way. We will occupy Tucson for the Confederacy. May I ask your name, sir?"

The Mexican lowered his lamp but not before Felton caught the reflection of disappointment in his eyes.

"I am Estevan Ochoa, Señor," replied the Mexican, with a hint of defiance.

Felton smiled flatly. The Mexican was short and almost frail looking. His light complexion confirmed his Spanish ancestry.

"With respect, sir," said Felton. "This country is at war. Your presence is required in the plaza tomorrow at eight o'clock. All the men of Tucson must be present."

Ochoa paused, his back stiffened. He was proud but not aristocratic. "Is that all, Lieutenant?"

"Yes, sir. Good evening."

"Good evening to you, Señor," replied Ochoa formally, then smoothly shut the door.

Untying his horse from one of the many iron hitching posts in front of Ochoa's house, Felton remounted. It was only a short distance to the next residence, but the roads were a quagmire and his boots were still relatively free of mud.

The second house was American in style—its adobe brick walls were neatly covered with plaster, and it had a framed roof. It was larger than the hacienda with fewer of its windows brightened by flame. A stone walkway led to a wrap-around porch. Felton secured his horse to a leafless tree branch that hung from the front yard of the house and out into the street. From where his horse stood, he dismounted onto the stones.

As he walked up the steps of the porch, the front door opened. The man standing in the doorframe was tall and had broad shoulders. With no lamp in hand, he appeared only as a dark silhouette. He held no light but his right hand was not empty. Felton knew trouble when he saw it and stopped where he was. Before he could announce himself, the man's voice boomed with authority. "Who are you?" he demanded, his right hand coming up.

"I am Lieutenant Felton of Company A," answered Felton with equal authority. "Texas Mounted Volunteers. At this moment, we are occupying Tucson in the name of the Confederacy. Who might you be, sir?"

"Confederates?"

Felton detected surprise in the response but nothing more. "The company will be occupying Tucson. They will enter town in a matter of minutes. May I ask your name, sir?"

A woman appeared in the doorway carrying a lamp. After handing the lamp to the man, she stepped back into the shadows. Now, the gloss of a heavy beard, a pair of deep-set eyes, and pistol barrel reflected flickering orange light.

"The name is Mosby. Sylvester Mosby. Are you going to fight Apaches?"

A third person now skulked in the shadows behind the woman. Judging by the build, Felton guessed it was a young man or teenage boy.

"You would have to ask Captain Hunter. You can do that tomorrow. All men of Tucson are required to be in the Court Plaza at eight in the morning. You understand, sir, this is war and..."

"I know damned well what it is Lieutenant," interrupted Mosby. "I was a Lieutenant too. I graduated West Point to get *my* rank."

The last comment was meant to be either a brag or an insult. Felton was unmoved. Mosby obviously thought himself an important man, but at the moment, he seemed more interested in the Apaches than a war of secession.

"We will see you in the plaza, sir. Goodnight."

Without a word, Mosby turned his back and shut the door. Felton had seen his kind before. Men like that were nothing but trouble and invariably reminded him of his father.

A pulsation of nausea hit Felton. He swore and jerked the reins from the tree. He didn't like to be reminded of his life in Tennessee. Being the son of a self-righteous preacher was a curse he had endured for years. Every day he heard the endless preaching and endless pulpit pounding of thou shalt nots. He was forced to listen to the lectures all over again during agonizingly long sermons on Sunday mornings. Neither of his parents were guilty of sparing the rod, especially when he fell asleep at church.

When Felton was sixteen, he had entered the Methodist seminary just to get away from home. Three years later, when he got word his father was murdered on the way home from a camp meeting, Felton left school for good.

At the funeral, he argued bitterly with his mother. He was not going to be a preacher and never wanted to be one in the first place. Why would God let someone like Pa get murdered? What good did all the church going do anyone? What good did it do, to never have any fun in life? He was through with self-denial. He was through with all of it!

His mother was weeping when he rode from their cabin; weeping in her black funeral clothes over the death of her husband, and for the loss of her son's soul. Hearing her sobs and wailing as he galloped away, Felton vowed he would never be that miserable. Life was too short and death the only sure thing in it. The best anyone could hope to do was outrun the inevitable as long as possible and have a hell of a time in the race.

Riding through the narrow streets to the north side of town, Felton passed a third house. All the windows were dark and there was only a wisp of smoke coming from the chimney. He looked it over closely and went on to the last wood-frame house he could find.

The windows of all three stories of what could have been a small mansion were brightly lit. A carriage with two horses was tied in the street. An orchard of some sort lined the sides and back of the house. He could hear music and see men and women through the lace curtains of the front window.

Caleb Felton felt a gust of wind brush against his cheek. The bite was gone from it. He turned and glanced to the west. Above the white peaks of saw-toothed mountains he saw a streak of red. He carefully studied the clouds. His mother had taught him well. The unusually cold weather was over. Tomorrow he would see the sun again.

Stepping over a puddle and onto another stone walkway, Felton took a moment to scrape the mud off his boots and knock some of it from his coat. He slid the red scarf from his neck and tucked it into his coat pocket. These people owned the best house of the four and were most likely sociable. If they were the least bit receptive to Confederate occupation, it would be in his best interest to make a good impression.

The wide steps leading up to the front door were made of large hand-cut stone. The heavy pillars supporting a raised porch were rounded and painted white. Suspended by two chains from the porch ceiling was a swing made for two. An oak rocker sat off to the side.

Felton wiped his feet on a rug that led up to the door. He was about to knock when he impulsively removed his buffalo coat and tossed it on the swing. The long coat kept him warm but also protected the only clothes he owned from the grime encountered on the march to Tucson. He was fairly presentable.

Felton adjusted his twin pistols and Bowie knife. Using the cast iron lion head attached to the massive wood door, he announced his presence with three metallic knocks.

The door was opened wide by a stout man with a wide smile showing under a well-trimmed mustache. He wore a black suit and tie and could have just stepped off any street in Atlanta or Nashville.

"Well, who the blazes are you, stranger and why are you standing out there in the cold? Come on inside and warm up."

Taking an immediate liking to the man, Felton said, "Don't mind if I do, sir."

A hand went out as Felton stepped into the foyer. "I'm Palatine Robinson."

Felton shook hands. "I'm Lieutenant Felton."

"Lieutenant? Lieutenant of what? Arizona Rangers?"

13

A second man walked out of the parlor and stood next to Robinson. He was taller, and slightly older, but also well dressed. The space between his eyes furrowed with suspicion. He held a glass of whiskey.

"Company A," replied Felton, eyeing the older man. "Texas Mounted Volunteers, Confederate States of America."

Both men suddenly let out howls of delight. The older of the two slapped his knee and broke into a jig. Dancing in tight circles, he yipped excitedly until two astonished women rushed in from the parlor.

The first to appear was a black-haired Mexican in her early thirties. The second was a beautiful brown-haired white woman close to the same age. Each wore dresses in the latest Southern fashion.

Thankful that an hour ago he had been in a barber's chair, Felton removed his hat and held it in his left hand.

"Gracious, me," exclaimed the white woman. "Palatine Robinson, what has gotten into you?"

"William," echoed the Mexican in accented English. "Are you loco?"

The one called William stopped dancing. Gulping the whiskey from his glass, he vigorously shook hands with Felton.

"Not by a large majority, Inez. This here is Lieutenant Felton. The damned Confederate Army has come to Tucson!"

Palatine Robinson reached for his wife's hand and brought her forward. "Lieutenant, may I present my wife, Charlotte."

Felton took her hand and bowed. "Charmed, Mrs. Robinson."

"This fine lady is Inez Oury."

Taking the hand of Mrs. Oury, Felton again bowed. "I am twice charmed, ma'am."

"This rough looking gent is William S. Oury. Genuine Texan. Former Ranger and he was a courier at the Alamo. He knew Davy Crocket and James Bowie personally.

"Charlotte and I are Virginians. All of us here are secessionists, sir. You are welcome in my house any time. In fact, I have extra rooms. If you are not aware of it, you will soon discover there are no hotels in Tucson. You and two others will sleep here, Lieutenant. I insist."

"A bed will be most welcome, Mr. Robinson. I accept your invitation. The Confederacy thanks you, sir."

Mrs. Robinson indicated the entrance to the parlor. "Lieutenant, come in and have some refreshment. There is one other of our household I want you to meet."

Felton glanced down at his feet. "I am afraid I may track in some mud, ma'am."

"Nonsense, Lieutenant. This is Tucson. You come right on in and have a seat. Palatine, get the lieutenant something to drink while I call on Bricela."

Robinson led Felton into the parlor and was followed by the Ourys. The room was furnished with plush carpet, two leather sofas, and another ornately carved rocking chair. A candelabra hung from a high ceiling and the walls framing a large stone fireplace were papered.

"Have a seat next to the fire, Lieutenant," said Robinson. "Would you care for whiskey or bourbon, sir?"

"Bourbon. If you don't mind, I will stand."

Oury laughed and slapped Felton on the back. "Palatine, his backside has been perched on a horse since leavin'...say, Lieutenant, where *did* you set out from?"

"Mesilla," answered Felton as he accepted the bourbon and took a sip. "Almost three weeks ago."

"Worst weather I have ever seen in Tucson," said Mrs. Oury. "We have been here for ten years now. It is never like this. Your journey surely was a bad one."

Felton shrugged. He was about to reply when Mrs. Robinson entered the parlor. "Bricela will be here momentarily," she said with a smile. "Bricela is my niece, Lieutenant. She came for a visit all the way from Georgia on the last Overland Stage that ran. When the company left for California, she was stranded here. That was, my gracious, seven or eight months ago.

"She was quite lonely as you can imagine, so we allowed her to adopt a house puppy shortly after her arrival. Goodness knows we have enough dogs in Tucson with no place to call home. She is looking for it somewhere upstairs. That poor pup is afraid of its own shadow. When she finds it she will be right down."

Oury sneered. "Injuns will eat dogs you know. The only good thing they ever did do. The red devils steal everything in and around Tucson they can get their dirty hands on except our mangy dogs.

"Speakin' of such, Lieutenant, you a Injun fighter? We need to kill ever last one of them Apaches. Wipe out the whole damned race. You have any run-ins with 'em comin' out?"

At the mention of "Apache" Mrs. Oury made the sign of the cross and whispered a few words.

Felton noticed the woman's curious reaction. "No, sir. The only Indians I've dealt with were Choctaws and Cherokees. We didn't see any Apaches. Too cold I would imagine."

"Oh, they was there," said Oury bitterly. "You just had too many troops. They never attack unless they're sure to win. Just 'cause you don't see an Apache, sure as double hell, don't mean they aren't within a bow shot of you. You can even step over 'em if they have a mind to lay still. They ain't nothin' like a tame Injun. These here are wild. You'll see soon enough.

"There ain't no kind of weather that affects 'em, neither. Hot, cold, don't make no difference. They ain't human. No human could live doin' what they do."

"They're a far cry from our southern Indians, Lieutenant," agreed Robinson. "A man has to witness what they can do before he can believe it."

Hiding his skepticism, Felton changed the subject."Captain Hunter is in charge of our company. He has called a meeting in the plaza tomorrow morning at eight. All the men of Tucson are required to attend. You may inquire as to his intentions to fight Indians then. He is already aware that it is a grave concern to all Tucsonians.

"I feel confident that if we do not encounter any Union forces he will do whatever he can for the citizens of the New Mexico Territory."

"Then there will be a celebration in Tucson, Lieutenant," said Robinson. "They will have music, dancing, games, races. You will all be welcomed as heroes. The Apaches are feared and hated by everyone."

Felton paused. The only Indians that he knew well had always been peaceful. "What started all the trouble with these Apaches? I had heard nothing of it in Tennessee before the war started."

Oury shook his head. "Up 'till one year ago everything was just fine and dandy. Cochise's people were even supplying firewood for one of the Butterfield Stage stations that I was head of, the one at Apache Pass.

"Of course, Chochise and his band were still raiding into Mexico, but that was none of our affair at the time.

"Anyways, a half white boy was stole by some Injuns from a man named Ward and he wanted him back. Ward claimed Cochise took him. Three months later the Yankees sent a lieutenant named Bascom to fetch the boy back from Cochise.

"Bascom knew Cochise was up at Apache Pass. You come through that pass and by the station, Lieutenant, on the way here. Did you see them graves by the station?"

"I saw them."

"Well, they was all my employees that Cochise murdered.

"But back to the story. Bascom camped by the station there in the pass and invites Cochise and some of his relatives into his tent friendly like. Then he tells him he wants the boy. Cochise says he don't know nothing about no stolen boy. Bascom says he and his folks are under arrest 'till the boy is give back. Chochise pulls his knife, rips a hole in the tent and runs out. Them Yankees shoot fifty shots at 'im and miss, but they kill the next buck that come through the hole.

"Bascom held the rest of Cochise's kin hostage and wants to trade 'em to get the boy back. Chochise comes back to the station and kills my men, then catches eight Mexican teamsters up the stage road and ties 'em to their wagon wheels and burns 'em alive. Bascom found the burned Mexicans, and Chochise had already murdered my men, so he hangs all of Cochise's kin over the graves of the Mexicans.

"That was last February. Since then, it's been nothing but blood, torture, and murdering by his bucks and squaws. When the Army pulled out, all hell, and I mean, all hell broke loose. Chocise has been running wherever he wants killing anybody he finds.

"Take my advice, Lieutenant. Don't never be taken alive by them red devils. Kill yourself first."

Mrs. Robinson put her hand up. "Please, gentlemen. I hear Bricela coming. Enough about those dreadful Apaches. She's heard about the Bascom affair often enough. I don't want her frightened anymore than she is already."

Felton started to ask another question but hesitated. He was in the process of remembering some forgotten thought. A small bit of information, hauntingly familiar, was trying to surface. He strained to recall what had crossed his mind but there was nothing.

His eyes narrowing, Felton glared suspiciously at his bourbon. Maybe he was just tired. Whatever eluded him must not have been important. Perhaps it concerned the oath to the Confederacy that was to be taken or what time the men were to assemble. Yet those were major details. What he missed was much more subtle.

His thoughts were interrupted by Mrs. Robinson. "In the parlor, Bricela. Come in and meet our guest."

Felton put on his gentlemanly smile. He turned toward the parlor entrance and prepared to meet a child.

He first caught sight of a blue velvet dress as it slowly appeared beyond the doorway. When the young woman turned into the parlor she was looking down at the small dog she held in her arms. Her light brown hair was streaked with waves of blond. A red ribbon, tied in a bow, held it back from her face. She was anything but a child.

"Bricela, I would like to present Lieutenant Felton," said Mrs. Robinson. "Lieutenant Felton, may I present my niece, Miss Bricela Verde."

The young woman casually looked up and straight into the Lieutenant's gaze. Her eyes were pale blue, strangely penetrating, and for Caleb Felton, profoundly disquieting.

Bricela Verde appeared only a few years younger than Mrs. Robinson and equally as beautiful. She was like no woman he had ever seen. In his years at the seminary, he studied the great portrait artists of Europe. He traveled throughout the South for more than a decade, but he had never seen or even imagined a face more angelic than the one before him.

Felton heard his own words as if he were standing in another room. The rote salutation was being repeated with practiced sincerity, but his mind was momentarily lost in a fog, drifting somewhere between reverence and awe.

After Felton finished speaking, Bricela hesitated. Her eyes were steady yet curious. She inquisitively turned her head before offering her hand.

"Lieutenant Felton," she said candidly. "What is the entirety of your name, sir?"

Mrs. Robinson was startled at the question. Before she could intercede for her niece, Felton took Bricela's hand and bowed. "Caleb R. Felton, Miss Verde." Straining to focus his concentration, he added, "At your service."

"Well, Bricela," chuckled Mrs. Robinson, "I always thought you were so shy."

Felton gently released Bricela's hand. The air seemed heavy, yet not uncomfortably so. Or was it the air? Her perfume perhaps? What was it about her eyes? Was it the color he found so perplexing?

Bricela's eyes narrowed. "What does the R stand for?"

The question brought a chuckle from everyone. Felton smiled and leaned forward to look at the black longhaired mutt she held.

"Why that is a military secret, Miss Verde."

"I hardly believe that, Lieutenant."

Still smiling, Felton leaned forward and looked at the puppy. "What is the name of your dog?"

Bricela kept her eyes on Felton as she scratched the dog under its chin. "This poor creature is named Robespierre," she said. "He was living alone in the streets and alleys. He seemed so lost. Aunt Charlotte thinks it's a silly name for a dog but I believe it fits him."

Felton stood erect. He hid his surprise by taking another swallow of bourbon. Robespierre was the name chosen for him by his mother in honor of her French grandfather. It was as hideous a moniker as it was uncommon.

"Why Robespierre?" asked Felton. "That name does seem a bit unusual, especially for a dog."

Bricela thought for a moment. Looking at nothing in particular, she wistfully squinted her eyes. "I really do not know why. The name just came to me...on the wind. It was as if destiny itself whispered it to me."

Felton stole another look at Bricela. Unexpectedly, he felt a knot growing in the pit of his stomach. This time it wasn't the recollection of his home in Tennessee that nagged at him. It was, however, an undeniable twinge of guilt, a sensibility that had not bothered him in years.

"Sometimes, Lieutenant," offered Mrs. Robinson, "Bricela is quite the mystic. Personally, I think she picked that name up in New Orleans. She visited there once and especially enjoyed the French Quarter. Of course, Robespierre is French."

"Do you speak French, Miss Verde?" asked Felton.

"A little. Have you ever been to New Orleans, Lieutenant?"

"A few years ago. My mother grew up in the French Quarter."

Offering his empty glass to Mr. Robinson, Felton said, "I need to return and make my report, sir, but if your offer still stands, I will return this evening with two other officers. We would greatly appreciate a good nights rest."

Robinson shook hands with Felton. "Absolutely, Lieutenant. We have plenty of room on the first floor. There's a back entrance you can use to come and go as you wish. Use the first door on the right as you enter.

"You won't disturb us at all. We are honored to have Confederate soldiers as our guests."

After shaking hands with Oury and giving one final look at Bricela Verde, Felton graciously excused himself and stepped out into the cool air. He took in a deep breath. Satisfied with the situation, he grabbed his coat from the swing and went down the steps to his horse. Captain Hunter would be in town by now and likely the men would be in the saloon celebrating. Swilling and Tevis would be waiting for him.

Felton reached into his coat pocket and pulled out the scarf. Looking back at the parlor window he thoughtfully ran it through his fingers. A moment later, he neatly folded the señorita's gift and shoved it deep inside his bedroll.

Rolling his coat, Felton tied it to the back of his saddle. When he jerked the second knot tight, the front door opened and closed. A woman wearing a shawl stepped onto the unlit porch.

There was a long silence. With the faint sound of creaking leather, Felton eased himself into his saddle. He sat motionless staring at the dark figure waiting for the woman to speak.

"Goodnight, Lieutenant." It was Bricela.

Felton stared even harder into the shadows. His pulse quickened. "Goodnight, Miss Verde," he said, slowly turning his horse toward the plaza. He could feel her eyes on him as the stallion walked into the night. He could sense her presence.

Bricela Verde walked back inside and into the parlor. The men were in another room but Mrs. Robinson and Mrs. Oury were smiling at her as she entered.

"Beau sabreur!" said Robinson. "Too bad he is so much older than you, Bricela. He reminds me a great deal of Palantine when he was younger. Very dashing and handsome."

Mrs. Oury laughed agreeably. "Muy guapo hombre."

"How old do you think he is, Aunt Charlotte?"

"Oh, I would say twenty-four or five. What do you think, Inez?"

"Yes. About that."

Bricela gazed thoughtfully out the window into the darkness. "I think we may have met before. Maybe in New Orleans."

"He will be staying here, Bricela. He and two other officers will be taking the downstairs rooms. You will have time to talk all about New Orleans. They will have news from the states as well. This is wonderful! Just wonderful."

"We will certainly have a *baile* now," smiled Inez. "We will dance and have games. We will start making plans! It will be like it was before the Union soldiers left us."

"We can have all the officers here for dinner parties," added Charlotte. "Bricela, you will finally have someone to talk to. I think you and the lieutenant will have much in common."

Bricela reached down and picked up her dog. "Yes," she said as she turned for the hallway. "We do.

"Goodnight Inez. Goodnight Aunt Charlotte. I'm going upstairs to work on my poetry."

Walking up the long flight of stairs, Bricela whispered to her dog as she petted his head. "He is older than they think, Robespierre, and there is something quite unusual about him...I like how he makes me feel."

Entering her room, Bricela put the dog at the foot of the bed. She removed a sheet of paper from a drawer. She took out a pen and bottle of ink and sat on the edge of her bed.

She dipped her pen and started at the top of a blank sheet of paper.

Beau Sabreur

He has strength like the sea...but is haunted by voices in the wind...

His eyes have power...causing her emotions to stir...

Felton tied his horse near an abandoned adobe in the Court Plaza but hesitated before entering the saloon. The heavy smell of tobacco smoke and liquor drifted through the open door and hung in the fresh night air. Dozens of boisterous voices blended with laughter while tinkling glasses accompanied a lively trio of fiddle, flute, and drum.

This had been his life for fifteen years and he allowed nothing to interfere with it. There were no entanglements or obligations. Since his father's funeral, he never looked back. Sentiment was for fools.

Bricela Verde, though, had somehow penetrated his inviolable barrier of selfish indifference. Her inquisitive gaze and the sound of her voice now strangely consumed his every thought. He depended on no man, was loyal to none, and made it a rule to never let any woman get close to him. Yet somehow, in the citadel of this self-imposed isolation, he could feel her presence, sense her standing beside him...as if she had been there before.

Felton swore. Shaking his head and trying to clear it, he walked into the den of celebration and looked around. At the far end of the low-roofed adobe, he caught sight of Tevis and Swilling leaning against weathered planks that served as a bar. He started through the thick mix of soldiers and Tucsonians, but his path was abruptly blocked by a young Mexican man.

He was shorter than Felton by several inches, and wore a blue sash around his waist with a pistol and knife shoved into it. His eyes blazed with defiance.

"You are the one. You have something that belongs to me. The scarf is mine!"

Felton thought quickly. It was a skill learned long ago and past experience made it easy to deduce what was at stake.

There were times he simply lied to such a man or sidestepped him all together. On occasion and for no good reason, he chose to stand his ground, spoiling for a fight. The posse that chased him from East Texas to Mesilla was the result of such an incident. But this Mexican was hardly more than a boy.

"No, amigo," replied Felton, deciding to lie just a little. "The scarf was merely loaned to me. The señorita was being kind to one who came to fight the Apaches."

The Mexican was unconvinced. "It is mine. You will give it back to me!"

There was no bluff in the young man's voice. He had come to fight, but if he made a wrong move and was not an accomplished gunman or knife fighter, he would be dead in seconds.

"I was going to return it my friend," said Felton, realizing he was now telling the truth. "I have it tucked away in my bedroll."

The Mexican's eyes still blazed. Anticipating his next demand, Felton smiled. "I can get it now if you wish."

Sneering, but appearing to lose some of his bluster, the Mexican pointed to the door. "I will go with you."

Felton shrugged. "Suit yourself."

Walking from the hard-packed dirt floor back into the mud and darkness, Felton rested his left hand on one of his Colts. "It's best if you walk beside me, amigo. I am Lieutenant Felton. Who might you be?"

Coming alongside Felton as they made their way across the plaza, the Mexican spoke boldly. "I am Jesus Maria Elias."

"Well, Señor Elias, there are over one hundred soldiers in Tucson tonight. You are a brave man, but bravery does not turn away lead bullets or a steel blade."

"It is better to die like a man than live like a dog," snapped Elias.

Felton took a few steps. "I suppose. But this evening I met a dog that has a fine life."

Elias glared at Felton. "You mock me?"

"No, no my friend...I mock only myself."

"Good," said Elias, his tone softening. "That is good. It is best to have no trouble."

Even in the starlight, the quality of the black stallion coming into view was obvious to Elias. "That is a fine horse, Lieutenant." The bravado was gone from his voice. "A stallion?"

"Yes. The best I've ever owned. I won him from a Frenchman. The man can't play poker worth a damn but he sure as hell can raise horses."

Elias stopped near the front shoulder of the horse. "I have such a stallion also. I raised him from a colt. The Apaches have tried to steal him many times."

Felton reached inside his bedroll as Elias admiringly rubbed the stallion's neck.

"I have turned the head of many women," said Felton, handing the scarf to Elias. "But they soon discover I am not what they want. You will look better in the eyes of your señorita if you return the scarf and say no more about it...ever."

The Mexican studied Felton for several seconds. He took the scarf and tucked it behind his sash. "Have you known so many women that you can tell me what to do with mine? I have known Juanita since we were children."

"How old are you?"

"I am nineteen years."

Felton looked down at Elias and thought of his nineteenth birthday. He woke up with a hangover, bruised knuckles and no idea why he was in a Little Rock jail. The only clue he ever had was the garter belt around his arm.

"In all that time you never thought there might be another woman for you?"

"No. There is no other. Juanita is for me."

"You are a lucky man. It is good to know what you want in this life."

"You gringos always want too much. A good woman, a good horse, and a ranch or farm to work. It is all a man needs. Mexicans are simple people, Lieutenant, but we are happy."

"Could be," said Felton, deciding he liked the man. "How about I show you there are no hard feelings and buy you a drink?"

Elias paused. "Gracious, Lieutenant. However, I must return the scarf tonight. I think maybe I have behaved badly to Juanita. She is better for me than tequila."

"Tomorrow, then," said Felton, extending his hand. "Call me Caleb."

Shaking hands, Elias nodded. "Yes, tomorrow. Tomorrow is a new day, amigo. This day will be forgotten. My friends call me Jesus."

To avoid the deeper puddles and mud, Felton walked around the edge of the plaza back to the saloon. As soon as he stepped inside, Tevis waved him to the back of the room.

Handing Felton a full glass of whiskey, Tevis smiled. "How'd it go with the rich folk?"

"No problems. I have a place for you, me, and Jack to stay. It's the Robinson place."

"Jack's taken on an abandoned adobe for him and his platoon but I'm game. I know that house and I've met Palatine a time or two. He's a good Southerner."

Noticing Felton had not taken a drink, Tevis stared at him suspiciously. "I hear Mrs. Robinson is quite a looker. You mind your manners, Caleb, or you'll get us both shot."

Felton took a drink. "Don't fret over it, James. She's a fine woman. She has her niece living there with her, too."

"A kid?"

"Not hardly. Early twenties, I'd say."

"She a looker like her aunt?" asked Tevis.

"Could be. Depends on your taste."

Tevis took a drink from his glass and grinned. "How does she taste to you, Caleb?"

A frown dulled Felton's demeanor. "She's too good for the likes of me."

"You get religion all the sudden?" goaded Tevis.

"She's too good for any of us, James. Except for the Captain, we're all a bunch of no-accounts."

Tevis took another drink and slapped Felton on the back. "That we are, amigo. That we most certainly are! But without us scoundrels to protect them, where would all the good folks be?"

"Mr. Robinson said we could come and go as we pleased but to use the back door. Our room is the first door on the right.

"I need to report to Captain Hunter. I may come back or turn in early so don't get so drunk you can't find your way home. The barber told me the Apaches have been known to come into Tucson at night."

"I'll show you the captain's quarters," said Tevis, starting to weave his way through the crowd. He pointed to the floor as he walked and spoke over the noise. "See that? Hard as rock almost. They get the dirt that way by mixing river sand with bullock's blood and cactus juice. Who would of thought? Blood, sand, and cactus mixing together into something useful."

Coming to the doorway, Tevis pointed to the east. "Go past those adobes there and you'll come into another smaller plaza. It's the Plaza de las Armas. He'll be in the big adobe. You'll see the light through the cracks in the door. The windows this time of year are covered with cowhide. In fact, most of these adobes don't have a nail in 'em. All the wood is held together with rawhide."

Felton walked from the cantina between a row of adobes. Crossing another plaza, he spotted light coming through a door jam. He knocked and waited. After making his report, he would return to the Robinson home. He wanted another look at Bricela Verde. He didn't like the way she made him feel. How could she be so different than other women? Maybe it was only because he hadn't seen a woman, any woman, in three weeks. That would explain it…or at least part of it.

Jack Swilling opened the door. He stood for a moment studying Felton. A smile raised his mustache.

"We been waitin' for you. Come on in."

"Have a seat, Lieutenant," said Hunter, pointing to a stool near him. The captain sat at a crude plank table. On it, a lamp's flickering amber light danced on a large map. He indicated another man standing off to the side. "Sergeant Holmes, come over and take a close look."

Holmes took a few steps, came alongside the captain, then stared at Felton. A moment later, he nodded. "He has an oily tongue and he's a good mixer. I'm with Jack. Grow some chin-whiskers and a mustache, dress 'im up some and he'll pass. Sure as hell's hot, he will."

"I'll explain, Lieutenant," said Hunter. "But first your report."

Felton glanced at Swilling, who was still smiling at the captain. "I spoke with men named Ochoa, Mosby, Robinson, and Oury. Robinson and Oury are for the Confederacy. I believe Mosby may be a neutral. I can't say about Ochoa."

Hunter wrote the names down. He motioned for Swilling to go outside. "Lieutenant, make certain we have no visitors."

After the door closed, Hunter stood and leaned over the table resting both hands on the edges of the map. "We've just received word that General Carleton is concentrating forces at Fort Yuma and may already be headed for us. He is using the mail route. At some point we will need to know his strength. His men will be spread out for miles due to water and feed restrictions. It will take time to get an accurate assessment. That is where you come in...should you agree."

"What is it you want, Captain?"

"Jack pointed it out but we all agree. You could pass for a Spaniard. Your Spanish is excellent. If you were to ride east with the story that you refused to take the oath to the Confederacy and were forced to leave Tucson, it would be very convincing. When you meet the column from California on its way to Tucson, you could ask to ride along so that you could return home with them. That would give you adequate time to gather the information General Sibley needs...if you are discovered, you will be considered a spy and most likely hung."

Caleb Felton smiled but there was no humor in it. "You are asking me to volunteer?"

"Yes, I am. I can send a rider, but he would only see the front of the column. I need to know what is behind the advance. There are rumors Carleton is a marching two thousand men across the desert.

26

"We need to know if that is true and know in time to get reinforcements from Sibley. If we don't, we could lose the entire Territory."

The face of Bricela flashed across Felton's thoughts. "How soon would I leave, sir?"

"Two weeks perhaps. Hard to say. We want enough time to pass so the entire column is on the road to Tucson.

"That will give you time to grow the mustache and beard the Spanish men wear."

"I'll need different clothes."

Hunter indicated the sergeant. "Amongst other things, Sergeant Holmes is a taylor."

"In that case, Captain, I volunteer."

"Very well, Lieutenant. Let's get started."

After Holmes took some measurements, Felton went outside and paused. Swilling was leaning against the adobe smoking a cornhusk cigarette.

"Want a smoke, Caleb? These Mex-style cigarettes are passable good."

"No. I'm done for the night. Tevis and I are staying at the Robinson's."

Swilling puffed smoke and grinned. "You volunteer?"

"You know damned well I did. I got you to thank for it."

"Not so much. Captain Hunter only brung you along with us 'cause you spoke such good Mex. I just pointed out the natural born color of your hide. Him and Holmes come up with the rest of it.

"When do you leave?"

"Two weeks. Maybe longer."

"Well, there ain't that many sportin' women in town anyhow. There ain't any whites that...hey now. I heard this evening, there's a white woman staying at the Robinson's...and she ain't married."

Felton ignored the last comment. Walking back across the dark plaza he said, "Goodnight, Jack."

Swilling started to take a puff from his cigarette, but his hand stopped halfway to his mouth. "You already treed the only woman in town, didn't ya? Damnation, Caleb. You beat all I ever saw!"

His reputation with women had never bothered him, but the idea of it being mentioned in the company of Bricela Verde suddenly made him feel ashamed. How would his staying in the same house reflect upon her, or even Mrs. Robinson? Perhaps it was better that he become a spy. The role fit him better than a soldier…and it would remove him from the presence of Bricela. There would be no temptations to re-sist…no complications.

The course of his life had been charted, and there was no room in it for someone as elegant and undefiled as Miss Verde. He should dismiss her and be done with it. She deserved a good man…a man like his mother once hoped and prayed he would be.

Buried memories stirred in the blackness of the night. Felton swore as he walked. He didn't know if his mother was still alive. Or what had become of his brothers and sisters. He'd never seen the grave of his fa-ther.

Standing on the stone landing behind the Robinson house, Felton tugged off his wet and muddy boots. With his boots in hand, he eased the door latch and stepped inside the back door. He was trying to wipe his soaked stockings on a floor rug when he looked up.

"You are back early," said Bricela.

Caleb Felton froze. He wanted to swear but he only stammered, "Tired…I." He tried to think of something other than how exquisite she looked in the soft glow of candle light. "I hope I don't make a mess."

"Nonsense, Lieutenant Felton," she said, cocking her head to one side. "No. No, that will not do at all. When we are alone I shall call you Caleb."

A jolt of something strangely pleasing yet resembling fear shot through Felton's body. His face stung with prickly heat. "Miss Verde…," said Felton in a near whisper. "I do not think that would be proper. In fact, we shouldn't be alone. I assure you that I have only the most honorable intentions, but…"

"I know you do, Caleb."

Felton felt off balance. He placed a hand against the hall wall to steady himself. He could not seem to focus his eyes or his thoughts. His wits, his charm, his relentless gaiety were all failing him.

"Where is everyone?"

"Uncle Palatine and Mr. Oury went to the saloon to celebrate. Aunt Charlotte and Mrs. Oury went to the Oury's to start planning the *baile*."

"I should go."

"Please. Put your boots down and come into the parlor and dry your feet. The parlor is proper enough, is it not?"

Bricela took the boots from Felton's hand and set them down. She turned toward the parlor. "Come along, Caleb. Please do."

After taking a few deep breaths to clear his head and wiping his feet more times than would do any good, Felton walked down the hall and took a seat off to one side of the fireplace. Bricela seated herself opposite him on a settee. They both looked into the flames and felt its warmth. For a full minute nobody spoke. Only the crackling logs broke the silence.

"When were you last in New Orleans?" asked Bricela.

Though he was alone with a beautiful woman, Felton found himself embracing no other desire than to be near her. It was a perplexing blend of comfort and satisfaction. "Two years ago."

"Oh."

"Why do you ask?"

"I feel as though we met prior to this evening. I was certain it was New Orleans. I was there a few months before coming to Tucson. You are sure it was two years ago and not one?"

Squinting thoughtfully, Felton had the vague sensation she was right about them having met. But it could not have been New Orleans. If they had met, he hoped she would not remember him well.

"I'm positive."

After another long pause, Bricela lifted her eyes from the flames and fixed them solidly on Caleb Felton. "Have you heard of reincarnation?"

Felton glanced at Bricela and back at the fire. "I studied it briefly in school."

"Do you believe it could happen?"

Felton shook his head and chuckled softly. "I don't believe in anything, Miss Verde. If I can't shoot it, spend it, eat it or...no, I don't believe it can happen."

"No? Why did you look at me the way you did when we met this evening? You looked at me...as if you recognized me."

Slowly Felton raised his head and looked into the pale blue eyes that held him. His first impulse was to admit nothing. Yet when they were introduced, she had somehow seen behind his debonair façade. If she were bold enough, or perhaps innocent enough, to ask such a question, he should have the decency to answer honestly.

Should he tell her he was instantly attracted to her? Should he confess that he was awed by her charm, and since their introduction unable to block her from his thoughts? Or was it better to do what he did best?

"I really don't know what I was thinking, Miss Verde. I hope I did not offend you. I must say, you are very perceptive."

Felton swore to himself. He had been on his own since he was nineteen, fought dozens of men and bedded countless women, but Bricela Verde was making him behave like a child. As he lied to her, he felt awkward and uneasy.

The blue eyes did not waver. "Your words say very little, Caleb Felton. People communicate in many ways. I can see well enough that there are some things you resist putting into words."

"Miss Verde...most of my life isn't worth putting into words. I'm not even fit company for someone like you. There was a time I might have been...but that was long ago."

There was a brief pause. Bricela asked, "If this were long ago...and you had just met me this evening...what would you say?"

The warmth of the flames and Bricela's soft voice were disarming. Felton lowered his defenses. For a moment, the skills he had honed to perfection and relied on to survive a life of self-interest and self-reliance would be set aside. There was no motive for insincere flattery or deception.

"I would say, Miss Verde... you are beautiful. But that can be said of many women...I would go on to say that you are like the ocean...fathomless, unchartable and yet mysteriously familiar. I would add that you are...the most intriguing woman I have ever had the privilege of meeting." Felton paused. "How was that?"

A smile of satisfaction adorned the face of Bricela Verde. "You should write poetry."

"The devil should write hymns."

"Your past is not important to me. A man can change if he wants. I can't believe you were all that bad. There is too much good in you. I know there is...I can feel it."

"Under different circumstances I would argue with you about that, but tonight I'm going to let it pass."

"Have you noticed, Caleb, how freely we speak to one another? We have only just met and we act as if...we are friends."

"Not very proper, is it?"

"For us...it is. Although, I don't think the world would understand. Nor would I ever tell anyone."

"I don't understand this myself, Miss Verde. Not at all. But I do find it…very pleasant."

"I would like for you to call me Bricela…when we are alone. Please."

Felton shook his head, but before he could protest, Bricela put up her hand to stop him. "I insist."

"I doubt we'll have much opportunity to be alone. I'll likely be out on patrols most of the time we are here."

"But when we are?"

Wrinkling his brow, Felton spoke uneasily. "How about for now, I call you Miss Bricela…at least for a while?"

"For a while."

Leaning forward in his chair and bowing slightly, Felton smiled, "I would be honored…Miss Bricela."

Steam rose from Felton's wool stockings. Watching the vapors swirl and disappear into nothing, he leaned back and searched for a way to preserve the moment. He wanted to fix the memory of it in his mind. He needed a word or maybe even three or four to define what was happening. The more he groped for a simple label, the more confused he became. There simply was no name for it.

Felton moved his feet away from the heat for a moment. "What brought you way out here to Tucson?"

"I heard of the giant *saguaros*, the *chollas,* and the San Xavier Mission from Aunt Charlotte when she visited us back east. When she returned to Tucson, she continued to describe this land in her letters. Eventually I decided I should have to see it for myself. All they said was true. It is a land like no other on earth. I actually do love it here."

"Maybe a person can get used to it, but it seems a bit God forsaken to me, like hell itself."

"It is not long until spring, Caleb. Wait until then. It is beautiful, more beautiful than anything you will ever see."

Looking admiringly at Bricela, Felton said easily, "I doubt that, Miss Verde. I doubt that very much."

Bricela blushed and pulled a strand of hair back behind her ear. She smiled faintly and gazed into the fire.

"Where will they hold the dance, the *baile?*" asked Felton, changing the subject.

"There is a long adobe at the end of Court Plaza. The floor is dirt but it is hard and smooth. The music is actually quite good even if it is only a small band. We have not had a dance in over a year. We will have a grand time. Everyone comes. Americans, Mexicans, Papagos. Young and old, they all come."

"You will have to save a dance for me, Miss Bricela. One dance or two would not seem improper."

"I will not have a *duena* to watch over me like a hawk as the Mexican girls do. I will be able to dance with whomever I wish…as often as I wish."

"If we danced more than two dances together, you and I might understand but others would not approve. Until some time goes by, until I can establish myself as more of a gentleman…or perhaps I should say, redeem myself in the eyes of others…I think it best we maintain appearances."

"I have not lived in Tucson long, Caleb, but one custom they have in the West is quite appropriate. One does not routinely enquire about one's past. All is new here. The past is forgotten or forgiven. We all start fresh. It is a hard country in some ways and we need strong men and women to settle here. It is a good place to build a new life."

"I'll mind my manners…now that I have a reason. Who knows…I might get used to being an officer and a gentleman. I suppose stranger things have happened."

Bricela turned to Felton. Her eyes flickered knowingly. "Oh, they already have."

CHAPTER 3

By the time Captain Hunter entered Court Plaza, the pastel pink of daybreak was fading to a lemon yellow. Almost ninety heavily armed privates were scattered around the edges of the plaza. The officers waited in front of the Shoo Fly where a sturdy crate and a flagpole had been set just beyond the *ramada* that shaded the saloon's entrance.

Hunter paused at the edge of the noisy throng of people. A faint breeze churned the cold air as the sun's rim cleared the eastern mountain peaks. Somewhere tortillas were being baked. The aroma of corn mixed with that of cigarette smoke and the smell of fresh manure. Several burros, with their wooden wheeled *carretas* hitched behind them, were scattered among the crowd. Dogs meandered through and between hundreds of legs. A few barked. Somewhere a pig squealed. A child's crying could be heard over the loud voices.

The Mexican men were wrapped in cotton blankets of various colors and each wore a large *sombrero*. Many of their hatbands were adorned with silver.

The few Mexican women present, wore calico skirts and muslin shirts. They covered their heads with *rebozos* or *tapalos*, wraps that left only one eye exposed to inspect the new visitors. Some balanced *ollas* on their heads while others carried their clay jars empty on their backs in baskets framed with *ocotillo* branches.

Anglo men were few in number. Most wore narrow brimmed hats and rough-cut business suits. Among the whites, only Palatine Robinson and Sylvester Mosby were well dressed. The clothes of Estevan Ochoa spoke of his Spanish decent and success as a businessman.

Hunter made his way through the gathering of Tucsonians. He saluted his men.

"Are all whites present?"

"Yes, sir," answered Tevis. "And all the English speaking Mexicans."

"What is the mood of the town?"

"For the most part, cheerful. A few whites don't seem too happy."

"Very well," said Hunter. He clinched his teeth and stepped up onto the makeshift platform. The murmuring ceased. A barking dog yelped and all grew quiet. Rays of sun began to warm the air.

"I am Captain Hunter, Confederate States of America. Tucson is now under Confederate control. We are at war with the Union and we will conduct ourselves accordingly.

"Many of you here are Neutrals. Some of you are for the secession and a few of you are not. Those of you that are not will have two days to reconsider your position. At that time, you will be asked to sign an oath to the Confederacy or face consequences.

"We have come to fight Union soldiers but are also here to secure this territory and protect its citizens and business interests from Apaches and Sonoran bandits. All we ask in return is your loyalty or at least your word of honor that you will not interfere with our cause.

"Spies will be hung. Those that do not take the oath will be forced to leave Tucson. Should you wish to speak with me, if you have any questions, my headquarters are in the Plaza de las Armas. Or you may also address any of my officers you see here with me."

Hunter paused and nodded to Sergeant Holmes who unfolded a flag and attached it to the flagpole.

Holmes pulled the rope and the heavy cloth rose high and gently unfurled. Seven white stars were set in a circle against a square of blue. Next to the stars, three broad strips, two red separated by one white, finished the flag of the new Confederation of States.

Again facing the crowd, Hunter forced a smile. "In the meantime, Mr. Oury has an announcement."

Hunter stepped down as William Oury took his place. "To celebrate the arrival of Captain Hunter and his men," boomed Oury in a deep and commanding voice. "There will be a Grand *Baile* this evening."

A cheer erupted from the people. Scattered shots erupted and a rag-tag band started playing a lively jig. Oury raised his voice over the music. "Today at noon, we will have foot and horse races on Calle Real. On Calle Alegria, we will have *olla* races for the women and the *correr el gallo* for our most expert horsemen."

Another cheer erupted. Oury stepped down to shake hands with Hunter and each officer. When he got to Felton, he again spoke over the noise of celebration.

34

"I saw that black you rode to the house last night. You should be able to give Jesus Elias a good run for the money. He's got a stallion that's never been beat."

"What is *correr el gallo* about? What is run the rooster?"

Oury laughed. "You got to be some kind of rider for that. They burry a chicken or rooster up to its neck in the street, then ride by at full speed and lean down trying to catch it by the head. The one that finally gets it has to ride off as fast as he can. The others chase after him, trying to steal it back. It's the big prize with the Mexicans. So far I've never seen a white win.

"Jesus has been the champion for quite a few years running. You best stick to a straight-up horse race. That you might be able to win."

"Thanks for the advice," said Felton. He caught a glimpse of Bricela standing alone in front of a whitewashed adobe. She wore a light gray dress with a high-necked lace collar. Her hair hung down over her shoulders. "I think I'll have a go at the chicken."

"Suit yourself," grinned Oury, who then disappeared into the crowd.

Some of the Mexicans were starting to dance in the streets. Dogs barked. Children laughed and screamed as they chased each other and darted like quail through groups of bystanders. Everyone seemed excited.

Felton made his way through the crowd toward Bricela. When he was almost near enough to speak, he noticed a young man leaning around the corner of an adobe staring at her. The onlooker was tall and thin, his face sparsely covered by an immature beard and raised pimples.

When Bricela saw Felton, she smiled and started for him. When she did, the man turned his head and glared into the plaza. His eyes met Felton's and filled with unmasked hatred. Mouthing words Felton could not hear, he ducked out of sight.

"I haven't seen them this happy since I arrived," said Bricela. "Isn't it grand?"

"Well, I just saw one person that wasn't so happy, at least not with me."

"Oh?"

"He was hiding behind a building, staring at you. When he saw me coming he laid his ears back and took off."

"Was he tall and skinny?"

"As a rail."

"That was Cade Mosby. He is Sylvester Mosby's son."

"You are aware he likes you?"

"Yes, I suppose he does, poor thing."

"He doesn't look more than seventeen or eighteen."

"The whole town feels sorry for him. Everyone says his father is too hard on him."

The last comment sounded all too familiar. Felton shoved the thought of his own father from his mind before it could take hold. It was too nice a day for bad memories.

"I haven't been to the river yet, Miss Bricela. Would you care to join me on a walk down to the Santa Cruz?"

"Why, certainly, Lieutenant. It is the first day of March and spring is in the air."

Placing her arm in his, she pointed the way. "I'll show you around town. We'll go over to the Calle de la Guardia, then down Calle Real to Calle de Mission and on down to the water's edge.

"The Calle de Mission leads to the San Xavier del Bac Mission, nine miles south of Tucson. After you subdue the Apaches, you must visit the mission. I have been to the churches in Santa Fe and California, but I am told the mission here is the most beautiful building anywhere in the West."

Walking across the plaza to its southern edge, the couple came upon a heavy wood post set in the bare dirt. It was too tall for a hitching post.

"What is that?" asked Felton.

Bricela shuddered. "That awful thing is a whipping post. I hate to think of what took place there. They should burn it. The Spanish were so cruel."

After walking a few minutes beyond the whipping post, they crossed to the far side of Calle Real. A large heavyset man with a thick black beard swept clouds of dust out the front door of an adobe.

Bricela waved. "Good morning, Mr. Warner."

Soloman Warner glanced at Felton and frowned. "Good morning, Miss Verde."

"Who is he?" whispered Felton.

"He owns one of the two remaining stores in Tucson. Before the Union Army left, he had an excellent stock of general merchandise. Most people just call him Soloman."

"Can we take a quick look inside?"

"Certainly."

Veering toward the store, Bricela spoke again to Warner. "This is Lieutenant Felton. He'd like to take a look inside your store."

Warner did not offer to shake hands. He kept his massive fists clasped around the broom handle.

"Sure, Miss Verde. But the Confederates already came lookin'."

Looking up several inches at Warner's disapproving scowl, Felton smiled. "If I see anything I want, I'll pay for it, sir. You can rest assured of that."

Stepping inside the low-roofed building, Felton glanced around at the half-empty shelves. Captain Hunter would likely requisition most of what the owner had left and only give him a voucher in return. It would be a bitter pill to swallow under the best conditions, but Tucson had been isolated for seven months, with no way to get new supplies. Warner would be put out of business.

Felton turned to leave but something caught his eye. He quickly looked away as if he had not seen it.

"I'll come back later, Bricela, when I have more time. I do think he has some things I can use."

Warner glared at Felton as they stepped back outside. "It'll take more'n a hundred Confederates to make it safe for any supply wagons to get through. Cochise is runnin' wild over the whole country."

"We expect reinforcements soon, Mr. Warner."

"Do you?" asked Warner derisively.

Felton tipped his hat.

"Good day, Mr. Warner," said Bricela.

As they walked away, Bricela again placed her arm in Felton's. "You'll have to excuse Mr. Warner. Normally he is very pleasant. He's fierce looking but actually very kind, especially to all the children in town. He gives them little pieces of ribbon and such just to make them happy. He is very well liked and respected."

A moment later, the last adobe was left behind and the cottonwoods that lined the Santa Cruz River came into view a few hundred yards ahead. Several times along the road they passed women draped with brightly colored *rebosos* that left only one eye exposed. Balanced on top of their heads without the use of their hands, they carried *ollas* of various sizes.

"Are they carrying water in those jars?" asked Felton.

"Water, barley, grain. Almost anything. Isn't it marvelous how they use no hands. The women, old and young, will race like that today. They will run with *ollas* on their heads and still use no hands to balance them.

"With a basket on their backs, the Papago women often carry two to three such jars at once. Most of them live at the San Xavier mission."

"How do they get along with the Apaches?"

"The Apaches are deadly enemies of the Papagos. The hatred goes back beyond memory. It is very intense.

"The Papagos are peaceful Indians, but if they need to fight they are as ferocious as their enemy. It is all so dreadful. This land is beautiful but it can be so harsh."

"It's rough," agreed Felton. "Seems like everything out here either sticks, bites, or stings."

Bricela looked up at Felton as they walked on. "You left the house before breakfast this morning."

"I didn't sleep well. About the time I finally fell asleep, Lieutenant Tevis and your uncle came through the back door.

"Your uncle and the lieutenant knew each other before this war started. Both came into the room and talked for a time. Most of the talk concerned the Apaches. Since they both had been...celebrating...quite vigorously, I did not believe much of what they said about them.

"I couldn't get back to sleep after that. I got up at first light and took a stroll around Tucson to work up an appetite. As I was returning to your home, Jesus Elias saw me and invited me in for coffee and something to eat.

"We talked awhile and he answered some questions I had about the game of Pull-the-chicken and how best to attempt it. They'll start at nine o'clock."

"Pull-the-chicken?"

Felton scratched his jaw and felt the stubble of the beard he was to grow. His time in Tucson would soon end.

"It's a horse competition. You ride full speed down the street and try to grab a buried chicken. Only its head and neck are above ground. The chicken ducks and bobs each time a horse or hand comes near it. It takes a lot of skill and a lot of luck to get hold of the chicken."

Bricela squinted and wrinkled her nose. "That sounds...dangerous for the riders, and a little cruel to the chicken. Won't its head come off?"

"Jesus says it comes out easy. When someone does get it he has to ride fast to get away from the other riders that chase after him. That's when it gets rough for the chicken.

"I gather Jesus is the favorite to win, especially with that stallion of his."

"I like Jesus," said Bricela. "I especially like how he treats his sweetheart, Juanita. He is very chivalrous."

Recalling the incident with the scarf, Felton smiled. "Yes, he is that."

"Juanita and I have become good friends. She is a Papago and her grandmother is a medicine woman. She is teaching me her language and their customs. Though I am Presbyterian, Juanita and I attend mass together. The catholic church of San Augustine is the only church in town."

"We rode past it yesterday when we entered town."

"What church do you attend, Caleb?"

Felton watched another woman with an *olla* balanced on her head before he answered. It gave him time to think of a response that would paint him in the best light without lying.

"I was brought up Methodist but I haven't been in a church of any kind lately."

Nearing the edge of the river, Bricela pointed to her right, indicating a crooked tree whose trunk was a foot in diameter. She said, "That is my favorite place in all of Tucson. Of course, we cannot picnic far away from town without armed escort. This is nearby and makes a very pleasant picnicking area.

"See how the tree has grown. It looks like the number two or a Z."

Walking toward the tree and the smooth sand at its base, Felton studied the bent tree trunk.

"Something fell on the tree when it was young but the tree didn't break. Whatever it was, it held the tree bent down for a year or two, then the tree tuned up toward the sun and kept growing. I've seen several like it in the woods back east."

Bricela took her arm from Felton's and, using her palms, lifted herself onto the bent portion of the trunk. She said, "See how it makes a natural chair?"

Since leaving the last adobe with Bricela at his side, Felton had merely glanced at her or kept her in his peripheral vision. Now, however, they were unavoidably face-to-face and he found himself staring into the same eyes that kept him awake throughout the long night.

There was a long silence. They did not speak nor did they touch. A faint smile of curiosity slowly grew on both their faces. Between them, in a realm where words had not yet found meaning, existed an obvious understanding.

"We should get back before someone misses us," said Felton.

Bricela's smile broadened as she helped herself off the tree and again put her arm in Felton's. "Yes, Lieutenant. We do not want the town talking. Would you be so kind as to escort me home?"

"Why, Miss Verde," replied Felton with polished formality. "I would be honored. Shall we?"

Bricela giggled softly, and then tried to look serious. "Yes, we shall, Lieutenant."

After returning to the road and taking a few steps toward town, Felton looked down in the sand at the tracks they had made only moments before. Now there were two sets of boot prints.

Felton stopped suddenly. "Excuse me for a moment, Bricela," he said, turning and looking behind him. "I want to look at something."

"What is it?"

Leaving her side, he smiled. "I'll be right back."

Looking casually at the opposite side of the road, Felton acted as if he had lost something from his pocket. Only briefly did he let his eyes check the tracks that abruptly turned and disappeared into the brush. The right boot heal was worn down more than the left and whoever followed them to the river had an unusually long stride.

Returning to Bricela, he took her arm and started again toward town.

"Well Lieutenant? What is the matter?"

"Can't fool you for a minute, can I?"

"No. In fact you cannot."

"Take a look down at our tracks and tell me what you see."

"Just our foot prints and those of sandals."

"There are two sets of boots down there. One is partially hidden in the grass. Don't look around but we were not alone at the river. Someone followed us and was likely watching.

"Judging from the length of his stride, he is long legged. If you look closely, you can see how his toes point outward."

Bricela sighed. "Cade, no doubt. Cade Mosby. He can be a pest."

For the next few minutes, the couple strolled in silence, enjoying the warmth of the rising sun. As they turned back onto Calle Real crowds were forming at the head of Calle del Alegria.

"It must be close to nine," said Felton. "I'd better saddle up. Will you be watching?"

"Maybe," shrugged Bricela. "I haven't decided yet."

"Will I see you afterward?"

Bricela smiled up at Felton. It was answer enough.

The entire length of Calle del Alegria was lined with excited Mexicans of all ages, a company of Confederates, and a sprinkling of white Tucsonians. Children threw rocks at dogs to chase them away while three men near the halfway point of the *calle* were busy burying an uncooperative chicken in the middle of the street.

To the west, a dozen horsemen assembled and prepared their mounts for the run. Holding the horses' reins, a Mexican boy beamed with pride as riders tightened cinches and checked stirrups

Smiles were universal. This was the *correr el gallo*. Winning was the object, but the brotherhood of sport reigned supreme.

Felton was braiding a loop into his horse's long mane. Jesus Elias was next to him doing the same to his bay.

"Your near stirrup?" asked Elias.

"Tied down to the cinch ring, just like you showed me. I took a hand-full of mane and tested it out on the way over. Along with this loop trick of yours, it ought to work fine."

"Some use leather strung from the horn," replied Elias, tugging on his finished braid. "I like the mane to hold onto. There is less chance to slide the saddle and end up in the *calle* for all to see."

"Some of the men," said Felton. "Told me on the way here that Comanches braid such loops and put their arms through. They shoot from under the horse's neck that way. Their saddles have something like a bone or stick for a cantle and they hook their leg around it instead of using the near stirrup.

41

"Those Comanche saddles aren't likely as good to sit on as ours, but I wouldn't mind owning one about now."

"The stirrup will work amigo. You can count on that. What you cannot count on is the chicken sticking her neck out for you." Elias walked behind his horse to the near side to double check his stirrup tie-down. He now spoke softly. "You see that skinny gringo with the big gray?"

Felton tested his braided loop and looked up. "Him? We almost met this morning…a couple of times. He was stealing a peak at Miss Verde from behind the corner of an adobe. He ran off when he saw me."

"That is Cade Mosby. He was weaned on a sour pickle, that one."

"Can he ride?"

"He thinks he can. He has a good horse but he is no *caballero*. He tries to win to be a man in the eyes of his father and Miss Verde. He forgets to have fun.

"His father is a *rico*. He would be much richer if the Apaches would not always be attacking his mine."

"He's using a leather loop on his horn," said Felton, taking a closer look at Mosby. "It's a long one at that."

"Es para nada. It will do him no good. He hopes very much to impress Señorita Verde, I think."

"I don't believe," grunted Felton, giving his saddle horn a hard jerk. "That Miss Verde will be here to see him even if he does win. She's hoping the chicken wins."

Elias laughed. "*Si*, amigo. That is Miss Verde. But she will be here, even so. Juanita has told me."

Unbuckling his belt that held the pistols and knife, Felton exchanged them with the boy for the reigns of his horse. "I'm all set."

With a grin that showed an even row of large white teeth, Elias nimbly swung into his saddle. "Arriba, amigo."

Felton and the other riders mounted in unison and all began to mill at the end of the street. Only Cade Mosby wore a frown.

A sombrero waved at the far end of Calle del Alegria and a young rider broke from the group. A cheer erupted from the onlookers. Within seconds, the *caballero* sent clods of dirt into the air at a full run.

Fifty yards down the street he leaned to his right. With his nearside boot hooked in the stirrup and his right knee bent, he slid to the right off his saddle. Letting his reins go he grabbed the leather loop that hung from his horn with his left hand and leaned even lower. He passed the chicken and reached for the head but the bird ducked away. His grasping hand narrowly missed.

The failed attempt was met with cheers and laughter as another rider bolted toward the chicken and quickly missed as well.

With each near miss, the spectators grew louder and more exuberant until finally only three contestants remained.

Cade Mosby had said nothing to anyone since the beginning of the competition. Now, waiting for his chance at the chicken, he sat next to Elias and peered across the Mexican at Felton.

"How old are you, Mister?" asked Mosby, as if he had a right to expect an immediate answer.

Elias smirked. He glanced at Mosby, shaking his head.

Felton took a deep breath and let it out slowly. "Older than you'll ever get unless you learn some manners."

With that comment, Felton spurred his stallion into a run and hooked his boot in the tied-down stirrup and leaned. Letting go of the reins and clutching the braided loop, he held his weight with his left foot and grabbed hold of the mane. His right hand was inches from the ground as the horse charged toward the chicken.

Felton snatched at the bird and came up with a few feathers that he released as he up righted himself. It was the closest anyone had come to pulling the chicken and the cheers intensified.

Felton slowed his horse and turned to watch. Instead of seeing Elias on his way it was Mosby.

Leaning to his side with the help of the long leather loop, Mosby got even lower than Felton had. His fingers grazed the dirt as he approached the bobbing head.

Twenty feet from the buried bird Mosby started to reach for the neck. His saddle slipped and rolled under the belly of the galloping gray. Mosby plowed into the dirt, rolling head over heals more times than anyone could count.

When he stopped rolling and was seen to be uninjured, both sides of the street erupted with laughter. Laughing uncontrollably, two men staggered from the crowd and helped Mosby to his feet and out of the path of the next rider.

Before the guffaws dulled, Elias was on his way. Sliding expertly to his right, he timed the hoof beats perfectly, and with cat-like reflexes shot his hand out for the bird. He passed the spot where the chicken had been, leaving only a puff of dust. Elias came up with the flapping hen, holding it high overhead, racing for the edge of town.

Immediately all the riders except Felton and Mosby gave chase. The posse soon disappeared at the end of the *calle* and headed for the plaza.

Felton knew he had the best chance of anyone to catch Elias, but he wasn't interested in proving whose horse was the fastest. At least not this way. *Correr el gallo* was Elias's game and he should enjoy it.

"That was quite a show, Lieutenant."

Recognizing Bricela's voice behind him, Felton did not turn to see who spoke. Taking off his hat, he held it over his heart. Taking a solemn breath, he leaned forward and placed a hand on his horse's neck. Straightening again, he said, "Pardon me, ma'am. I was observing a moment of silence for that poor unfortunate chicken."

Bricela rolled her eyes. "Very amusing."

Felton turned and feigned surprise. "Why Miss Verde, how do you do?"

Felton replaced his hat. He dismounted and faced Bricela, who stood less than a foot from him. A wisp of a smile adorned her natural beauty. She was as angelic in the midday sun as she was in the parlor's gentle firelight. Her pale blue eyes, faintly curious and entirely unpretentious, were studying him.

"You have an unusual brand on your horse, Lieutenant. Is it a two or a Z?"

"It's a Z, and there is a story that goes with it. If you walk me to the plaza by the church where we have made our corral, I will tell you all about it."

"Of course, Lieutenant."

Leading his horse by the reins, Felton and Bricela started through the empty lots between the scattered adobes heading south toward the Church of San Augustine.

"A Frenchman," said Felton. "Owned this horse and I won it from him in a card game. It was put up as a wager but he hadn't ridden it to town. After the game we rode out to his ranch to get it.

"The black looked sound enough but just out of curiosity I asked how fast he was.

"The Frenchman had a heavy accent. He said, "He iz az fazt az zee can be!"

"I said, "As fast as zee can be, you say?""

"Wee, wee," he said. "Az fazt az zee can be!""

"So we saddled Z here and I took him for a ride. He was the smoothest and fastest horse I'd ever ridden or seen ridden. I asked the Frenchman if he had any more like him, and I'll be da…I'm mean…I was taken back to see that he was breeding a small herd of blacks just like this one.

"I let the Frenchman in on my joke, even though I had to explain it a few times. I said he should brand all his horses with a Z. They would surely become famous for their gait and their speed. Everyone would remember when they saw that brand on a horse, it would be as fast a Zs can be."

"Did he take your advice?"

"As a matter of fact, he did. So if you see a horse with a Z on it, you can bet he'll be a fast one."

"Don't you think that is a bit odd?"

"What?"

"This morning I showed you my favorite tree—the one that had grown into a Z, and now you show me your favorite horse, a horse with a Z."

The similarity of the brand and the tree had not occurred to him. He immediately thought of her dog, Robespierre. He thought of his middle name. Felton shrugged. "You have a black dog and I have a black horse. It's just a coincidence. I mean sometimes things just happen at the same time."

"I know what coincidence means, Lieutenant," said Bricela, without malice in her tone. "Do you deny that you feel as though we have met before or somehow been very close at some other time or place?"

Felton looked down at his feet as he walked. "I'm not ready to answer that question yet."

"Please try. It is important."

Glancing up at the stallion, Felton hesitated several seconds. His experience told him not to answer, but Bricela had a way of weakening his resolve.

"I can't deny there is…something."

"Something?" questioned Bricela. This time her voice flickered with irritation.

"What I mean to say is…I can't explain it."

"Try…please."

45

Taking a few more uneasy steps, Felton said, "Well, if I were the romantic sort, which I am not, I might say I feel as if...it's kind of like there is a voice inside my head. I should be able to understand what's being said, but I can't quite make it out."

"So is it also coincidence that I should feel the same?" asked Bricela. "For me it's like an echo carried on the wind. It is an awareness, a type of a communion...but it's...much more than that."

"We've only just met, Bricela. You'll have to pardon me, but what you're suggesting makes no sense."

"If it made sense, we would be able to explain it. Neither you nor I can describe what exists between us. It is real, nonetheless. You can't deny that."

Coming to the edge of the church plaza where the Confederates corralled their horses, Felton stopped. "What I will admit is that there are some things that can't be explained. I say, at least for now, let's leave it at that."

Bricela was about to protest but a voice behind her interrupted.

"Don't unsaddle him, Caleb," advised Tevis, as he rode up beside Felton. "Captain Hunter has organized some patrols."

Tipping his hat to Bricela, Tevis continued. "Good morning, Miss Verde."

"Good morning, Lieutenant."

"What kind of patrols?" asked Felton.

"Well, you and I are going to see the Papagos at the San Xavier Mission. Lieutenant Swope is coming along but taking his patrol on down to the Mosby mine. The Apaches need to be cleared out.

"Jack Swilling is the most experienced Indian fighter among us. The captain has assigned his platoon and two others to scout outside Tucson to search for sign."

"Will you miss the dance?" asked Bricela.

Shaking his head, Tevis grinned. "Not me and Caleb. We're taking our platoon down and will be back before dark. We're trying to recruit a few Papago scouts is all.

"Some civilians will tag along to visit relatives and such. They've been afraid to go without an armed guard on account of the Indians.

"We'll be escorting them down and back with twenty men."

"Can anyone go?" asked Bricela. "I have yet to see the mission. My friend's grandmother is there, and I do want so much to meet her."

46

"There will be two or three wagons for sure. Likely there's still room for you."

"When do we leave?" asked Felton.

"Half an hour. We'll form up in the main plaza."

"If you gentlemen will excuse me, I must be on my way. I will see you both in the plaza."

Both Tevis and Felton tipped their hats and watched Bricela hurry away.

"You two make a dandy looking twosome," said Tevis. "That was quite a show you put on with that chicken run."

Felton continued watching Bricela until she disappeared beyond some adobes.

"You lived here for a while, Tevis. What do you know about Mr. Mosby, the man, not the kid?"

Tevis rubbed the neck of the stallion. "Thinks he's the biggest rooster in the hen house. I suppose some would say he's a good businessman, but a good many others would say he's ruthless. All he cares about is money. He'll take the captain's oath because it suits his interests and for no other reason."

"Know anything about his kid?"

"Not much. He's cocky now that he's grownup some and on account of his father's money, but it's all show. When I lived here he was a little runt. He was all the time getting picked on at school. People in town didn't feel too sorry for him. Some folks just resent people with money. Word was, though, he asked for most of what he got by shooting his mouth off.

"They're still laughing about how he fell off his horse this morning."

"He was trying too hard," said Felton. "He wanted to impress Miss Verde."

"I'd say you beat him to it. You can't blame him for trying. She's the only white woman around that's anywhere near his age. He must be twenty by now."

Other Confederates came toward the corral to lasso their mounts. They seemed well rested and in good spirits. Jack Swilling was among them.

"If I was you," said Swilling as he came near. "I'd leave that loop in your mane. Could come in handy fightin' Apaches."

47

"I was thinking the same thing," agreed Felton. "Too bad you're going to miss the *baile*."

Swilling swore. "I'd rather fight Injuns. You may get your chance, too. That mission is only eight or nine miles out, but that don't make no mind to an Apache. It don't matter none at all if you see no sign of 'em. None at all. They can be anywhere. You best learn to always be ready for trouble. I mean all the time…especially when you feel the safest. That advice alone will keep you alive out here longer than any other."

"Jack's right, Caleb. You're the least experienced Indian fighter in the company, and there's plenty to learn. The trick is living long enough to learn it."

Felton smiled amiably. "I fought a Cherokee in a bar once."

Neither Swilling nor Tevis returned the smile.

"Once you see what they do…you'll understand," said Tevis. "They're worse than animals…much worse. Men, women, children. It doesn't matter to them. You'll learn. You'll learn the same way we did."

CHAPTER 4

Built on a low-lying mesa, the white dome of Mission San Xavier del Bac could be seen for miles. Surrounding the church, the Papago *ramadas,* made of adobe bricks and ocotillo poles, blended perfectly with the desert. The approach to the church and the adjacent Indian village lay across a sea of sand punctuated here and there with a mesquite patch or occasional fifty-foot saguaro. Beneath the giant green sentinels, a few cholla and barrel cactus helped break the emptiness of the tableland. With such scant cover, even the hated Apaches would have difficulty concealing themselves. Once on the mesa, the column of three Confederate platoons and two wagons relaxed their vigilance.

Lieutenant Swilling led two platoons ahead of the wagons while Tevis and Felton's platoon maintained the rear guard. Bricela rode in the second wagon along with four Papagos, Jesus Elias and Juanita. The lead wagon was driven by Sylvester Mosby, and carried three armed men and supplies for his Patagonia mine forty miles to the south.

As the head of the column continued past the mission, the rear wagon stopped in front of it and the passengers started unloading. Swilling continued on the road to Magdalena. A moment later, the rear guard halted their horses in the shadow cast by the massive church belfry.

Lieutenant Tevis turned to Felton. "You talk to anyone around the church that speaks Spanish and I'll go out into the village and see what I can find. We need scouts that are willing to help us with the Apaches and the Union soldiers. Let them know they have to do both or we can't use them."

"Alright. Anything else?"

"Keep a close eye on those that came with us who want to go back to Tucson. I don't want to have to go looking for them and miss the dance. We shouldn't be here more than an hour."

Felton dismounted and tied his horse. "I'll be within shouting distance of this church and so will everyone else. I've got a dance or two reserved for me."

Glancing at Bricela who was brushing dust from her dress, Tevis said, "She'll have a full dance card tonight unless she has one of those *duenas* to guard over her."

As Tevis and the remainder of the platoon started for the village, Felton called out, "If you get this done quick, Lieutenant, I'll put in a good word for you."

Bricela and Juanita went inside the mission. Elias came over to Felton and rolled a cornhusk cigarette.

"Do you go inside, amigo?"

Felton watched Elias carefully. Rolling tobacco in a cornhusk was a unique custom and to pass for a Mexican, Felton would need to do it expertly.

"No."

"It is very beautiful."

"Maybe later. I'm supposed to look for Papago scouts. They have to be willing to scout for Union soldiers as well as Apaches."

"Buena suerte. The Papagos sold a lot of grain to the soldiers. They want to fight no one but the Apache. They hate the Apache. They like the soldiers. You will not get any scouts here."

"You sure?"

"Yes."

"How about you teach me how to roll a smoke like that."

Elias nodded and pointed to some shade near the mission doors. "Not in the sun. It will take you too long."

For the next ten minutes Elias showed Felton the tricks of using the husks as paper. He finally rolled one without spilling tobacco onto the sand.

"Now you must practice, gringo," grinned Elias. "It will come with time like all things. Soon you will be a damned greaser like me."

The heavy door to the church swung open. Juanita and Bricela emerged, both seemingly humbled by their experience.

"You must see it, Ca…Lieutenant," sighed Bricela. "It is magnificent."

Felton lit his cigarette and took a puff. "I will, later on. Elias has just taught me to roll a Mexican smoke."

Juanita shook her head. "Men. Always the same."

"I think Caleb has seen many churches," said Elias. "But maybe he has not seen someone like your grandmother. He will want to go inside the *ramada* and meet her."

"My grandmother is a medicine woman," offered Juanita. "She is called Owl Woman—she sees in the darkness what others do not. Her home is just behind the mission."

"I'd like to meet her, Juanita. You two go ahead. Elias and I will finish these husks and come visit."

Taking Bricela by the sleeve, Juanita turned up her nose. "Come Bricela. We will leave these two to their smoke."

Felton watched the women round the corner of the mission. He glanced cheerfully at Elias. The Mexican was suddenly serious.

"Did I say something wrong?"

Crushing his cigarette, Elias said, "We go now."

After one last puff of tobacco, Felton dropped his cigarette and smothered it with the sole of his boot. "I'll apologize to Juanita, Jesus. Sometimes I forget my manners."

"Come," said Elias. "Juanita is not the problem. It is the medicine woman we must not offend."

Stepping out of the shadows, the sunlight reflecting off the white-washed mission was almost blinding. Heat radiated from the towering walls like an oven. Following Elias, Felton squinted back at the church. It was bigger than any he had seen, but that was the only difference. They were all the same. At least this one was good for blocking the sun.

The front of the *ramada* was shaded by a crude layer of sticks held up by crooked mesquite logs. Ocatillo lined the adobe bricks on the outside and a chimney poked through the dirt roof. The door was open.

Elias removed his hat and entered. Felton did the same.

The one-room adobe had no windows. It took them a moment to adjust to the dim light. In a far corner, Felton could make out a fireplace. In another, a white sheet of muslin hung down from the drab walls and out onto the floor to form a type of shrine. Carefully arranged on the muslin was a picture of the Virgin Mary and a crucifix. Next to them were bits of ribbon, some colored beads, and small pieces of ornate pottery.

Bricela and Juanita were sitting on a hemp matt. Across from them, a pair of black eyes peered out from underneath a white *rebozo*.

The medicine woman's eyes were fixed on Felton. She spoke but not in Spanish. Juanita responded and the older woman repeated the same words. Juanita spoke again in Papago. The medicine woman calmly repeated what she had already said.

Juanita turned toward the two men. Her face was filled with confusion.

"Please sit down, Lieutenant," said Juanita. "Next to Bricela. Elias, you sit next to me."

With no introduction of any sort, the men took their places. Owl Woman's eyes had not left Felton since he had entered. They now drifted to Bricela and back to Felton. For several seconds she studied them both. She spoke as Juanita interpreted.

"Grandmother says that," Juanita paused. "Some of our Papago words have no English word. No word in Spanish either. I will do my best to tell you what she sees.

"Grandmother says that you, Lieutenant, and Bricela have…medicine…you have a…joyous sadness.

"Grandmother says…you are like eagles that soar but cannot land…no…that are unable to land.

"Grandmother says…again…that you and Bricela are…this is a word you cannot…there is no word…but the closest is…that you are…twins."

There was a long silence before the old woman spoke again.

"Grandmother wants to know what you think, Lieutenant."

Sitting in the dim light of the adobe with Bricela by his side, Felton stared into the penetrating eyes of the medicine woman. Since his fathers death he had believed in nothing he could not see or touch. Yet Bricela was a reality he could not explain any better than the words of Juanita's grandmother. What did she mean by "sad joy"…or "twins?"

Owl Woman suddenly laughed. She put her hand on Felton's knee and spoke.

"Grandmother says it is good to doubt an old woman."

Felton grinned and nodded.

The woman's eyes narrowed. She spoke softly through a smile.

Juanita cocked her head. She shrugged. "Grandmother says you will soon come to meet the woman who lives in the big water. You will no longer doubt an old woman's words."

Bricela leaned forward, her eyes on the medicine woman. "Juanita, ask her if there is *any* way the eagles may land together."

"What?"

"Please," pled Bricela. "Ask her."

Juanita repeated the question to her grandmother.

Owl Woman put one hand on Bricela's knee and the other on Felton's. She closed her eyes and rocked back and forth. In a low, monotonous tone, she muttered, and then half whispered a continuous chant. Her wrinkled skin flushed.

Felton looked at Bricela, then at Elias and Juanita. All three stared expectantly at the medicine woman. The answer they waited for would have no more meaning than anything else Owl Woman had said. Prophecies and fortune telling were always performed with an element of vagueness. Indian medicine was no different than other parlor tricks he had witnessed.

After several minutes, the ceremony ceased and Owl Woman slowly opened her eyes. She spoke to Bricela.

"Grandmother says such a thing can be, but she cannot see. It is too far."

Placing her hand on Owl Woman's, Bricela smiled. "Thank you."

Understanding the meeting was over, everyone but Owl Woman stood and started for the door. When Bricela was almost out, the medicine woman spoke two words.

Walking back to the wagon, Bricela looked quizzically at Juanita. "Did she say goodbye?"

Juanita stopped and glanced back. "No. She said…'be strong'."

"Who was she talking to?"

Juanita turned and stared ominously at the heat waves far out on the desert horizon. "I think…I think she spoke to all of us."

"Strong about what?"

"I do not know," said Juanita, starting again for the wagon, but this time with a quicker pace. "It is her way. She does not explain everything she sees or everything she knows. Sometimes it is not good to know too much."

Seeing Tevis and his platoon returning at a gallop, Felton and Elias helped Bricela into the back of the wagon.

"It looks like Lieutenant Tevis is done early," said Felton. "Just as well. I haven't been to a dance in ages."

Bricela eyed Felton uneasily. "We need to talk about what Owl Woman said, Lieutenant. I need to explain something to you."

Elias took the driver's side of the springboard and Juanita sat next to him. Each held their heads low and did not speak.

Tevis was approaching fast. "At the dance," said Felton, mounting his horse. "We can talk tonight."

"Done already?" asked Felton.

Tevis came alongside in a cloud of dust. "I didn't get any scouts, but I did get information the Captain will want right away. You have any luck?"

"No. Elias says these Papagos won't go against the Union. There's nothing in it for them."

"I agree," said Tevis, who then rode to the wagon.

"Are the other Papagos coming back with us?"

Juanita shook her head. "They will stay with their families. We are all that will return."

"Good. We'll lead out. Stay right behind us, Señor Elias. No straggling."

Tevis returned to Felton and led the platoon north at a fast walk.

"I never will understand how they do it," explained Tevis. "The Indians know things long before the whites. They told me a large force of Union soldiers is gathering at the Yuma crossing. There are over a hundred supply wagons already there and more arriving every day. They said a small Union force crossed the Colorado a few days ago and is heading up the Gila toward the Pima village.

"The Union has been stockpiling hay and grain there and at several stations along the Overland Stage route. They're preparing for an assault on Tucson as soon as they get all the forces assembled at Yuma.

"They're telling everyone the Army's on a campaign against the Tonto Apaches, but those Indians are too far to the north. They're headed where the stockpiles are and then straight for us."

"Sounds like we better enjoy the dance tonight," said Felton. "Tomorrow we go to work."

As the platoon and wagon rode up the Calle de Mission, Felton looked at Tevis. "I'll be at headquarters directly. I have to make a stop at Solomon's store first."

"It'll take a few minutes to gather the other officers," said Tevis, watching Felton veer away. "Don't take too long."

Passing by the wagon, Felton smiled at Bricela. He dismounted in front of the store and went quickly inside.

"I was just closing up," grumbled Soloman from behind a counter. "It's getting late. Besides, you Confederates already took most everything I got that's worth anything."

Pointing to a shelf above the counter, Felton said, "I want that brooch."

Soloman turned and studied the polished white ornament centered on a red lace ribbon. "You got silver or gold to pay for it?"

"How much?"

"That there is ivory. I made it myself from a piece I traded from a Pima."

"Where did a Pima get ivory?"

"Said he found it. They come across it time to time. It's elephant tusk. That's why it has a little yellow in it. It's old."

"How much?"

Folding his arms, Soloman scowled at his empty shelves. "That would cost the likes of you a gold Eagle."

Felton raised an eyebrow. "Ten dollars?"

"A man has to make a livin' somehow. What else do I have to sell now?"

"Let me take a look at it."

Soloman seemed surprised at the request, and took the brooch from a small display box. Handing the necklace to Felton, he muttered, "Carved and polished it myself. Took me a good while."

Admiring the workmanship and recalling the red ribbons Bricela wore in her hair, Felton laid the brooch on the counter and reached into his pants pocket. He laid down a silver three-dollar trime. From another pocket he retrieved a one-dollar gold piece and two quarter Eagles.

Using a big finger, Soloman moved the coins around. "That's only nine dollars."

"You won't dicker some?"

"Ten dollars is ten dollars."

"Throw in the box for ten dollars."

"Deal…if you got the other dollar."

Felton grinned as he took back the trime and the gold dollar. "You drive a hard bargain, Mr. Soloman."

As the merchant smugly reached for the brooch, Felton produced a five-dollar gold piece from the palm of his hand and slapped it down on the counter. "Ten dollars…and the box."

Captain Hunter was pacing the dirt floor of the adobe when Felton stepped inside. The sun had set and lamps were already lit. After Felton, came Tevis and Sergeant Holmes. The rest of the officers were already present.

Hunter stopped pacing and faced his men. "We just had a Mexican courier come in from Los Angeles. He confirms what the Papagos told Lieutenant Tevis this afternoon. "A large army of up to two thousand men is gathering at the confluence of the Gila and Colorado rivers. The express rider reported that General Carleton is undoubtedly in charge of the operation. He has been sending camel riding couriers, Hi Jolly and Greek George, back and forth from his headquarters to Yuma. Colonel Rigg is now in Yuma organizing an advance guard. Yuma is three hundred miles from Tucson, but he sent workmen ahead of his column. They've been stockpiling feed for weeks at stage stations along the Gila, especially at the Pima mill run by Ammi White. White is a Unionist and has hundreds of pounds of grain ready for Carleton's forces.

"Lieutenant Tevis' sources report a small armed force has already crossed the Colorado River and is on its way to protect White's mill and to scout out our strength.

"Tomorrow at sunrise, we will leave in force. We should arrive in time to intercept and capture the Union scouting party at the Pima village. That is ninety miles from here. From that point on we will burn all stockpiles as far west as we can. Carleton must be delayed until we can get reinforcements from General Sibley.

"I have reason to believe there are Union spies here in Tucson. Messages have been getting through about conditions here for several months. Keep this information about our departure to yourselves. Go about the dance tonight as if nothing is known. We will leave before daybreak and it will be a forced march, gentlemen. We must not allow Rigg to discover our strength here in Tucson at any cost."

It was after dark when Felton and Tevis left Captain Hunter's adobe and returned to the Robinson home. Lamps were lit in the rear entrance but the Robinsons and Bricela were gone. A hint of perfume met the two men as they entered the back door.

"They've already gone to the dance," said Tevis smelling the air. "Miss Verde and Mrs. Robinson will sure enough be the bells of the ball."

56

Felton thought of the small box he had placed inside his coat pocket. He wanted to privately give the brooch to Bricela before the dance. Now he would have to wait. He was leaving tomorrow and could be gone for weeks. Hopefully, it would not seem too forward presenting the gift at the dance. Certainly Bricela would understand. How would her aunt and uncle react? Though it seemed much longer, they had only known each other a few hours.

He would have to think of a way to present the brooch and offend no one. It was a delicate situation for all concerned. And, when viewed from the outside, quite absurd.

"Are you going to shave?" asked Tevis. "You're looking mighty rough around the edges for someone going to a *baile*. These are big events out here."

"You haven't heard."

"Heard what?"

"Jack volunteered me to be a spy. I'm supposed to pass for a Spaniard, a gentleman from Sonora. At some point, I was going to be sent west. Now, I can see I'll be headed for Carleton's forces. It seems likely I'll leave tomorrow."

Tevis' eyes narrowed. "That's dangerous, Caleb. They hang spies, or shoot them."

"So I've heard. I'm growing a beard like Ochoa's. They're making up some new clothes for me. I should be fine. Let's just wash up and get over there."

In their room a pan of water had been set on a dresser, as was a bar of soap and a towel.

As Felton washed his hands and face, Tevis looked into a small hand mirror and combed his hair.

"When we first walk into the dance hall," explained Tevis. "They are going to break an egg over our heads."

Felton toweled off his face. "A what?"

"Actually, it's an egg shell filled with colored paper. It's some sort of tradition, so don't act surprised. Don't wait to be presented to anyone. It's not like our dances back home. Here you can talk to anyone you choose and ask any woman you want to dance with. Everyone is there for a good time. All ages come."

"What kind of music do they have?"

"Usually, a flute, harp, some pipes, a drum, and a fiddle. They don't sound bad. Besides, it's the best music you're going to hear for three hundred miles."

"Do we go armed?"

"Always."

Felton traded the towel for the mirror. The stubble on his face was going to need some explanation.

The adobe chosen for the dance was next to the Shoo Fly Saloon. It was one of the largest buildings in Tucson and had been reserved for such occasions. Lamps burned outside the doors, illuminating the plaza. As Tevis and Felton neared the *baile,* they caught sight of a man emerging from the shadows. He disappeared, only to reemerge again. He appeared to be dancing. They stopped and watched him.

He spun in slow circles, and then started to waltz. Holding his arms around an invisible partner, he spoke softly. He threw his head back and laughed.

"We do not know his name," said a voice from the darkness. Estevan Ochoa stepped into the light. "He came into town one day, the sole survivor of an Apache massacre. He has acted this way since that time. What he saw, what happened to him no one knows.

"He is harmless. We all feed him and care for him. He was scared out of his mind. He has never recovered. It has been years."

"What could have been that bad?" asked Felton.

Ochoa glanced at Tevis, then at Felton. "You are new here. You have not seen what the Apaches can do.

"Señor Tevis, Señor Swilling, and many of the others can tell you the stories, Lieutenant Felton. You will have to see with your own eyes to understand. No words are possible. Words, no matter how cruel, could describe what this man has seen."

Felton watched the dancer. "How do you know it was Apaches that caused it?"

"When he first came to Tucson, he would not stop talking. He talked crazy, but enough was understood. We went to look for his people...and we found them. Some he had called by name. Most of them were dead before we got there...some we killed ourselves."

"You killed some Apaches?"

"No, Señor. We put to death what remained of some of the Mexicans."

"Enough of this kind of talk," said Tevis, trying to lighten the mood. "Let's enjoy the dance while we have it."

"Certainly, Señor Tevis," agreed Ochoa. "First I would have a word with the Lieutenant, if you please."

Tevis shrugged. "Meet you inside, Caleb. Don't be too long or all the women will be danced out."

Ochoa rolled a cornhusk cigarette. Pointing to the tobacco, Felton asked, "Do you mind?"

Handing the makings to Felton, Ochoa smiled approvingly as he watched Felton make his own smoke the Mexican way.

"I spoke to Señor Soloman this evening," said Ochoa. "He likes you. He says you are different from the other Southern Confederates here."

"I try to get along," said Felton, awkwardly finishing his cigarette then taking a light from the end of Ochao's.

"I feel I must tell you something," said Ochoa. "Something of which Señor Soloman believes you are not aware."

Felton blew smoke into the cool desert night. "Like what?"

"You are making enemies of the Mosby family. They are powerful and dangerous to those that get in their way."

"I've done nothing to them. Why should I be their enemy?"

"May I ask your age, Lieutenant?"

Felton laughed softly. "You're the second person today to ask me that."

"And the first?"

"Cade Mosby," replied Felton, immediately suspicious. "What's the connection?"

"The connection, Señor, is Miss Verde."

"Oh, that. Well, jealousy is an old story Señor Ochoa. A story I am more than familiar with."

Ochoa took several puffs on his cigarette before he spoke again. "How old are you?"

"Close enough to call it thirty-four."

"I would have thought younger but it is of no matter," said Ochoa. "A few years would still make no difference."

A thought was beginning to form in Felton's mind. He blocked it before it could surface. "Why?"

"Señor, Miss Verde has just recently seen her fifteenth year."

Caleb Felton's mind went blank. He could hear the blood pulsating in his head. There was no thought, no sensation at all. For several seconds he was speechless. From seemingly far away he heard himself repeat the word. "Fifteen?"

"She looks much older, it is true. It is an easy mistake to make. I did not think you knew."

"Fifteen?" repeated Felton. This time his mind was clearer as he grasped the meaning of what was said. "You are certain?"

"Yes. There is no doubt."

"She's barely more than a child."

"In years, Señor. In years only. Still, it is the way of things. For you my friend, it is a joyous sadness you must endure. If she were thirty and you fifty, it would not be so frowned upon. But there is no hope for the two of you."

"Why didn't she tell me?"

"*Quein sabe,* Señor. A young woman, an older man. Who can say?"

Felton dropped his cigarette but did not crush it. "Thank you for telling me before I made a complete fool of myself."

"What will you do now?"

"I leave tomorrow. I'll go to the dance tonight. Everything will go back to the way it was. I will go back to what I was. I was headed straight for hell anyway. That makes Miss Verde as close to heaven as I'll ever be…at least I'm going to have this one night with her."

"Lo siento mucho, Señor. I will leave you to your thoughts. I go to the *baile* now."

Felton stood in the darkness. He looked down at the cigarette glowing at his feet, then at the hapless Mexican dancing insanely in and out of the shadows. Whether he heard the music from the dance or from memories of better days, Felton could not say. In his imaginary world, he had at least found happiness.

Perhaps all happiness was an illusion, a short-lived fantasy that existed in moonlit shadows and soft fire light. Bricela Verde seemed real enough. From the moment he saw her, there existed a harmony, an intimacy that was impossible to explain.

There was a purity about her, an innocence that inspired a sense of reverence. He wanted to touch her, to caress her. Yet for the first time in his despicable life, his passion was devoid of lust. From the beginning, it seemed like a dream or an awakening from a long forgotten memory. Now it was over.

Felton swore and crushed the fire out of the cigarette with his boot heel. He was a scoundrel and she an angel. He would never have her. He had been living a fool's life and this was the long awaited punishment of God.

Passing the dancer, Felton removed his hat and stepped through the door of the *baile*. A young girl on a ladder immediately crushed an egg over his head, dusting him with bits of yellow and blue paper. Candles were lit along the walls and by each hung a picture of a Catholic saint. A small fire burned in a corner fireplace. Along the walls low benches were built of rough-cut cottonwood. Only a few were occupied. The packed-dirt floor was crowded with couples laughing and dancing to the lively tunes of the band that was somewhere in the front of the hall.

Felton caught a glimpse of Bricela dancing with Captain Hunter. Instead of feeling the sting of foolishness experienced a moment before, he realized nothing had changed. He still felt the same fascination and, however it might be defined, the same admiration. The bitter disappointment of losing her had vanished.

Perhaps from the beginning he knew he was not good enough for her. Or could it be the uncertainty of war tethered his emotions and unknowingly constrained him. Whatever prepared him for this night somehow left him dispassionately resigned to his fate.

Placing his hat on a bench, Felton worked his way around the dancers until Bricela spotted him.

The dance ended and she quickly came over. Felton noticed the red ribbon in her hair and smiled. Being in love with her would have to be enough. There was no hope in it, no future. Just being with her, enjoying a brief existence near her, was all he could ever have.

Reaching inside his jacket, he took out the box and handed it to her. He gave it no more thought. It was purely a gift. He no longer cared what others might think.

"This is for you, Bricela. I want you to remember me."

Bricela's eyes flickered with discomfort. "I don't require anything to do that, Caleb."

A torrent of churning emotions mixed within Felton. The words of Owl Woman echoed in his mind…a joyous sadness…almost the same words Ochoa just spoke in the plaza. It was as close a description as anyone could hope for.

"I know, Bricela. But we are leaving tomorrow for a while...and this is war."

"Don't say that, Caleb. Nothing will happen to you. I know it will not. I know it."

"Just the same, I want you to have it. I think it is more for my benefit. I want you to have something I gave you."

Bricela smiled weakly and opened the box. "It is beautiful, Caleb. The red ribbon matches the one in my hair."

Watching her tie the necklace, Felton said, "It's ivory. Soloman Warner made it."

"It is lovely. Especially since it came from you."

"Shall we dance?" asked Felton, extending his hand.

"Certainly, Lieutenant Felton."

Felton held her at a distance. His left hand felt the softness and warmth of her fingers while his right held her gently around the waist. He looked deeply into her eyes. He knew they would never be as close as they were at that moment.

As they danced, Felton thought of Owl Woman. She had only been guessing but was good at her craft. Two eagles that could not land, she had said. Their feelings for each other must have been obvious to the medicine woman as well as the age difference. She was a wise old grandmother and, no doubt, could show a gypsy fortuneteller a few tricks.

As soon as the tune ended, Felton was tapped on the shoulder. He turned to see the bruised and pimpled face of Cade Mosby.

With words carrying the smell of whiskey, he said, "I'll have the next dance."

Felton's stomach twisted. He managed a courteous smile. Bowing to Bricela, he stepped out of the crowd and went to the bar. Several men leaned against it including Estavan Ochoa and Soloman Warner.

Warner nodded. "Buy you a drink, Lieutenant?"

"I could use one. Thanks."

Indicating the brooch, Warner added, "Looks mighty good on her."

Accepting a glass from the bartender, Felton toasted Warner and Ochoa. "Here's to fools every where."

"To fools," said Warner.

"*Salud*," said Ochoa.

Just past midnight, the *baile* started to wind down. To avoid arousing suspicion, most of the soldiers began leaving an hour before, in twos and threes. Hunter knew there would be Union sympathizers in Tucson, and their departure for White's mill was to be a closely guarded secret.

Of the officers, only Felton remained for the last dance. Bricela had promised it to him. When Mosby asked for it and was politely refused, he stormed from the hall. Now the band was announcing the final tune and couples were taking their places on the dance floor.

Elias and Juanita were in the center of the room where Bricela and Felton soon joined them.

"Our last dance," said Felton.

Bricela took his hand as the band started playing a slow, mournful tune. Felton once more put his hand around her waist. She looked up at him.

"I danced with Mr. Ochoa twice this evening."

Felton stiffened. "He is quite a gentleman."

"He said he spoke with you in the plaza before the dance."

"He did," replied Felton. "He did."

They danced slowly for several seconds, each trying to read the others eyes. Finally, Bricela spoke.

"It *is* meant to be, Caleb. No matter what you think now."

Felton smiled. She was so beautiful. "Bricela...it makes no sense."

"Since when, Caleb...since when does love have to make sense. It never does if you think about it. It is its own form of senselessness."

Felton wanted to tell her she was too young to understand the love between a man and woman. Having never experienced it himself, he said nothing. He refused to mention her age. It would only insult her. He wanted the night to be perfect...if not for himself, at least for her. She would have the memory of him, even if it were a fairytale. He could at least give her that. That was far better than the truth.

"I am afraid Owl Woman was right," he said.

"I will wait."

"For what, Bricela? We are 'two soaring eagles that cannot land', remember? But it doesn't mean we can't see each other from time to time."

"She only said it would be a long time, Caleb. But it *was* possible. Juanita says her grandmother only sees pieces, not everything. Just pieces of what is to be."

63

The tune was ending and Felton struggled to tell her how he felt. He wanted to say it just once.

"Bricela, you do know how I feel about you?"

"Yes…but I would like to hear it."

Before he could speak, the last notes of the band fell silent. Realizing the finality of the moment, Felton gently embraced her. Saying nothing, he stepped back and paused. Forcing a smile, he took her hand and kissed it.

Feeling elated and nauseous at the same moment, Felton said, "I'll meet you outside and walk you home with your aunt and uncle. I need some fresh air."

Grabbing his hat, Felton went out the door and stood in front of the Shoo Fly. Fighting the urge to vomit, he leaned against the wall next to an oil lamp. Tugging on his hat he inhaled deeply but it did no good. He bent forward just as bits of pulverized adobe slammed into the side of his face and a roar and flash of gunpowder exploded from the darkness.

Diving into the shadows, Felton drew one of his Colts. He rolled and came to his feet. He could hear someone running, then nothing.

Elias was first through the door of the dance hall, quickly followed by Palatine Robinson and Bill Oury.

"What the hell happened?" roared Oury. "Someone take a shot at you?"

Felton wiped the dirt from his face. "Could be," he said honestly. Then lying, "Likely it was just some drunk shooting at the moon."

The shot had come from forty to fifty paces away and in poor lighting. Someone knew how to shoot and shoot well.

Bricela, Juanita, and Mrs. Robinson came out next. Bricela tried to hide her concern but it was futile. She went to his side, took a lamp from the wall and held it close to him. She saw pinpoint drops of blood forming near his temple.

"You're bleeding," she exclaimed.

Looking at his hand, he saw blood mixed with dirt. "Just the ricochet, that's all."

Felton glanced at Robinson and Oury. They had been drinking heavily, but were still sober enough to walk home. Elias had come to the dance unarmed.

"I was going to walk home with you all, but I think I'll take a look around first. We don't want a drunk shooting up the town. Bricela, you should go along with them."

Bricela started to protest but wisely did not. So far, only Ochoa and Warner had any idea of her relationship with Felton. It was best to keep it that way.

Felton waited until the Ourys and Robinsons left with Bricela. He took the lamp and went to where the shot had been fired. The ground was still soft from the recent rain and would leave a fair track. Between two adobes that formed a narrow alley, Felton found what he was looking for. The shooter wore boots, not Mexican sandals. He stood for a long time waiting for his shot, and in doing so left several clear prints. The right boot heel was worn more than the left, and the toes unmistakably pointed out more than normal.

Leaving the lamp behind, Felton ran across the plaza toward the home of Sylvester Mosby. He had gone to his mine, but his son was still in Tucson.

Mosby had run in the opposite direction of his home and would be circling now to get back before he was discovered. Guessing he would enter the rear of his house, Felton quickly hid in the shadows near the back walkway. He had not waited long before the crunch of sand under hard boot leather sounded from the blackness.

A tall figure appeared and paused. He shoved a pistol into his pants, using his shirt to conceal it. When he finished tucking his shirt, Felton stepped from the shadows.

Mosby turned but a fist flattened his nose and sent him backwards. He landed on his back with a thud. He didn't move.

Felton rubbed the knuckles of his right hand, then jerked Cade's pistol from its hiding place. He smelled the barrel. It had recently been fired.

Cade Mosby was a jealous coward but he could shoot. He was nineteen, old enough to be considered a man, but there was no reason to kill him. Everyone deserved the privilege of being a fool at least once in their life.

Bricela put on her nightgown and robe. She went downstairs to stoke the fire. Lieutenant Tevis was in his room. Her aunt and uncle had gone straight to bed. After adding wood to the fireplace, Bricela sat and gazed into the growing flames. Someone had tried to shoot Caleb Felton. He seemed well liked by almost everyone. Only one man she knew of had any grudge against him. Something told her that man was the type to hide in the darkness as the shooter had done.

She could not get Cade Mosby out of her mind. He was as obnoxious as his father, but without the backbone to be successful at anything. He had been taught to take what he wanted at the expense of others, but lacked the fire of ambition that burned in his father. He had inherited too much of his mother's desire to merely be handed an easy life.

If he did take a shot at Caleb, and Caleb caught him, what then? It was attempted murder and all because of her. If Mosby hadn't missed, Caleb would be seriously wounded or dead. None of this was supposed to happen. It was a private affair, a precious moment in her life that bordered on the sacred. It wasn't supposed to be like this.

Hearing the back door open, Bricela rushed from the parlor into the hall. Felton stood there as if nothing was wrong. He smiled at her. His eyes were soft and understanding.

Bricela went to him. She hesitated, then put her arms around him and laid her head on his chest.

"I was worried," she whispered.

Felton gently pushed her back and motioned toward the parlor. When they were seated by the fire, he spoke easily.

"Everything is fine, Bricela. You shouldn't worry about me."

"Did you find out who shot at you?"

A grin from Felton brightened Bricela's mood. His smile always lifted her spirits.

"He won't try it again."

"Who was it?"

"No one important. He'll look like a raccoon for a few weeks…if he shows his face that is."

"The night was so perfect, Caleb. I dearly wish it had not ended that way."

Felton brushed a strand of hair from Bricela's forehead. "We both agree on that."

Bricela could not resist. Even though she had no doubts, she had to ask. She desperately wanted to hear Caleb say it, at least once.

"Caleb…do you love me?"

There was a moment of silence. She looked expectantly into the flames of the fire. Her heart pounded.

"Yes, Bricela. I cannot explain it or begin to understand it. The feeling began the moment I saw you, it was there at the river, it was still there when I discovered your age. It's here now and hasn't changed. It will never change…no matter what happens in the future. No matter how our lives may turn out…I will always care for you."

Tears rolled down Bricela's cheeks. She smiled and looked at Felton.

"That is so beautiful…and so sad."

Felton took her hand, caressed it for a moment. He kissed it. He stood slowly and took one last look into her pale blue eyes. "Good night, Miss Verde."

Bricela's lip quivered though she forced a smile. Another tear streaked her cheek. "Good night, Lieutenant Felton."

Wiping her tears away, Bricela went to the entry of the parlor and watched Felton go down the hall and into his room. He did not look back.

Ascending the stairs to her room she whispered, "You're not going to be rid of me that easily, Caleb Felton. Too much unites us. Too much bonds us. Too many signs confirm us. We both see it. We sense it. We know it."

Closing the door to her room, she went to the bedside stand. There was a bottle of ink next to an unfinished poem. She read what she had written the night before.

There were obstacles to his affection
That blocked their sunlit path
In vain she tried to pull him from their shadows
Just to know the feeling of love
Yet in all life's beauty, there she remained
Being chased by the laughter of the wind

Putting pen to paper, Bricela started to write.

Emotions rain down like tears of a wandering angel
Painting blurred pictures in her mind
The parting words are softly spoken
The moment safely tucked away
In that sadness of a passing joy
To ease the broken pain

She reserves a place in her heart for him
And holds a smile in silent love
For in time, and time again
Their destiny's pilot is reunion

CHAPTER 5

Sixty men and three wagons rode quietly out of Tucson before the break of day. By sundown they were making camp at the abandoned Picacho stage station forty-five miles northwest of Tucson. Towering above the station like an enormous castle, a red-brown mountain peak of rock cast a dark shadow over the scattered thickets of mesquite and soldiers.

After sending scouts ahead, Captain Hunter ordered small cook fires to be used, and only then under the branches of the mesquite and palo verde trees. He wanted no smoke rising into the clear desert air.

The men scattered into the brush with their horses to make camp. Hunter and the officers unsaddled in the pole corral and went into the flat-roofed adobe station. In the fading light, Hunter walked across the dirt floor to the crude table used to feed the passengers of the stage line. He took out a map, unfolded it, and set it down on the dusty tabletop.

Lieutenants Swilling, Tevis, and Felton along with Sergeant Holmes gathered around.

Hunter lit a candle. Hunching over, he rested a finger on the map. "We're here, at Picacho Station," he said, sliding his finger along a line of black ink. "Another forty-five miles up this stage road is the Pima village. Near the village is White's flourmill and trading post.

"My spies tell me that White has sold fifteen hundred sacks of wheat to the Union and stockpiled them at his mill for General Carleton's Army. From Fort Yuma, all along the way to the mill, Carleton has been sending men ahead of him to cut and stack hay."

Hunter moved his finger again and tapped it on a black rectangle. "From the mill to Stanwix Station is another fifty miles. There are at least six stations in that stretch that have hay set aside for his cavalry and stock teams.

"Stanwix station to Fort Yuma is about ninety miles. I doubt we can go farther east than Stanwix before we encounter resistance. We will go as far as we dare. Carleton needs the feed to move across the desert. We have to delay his advance as long as possible until our reinforcements arrive from Mesilla."

"A small Union force crossed the Colorado River yesterday and is on the stage road headed for Tucson. We will leave at three tomorrow morning to arrive at White's mill before the Union patrol. We'll take White prisoner. When Carleton's men arrive, I'll impersonate White."

Hunter paused and studied Felton's appearance.

"Lieutenant Felton. Sergeant Holmes has your clothes ready. You need to darken your beard with charcoal. You and Lieutenant Swilling will leave at two with one platoon for escort. Within a proper distance, you are to leave the platoon and enter the village posing as a Mexican expelled from Tucson. Use your own judgment regarding what to say to White in order to gain his confidence. Once you have the opportunity, arrest him and hold him.

"Any questions?"

Felton rubbed his chin with the back of his hand. "If the Union soldiers are already at the mill when I ride in, what then?"

"In that case you must do your best to escape and report back to Lieutenant Swilling."

"Lieutenant Swilling, when you have secured the mill, send a courier to report to me."

"Yes, sir."

Sergeant Holmes handed Felton a sombrero with a silver-studded hat brim, a red sash, and short-waisted jacket.

Felton took off his hat, replaced it with the sombrero. He put on the jacket. It fit perfectly.

Swilling shook his head. "Damned, Captain if he don't look like a greaser. With that sash and them pistols, he'll pass sure as hell."

Hunter nodded. "If I were you, Lieutenant, I would speak only Spanish. White likely speaks some like we all do. You can get your point across about being sent out of Tucson. If he gets suspicious, kill him."

"What does he look like," asked Felton, suddenly uneasy at the thought of killing a man he had no quarrel with.

"I've seen him," said Tevis. "He's tall and thin and his face looks like old boot leather. You'll know him on sight."

"Inform only the men you'll need," said Hunter. "I want all fires out before dark."

Walking out of the adobe, Felton unbuckled his gun belt and wrapped the sash around his waist. He buckled his belt again and looked at Swilling and Tevis. "I kind of like this outfit," he said. "What do you gringos think?"

"Too bad your beard isn't fuller," observed Tevis. "That's the only draw back I can see."

"A little more trail dirt and some fire-black and he'll pass," said Swilling. "That sombrero cinches it."

"I have another pistol in my blanket," said Felton. "I'll add it to the sash. That'll help."

"Where'd you come across another pistol?" asked Tevis.

Felton shrugged. "Took it off someone last night after the dance."

"Took it?" asked Swilling.

"He got careless with it at my expense. It's engraved and has eagles carved on both sides of its ivory grips. It's a .44, but it'll go well with the silver hatband. Four chambers are still capped and loaded."

"Them Yankees like the .44," offered Swilling. "If we catch us some of them fellers, we can get you some caps and balls."

"Let's make sure it's us that does the catching," cautioned Tevis. "If they catch Caleb and find out he's with us, they'll likely shoot him."

"That won't happen, boys," said Felton. "Unlike the two of you, I'm a total stranger in the territory. I'm the right color and I ride a stallion like the Mexicans. This will be easy as falling off a log."

"Let's give the captain's orders to the men and get back to the station," said Tevis. "I'm hungry even if it's only bacon and coffee. Maybe Holmes brought some of those corn tortillas along."

Swilling wiped saliva from the corners of his mouth. "If'n we get to that flour mill early enough, we'll be eatin' hot bread. All we can hold."

The Lieutenants split up and passed Captain Hunter's orders to the men. Before returning to the station for supper, Felton went to the corral to retrieve his blanket. He was bone tired. After eating, he wanted nothing more than to roll up in a corner and fall asleep.

Thoughts of Bricela kept him awake the previous night. When he finally started to drift off, Tevis shook him. In a matter of minutes they were saddled and forming a column of twos for their ten-hour march.

Felton hoped to sleep in the saddle on the way to Picacho, but Swilling wanted him to know what lay ahead and kept him awake throughout the long march. He advised Felton of the terrain to the west and the tactics of the Apache. Along the stage route, at what seemed every half mile, Swilling pointed out piles of stones. Each was a grave of someone killed by Indians. The ones marked with crosses made of Spanish bayonet or mescal were Mexicans of the Holy Mother Church. The numerous graves without such markers were Americans. There was a story behind each tragedy and the First Lieutenant knew the gruesome details of most of them.

Swilling's tales of murders inflicted on hapless travelers were blood chilling and revolting. How much of what Swilling recounted was fact and how much exaggeration, Felton could not guess, but if the stories were even faintly accurate, the Apache was like no Indian he had ever heard of.

How could they possibly run a horse to death or travel one hundred miles in a day on foot? What human could be so cruel to a captured prisoner? What Swilling claimed they did to women and children, Felton simply blocked from his mind. It was unthinkable.

Inside the pole corral Felton went to the fence rail where he had forked his saddle. He reached for the leather straps that held his blanket then paused to look at the fading sunset. He could not help but think of Bricela. She should never have come to such a place as New Mexico Territory. Even if half of what Swilling said was true, she shouldn't be anywhere near Tucson, or Mesilla for that matter.

This was a land of heat and cold, of scorpions, and cactus. It was a place of constant danger and death. Bricela was a delicate flower in a land of desolation and thorns. She was innocent, overly romantic and somewhat of a mystic. A young woman like her belonged back east where it was civilized. Not in Tucson, with its crumbling mud houses, dirt streets, and abandoned churches.

The war of secession had trapped her in the middle of nowhere with no way to escape. Bricela believed fate brought him to Tucson and destiny had thrown the two of them together. For what purpose? What purpose was there in having her become attracted to a thirty-three year old man and then shed tears over him? Or for Bricela to be surrounded by blood thirsty savages or see white men kill each other in battle?

Swearing softly, Felton took another look at the sunset. The color was almost gone. His eyes drifted higher to view the evening star. While his eyes held on it, a thought suddenly occurred to him. Until he met Bricela, his life had no direction, no meaning other than pursuit of self-satisfaction. Now something was undeniably different. He cared for someone. He cared in a way he could never hope to explain. At this moment in time, she needed him. She needed him to help her get back to where she belonged, to take her home.

He could at least do that for her. If he was worthy of nothing else...he could accomplish that much. He could protect Bricela Verde until she was safe.

Felton stared at the star, recalling his attempts to define his feelings for her...even after he knew her age. Certainly protecting her was a part of it, at least a piece of the confusing puzzle. And it was perhaps the only piece that would ever fit into his misspent life.

Swilling reined his horse to a stop just as the sun crested the eastern mountain peaks. He saw a set of white buildings five miles ahead, surrounded by fields.

Felton and Tevis rode up next to Swilling.

"That it?" asked Felton.

"Yep," replied Tevis softly. "A mill, house, and trading post all in one spot, all painted white. It's called Casa Blanca. It's pure coincidence it belongs to a man named Ammi White. When the Indians and Mexicans say Casa Blanca, they're speaking to the color of the house, not his name."

"The mill's next to the house," said Swilling. "The Pimas are friendly, so if you pass by any don't give 'em a thought. Just get White if he's alone. If the Union soldiers are already there, try to get back and warn us. Otherwise, we'll ride in casual like, in about a half hour. The captain will be another half hour behind us."

"No problema, Señor," replied Felton with a rare salute to Swilling.

"Hasta luego," Felton said to Tevis.

Felton put the black into an easy canter and in a matter of minutes was in front of the whitewashed adobe of Ammi White. A quick look around revealed no other horse tracks. There was a good chance the Union troops were not there.

Before Felton dismounted, a man opened the door and stepped out of the adobe. He shielded his eyes from the rising sun with one hand and held a double-barreled shotgun in the other. He was well over six feet tall with a prominent Adams apple and dry, wrinkled skin. There was no doubt he was White.

"Buenas dias, Señor," greeted Felton.

"Who are you and what do you want," grumbled White.

Felton smiled. "Lo siento mucho. No comprendo."

White studied Felton closely. "You no *comprendo*, eh."

"*Si*, Señor."

"De donde?" asked White.

Captain Hunter was right. White spoke some Spanish but very poorly. He wanted to know where he had come from. He would want to know why.

"Tucson. Los Confederates esta muy malo, Señor. Soy para el Union."

"Confederates in Tucson?"

"Si. Hay muchos."

"How many? *Cuantos?*"

If White had received word and already knew how many men were in Tucson, a lie at this point could get him killed. Telling White the truth would do no harm if the miller were taken captive.

Felton shrugged. "*Cien.*"

White seemed pleased with the answer. Felton rubbed his stomach.

"Tengo hambre, Señor."

Easing his grip on the shotgun, White motioned for Felton to dismount and come inside. "*Comida*, eat."

"Muchas gracious, muchas gracious, Señor," replied Felton, quickly dismounting and tying his horse.

White set his shotgun down just inside the door and went into the adobe. It had four large rooms separated by two walls and another door. He indicated for Felton to take a seat on a bench next to a rough-sawn table. White went into an adjacent room and spoke. A woman answered but not in English or Spanish.

Felton removed his sombrero and set it on the table. He took out a cornhusk and some tobacco. When White looked back at him, Felton held up the tobacco and asked, "Esta bien?"

"Sure, go ahead," said White. "Nosotros tenemos heuvos y carne."

The man was hospitable and Felton hadn't had eggs in weeks. He would hate to have to shoot him.

White came back from the kitchen and sat across from Felton. He took out a pipe and Felton offered him his tobacco pouch.

"Don't mind if I do," said White. He took a pinch of tobacco and tamped it into the blackened bowl of his red clay pipe.

Felton lit his cigarette and handed the match to White. The smell of ham cooking drifted from the next room and mixed with the aroma of tobacco. It would be at least fifteen minutes before Tevis and Swilling arrived with the platoon. Almost time enough to eat.

"Adonde va?" questioned White. His tone was friendly.

"California. Para vivir con me tio."

"California, you say?" smiled White. He took several puffs on his pipe. "Mr., you're gonna run into a pack of *Californios* before you get too far."

Smiling as if he did not understand, Felton repeated, "Californios. Si. Mucho gusto."

"Usted va Los Angeles?"

"No," answered Felton. "San Bernadino."

"Never been there," muttered White. "Been to Los Angeles, though. They grow oranges there. Sweet as sugar."

As Felton finished his cigarette, a short heavyset Pima woman brought out two plates of eggs and ham. She disappeared into the kitchen and returned with coffee and fresh bread.

Thankful that White was a man of few words, Felton ate in silence, enjoying fried eggs and bread still hot from the oven. He was pouring himself a second cup of coffee when he decided the time was right.

With his left hand, he raised the tin cup to his lips and blew steam away from its rim. His right hand went under the table and eased the ivory-gripped Colt Army from his waistband. He sipped coffee. It was freshly ground and strong. White's pantry had been well-stocked from California.

Seemingly enjoying his coffee, White suddenly looked toward the door. The sound of horses caught his attention. So did the raspy clicking of the revolver's hammer as Felton raised the pistol over the table and casually pointed at White's chest.

"You serve a good breakfast, Mr. White. Get ready for more guests. They'll be hungry."

Staring wide-eyed at the pistol, White froze. He failed to notice Felton spoke with no accent. "What the hell? Who are you? Some damned Sonoran bandit?"

"No, sir. I am Lieutenant Felton, Confederate States of America. You are my prisoner."

A knock came at the door.

"Come on in," said Felton. "You're late for breakfast but the kitchen's still open."

With pistols in both hands, Swilling kicked the door and it swung open. Seeing Felton at the table, he slowly holstered his pistols. Calling to Tevis, he ordered the men to hide the horses and post a guard before coming inside. He also sent a courier to hurry Hunter along.

"Looks like you got the drop on him," admired Swilling.

"Mr. White, this mangy looking gentleman is Lieutenant Swilling. He's in charge until Captain Hunter gets here."

Tevis came inside and looked at White, whose face was a portrait of shock. "For a Yankee, he doesn't say much does he?"

"Serves up a good breakfast, though. There's an Indian cook in that other room. If you catch her before she bolts out the back, you can put her to work."

Several of the privates entered through the front door. A few entered through the kitchen's rear entrance. A private ushered the Indian into the room where Swilling and Felton waited. She showed no expression.

"She your cook?" asked Swilling.

White's eyes narrowed. "She is. She don't speak English or Spanish. I ain't tellin' her to fix food for no Rebels."

"Mr. White," said Felton, still pointing the pistol at the miller's chest. "You are speaking to Confederates. And you should be grateful that Captain Hunter is in command and not me. He is a gentleman. Personally, I would shoot you for aiding the enemy...but the captain insists we use good Southern manners. First, he will conduct a trial for you. Then he'll hang you."

Tevis shook his head. "So much formality for a man that won't feed weary travelers. It's a waste of time when a bullet is so easy and quick. The men are hungry. They don't want to wait for a trial...no matter how short it will be. Maybe we should shoot him now and just tell Captain Hunter he got ornery."

Swilling tugged on his mustache and thought for a moment. He drew his pistol and cocked it. "You're right. My belly is empty. Let's get it over with."

"Stop!" bellowed White, putting up both hands. "She'll cook for you."

Feigning disappointment, Swilling slowly uncocked his pistol. "Well, it's a fair trade by and by. Tell your cook to make enough for eight hungry men right off, and to keep on a cookin'. There's more behind us."

White gave the orders and the stoic Indian was escorted back to the kitchen.

Taking White's coffee cup, Swilling sat next to Felton. Tevis went to the kitchen and the men found places to sit against the walls.

"Did he tell you anything about who's comin'?"

"No," said Felton. He uncocked the Colt and set it on the table in front of him. "His Spanish isn't so good."

"When Captain Hunter gets here, he's goin' to take White's place. Most of the men will hide out 'til we know what we're facing."

"Well, if Mr. White here has stockpiled fifteen hundred sacks of wheat and flour, he's expecting a lot of company."

Swilling nodded. "If Carleton has done sent out his advance guard, he won't be far behind. There ain't enough water in the desert to send out a large force all at once. They'll have to send 'em two or three companies at a time. The first bunch after the advance guard is likely to be two to three hundred men."

"Those aren't good odds, if you ask me."

Swilling took a gulp of lukewarm coffee. "That's one reason we're mounted on the best horses west of the Mississippi. When we have to, we plan to fight some, then hightail it. Just slow 'em down 'til General Sibley or Colonel Baylor reinforces us."

"None of you is wearing uniforms," complained White. "How's a body to know you're soldiers and not common folk? If Carleton catches any of you, he'll hang you for spies."

"Except for this dashin' Mexican next to me," said Swilling pleasantly. "We're made up of Arizona Guard, Texas Rangers, and West Texans. Our uniforms ain't made it this far west. If Carleton knows what's good for him, he'll respect that...or we'll make it a point he does.

"You've been out here long enough to know what we can do if we have a mind to, don't you, Mr. White? Ask yourself who we been fightin' while your Yankees has been livin' high on the hog in the big cities?"

Swilling's eyes hardened at White. "If Carleton or any of his men hang one of us, we'll show him and his eastern lily-livered bastards how to kill men Apache style. Ever' last one of my platoon can and will do it."

White's Adams apple bobbed up and down. Swallowing hard, he had nothing to say in response.

Felton glanced at Swilling. There was fire in his eyes. He wasn't bluffing. The change in the lieutenant was unsettling. Would someone as seemingly refined as James Tevis actually kill a man as Swilling claimed the Apaches often did? Was any civilized man capable of such unthinkable brutality? If he was, how thin was the skin of civilization?

A private came out of the kitchen with a fresh pot of coffee and more cups. Swilling eyes shifted from White to Mosby's ivory-gripped revolver on the table.

"Mind if I take a gander at your new pistol?"

"Go ahead."

Palming the revolver, Swilling felt its weight. "It's heavier than the Navies. Shoots a bigger ball, too."

Rubbing a finger along the barrel, he studied the engraving. "It's silver plated. Could be one of a matched pair.

"Tevis told me you took it of'n the one that took a shot at you after the dance. Likely he'll be a wantin' it back."

"He's welcome to try and take it," said Felton. "Next time I won't be so accommodating."

Swilling handed the Colt back to Felton. "Should'a killed 'im. Likely you'll have to sooner'n later."

Felton looked at the ivory grips. They had been checkered for better handling. An eagle with outstretched wings was carved on both sides. Birds were a common decoration to such grips, but usually on one side only. With such craftsmanship invested in the pistol, Swilling could be right. It might be one of a set, with Cade Mosby in possession of the other.

Frowning skeptically, Felton thought once more of the old Papago medicine woman. Two eagles that soar but cannot land, she had said. Twins, she said as well.

Turning the pistol from side to side, he studied the grips more closely. The eagles had been carved identically. But these eagles had landed on the grips of a Colt pistol, hadn't they? They were soaring nowhere. Why was he thinking of such nonsense? He and Bricela had almost nothing in common and yet the Owl Woman had called them twins, at least that's what Juanita had translated. The old woman had simply sensed their attraction to each other and guessed the age difference between them. That would explain the comment about the soaring eagles. Nothing else rang true. They were not twins, and there was no "woman that lived in the big water" that she had spoken of either.

Yet there was something in the way the old Papago stared at him. Something she seemed to *know*. He played enough poker to recognize the look in her eyes. What could she possibly have had up her sleeve? The two of them had never met.

On the other hand, there was the nagging sensation that he and Bricela were more than recent acquaintances, more than simply a young woman and a man beginning to care for one another. For this, there had to be an explanation. The harder Felton searched for an answer the more it eluded him. It constantly remained just beyond his grasp.

Felton replaced the pistol in his sash. "Nobody will come asking for this pistol. Just the same, I'll keep it out of sight when we get back to Tucson. I don't want trouble on account of it."

Tevis returned with two plates of ham, eggs, and fresh biscuits. He placed one in front of Swilling and sat down at the table. He began to eat.

"When the captain gets here," he said between mouthfuls. "We're loading all the flour we can carry onto our three wagons and taking it back to Tucson. They'll be happy to have some bread for a change instead of tortillas."

"What do we do with all the rest? There'll be at least a thousand sacks left behind."

"Burn it I suppose. We can't leave it for the Yankees. If they aren't too close, we can come back for more."

Felton stood. "I'm going to see what kind of trade goods White has in his post."

"Take a look at the mill while you're at it," said Swilling. "We can't be leaving it for the Yankees, but if we lick 'em and push 'em back to California, we'll be needin' it for ourselves. See if you can figure out how to take some of the parts off'n it."

Walking out the front door of White's home, Felton saw no one. Only his stallion remained in sight. Even the tracks of Swilling's platoon had been wiped from the road. These Confederates knew how to lay a trap.

The trading post was well supplied. Felton found two boxes of .44 caliber balls along with a full tin of caps and shoved them in his pockets. There was much the captain would take to supply his men and that meant less room in the wagons for food. The war was going to leave everything in short supply.

The flour mill was run by a steam engine. After studying the machinery, Felton discovered several belts that could easily be removed along with some crucial gears. It would be a simple matter to dismantle it, but what they would do with the hundreds of stored flour sacks, he had no idea.

Felton returned to White's house as Captain Hunter and his fifty troops rode up. Swilling came out of the adobe.

"No problems, Captain. White's inside along with his Pima cook. We ain't seen no Yankees so far."

Felton added what he had learned. "There's a well-supplied trade good store next to the mill. The mill is full of flour sacks and runs on a steam-powered engine."

Hunter dismounted and ordered his men to disperse around the buildings and hide the horses. Some men he sent to the trading post with orders to take anything useful and load it into one wagon. The other two wagons were to be filled with flour.

The captain turned to Sergeant Holmes. "Take some men and destroy the belts to that mill. Dismantle the mill as much as you can and hide the parts where we can find them later."

"Yes, sir. And the extra sacks of flour and wheat, sir?"

"Send a rider to the Pima village. Tell them it's theirs and that it's a gift from the Confederacy. Tell them to come get it now. They need to take all of it back to their village."

"Any difficulty in arresting Mr. White?"

"No, sir," replied Felton. "He didn't lift a finger."

"Let's go have a look," said Hunter, and went into the adobe followed by Swilling and Felton.

White still sat at the table next to Tevis. The miller glanced up sullenly as Hunter entered.

"You are Mr. White?"

"Yea, that's me."

"I am Captain Hunter of the Confederacy. Mr. White, you are a known Unionist and have sold supplies to the Union Army. We are confiscating your property for the Confederacy and placing you under arrest.

"Lieutenant Swilling, take Mr. White to the mill and have him held prisoner. If he tries to warn anyone of our presence, leave orders that he is to be killed immediately. Otherwise, make him as comfortable as possible.

"Send the men in here four at a time to be fed."

After Swilling left with his prisoner, Hunter and Felton sat down. Felton rolled a Mexican smoke. Hunter poured himself some coffee.

"Did White suspect at any time that you were not Mexican?"

"No."

"Good. Depending on what happens here, I may send you on ahead. I have spies about but they have heard very little from Yuma. I suspect there are still some Union spies in Tucson as well.

"I believe the spies are leaving Tucson for Sonora and heading west to California. I may send you in that direction to see what you can discover. I have not decided yet."

"Captain," said Tevis. "We beat the Yankees to this village but it couldn't be by much. What are your plans?"

"I will answer the door when they arrive, and if they do not know White by sight, I will impersonate him. You two lieutenants and a few men will be lounging inside. The men will conceal their weapons. You, Lieutenant Felton, will continue to act as a traveling Mexican. The men inside will pose as mill workers. The remainder of our company will remain hidden outside. We will try and take the Yankees without a shot if we can. We should outnumber them at least three to one. I want no unnecessary bloodshed.

"Before I announce who we are, I hope to gather as much information as possible. They know White is a Union sympathizer and hopefully they will speak freely."

"It will be close quarters if shooting starts," warned Tevis.

Hunter took a drink of coffee. He never smiled. "That it will, Lieutenant. Lieutenant Felton will be the only one visibly armed. Likewise, if things go wrong, Lieutenant Felton, you will be first to draw their attention...and their fire."

The hours rolled slowly by. The Confederates continued to come and go from the mill in small groups to get more coffee or food. Anyone that might be watching would think nothing unusual was occurring.

Hunter ordered the cook to bake bread and keep baking it. He wanted the smell of fresh baked bread in the air when the riders approached. It was the universal aroma of home. It would be disarming to all but the most wary, and anyone arriving after dark would be thinking of food and comfort.

It was near midnight when a sentinel reported the sound of galloping horses. Hunter ordered everyone to their places. A minute later, a heavy knock came at the front door.

One of the privates slowly stood and picked up an oil lamp. He casually opened the door.

"Who are you?" asked the private.

"Americans," a voice reverberated through the closed door.

The private slowly opened the door and held the lamp high. A tall square-jawed man with a close-cropped black beard stood erect in a neat Yankee captain's uniform. "Does Mr. White live here?" asked the captain with a distinct Irish brogue.

"Yes, he does," answered the private.

"Give him Captain McCleave's compliments, and tell him I want to see him."

The sentinel went into the dining area and returned with Captain Hunter.

"Are you Mr. White?" asked McCleave.

"Yes. Who are you and what do you want?"

"I am Captain McCleave of the First Regiment Cavalry, California Volunteers. I am here with three men. We are Union soldiers. We require supper and forage for our horses."

Hunter smiled agreeably. "Very well, Captain. You're welcome here. In fact, I have been waiting for your arrival. Take off your weapons and make yourselves at home. I am glad to see you. I have been stockpiling goods for the Union for weeks."

McCleave signaled his men to come in. After hanging his weapons on a wooden peg on the wall, he took a seat in an armed chair. His men kept their pistols, and all sat at the table. McCleave nodded to Swilling and Felton who nodded in return. He took out a pipe and filled it with tobacco.

"Supper will be in a few minutes, Captain," said Hunter. "We have ham and beans and of course, bread and coffee."

"That's Jack," offered Hunter, pointing to Swilling, who sat against the wall pretending to repair a cast iron gear from the mill. "He's my head man in charge of the mill workers. That Mexican standing next to him just rode in today from Tucson. He doesn't speak too much American."

McCleave lit his pipe. "Tucson, eh?"

Looking at Felton, McCleave tried his hand at Spanish. "Soldatos en Tucson?"

"Si, Capitan. Mucho."

"How many, uh, *cuantos*?"

Felton tried not to laugh. He had never heard Spanish spoken with an Irish accent. "No se. Muchos."

Taking a puff on his pipe, McCleave's eyes narrowed. "We have spies in Tucson. We received word from them at Fort Yuma that you could be in danger, Mr. White, including all your forage and flour. That's why I rode ahead to check on your situation."

Hunter paused and looked at the three other Yankees. "You only have three men with you, Captain. What would you have done if the Confederates were already here and I were a prisoner?"

"I was in a hurry, Mr. White. Major Rigg was quite concerned about our forage supplies. Despite the risk, I was sent ahead. I left six of my men at the Maricopa Wells station and proceeded posthaste. Behind them, I have another detachment of mounted soldiers already in route.

"At Fort Yuma we are amassing a force of over two thousand men. We will have infantry, cavalry, and artillery that include six- and twelve-pound howitzers. Our equipment is being personally scrutinized by General Carleton himself, down to the type of shoes and leather they're made of. When we begin our march, nothing will stop us."

"When might that be?" asked Hunter, surprised at how much McCleave was divulging.

"We should be in control of Tucson by the first of June. No later. Of course, from Yuma we have to dispatch the men at intervals due to scarce water and supplies, but all has been planned."

"When do the first detachments start across the desert?"

"I should say within the week, Mr. White."

"You say General Carleton is heading this whole army. What kind of man is he?"

Pompously plucking at the tips of his buckskin gloves, McCleave removed them as a smirk grew under his beard. "The general and I served together in the Dragoons before the war. He was a captain and I was his first sergeant. We are close friends. He personally asked me to join his command. That is why I took the initiative to come here and secure the provisions for his advance."

Hunter acted impressed. "So it's Carleton in command, Rigg, then you."

"Yes. The Confederates have no such chain of command. Their military presence in Tucson is quite primitive."

Hunter gave McCleave several moments to continue but he seemed to be finished dispensing information. The room was quiet. The smell of fresh bread and pipe smoke filled the air.

Hunter came to his feet. "Captain McCleave of the First Regiment of Cavalry, California Volunteers, I am Captain Hunter of the Confederate Army. You are my prisoner."

Immediately, the door to the other room flew open and the rest of Hunter's men burst in. McCleave stood, half in shock and half in rage.

"I will not surrender, sir!" he declared. "I will not surrender!"

Hunter calmly drew a pistol from his inside coat pocket. "If you do not, sir, I will blow out your brains."

McCleave started to protest but then slowly sat down in total humiliation.

"Captain McCleave, if you swear an oath to take up no arms against the Confederacy, you may enjoy your freedom while you are amongst us."

McCleave mustered all the defiance he could. "I will take no such oath."

"Then you will remain under close arrest." Hunter holstered his pistol, keeping his eyes on McCleave. "Lieutenant Tevis, you are in charge of Captain McCleave. Show him every courtesy as an officer. Shoot him if he tries to escape.

"Lieutenant Felton, your services are again required. Lieutenant Swilling, you and your platoon will accompany Lieutenant Felton to Maricopa Wells at once. It is best we have the six soldiers at the wells back here before dawn...alive if possible."

Knowing the next stage station at Maricopa Wells was less than ten miles from the mill, and that Apaches almost never attacked at night,

Swilling took his time leading the platoon along the stage road. He wanted the six remaining soldiers cooking breakfast when Felton knocked at their door.

An hour before sunrise the platoon rode up a slight grade and onto an alkaline plane covered in pale-green salt grass. It was three more miles before Swilling spotted the gray outline of the flat-roofed adobe at the wells. He and his men quietly dismounted and lead their horses into a warm morning breeze that drifted in from the west. When he spotted a wisp of smoke rising from the chimney, he halted.

Whispering to Felton, he said, "Go on in like before. We're comin' right behind you in one or two minutes. So be quick about gettin' the drop on 'em. They got you six to one. It's likely some of 'em, maybe all of 'em, will be wearing their pistols."

Felton adjusted his two Navy Colts and his newly acquired Army pistol. This would be far more dangerous than dealing with a single unsuspecting mill owner. These were soldiers.

"Don't be too long, Jack," said Felton, stepping up into his saddle. Leather creaked as he uneasily shifted his weight. "I can bluff them some but the sooner they know they're surrounded the better."

"You ever shot anybody? Ever got your man?"

"No. I grew up hunting with a rifle and shotgun, but pistol shooting isn't my game."

"As close as you'll be in there you won't miss. If it comes to 'shoot Luke or give up the gun', you be the first'un to shoot. And keep on shootin' once you start."

Felton pulled his sombrero down low. He had been in close scrapes before but never anything like this. His heart rate climbed. This was war. When he signed on with Hunter, it was merely to get out of Texas. He had no feeling about cession one way or the other. He had no feelings in general about much of anything. Now he was a Confederate facing a room full of Yankees that would kill him if given a reason.

Swilling reached up and shook Felton's hand. "Buena suerte, amigo."

"Vaya con Dios," returned Felton. He gently nudged the stallion into an easy walk.

The phrase "Go with God" was common among Mexicans. Now, facing the reality of death, he felt the sting of hypocrisy in his choice of words. Felton started to swear but instead chastised himself. "A little late in the game," he muttered. "To be bringing God into it."

Bricela's face appeared in his mind but was quickly forced from his thoughts. Thinking of her now could get him killed.

In front of the station, Felton eased out of the saddle and tried to look relaxed. It was still dark but his movements could easily be seen in the starlight.

"Hola a la casa," he announced. Remembering the Apaches also spoke Spanish, he added in accented English, "I am recently from Tucson, Señores, and would like something to eat. I can pay."

The station door opened a crack. A faint glow of lamp light could be seen.

"Did you come by the flour mill? White's mill?"

"*Si*, amigos."

"You alone?"

"*Si*"

"Why didn't you stop at the mill? Why'd you keep on riding?"

Felton thought quickly. He was at least good at that. "I must see my señorita in Los Angeles before she marries another hombre. I ride hard. I was so tired, I fall asleep in the saddle. My horse is a good one and he keeps the road. I wake up and here I am."

The door opened wider and a gruff-looking sergeant stepped out for a better look. He held a carbine in his hand and wore a pistol around his waist. "Alright. Come ahead."

Felton grinned sheepishly and tied his horse. "*Gracias*, Señor.*"

Inside the station, a soldier was heating some water on a cast iron stove and two were rolling their blankets. Two more sat at a table. All looked at him as he walked in. Each man wore a pistol. With Swilling right behind him, he had to make his move quickly.

Pausing by the door, Felton allowed the sergeant to pass by him on his way to join the others at the table. Still smiling, Felton removed his sombrero with both hands and held it in front of him. The size of it covered the two pistols on his hips.

"Hola, hola," he repeated, half bowing to the soldiers until each regarded him as harmless. The sergeant laid his carbine on the table.

As soon as their attention was diverted, Felton let go of his sombrero and in one smooth movement drew and cocked both Navy pistols. "Don't any of you go for your guns or many of you will die," he said, still maintaining his Mexican accent.

The soldiers froze. The sergeant's eyes betrayed his intentions. "You damned greaser bandit. You think we'll put up with the likes of you?"

Felton spoke in a polished southern accent. "Before you go for that carbine, Sergeant, consider the fact that you are surrounded by an entire platoon of Confederate soldiers. My captain wishes to take you all alive, but we'll kill all of you if you insist. We already have Captain McCleave and his three men."

The mention of McCleave and his men was enough to defuse the sergeant for the moment. But he was no fool.

"So where is this platoon? I don't hear nothin' outside."

Felton stalled. "They are awaiting my signal. If you choose to surrender, I will give the signal."

The sergeant's eyes narrowed. "What if we don't surrender?"

A smile grew on Felton's face. "The boys in the platoon will see that what I claimed I could do is true. I will collect my bets."

"What bets?" snorted the sergeant.

"That I can kill all six of you before you get me. They say I can't...I say I can. Want to try me, Sergeant?"

Before the sergeant could reply, the door was kicked open and Swilling jumped inside the station with a double-barreled shotgun in hand. He was followed by a half-dozen screaming soldiers. Bloodcurdling Rebel yells filled the air.

As the yelling subsided, Swilling swore. "Damn, Felton. You taken all the fun outa this war. I was itchin' to get me a war record."

Felton holstered his pistols. "Close enough for me, Jack. The sergeant there was about to call my bluff."

"So there weren't no bets?" snarled the sergeant. "You're nothing but a blowhard!"

"No bets, Sergeant. But this is Lieutenant Jack Swilling and these men are his Texas platoon. Before this war started, they hunted Comanche and Apaches for a living. They don't bluff about anything.

"Had you killed me, you all would have died. This is much more civilized, don't you think? Captain McCleave thought so. He surrendered like a gentleman and is being treated as such. Behave yourselves and you will receive the same consideration."

CHAPTER 6

It had been two weeks since Bricela awoke and found Caleb gone. She asked her uncle if he knew when the soldiers might return. All he divulged was that the men had left quietly and secretly. That same evening Sylvester Mosby returned from his mine and told everyone he had seen no apaches anywhere. He needed more workers. Jesus Elias signed on along with ten other Mexicans.

The remainder of the Confederate company that had stayed in Tucson told her nothing of Captain Hunter or the missing lieutenants. All they said was that they themselves were patrolling Tucson for Apaches and had seen no sign.

Four days after Caleb and the other soldiers disappeared, Elias left for the mines. Since then Bricela, Juanita, and her older sister Maria, went each morning to Saint Augustine's Church to pray for everyone's safe return. They were coming out of the church, the day already growing warm, when Captain Hunter and three dozen men rode into the church plaza.

The women stood near the church wall as the Confederate soldiers, dirty and tired, dismounted. The women didn't recognize ten of the men. They wore blue uniforms and had no weapons. One had captain's bars on his shoulders.

Though he was bearded and covered in cream-colored dust, Bricela easily recognized Lieutenant Tevis. Anxiously, her eyes darted over the rest of the soldiers. "I can't see him, Juanita. Do you see him?"

"Who, Bricela? Who is missing?"

Briclea caught herself. She had not told Juanita of her feelings for Caleb. It was something even her closest friend would find difficult, if not impossible to understand.

"The other lieutenant that was staying with us, the one your grandmother said was my twin. Lieutenant Felton."

"Oh. The handsome one," said Juanita with a faint smile. "You look for him."

"Those men in blue," asked Maria. "Are they the enemy of your friend's army?"

Continuing to search the men, Bricela nodded. "Yes, I believe so."

"Maybe they had a fight. Maybe Elias's friend is hurt or..."

"No," interrupted Bricela. Her tone was confident and calm. "No, I would know if he were hurt...or worse. He is fine—just not here with these men."

Maria looked questioningly at her sister Juanita.

"Grandmother...she says they are...Grandmother says Bricela would know such a thing."

"He is the one Elias told me of?" questioned Maria.

"Yes. He and Elias are friends. He is the lieutenant that played run the chicken."

Maria smiled. "Mucho bueno hombre."

"If you two will excuse me," said Bricela, stepping away from the church. "I want to talk to Lieutenant Tevis."

"Mañana, Bricela," said Juanita.

"Si, Juanita. Mañana a la Mission," replied Bricela.

Walking slowly toward the men as they led their horses into the corral, Bricela waited until Tevis passed near her.

"Lieutenant Tevis," she called.

Tevis smiled and came toward her. He brought the large man with captain's bars with him.

"Miss Verde, good morning."

"A fine day indeed, Lieutenant," replied Bricela. She was suddenly uncomfortable with the presence of the other man.

"Miss Verde, may I introduce Captain McCleave of the Union Army. He is to be our guest for a while."

McCleave took off his hat but did not smile. "It is a pleasure, Miss."

Bricela blinked as the words Tevis spoke began to register. "Pleased to meet you, sir."

"Miss Verde, I am certain you have many questions but I must first attend to the good captain, here. After I clean up, I will come to your house if the room is still offered. I will tell you all about our adventures."

"Yes, Lieutenant. The room is still yours...and Lieutenant Felton's if he returns."

Tevis grinned broadly. "Oh, he'll be along. You may not recognize him when you see him, but he'll be along. Wait until you hear what he

89

did. The man has more pluck than anyone I know. He surprised the…he surprised all of us."

Bricela felt a chill go down her spine. "I will have tea ready, Lieutenant. At your convenience."

Hurrying to catch up with Juanita and Maria, Bricela quickly gave them the news that all was well, then went home.

Mrs. Robinson was in the kitchen when Bricela rushed inside to meet her. "Aunt Charlotte, the soldiers have returned," announced Bricela. "They have some Yankee prisoners and one of them is a captain. I think Lieutenant Felton may have had something to do with their capture."

"Yankees! Here? Was anyone hurt?"

Bricela excitedly put a teapot on the stove. "No. I don't think so. Lieutenant Tevis is coming to tell us all about it."

"And Lieutenant Felton?"

"He will be along later," answered Bricela. She stiffened her lips to fight off a smile. She rubbed her eyes to hide the flush in her cheeks. "I don't know when. But he is safe."

Mrs. Robinson's brow wrinkled. Placing a gold-rimmed serving plate in a cupboard she said, "War is such a dreadful thing. Your uncle and Mr. Oury have both endured the horrid experience. The stories they tell are so awful."

Only half-listening to her aunt, Bricela thought of Caleb. They would have so much to talk about, so much to try and resolve. Or maybe just to wonder about. He would soon be by her side and they could walk together once again. It was such a simple pleasure…and for now it was enough. She was young but she would be patient. In a few years no one would question their affection for one another. Time was not their enemy. It was merely an impediment to an inevitable outcome.

"How did you know the men were Yankees?"

"Lieutenant Tevis introduced me to the captain."

Mrs. Robinson drew a breath. "My word! You were that close to a Yankee?"

Bricela was opening a tin of tea. She paused to think. "He seemed just like any other man. The captain, I mean. He did not look dangerous. Lieutenant Tevis certainly does not look dangerous.

"They both behaved like gentlemen. I can't see why they should want to hurt one another."

Taking a step toward her niece, Mrs. Robinson put her arms around her. "Oh my sweet Bricela, if it were only so. You must be strong child. You must be strong."

Releasing Bricela slowly, Mrs. Robinson stood back and gazed at her with tear-filled eyes. "I fear this whole affair will be a horrible ordeal. I hoped we would escape the war in Tucson, but it has come to us even here. You are so young."

"Aunt Charlotte," said Bricela, noticing the anguish in her voice and the tears. "Are you alright?"

"I am going to lie down for a while," said Mrs. Robinson. Her shoulders slumped as she started despondently down the long hallway. "I don't feel well. Please excuse me, Bricela."

The water in the teakettle had been ready for a full hour before Tevis showed up at the back door. It had been two weeks since he had slept in the house. He politely knocked before entering. Bricela met him and escorted him to the parlor settee. She brought in tea.

She handed him a cup and saucer and took a seat in the padded chair across from the settee. "Lieutenant, tell me all about your outing."

Tevis sat down and took a sip of tea. Keeping the cup clinched between his fingers, he set the saucer down on a small table. He shook his head and smiled.

"It was easy, thanks to Caleb. Excuse me. I should say, Lieutenant Felton."

"You may call him Caleb. He is your friend."

Tevis nodded agreeably. "Caleb was dressed up like a Mexican. He can speak Mex like he is one. I swear, not even a Mexican could tell the difference with the clothes our sergeant made for him. He had a sombrero with a silver hat brim, too.

"First, the captain sent him alone to the mill up by the Pima village. He was to capture the man that ran the flour mill. So Caleb goes in and gets the drop on Mr. White, smooth as silk."

"Gets the drop?"

"Oh. That's when you draw your weapon before the other fella has a chance to get at his."

"Is that difficult?"

"Sometimes yes, sometimes no. This time it was easy enough but there was a second time after we captured the Yankee captain.

"We took over the miller's house and let Captain McCleave walk into a trap. He had only three men with him. They gave up without a fight. McCleave had left six of his soldiers at Maricopa Wells and Captain Hunter wanted them brought in the next morning.

"And he sent Lieutenant Felton with you to get them?"

After taking another drink of tea, Tevis smiled and leaned forward. "This is where Caleb showed his grit."

"His what?"

"My apologies, Miss Verde," answered Tevis as he leaned back again. "That is vulgar Texas slang. I mean his courage. Some would say, his caliber."

Bricela's eyes widened expectantly. "I understand."

"Captain Hunter sent a platoon along with Lieutenant Swilling, sure enough. He trusted Caleb to get the job done and sent him in first by himself...to face six men."

Slowly, Bricela put her hand over her mouth as she listened.

"Caleb went into the stage station at the wells just like he did at White's mill. He waits until the time is right, then pulls both his pistols and holds off all six armed Yankees until we burst through the front door. Six to one, Miss Verde! Six to one!"

A jolt of fear shot through Bricela. Doing her best to conceal the rush of anxiety that followed, she said nothing.

"You know the funny part of it? Caleb bluffs them. Caleb has never even shot a man, much less killed one, but he plays the role of a marksman like he's on stage. He makes them believe he just might be able to kill all of them before they kill him. They were still trying to make up their minds what to do when we charged in. Doesn't that beat all you ever heard?"

Taking her hand away from her lips, Bricela struggled to speak. "But...but what if they had... he could have been killed. What if they hadn't believed him? Poor Ca...Lieutenant Felton would be dead."

Tevis sat back and waived a disregarding hand. "Not him, Miss Verde. He has the luck. He's always had it from what I gather. He's had quite an exciting life."

"So, when will he return?"

"Not long, I would imagine. Captain Hunter sent him on with Lieutenant Swilling and some men to reconnoiter the Yankees. They'll go east on the stage road toward Yuma until they make contact and report back. They're going to burn all the Yankee supplies they find along the way.

"There are too many of them and they're too well armed to be attacked by the Apaches. They won't get into it with the Yankees. So, a few days I suspect."

Bricela folded her hands and rested them in her lap. Despite her efforts, her brow wrinkled with disappointment. "A few days?"

Tevis glanced curiously at Bricela. "More or less."

Captain Hunter sat in his adobe headquarters waiting for the next Tucsonian to be brought in. A small table was in front of him. On it lay a written oath to the Confederacy, a pen, and bottle of ink.

Hunter stared at the oath. The men in Tucson had been given more than enough time to make their decision. They were treated as well as circumstances allowed but only a handful signed the oath of allegiance to the Confederacy.

Hughes, the butcher, Warner the store owner, Fritz Contenzen, Meyer the druggist and Brady—all good men—had chosen the Union. One by one they were asked to swear their allegiance and each had refused.

There was no choice but to order them out of the Territory. The last man on his list was Estevan Ochoa. Surely he would stay or at least sign as a neutral. He was an honorable man and part owner of a large freight company. Ochoa's partners lived in Mesilla and Hunter knew both of them well. Their company would be a valuable asset to General Sibley.

The doorway darkened and Hunter looked up. A soldier directed Ochoa to the table. Hunter stood and shook hands with Ochoa. They remained standing.

"Mr. Ochoa, I presume you know why you are here?"

"Yes, Captain, I do."

"Mr. Ochoa, you realize of course that the United States no longer exists. I trust, therefore, that you will yield to the new order and take the oath of allegiance to the Confederacy and thereby relieve me of the necessity of confiscating your property in the name of the government, and expelling you from the city."

"Captain Hunter," said Ochoa politely. "It is out of the question for me to swear allegiance to any party or power hostile to the United States government. For to that government I owe all my prosperity and happiness. When, sir, would you like for me to leave?"

"Immediately," replied Hunter with as much gentility as Ochoa. "You may take your favorite mount together with arms, ammunition, and as many provisions as you can quickly collect."

Ochoa bowed. "*Gracias.*"

"Will you go to Sonora as the others have chosen to do?"

"No. I will travel to Mesilla."

The captain extended his hand once again. As Ochoa took it Hunter said, "God's speed to you, sir."

The tons of forage at Burke's Station that had been stored for Carleton's California column was set on fire just after sunup. Swilling had left nothing but ashes at all the other stage stations east of Burke's. Now, a mile ahead of the slow-moving column of Confederates, another flat-roofed adobe building came into view. The stage road ahead rose and fell through several arroyos. In the glaring sunlight, the path before them seemed empty.

"That'n is Stanwix Station," said Swilling. "It's only eighty miles to Yuma now. I don't know how we come so far without seein' no Yankees."

Felton was tired. He was unaccustomed to long rides with so little sleep. He wiped his bloodshot eyes and squinted at the distant station that danced in shimmering heat waves.

"That McCleave sure stuck his neck out coming all this way without support," observed Felton. "I wonder what he was thinking. His Yankee general friend is going to be madder than a wet hen when he finds out how foolish he was."

Suddenly jerking his horse to a stop, Swilling put up his hand to halt the column. Felton said nothing but looked in the direction of the station. There was a wisp of dust, then a flicker of movement.

Two rider's heads rose from the trail as they rode out of an arroyo less than seventy yards away. When they saw the forty men in front of them, they drew up as well. Both men wore blue.

"Surrender, boys," commanded Swilling. "We got you outnumbered."

The two Yankee vedettes spun their horses. Confederate rifles blasted at the fleeing targets. One man slumped but did not fall. Swilling kept his reins tight.

"Well, that tears it. Them two is lookouts for damn sure. The rest'll be along directly."

"We're not going to chase them?"

Swilling shook his head. "Just sit tight, Caleb. Keep your eyes on that road up yonder."

A minute passed. Then five more. The sun grew hot on Felton's shoulders. The air was still. At midday nothing moved. The men and horses to the rear were perfectly silent.

Pointing to the west, Swilling said, "Here they come. Hell's a poppin' now."

A long cloud of dust was rising two miles beyond the station. A large force was coming toward them, likely at a full run. Swilling sat lazily in the sun.

Felton squirmed, his saddle leather creaking under him. He anxiously glanced behind him but the other men seemed as unconcerned as Swilling.

"What do we do now, Jack?"

Swilling took off his battered hat. He casually ran his fingers through his long hair, shoving it straight back.

"That big dust up yonder means them two was advance guard of a mighty big bunch. Bigger'n us by a site. So we hightail it. Them Yankee horses'll never catch us. I just wanted a gander at how many they might be so I could tell the captain."

"How far do you think they'll chase after us?"

"Oh, could be ten, twenty mile," said Swilling, tugging his hat down tight.

"It's a hundert fifty miles to Tucson from here. You ready for a good hard ride back to town?"

Felton tightened the hurricane strap of his sombrero. "I was ready five minutes ago."

The pursuing cavalry gave up the chase in less than an hour, but the Confederates passed the bend of the Gila River still at a gallop. By late afternoon, they passed the Pima village at a trot. By midnight, Swilling brought the Rebels to a halt at Picacho Station. They were nearly one hundred miles from the shots fired at Stanwix.

Guards were posted. Saddles were loosened but remained on the backs of sweat-stained horses. Small fires were built. Men ate what meager rations they had left.

Felton threw down his blanket and sprawled out next to a handful of burning mesquite branches. From his pocket he took out his last piece of jerked meat. Even his bones ached.

Seemingly unaffected by the long ride, Swilling stood next to him and gazed up at the star-filled sky. He rolled a smoke and squatted by the fire and lit it. "This is Picacho Pass. It's a good spot to leave a rear guard. Out from the station here, there's a patch of rock sittin' all alone. I'm gonna leave Sergeant Holmes there with nine men.

"It's only forty or so miles back to Tucson. We can send couriers back and forth from here to keep an eye out for them Yankees. No tellin' what they'll do next."

"How many of them do you think there were back there?"

"I figure a couple a hundert. We can handle that many...but what's behind them? That's what I been wonderin'. How far back are the rest?"

Felton closed his eyes as he chewed. He could see Bricela sitting on the bent tree. She was smiling, her eyes full of life. "Right now, I just want a bath and some sheets to slide between," moaned Felton. "I want to shave off this beard. It itches."

Swilling smirked. "You best not count on that, amigo. You're the only spy we got and you're a damned good'un. When the captain hears about Stanwix, I got a feelin' he just might want to send you back down the road we just come up."

"I should have let that posse catch me back at Mesilla," muttered Felton. The image of Bricela was replaced by the forms of the two fleeing vedettes. "I doubt they would have hanged me."

After blowing a column of cigarette smoke into the desert air, Swilling asked, "What was they after you for, anyhow?"

"They were going to claim I was cheating at cards."

"Was ya?"

"No. They just used that as an excuse. There was a particular woman that, at that particular point in time, looked mighty passable. Turned out, she was the sheriff's wife."

Swilling took another puff on his smoke. "That being a Texas town, they would'a hung ya."

Closing his eyes, Felton stretched and put his hands behind his head. "So…they were out to hang me in Texas…and someone in Arizona tried to shoot me. Seems I could use some reforming."

"A wolf's got to eat with the teeth he's got, Caleb. You're a scoundrel, alright. They make the best spies. You best not go to reformin' 'til this damn war is over."

"We sure enough started things rolling this morning," said Felton. His eyes opened to a starry sky. Bricela was only fifteen. He had been a fool not to see it. Even if she were older, he wasn't the man for a woman like her. "You're right, Jack. I've got no reason to change. Even if I wanted to, the rut I'm in is way too deep."

Silhouetted by a fading red orange sky, thirty dusty soldiers rode in silence past the first adobe of Tucson. They turned down Calle Real, then headed toward the corrals at Saint Augustine's Church. Before resting or eating, even before storming the cantinas, the men would care for their horses. The mounts had been called on to outrun a company of Yankees, then carry their riders over one hundred and fifty miles in less than two days.

A large, well-equipped army was marching toward Tucson from California, and the superiority of the Texas horses was the only advantage the ragged Southerners possessed. If reinforcements did not arrive soon, the only chance for survival would be another rapid retreat.

Felton shoved back his sombrero and wiped his forehead with the back of his grimy sleeve. He glanced in the direction of the Robertson's house. Bricela would be sitting down to supper and may not have heard he was back. It would be better that way. They would have little to say to each other now. He would sleep in the plaza with the other men.

He was too filthy to enter the Robinson's house, anyway. After his stallion was rubbed down and fed, Felton's first stop was going to be the bathhouse. Whether the Mexican that ran it was there or not, he would have a hot bath and wash the smell of campfire smoke and sweat from his hair and beard. His beard could use trimming but it would not be shaved off. Masquerading as a Mexican and spying was better than being in Tucson. At least then he could do no more damage to Bricela.

Swilling rode up next to him. "I'm headin' to the Shoo Fly after reportin' to the captain," said Swilling. "You goin' to those rich folks' house to get that bed you been pinin' over?"

"Nope. I'm going to roust out that Mexican barber that gave me a shave the first day I rode in. He runs a bathhouse, too. After I've scraped off this trail dirt, I'll eat at the Shoo Fly and bed down in front of the church. I've been gone too long from the Robertson's. We need to get reacquainted before I take advantage of their hospitality."

"We got room in our 'dobe."

"*Gracias*. I'll take the stars. There're likely less varmints crawling around in the church yard."

"Suit yourself."

"What do you think Captain Hunter will do now that we know the Yankees are headed our way?"

Jack looked down at the dirt in the street as they rode. "Don't see any sign that reinforcements has got here. Maybe the capt'n had some couriers come in since we been gone. He can tell when more men might come along.

"If they ain't here directly, we got no choice but to cut and run."

The column reined left onto Calle de la Mesilla. The dull thud of horse's hooves echoed off empty adobe houses as they rode toward the corrals in the church plaza.

"What do you think will happen to the Southern sympathizers if we have to leave?"

Swilling grunted. "The cap'n was goin' to boot the Yankee folk out of town. I suppose the Yankee officers will do the same. If'n this war keeps up there won't be no whites left in Tucson."

"If the Union takes Tucson," said Felton. "Those men Captain Hunter asked to leave will likely come back. They own property and all the men I've met here are tough and independent. If they weren't, they wouldn't be here in the first place. Even the Apaches can't drive them out."

"I don't mind fightin' the Union," said Swilling, lowering his voice and glancing over his shoulder. "But I'd sooner be fightin' the damned Injuns as these Yankees. Nothin' is worse than a Comanch' or 'Pache."

Felton thought of McCleave and Ammi White. He never cared for politics and Tucson was a long way from the South or North. But the South was his home. Northerners were trying to invade his country, to take it over and change it. The thought of such aggression angered him. Was it worth dying over? The colonies separated from England, Louisiana from France, Texas from Mexico, and now the Confederacy from the Union. Was it worth going to war to try and stop what Americans had done time and time again?

Maybe the Apaches felt the same about the whites and Mexicans, that these strangers were invading their country. But this was a big country. There was room enough for everyone. Why were the Apaches at war with the whites and Mexicans? With so few warriors, they could not hope to win. Life on a reservation could not be so bad. Diplomacy was far better than war.

"I heard that a Lieutenant Bascom stirred up the Apaches," said Felton. "Is that true?"

Swilling turned his head and spat. "True enough, I suppose. Ol' Bascom got Cochise to murderin' Americans, but Cochise and his bunch never stopped crossin' the boarder to murder and steal from Mexicans. Mangas Colorado is another 'Pache. His tribe's been murderin' whites all along, same as he does Mexicans.

"I fancied all along it was only a matter of time 'fore Cochise found some fool reason to kill some whites. He only put up with us 'cause he knew we was against Mexico. To him we was allies up 'til that Gadson Purchase. That ended the war with Mexico, ya see.

"I knowed then it wouldn't be long 'til Cochise went to killin' whites. It's what 'Paches do. They live on plunder and they enjoy the murderin' and torture. They's like land pirates, only worse. When they take a man captive...or a woman...no, sir. No pirate was ever like that. I'll allow as the meanest pirate that ever lived was not near so bad as a ever'day 'Pache buck. Pirates was white men. These are Injuns and they need killin'. They don't understand nothin' but killin'."

The men rode to a rope picket line, tied their horses and unsaddled them.

Swilling and Felton had just dropped their saddles when Captain Hunter appeared. Swilling and Felton saluted and received one in return.

"What do you have to report, Lieutenant?" There was anxiety in Hunter's tone.

"We run into a couple companies of Yankee cavalry at Stanwix Station," explained Swilling. "We fired at two of their vedettes. They took off and brung the cavalry. We outrun 'em after about ten mile or so, and then they seemed to have give up.

"We got to Picacho Pass and I sent a man up the peak as lookout. He could see way down the road. There weren't no dust all this mornin'. So I left Sergeant Holmes and nine men there as sentinels. Their camp is out a mile from the station by a stand of rock."

Hunter looked grim. "McCleave was telling the truth, at least about the companies following him."

"Any word from General Sibley?" asked Felton.

"None."

"We burnt all the forage from here to Stanwix, Cap'n. That'll slow 'em down."

"How far can your sentinels see down the stage road?"

"On top of that rock they could see dust risin' at fifty miles. If they spy a lot of it, they's ordered to hightail it back here and report. If it's just a few comin', they's to kill 'em and send a courier."

Hunter thought for a moment. He glanced at Felton. "We need to know where the main force is, the number of men and type of artillery." Hunter paused. "Get some rest, gentlemen. We will have an officers meeting in my quarters at sunup."

After Hunter left, Swilling turned thoughtfully to Felton. "Take extry good care of your black there, Caleb. I got a feelin' you and him ain't goin' to be restin' too long. You see the look the cap'n give you just now?"

"I did. But it's like you said, Jack. A wolf's got to eat with the teeth he's got. It's best I do what I'm good at."

Felton fed the stallion some oats and rubbed him down for a half hour before going to the barber's adobe. He looked through the square opening that served as a window. The barber chair sat in darkness. A light flickered under the edge of a tattered blanket that served as a door to the back room.

Placing his palms on the window ledge, Felton leaned in. "I'll pay gold," he said, raising his voice. "For a shave and a bath."

The blanket slid to one side. A stoop-shouldered, wiry Mexican appeared. Arthritic fingers held a candle that illuminated his face. "Ah. Señor Lieutenant," said the barber, hurrying to the front door and opening it. "I saw you ride in and started the water. Come in, come in."

"You guessed I was coming?"

The old man shrugged and turned toward the back room. "Mexican Army, Union Army, Confederate Army, no matter. Always the officers want to be clean. It is not hard to know you will come, Señor.

"When officers are in Tucson, I do a good business."

Felton followed the candle light into the back room where other candles burned on iron holders jammed into the cracks in the walls.

"How did you recognize me? I thought I looked like one of your people."

Placing the candle on the flat surface of an overturned *olla*, the barber looked Felton over carefully. "You look Mexican, but you ride like an American. Any man long in this land can see these things, Señor. You are a hard man to miss, Mexican or gringo."

Felton took off his sombrero and wiped his forehead. "What do you mean by that?"

Without answering, the Mexican held up a halting finger and waved it back and forth. Turning quickly, he hobbled out the back door and returned with a steaming bucket of water. Stepping alongside a tub held together with hundreds of rivets, the old man poured in another gallon of bath water.

Slowly straightening his stiff back, the barber said, "Owl Woman...she speaks best of what I try to say. She says you have medicine. You have what other men do not. You have medicine."

Felton's eyes narrowed. "Are you Papago?"

"No, Señor. Owl Woman is known to all here, Papago and Mexican. She sees much. She can also cast spells...and remove even the most powerful spells of others."

Felton scratched his beard. He knew of Creoles in Louisiana that believed such superstitions. His sea captain grandfather told tales of fortune tellers and claimed he'd even seen witches in Haiti cast spells. But then again, he spoke of ghosts and sea monsters as well.

"Is having this medicine a good thing or a bad thing?"

The Mexican's face wrinkled as he studied Felton. "That is up to you, Señor Lieutenant. Owl Woman cannot see such things for men. A man *chooses* his path. It is how God made us. We all have to choose...good or bad. Medicine or no medicine."

"You know anybody else around here with this medicine?"

"*Si*. Owl Woman says the same of Cochise and Mangus Colorado. Medicine is what makes many men chiefs. Those two have medicine."

Felton smirked. "I'm no chief. In fact, I'm not much of anything."

The barber turned to get another bucket. "A man can change, Señor. Get in the tub. I will add water once more."

A knock came at the front door and Mrs. Robertson answered it. A small boy in soiled linen looked up. He was breathing hard.

"May I help you, young man?"

"Miss Verde, *por favor*."

Mrs. Robertson turned to call for Bricela. She was already coming down the hall. "There is a boy here asking for you, Bricela."

Bricela's step quickened until she came alongside her aunt. "Good evening, Manuel," said Bricela. She suppressed all signs of excitement. "Aunt Charlotte, this is Juanita's nephew, Manuel. What is it, Manuel?"

"They have returned, Miss Verde. He is with them. He takes a bath now."

Both women blushed. Bricela cleared her throat. "Thank you, Manuel. I will see you tomorrow."

The boy grinned. He ran down the porch stairs and into the night.

Mrs. Robertson eased the door closed and glanced quizzically at her niece. "What, pray tell, was that about?"

"I asked him to tell me when the other soldiers returned," Bricela replied. Lying was unbecoming for a lady—she only bent the truth. "I thought it best we know when to expect Lieutenant Felton's return. Manuel was gracious enough to help.

"So much time has passed since he stayed with us he may feel it improper to come back, especially this late in the evening. We should send word that he is still to be our guest."

"Yes. Your uncle Palatine is out and about. He will surely tell the Lieutenant. The men always gather at that ghastly Shoo Fly."

Bricela opened a hall closet and took out a shawl. She threw it over her shoulders and looked expectantly at her aunt. "I'll go to the plaza and tell Uncle Palatine that Lieutenant Felton is here. The lieutenant may not visit the Shoo Fly this evening. And of course, we all want to know what happened on his patrol. Aren't you curious to find out what has happened since the capture of Captain McCleave?"

"Yes, dear, we're all anxious to hear the war news. Can't it wait until morning?"

"Aunt Charlotte, the lieutenant has been away from a comfortable bed for three weeks. As for the news, I should like to know tonight. I will worry over him...it...all night if I don't know what has happened. I won't sleep a wink."

"Oh?" questioned Mrs. Robinson. She studied her niece closely for a moment. A faint smile turned her lips. "Oh," she said softly. "I see."

"May I go? The plaza is well lit and Captain Hunter's men are everywhere. I will be safe."

"Alright. Go straight to the saloon and ask for Palatine."

"I will Aunt Charlotte," said Bricela, leaving quickly out the door.

Halfway across the plaza Bricela heard a familiar laugh. There was no question when Uncle Palatine felt the warming effect of too many drinks. He was normally in a good mood. A few shots of bourbon or cheap whiskey only improved his outlook on life.

Bricela stopped a few feet in front of the Shoo Fly. The air was warm and heavy. A pale blue haze encircled two Confederates and a Mexican who stood outside talking and smoking together.

"*Por favor*, Señor,*"* interrupted Bricela, preferring to single out the Mexican.

The Mexican looked over his shoulder. He removed his hat and holding it in front of him with both hands, approached Bricela as if she were royalty. "Yes, Miss Verde. How may I be of service to you?"

Bricela started to ask for her uncle but thinking better of it said, "I am looking for Lieutenant Felton...or Lieutenant Tevis. Do you know them?"

"*Si*. Only Señor Tevis is inside."

"Will you please tell him I wish to speak to him?"

Bowing, the Mexican answered, "*Si*, Miss Verde. Pronto."

A minute passed before Tevis walked out of the cantina and over to Bricela.

"Good evening, Miss Verde. Are you looking for your uncle? He's here, a bit snake bit by the coffin varnish they pass off as whiskey, but he's here. Want me to bring him home?"

"No. I am looking for Lieutenant Felton. I received word that he is back in Tucson. I wanted him to know he is still welcome at our home."

"He was over at the barbers getting cleaned up. Lieutenant Swilling said Caleb was going to get some sleep out by the church where we keep our horses. We have an officers meeting in the morning and we'll know more then. The captain may be planning on sending Caleb right back out."

"So soon?"

"I can't talk about the particulars. Tomorrow maybe you can get some answers."

"All the more reason he should rest at the house tonight. Why would he sleep at the corral?"

"Beats me, Miss Verde. I was wondering on that myself. Some men get used to sleeping under the stars."

"Thank you, Lieutenant," said Bricela. She started for the church.

Tevis took two quick steps and caught up to her. "You're not thinking of going over there by yourself?"

"I most certainly am," snipped Bricela. She continued walking.

"It's best I escort you. Or I can get your uncle."

Bricela put her arm through Tevis'. "If you don't mind."

"My pleasure. Watch your step. The ruts in the street are hard to see at night. It's easy to twist your ankle."

One hundred feet east of the Shoo Fly, the ominous black outline of the whipping post took form. Bricela's eyes lingered on it as they past by. She felt uneasy and shuddered.

"Are you cold Miss Verde? Perhaps we should go back."

"No, I am warm enough. I just felt...something...something horrible when I looked at that awful post. Why doesn't someone remove it?"

Tevis patted Bricela's hand. Glancing back over his shoulder, he said gently, "Young women should not concern themselves with such matters. Military life can be a hard one...and it can at times be cruel. With some men, discipline must be harsh. Without it, there can be no order.

"That was put there by the Mexican Army. In the military outposts along our frontier, they're used by our own armies. Unfortunately, they serve a purpose."

"Would Captain Hunter ever use such a thing?"

There was a moment of silence as they continued east past a cluster of single adobes.

"The captain is a gentleman. He would prefer not to resort to that severe a punishment. But I believe he would if, say, a soldier deserted...or someone harmed a woman."

Crossing Calle del Arroya, Bricela thought of Soloman Warner, his store and the necklace Caleb had purchased from him.

"It is sad that Mr. Warner and Mr. Ochoa were told to leave town. They are such nice men."

"They are, indeed. Yet the captain must be mindful of Union spies. Even though the Apaches are bad, couriers still cross the desert, both Union and Confederate."

"We have spies in Yuma. We knew the Union had spies here in Tucson. The captain only did what he had to."

"All of the men ordered to leave could not have been spies."

"No. But this is war, Miss Verde. It doesn't pay to take unwarranted chances when lives hang in the balance. At least one in that number of Union sympathizers was a spy. We just don't know who it was."

A few steps in front of the couple, the backside of a row of abandoned adobes formed a blank wall and marked the beginning of another street. Turning south on Calle del Alegria, the smell of horses filled the air.

"You speak of spies," said Bricela thoughtfully. "Would Lieutenant Felton have been considered a spy...if, instead of our capturing Captain McCleave...the Yankee captain and his men had captured him? You told me he was disguised as a Mexican."

Tevis glanced down at Bricela. "Now that is a mighty good question," he muttered. "I never thought of it that way, but now that you bring it up, I suppose he could have been looked upon as a spy."

"What would they have done to him?"

A voice boomed from the shadows at the end of the adobe wall, "Who's agoin' yonder?"

"Lieutenant Tevis and a guest to talk to Lieutenant Felton."

A soldier stepped from the darkness, his face hidden under a drooping broad-brimmed hat and a long beard.

"Evenin' Lieutenant," said the guard in a slow, thick Texas drawl. Realizing there was a woman present he added, "Evenin' ma'am."

"Good evening, sir," returned Bricela. "But it is 'Miss'."

"Yes'm."

"Has Lieutenant Felton been here long?" continued Bricela. "Is he asleep?"

"No'm. He ain't asleep. I'll fetch 'im fer ya."

"Thank you, sir. You are so kind."

When the guard was out of sight, Bricela eased her hand from Tevis. She peered up at him, trying to see his face. "You didn't have a chance to answer my question, Lieutenant. What would have happened to Lieutenant Felton?"

Tevis hung his head and rubbed the back of his neck.

"You shouldn't worry about that, Miss Verde. Caleb won't get caught."

"If he is," insisted Bricela. "What then? I want the truth. Would he be tied to one of those horrible posts?"

Tevis took a deep breath and let it out slowly.

"No. They would execute him. That's what usually happens to spies in the military."

Bricela stiffened at the blunt answer. She quickly reassured herself that Tevis' first response was the right one. Caleb had not been caught nor would he be. He had returned safely...even after he was sent alone into the heart of the Yankee Army. "In that case, I pray he is finished spying."

Footsteps sounded from the church plaza. Two dark figures appeared.

"I got 'im fer ya, Miss," announced the guard as he and Felton came near.

"Thank you again."

Felton immediately recognized the sound of Bricela's voice. "Miss Verde, good evening. This is a pleasant surprise. What can I do for you?"

They were not alone, appearances had to be maintained, but Bricela still felt a twinge of rejection in the polite response.

"I received word you had returned this evening. I wanted to assure you that you are welcome at the Robinson house just as you were before."

"It's late," said Felton. "I don't wish to impose. Perhaps tomorrow."

Bricela could not see Felton's expression. His tone remained formal. The cool reception caused some uncertainty, but she continued the performance. "You are very considerate, Lieutenant. Uncle Palatine is so fervent in his support of the new Confederacy, I fear he may be somewhat offended if you do not accept his hospitality. He is also anxious to hear the news of your last patrol."

Felton sighed. For a moment there was silence. "If I am not impos-ing," relented Felton.

"I assure you, Lieutenant, you most certainly are not."

"Thank you, James," said Felton. "I'll escort Miss Verde back to her home. I assume you were at the Shoo Fly with the boys."

"I was and you are welcome," said Tevis. "Good evening, Miss Verde. I'll see you at breakfast."

"Good evening, Lieutenant Tevis."

Tevis headed back up Calle del Alegria. Felton took Bricela down the street toward Calle Real. It was a much longer walk home. The thought that Felton chose the route on purpose restored Bricela's shaken confidence. She smiled and put her arm through his. "For a mo-ment I thought you would not come," she said.

"Come where?" asked Felton. "Back to Tucson?"

"No. Back to our home."

Felton cleared his throat. "So did I. You have a strange effect on my better judgment."

"Oh? What, dear Caleb, did your better judgment tell you to do?"

"It doesn't matter. I never listen to it anyway."

Bricela laughed. They walked easily in the quiet of night. She glanced at the quarter moon rising above the mountain peaks. It cast its soft light on Caleb's face. Her shoulder gently pressed just below his. Her free hand now rested on his arm. It was the perfect night, the night she would surely be kissed for the first time.

Caleb Felton was handsome and gallant. He was dashing and his bravery had been the talk of Tucson for weeks. When the Mexican women spoke of him, there were whispers and giggles of excitement, a desire that he might at least look their way. Though he was older, he had chosen her. He was in love with her, in love with Bricela Verde. From the moment of their first encounter, they knew their destinies were intertwined.

"I worried about you, Caleb. Especially after Lieutenant Tevis told me what you did at White's mill and Maricopa Wells. Everyone has been talking about you."

Chuckling easily, Felton said, "Don't believe everything James tells you. Likely, he embellished his tales. It was nothing but foolishness."

"Modesty, too," teased Bricela. "It is no wonder you are causing such excitement among the women of Tucson."

"Merely a flash in the pan," said Felton. He paused. He added seriously, "They don't know me. No one here knows me."

"I do, Caleb. We are twins, remember, like Owl Woman said. We knew each other from the beginning."

Felton shook his head. "I won't deny there are things about you I don't understand...but I'm not ready to put much truck in Owl Woman's opinion."

"I want to see her again," said Bricela. "I want to ask her some more questions. I'm curious about what she does, how she does it. You could see by her little shrine she was Catholic, yet she still practices the Papago ways."

"Unless she comes to Tucson, you'll have to wait for another armed escort. The Apaches are out there somewhere. Jack Swilling says since they haven't been seen in a while—they're sure to show up soon. It's their way."

Turning right on Calle Real, Bricela wondered when Caleb would stop, when he would take her in his arms and gently kiss her. Perhaps it would be in front of Soloman Warner's store or at the edge of the main plaza. He would not chance being seen by anyone. It would have to be soon. She felt her heart pounding in her stomach.

"I may be sent out again very soon. If I am...if I am, I may not return for a long time."

Bricela's heart sped up. He would want something to remember her by, something special.

"You know how I feel about you, Bricela. I know you won't forget me completely...I want to think you will remember me from time to time...that you will hold a small place for me in your heart."

Felton stopped walking. The silver outline of Warner's store was to Bricela's left, the main plaza entrance to her right. She wanted to remember every detail.

Without understanding fully, Bricela said softly, "I will never forget you, Caleb. Never."

Felton smiled down at her. His eyes were full of unspoken thoughts. He took her by the shoulders. She readied her lips, tilted her head back ever so slightly, and closed her eyes. She felt his lips kiss her forehead.

Bricela waited a few heartbeats. She opened her eyes. There was no second kiss. No kiss like the one she had long imagined and so often dreamed about. He had kissed her as if she were a child!

Wanting far more than he had given, she looked expectantly into Caleb's eyes. Instead of seeing love, there was a confusing blend of sorrow and pain.

He took her in his arms and held her.

"You are as close to heaven as I'll ever be," he said tenderly. "I just want to hold you tonight."

Bricela slowly put her arms around Caleb Felton. Her fingers sensed the muscles in his back. She leaned her head on his chest, felt its warmth and heard the slow beating of his heart. She was at ease and yet strangely ecstatic. She wanted to laugh and to cry. Under the moon and stars, in that instant, she experienced more than she could ever hope to understand, what she could never explain—something she would not have dreamed possible. She smiled as she would but once in a lifetime. It was better than a kiss. It was a union of souls, a moment that would last forever.

"Twins," she whispered to herself. "Twins."

They had not held each other long enough, yet with unspoken mutual consent, they separated. Looking into each other's eyes, the space between them slowly grew until Bricela was once again by Caleb's side. They walked together arm in arm with the moon at their backs.

"I don't want to go home right now." said Bricela. "I don't want this night to end."

Caleb nodded. "Nor I, Bricela. But sooner or later it's over."

"Oh, it's not over, Caleb. It's a new beginning. I just don't want to miss you tonight."

They turned off the main street. In a matter of seconds they would be at the Robinson's door.

"Time to go back to Lieutenant Felton and Miss Verde," said Felton.

Bricela smiled and looked up at Felton. The moonlight illuminated her face and her innocence. "For now, Lieutenant. For now."

With Bricela listening, Felton conversed with Palatine Robinson and Bill Oury until past midnight. He was still the first to arrive at Captain Hunter's quarters for the officers' meeting the next morning. He was drinking coffee with Swilling when Tevis came through the door.

Tevis filled a cup of his own. He took a sip and smacked his lips. "That tea at the Robinson's is good enough and I'd never tell Mrs.

Robertson, but I like my coffee. Where'd you eat this morning, Caleb? We missed you at breakfast."

"I didn't eat. Wasn't hungry."

Two more officers came in. Hunter emerged from an adjacent room with a small wiry man dressed in sweat-stained buckskins. Hunter's eyes were darkened with fatigue. He held a small piece of paper in his hand.

"I've just received word from General Sibley that he is fully engaged against General Canby near Santa Fe. He can send us no reinforcements. Our orders are to remain in Tucson as long as possible and to gather as much information about the column from California as we can.

"He hopes...He hopes to send us reinforcements soon.

"No riders have come in from Picacho Pass. We can assume there was no immediate sustained pursuit since our engagement at Stanwix Station.

"Gentlemen, if you have any suggestions as to our next move, now is the time."

Felton waited a few seconds before he broke the silence. He did not want to seem too eager. His decision to leave Tucson must appear to have been spontaneous. He would leave Bricela behind but not as he left other women. This time, for the first time, he cared what a woman thought of him after he was gone.

When Tevis or Captain Hunter informed her of his sudden departure, she would believe a sense of duty and gallantry took him from her. She could always hold onto that.

By leaving, he was protecting her. In time, she would understand what he did was best. Thinking him to be more noble than he had a right, Bricela's romantic vision of a dashing lieutenant would last a lifetime. It wasn't much. It was a lie. It was all he had to give.

"Captain Hunter," said Felton, "I can get the information we need and with no risk to our men. I should go immediately to Picacho and if all is well there, proceed as far west as necessary to reconnoiter the entire strength of the Union forces.

"I can either return or send a Mexican rider back via Sonora and up through Tubac."

All eyes turned to Felton. He suppressed his guilt. He wasn't brave as they would assume, nor was he devoted to the Confederacy. How differently would they think of him if they knew he was escaping Tucson to avoid hurting a fifteen year old girl? How would they look at him if they discovered he was in love with her?

Volunteering was better than desertion and distance better than heartbreak. Leaving, and leaving soon, was his only choice.

"I go along with Caleb's idea, Cap'n," offered Swilling. "We chewed it over on the way back. I don't see there's much else we can do."

Tevis and the other officers agreed.

Hunter thought for a full minute as he studied the dispatch in his hand.

"We have one advantage and that is McCleave. I have come to understand that he is a good friend of General Carleton and that Carleton does not hesitate to show favoritism in his ranks.

"If you are discovered as a spy, Lieutenant Felton, you will offer yourself for prisoner exchange. You will be safe from the firing squad or the gallows if Carleton believes he can trade you for McCleave. And he can. You have my word."

"I understand, sir. I will leave at once."

Chapter 7

Giving his stallion a much deserved rest, Felton borrowed a smooth-gaited bay gelding from one of the privates. It liked to run and the farther Caleb Felton galloped from Tucson the better he felt. Before Old Pueblo was a mile behind, the tangled knot of emotions that had plagued him throughout the night began to unwind. It was the opposite of what he expected.

Judging from the classic literature he studied in the Methodist seminary, and from what other miserable souls had told him about love, he should be distraught with grief or at least heartbroken.

Despite his attempts to deny it, Bricela captured his heart the moment they met. No other woman had ever come close to doing that, yet leaving Tucson for the last time was far easier than it should have been. In fact, he was glad to be going.

Swilling had told him to scour the desert for Apaches as he rode and Tevis advised him to devise a plan for spying on the California column. But Felton had been in the Territory for months, and not seen so much as a moccasin track. And if McCleave was one of General Carleton's best, the Yankees were nothing to worry about. On the other hand, it was a nice morning to be astride a good horse, enjoying the freedom of the open road.

Riding west at a gallop, the rising sun warmed Felton's back as a beautiful morning grew into a grand day. For countless miles his thoughts drifted from Bricela to the colors of the desert, the deep blue in the sky above him and then, with a smile, back to the young woman that had walked with her arm through his in the moonlight.

He would miss her like no other and certainly long to see her smile and feel her gentle touch. He would never meet anyone like her or share the same mysterious closeness. These things Felton accepted as his fate but no matter how long he pondered his decision to leave Tucson, no matter how hard he tried to understand it, he could not explain his unfading optimism and pleasant disposition. All he knew for sure was that he felt better than he had in weeks and had covered forty long, monotonous miles in what seemed like minutes. Nothing was as it should be yet at least one thing was clear. For the moment, what he was doing for Bricela had to be.

Just shy of noon Felton reached the base of Picacho Mountain. After passing a stand of ancient saguaro, he caught sight of the squat adobe station and veered off the stage road. He cleared his head. Now, it was time to think of war.

A mile distant, a small ridge of jagged rock rose thirty feet above the mesquite and cactus. He would find the Rebel picket hidden there.

After winding his way through the cacti until he was hidden from the stage road, Felton stopped under the meager shade of a palo verde. He removed his close-fitting Mexican jacket and sash and tied them to his pommel. It was only April but he was starting to sweat. Shoving his Army pistol into his waistband, he slid his sombrero off and thoughtfully wiped the grit from his face and beard. After nooning with Sergeant Holmes and his platoon, he would continue west, deeper into enemy territory and further from Bricela.

He uncorked his canteen and raised it. Before the water touched his lips, he froze. The answer to the question that had been gnawing at him since leaving Tucson suddenly burst into his consciousness.

Lowering his canteen, he laughed and swore. He shook his head, then laughed and swore again. This time his epithets were tempered with awe.

"What'cha laughin' at Lieutenant?" asked a voice from behind a mass of cholla branches.

Sergeant Holmes appeared. Seeing the gleeful expression on Felton's face and hearing his laughter, Holmes began to grin himself. "You ain't goin' loco er ya?"

"No, my good sergeant," replied Felton merrily. "I have just now discovered what it feels like to do…what my daddy used to call, 'the right thing'."

Holmes took off his battered hat and scratched at the matted hair underneath. "You talkin' 'bout what you done at the wells?"

"No, sergeant. That was doing what came naturally to a scoundrel like me. I'm talking about something entirely different. For the first time in my useless life I did something for someone else…something I…Caleb R. Felton did not *want* to do.

"You know what, Sergeant? It feels good. It makes a man feel *good*! Can you imagine anything so preposterous?"

Putting his hat back on, the sergeant said, "Pre what?"

"Ludicrous," chuckled Felton. "Ludicrous."

"I don't speak no Spanish, Lieutenant. You best palaver to me in American."

Felton dismounted and led his bay to the Confederate. "You got any coffee going, Sergeant?"

"Shore 'nuff, we do. Come on."

With Holmes leading, the two carefully picked their way through the maze of cactus toward the ridge of rock less than two hundred yards to the north.

"We set up in a small clearing at the base of that rock pile," said Holmes. "We ain't seen hide ner hair of any Union Army. The boys is gettin' restless.

"You got any news fer us from the captain?"

"No. I'm headed up the road to find out what we're up against. The disguise you sewed for me is being put to the test again. When I get what I'm after I'll report back."

The sergeant was about to speak when he slid to a stop and threw up his hand. Before he offered an explanation a pistol shot rang out. A volley of rifles followed. General fire erupted.

Felton and Holmes ran toward camp as the firing continued. When they were within fifty yards Felton, stopped to pull his rifle from its scabbard and tie the gelding. He tossed his bulky sombrero at the feet of the horse and followed after Holmes.

He had taken only a few steps when a bullet buzzed past his ear. He spun and fired from the hip. A man in blue dropped out of sight behind a clump of prickly pears as Felton dove behind a dead mesquite. The general firing slowed. There was no doubt Yankees had discovered the picket post.

Felton crawled until he found Holmes' tracks. More firing erupted from his left and right but he could see nothing but clouds of blue white smoke filtering through the brush. Which army it came from was any-one's guess. He remembered some advice Swilling had given him—that sometimes the first man to move in such a situation, was the first man to die. Felton lay motionless and listened.

He could hear voices but nothing distinct. He saw a patch of blue slipping slowly through the thicket. Without thinking, he snapped a shot at his target. It too disappeared. There was movement after the smoke cleared. Likely he had missed. No return fire came his way, but his position had been given away. He crawled toward the rock ridge. If anything, the Confederates would hold that position.

To his left he saw the clearing. In the center, a small fire smoldered near a few pots. A blanket was unrolled where men had been sitting. Playing cards were scattered over the blanket and sand. A body, dressed in a blue lieutenant's jacket was sprawled nearby. His neck had been broken by a bullet. Beyond the dead lieutenant two more Yankees lay face down. The sand around them was red. One was moaning in pain.

Felton crawled more slowly. He expected a heavy lead ball to plow through his flesh at any moment. In his mind, he saw Bricela for a moment. He shoved her from his thoughts. Sand caked the back of his hands and face. Sweat trickled down his back. Between the random shots there was absolute silence. He could hear his heart pounding.

Ahead, he saw a flicker of brown. He held his fire. It moved again but there was no blue. Felton decided to take a chance.

"Sergeant Holmes," he whispered."Is that you?"

A voice answered softly. It was not Holmes. "Who are you?"

"Felton."

"Over here Lieutenant. We got you covered."

Felton crawled to the man's side. It was a private but not one he knew by name.

"Fancy seein' you out here, Lieutenant. Come just in time. You by yerself?"

"Yes. What happened?"

The private turned his head and spat a stream of brown tobacco onto the sand.

"They caught us nappin' sure enough. Two of the boys was playin' cards when that dead lieutenant and his men come out of nowheres. He throws up his pistol and fires off a shot. Says for us all to give up to him. The two playin' cards had no chance so they give up. We lit into 'em from the brush and emptied three saddles and kilt the lieutenant. We just been pot shootin' since then."

"Any of our men hit?"

"Don't think so. I think they got the drop on Sergeant Holmes. I bet he's a prisoner sure enough."

"How many of them are there?" asked Felton, realizing he was now in command.

"Best we can cipher they's twelve or thirteen. Four of them is down and three or four of ours is taken. That leaves eight of them and six of us."

Felton thought for a moment. "These Yankees were likely headed for the station thinking our picket would be there. That's the way Captain Hunter had it figured. They stumbled onto you out here instead.

"The chances they're not alone are good. I don't know about you, but I'm a gambling man, and I don't like these odds. I say we get back to Tucson and tell Captain Hunter what happened. Otherwise, if we wait we could get cut off. They could walk right into Tucson without warning."

"Sounds good to me, Lieutenant. I'll spread the word."

The private started to leave. Felton stopped him. "One more thing. Get the men together and go as fast as you can. Don't wait for me. I won't be going back with you."

The private's eyes narrowed on Felton. He smiled knowingly. "Got your Mex outfit with ya?"

"I do."

"Anything you want me to tell the captain?"

"No...do you know who Miss Verde is?"

"Shore. I don't say nothin' to her, but everbody knows Miss Verde."

"Tell her...I'm alright."

The private chewed his tobacco thoughtfully. "Sure 'nuff. That it?"

"That's it."

During the half hour it took Felton to find his horse, less than a dozen shots had been exchanged, and none of them fired in his direction. Before returning to the stage road, he cleaned and reloaded his pistol then carefully wrapped the red sash around his waist. After beating the dust from his Spanish jacket and buttoning the silver button that held it closed, he brushed the sand from his face and hands. Now he was to become a wealthy Mexican Don, a rancher and gambler of noble Spanish decent. Caleb R. Felton no longer existed.

With one last look over his shoulder, Felton tugged his sombrero down low and carefully led his mount back to the edge of the road. Drawing his razor-sharp Bowie knife, he took one swipe at an inch thick mesquite branch and dropped it onto the desert sand. He sheathed his knife, then brushed away the last thirty feet of his tracks that led toward the picket. Should the Yankees backtrack him, only an expert trailer would know he ever left the road.

He spurred the bay into a run and in a matter of seconds, slid to stop in front of the abandoned stage station. Once the Yankees discovered their enemy had fled back to Tucson, and with wounded men to attend, they would certainly show up at the station.

Felton scanned the bare ground near the adobe and saw no fresh tracks. He dismounted and braided a loop in the horse's mane. He would also tie down the near stirrup as only a Mexican that played Pull-the-chicken would do. He needed to look the part of a Mexican and wanted every detail to be convincing.

After securing the stirrup, Felton studied the desert once more and listened for several seconds. There was no sign of Yankees. He rolled a cornhusk cigarette. He quickly smoked it halfway down and gently extinguished it with the toe of his boot. If any one of the California Yankees was an experienced Indian fighter, this small touch of authenticity would not go unnoticed.

Felton heard the muffled sound of a horse's hoof kick a stone. The sound had come from somewhere to the north, shielded from sight by a grove of cholla and ocotillo. He took the reins of the bay and led him inside the adobe and closed the door. He would not have long to wait.

Heavy plank shutters, peppered with old Apache bullet holes, covered the two front windows of the stage station. Each had large shooting portals. Felton peered out of one of them. He could see up and down the road for at least a mile.

Dust was rising far to the west. Two hundred yards to the east a horse appeared. It was quickly followed by others. All were headed toward the station. When the last horse joined the Yankee platoon, Felton counted twenty-two men mounted and three men walking. One soldier was being held on his horse by men that rode beside him.

As the riders grew near, Felton could see that the lead rider wore civilian clothes. Judging from his mannerisms, he was likely a scout hired by the Army. If that were the case, he would be a man familiar with the area and the people of Tucson. Felton would especially have to watch what he said and did around him.

Felton took in a deep breath. He let it out slowly. His heart pounded. It was time. He was an experienced bluffer and had a plan. If all else failed, his ace in the hole was the name of Captain McCleave.

Stepping out into the open, Felton waved his hands excitedly and shouted, "Amigos! Americanos! Amigos, aqui!"

The patrol halted. An order was given and a private galloped toward Felton with his pistol drawn.

"Who are you?" he demanded.

Felton smiled. The private was trail hardened and no fool.

"I am Carlos Ramirez Fuentes, Señor," offered Felton in a heavy Mexican accent. "Lately removed from Tucson by those calling themselves Confederates."

"You alone?"

"*Si*, except for my horse. He is inside. I heard shooting and think they are Apaches murdering someone. I ride fast here.

"You save me from the Apache devils, Señor. Muchas gracias."

The private glared at Felton. He dismounted and went inside the station. He emerged seconds later and waved to his commanding officer.

Without being told, Felton retrieved his horse as the patrol advanced. A quick glance told him the men on foot were Confederates. One of them was Holmes. Their hands were tied behind their backs, but they held their heads high.

Felton grinned at the private. "A man must protect his horse, no?"

A young lieutenant ordered the prisoners taken into the corral. Guards were posted and the wounded man carried inside the station. His neck was wrapped with bloody handkerchiefs.

The lieutenant and the scout approached Felton. The scout looked down at the cigarette as the Yankee's eyes narrowed suspiciously.

"I am Lieutenant Baldwin. This is my scout, Mr. Jones. Who are you and what are you doing here?"

Felton bowed. "I am Carlos Ramirez Fuentes. I was told to leave Tucson by...by *el cazador...Capitan* Hunter is his name."

Jones pulled Felton's rifle from its scabbard. He smelled the barrel, then shoved it back into place. "I Was you, lieutenant, I'd have a look-see at them pistols."

Extending his hand, the lieutenant said coldly, "Your pistols Mr. Fuentes."

Making no sudden moves, Felton took both Navies at once and handed them to Jones. After he had inspected the caps and cylinders, Felton handed the scout the recently cleaned Army. So far their every move had been anticipated.

"They ain't been fired," said Jones.

Baldwin sighed. He seemed to relax but his face was lined with worry. "Return his weapons, Mr. Jones. I'll leave no man unarmed in Apache country."

"*Gracias*," said Felton, accepting his pistols. "Did you kill many Apaches today?"

Before Baldwin could answer, Jones asked pointedly, "Who do you know in Tucson? I never seen you before."

"I visit my señorita there. I am from Sonora."

Jones' eyes flickered.

"Who might that señorita be? I know 'em all."

"This one," smiled Felton. "Is called Juanita."

"That the same Juanita that Jesus Gonzales is sparkin'?"

Felton shook his head gravely. "That is why I am here, Señor. Jesus is a jealous hombre. To be rid of me, he tells the *capitan* I am for the Union. Because of his lies I am told to leave Tucson. So it is that I now go to Los Angeles...and it is not Jesus Gonzales. You try to trick me. No, his name is Jesus Elias, not Gonzales."

"Are you for the Union?" asked Baldwin.

"I am only for me, Lieutenant. We have enough war in Mexico to keep us happy."

"So why are you here on the road to Yuma and not headed back to Sonora?"

"The Apaches are bad on the southern road. It is time I leave Sonora. There are more señoritas in Los Angeles I have not met.

"I am here because I hear the shooting and run to the adobe to get away from the Apaches. It is you who fight the Apaches for me."

A private came out of the adobe and looked Felton over before turning to the lieutenant. "Private Leonard is bad off, Lieutenant. He got it in the neck like Lieutenant Barrett. He ain't gonna make it through the night. Who ever heard of shooting a man in the neck like them Rebels done?"

Jones turned his head and spat."You California boys is mostly miners and such. Them Rebels growed up hunting their food. A neck shot comes natural to 'em. Saves the meat."

Baldwin stared at Jones for a moment. He slowly turned his head to the west. Below the rising dust on the stage road, dark figures could be seen advancing at a gallop in a column of twos. "Captain Calloway is not going to like this," muttered Baldwin.

"Ain't yore fault, Lieutenant," said Jones. "I told Barrett to hold up and wait for ya. Like all Irishmen, he was bullheaded and wouldn't listen. Got him kilt. Like to have got us all kilt. Them Rebels can shoot.

"We didn't hit one of them and they got six of us. We brung two hundred and seventy men out here and not one dead Reb to show for it."

Baldwin stood waiting for Calloway's column to arrive while Jones and the private went to the corrals. Felton stayed where he was. He leaned against a porch post and thoughtfully rolled another cigarette.

The force gathering at Picacho Peak was three times the size of Hunter's company and Tucson was a mere forty miles away. The men stationed at the picket post that had ridden back to town would know nothing of the approaching companies. Captain Hunter may be able to hold off these men but what if there were more soldiers behind Calloway's command? Did they bring artillery? These were questions Felton would have to answer before reporting to Hunter. When Felton had the information he needed, would there be time enough to warn Hunter?

A hundred yards from the station the cavalry column slowed to a walk, then to a halt. A half-dozen dust-covered Yankees rode forward. A man with captain's bars was in the lead.

Salutes were exchanged.

"Report, Lieutenant," ordered Calloway.

Lieutenant Baldwin stiffened. "Sir, I regret to report that our patrols did not link up as planned. Lieutenant Barrett and his patrol engaged the picket post before we arrived. We captured three Confederates. We lost Lieutenant Barrett and one private. We have four wounded. One not expected to live."

Even under a heavy layer of dust, Calloway appeared to pale. His eyes widened with uncertainty. For a moment he was speechless.

"And the Confederates. Their losses?"

"None, sir. None that we can tell. Only three prisoners."

"Have you interrogated them?"

"They are refusing to talk, sir," answered Baldwin. As if the thought suddenly occurred to him, he turned to Felton. "This man says he has just come from Tucson. We were about to question him about the Confederate forces."

Eyeing Felton, Calloway anxiously leaned forward in his saddle. He was clearly shaken by Baldwin's report. Felton instinctively knew it was his chance to buy some time.

"How many men do the Confederates have in Tucson?" growled Calloway, with more fear than ferocity in his tone. "What type of fortifications do they have?"

Felton took the last puff from his cigarette and dropped the butt. He looked up at the captain and scratched his jaw.

"I think, maybe five hundred men. Many come just yesterday, I think. They dig ditches all around the town."

"Artillery? Do they have big guns?"

Seeing Calloway's growing agitation, Felton lied some more. "*Si.* Two, maybe three. I was not there long before I leave. They say more men will come from Texas soon."

Calloway slumped. "Fortifications and reinforcements. Five companies could be headed for us as we speak and we don't have enough supplies to make a stand."

"I suggest, sir," offered Baldwin. "That we proceed with all haste to Tucson and surround the town. We can still satisfy General Carleton's orders to retrieve Captain McCleave by cutting off all escape routes so that they cannot retreat with the captain. We can take them by surprise and..."

"No, Lieutenant," interrupted Calloway. "First we lost McCleave and now Barrett is dead. We will regroup and fortify near the Pima village at White's mill and wait for Colonel West and his command.

"We will leave at first light."

Felton glanced at Baldwin from the corners of his eyes. Carleton wanted McCleave badly. Calloway was giving the orders but seemed unnerved. Baldwin, on the other hand was, another story.

"Señores," said Felton casually. "You speak of one called McCleave. He is no longer in Tucson. He leaves already with some soldiers for Mesilla. He is gone."

All eyes turned to Felton.

"Are you certain," demanded Baldwin. "How do you know it was him? What did he look like?"

"He was a big man. He has a beard...and he talks like no one I hear before. His words are strange to me."

Baldwin swore. He had to have known McCleave spoke with a brogue. Calloway, now with no reason to continue on to Tucson, regained some of his composure. The ruse was working.

"At first light," repeated Calloway, wheeling his horse. With the officers following, the captain returned to the column.

"The news I bring is bad, Lieutenant?" asked Felton.

Baldwin looked long and hard at Felton.

"You will stay with the column, Señor Fuentes. Any attempt to leave without permission will get you shot or hanged. Do you understand?"

"*Si*, Lieutenant," returned Felton smiling. "Should you return to Tucson soon, I would ask to return with you…Los Angeles is very far and my Juanita is so close."

Waving his hand in disgust, Baldwin walked away. "You will come with us to the Pima village. The rest of it is up to Colonel West."

Felton watched the lieutenant until he was inside the adobe and out of sight. Holmes and two privates were in the corral and it was best to stay clear of them. Even a casual glance of recognition could prove a fatal mistake.

Mounting the bay, Felton rode easily through Calloway's soldiers as they prepared to bivouac along both sides of the road. Most of the men merely glanced his way, then went about their routine.

A pair of mountain Howitzers rumbled onto high ground behind the station. Guards scattered out into the desert in every direction. The bulk of the men were picketing their horses and finding shade where they could. Each wore a pistol and knife in addition to a Sharps carbine that hung from a wide leather shoulder strap. Unlike Hunter's ragged Confederates, everything from their narrow-brimmed hats to their boots were Army issue. These men were well disciplined and well equipped.

At the rear of the column, a canvas wagon had pulled into a small clearing. A team of mules was being unhitched by someone dressed in stained buckskins. He was the only man in sight without a uniform. Hoping he might prove to be a neutral, Felton rode toward him.

The teamster was bent over, working with his back to Felton and swearing to himself. For a moment, Felton sat his horse, listening. The ingenious combinations and almost poetic rhythm of curse words had to have been the most scorching string of epithets ever unleashed into the deserts of New Mexico Territory.

When the gray-headed teamster paused to unhook a singletree, Felton spoke up.

"Where it is, amigo, you learn to swear with such eloquence?"

The driver straightened and turned to face Felton. His eyebrows were gray and bushy, as was his drooping mustache. A small gold ring hung from his left ear lobe and a scar crossed his cheek on the same side. He was wiry and no more than five foot seven. He squinted at Felton for a moment, wiping the sweat from his wrinkled forehead with the back of his hand. "Mostly," said the teamster. "I learned that fine art on the high seas. Only a sailor has the time to compose such spicy commentary."

Felton laughed. Judging by his speech and appearance, this was no ordinary teamster.

"My grandfather was a Portuguese sea captain, Señor," offered Felton, with a friendly smile. "He failed to master your craft as well as you."

"A seaman, you say? Well make yourself at home boy. Where do you hail from?"

Felton dismounted and tied his bay to a palo verde as the teamster went back to work on the harnesses.

"Sonora and Tucson. Picacho Peak. Anywhere is my home."

"You got sailor blood in your veins alright. Never like to anchor too long in one port myself."

"And you, Señor? What takes you from the deck of a ship to the seat of a wagon?"

The teamster took a step toward Felton and extended his hand. "The name's Soleil. Call me Soleil, plain and simple."

Felton shook his hand. "Carlos Fuentes."

"Back in forty-nine I was down under...Australia...on a whaler out of Boston. That's when we got word of the gold strike in California. We got the fever and sailed up to San Francisco. Every last one of us jumped ship and went to the gold fields. We weren't alone. The whole bay was full of empty ships that year.

"Well, one thing led to another and here I am a muleskinner. No gold strike to speak of yet. I hear there's still plenty to be had in this country. Why, more than half the men in this army are miners. A good many signed up for the same reason I did, to be the first ones here. I was too late and lost out on the rush of forty-nine, but we'll beat the rush this time.

"These men are tough. They'll fight the Confederates sure enough, but when that's done they'll head for the gold fields same as me."

While Soleil hitched his mules to a picket line, Felton removed the saddle and blanket from the bay. This would be as good a place as any to settle and the teamster was talkative.

When Soleil returned, Felton pointed at the wagon.

"What, then, is it you do for the Army?"

"I'm in charge of the supply wagon, but we don't have much. The men mostly eat jerked beef and hardtack. A few have pemmican. I have some medical supplies and bed rolls for the officers and a water barrel. I'll be the ambulance should we have the need, but mostly I'm hauling the grain we got back at the Pima village.

"The Confederates burned all the hay stacks we had put aside. They gave the grain to the Indians. The Pimas turned around and sold it to us when we rode in. The Rebels were trying to treat the Indians right but this is war. They should have burned all of it. In war it doesn't pay to be civilized. The cutthroats are the ones that win, at least at first."

Felton unrolled his blanket near his horse and sat down in the shade. A Spaniard of his character wouldn't be expected to expend too much energy working. His image was to be that of a shiftless gambler, a no-account womanizer…which was what he was.

"I don't think, amigo, the gold is so easy to find. The Apaches kill everyone. The people of Tucson, Tubac, Sonora…all live in fear. Gold does a dead man no good."

Soleil hung his harness leathers on the side of the wagon. He took a box from under the seat and set it next to Felton's blanket. Using the box as a chair, he sat and tossed his battered hat onto the sand. "We'll fight the Apaches. These Californians aren't run-of-the-mill. Carleton handpicked them. Most of them already came across the deserts and plains to get to the gold fields. They're tough and they've seen Indians before.

"Besides, when a man gets the fever, there's no stopping him."

Felton shrugged and removed his sombrero. Soleil knew how the men had been selected and that Carleton had done it personally. He would know more. "Maybe it is for me not so different. I chase the women. It is like a fever, too, I think. There is no cure for it. I look for a special one and never can find her. For this, I go to Los Angeles as soon as I can get past the Apaches and Yumas. Are there more soldiers on the road to Yuma?"

Soleil swore and said, "Why, there's soldiers stretched from here back to Yuma and then some. Carleton has them spaced a few days apart so that they don't run the water holes dry.

"We're out front to try and get Captain McCleave back from the Southerners. We're just the first of more than two thousand men. Behind us, there is Colonel West, then Cremony, then a dozen more. They just keep coming. First the cavalry, then the artillery and infantry.

"General Carleton is a despised man. Even his officers don't like him. But he does know his military. These soldiers are well prepared and outfitted. The only thing slowing down the advance is water and forage. He's calculated that pretty well, too."

"Is good for me," said Felton. "I can soon be in the arms of a beautiful señorita."

The sound of boots grinding sand caused Soleil to glance to his left. Three men were approaching. The one in the lead was over six feet tall and barrel-chested. His cheekbones were high and his lower jaw squared off like a beam. On sleeves stretched tight by massive biceps, yellow sergeant's bars caught the sunlight.

"Look what the tide washed in," muttered Soleil, coming to his feet. "What can I do for you, Sergeant Turner?"

The sergeant tossed a canvass bag at Soleil's feet. "You know what I want," grunted the sergeant as he eyed Felton and the bay.

"You already had your forage ration, Turner," said Soleil. "I follow the captain's orders, not yours."

"Calloway's turning back," said Turner. "He's yellow. Me and some of the boys may not want to turn tail, so fill it up. Keep your mouth shut about it."

Soleil kicked the bag back toward the three men. "Fill it yourself."

Turner snickered. He took a second look at Felton's gelding. He went to it and rubbed his thick hand along its neck. "I seen you ride past, greaser. You got a good mount. It ain't gaunt like mine from lack of forage. Must be sixteen hands."

Felton could read men as others would a book. He knew what was coming and casually removed his spurs. Some men used the large rowels as weapons in a fight. Felton preferred being able to sidestep and pivot without getting his feet tangled.

He had seen such men as the sergeant many times. They were usually bigger than most. They were tough and walked with a swagger,

125

their confidence the result of numerous victories in barroom brawls. Most would kill at the drop of a hat.

"I think maybe, Señor Sergeant," said Felton, lazily coming to his feet and scratching his head. "He is not so big as you say. But he is a fine horse, no?"

"You hear that, boys?" said Turner. "The greaser just called me a liar."

"Yeah, Serg," agreed one of the privates. "We heard it plain as plowed ground."

"Well now, Mr. Greaser," smiled Turner. "Since you called me a liar, I'm going to give you two choices. You can give me this horse…no, let's say I'm taking it for the Union Army and you're giving it to me personal…or I beat the daylights out of you and then I take it anyway.

"Now which way sounds best to you?"

Turner was at least two inches taller and forty pounds heavier than Felton. He was strong. Turner would start with his fists then, if that failed, resort to wrestling, biting, and gouging. He would stop at nothing.

Taking a step back from the sergeant, Felton took off his jacket, then his gunbelt and extra pistol. He handed them to Soleil.

"The sun is still very bright, Señor. I think maybe you have a hard time beating the daylight out of anyone. Even a lowly greaser like me."

One of the privates ran to announce the fight while Turner removed his weapons and hat. In seconds men formed a jostling ring of blue around the wagon.

Soleil looked up at Felton, then down at the Mexican's scarred knuckles. "Do you know what you're doing, Carlos? He could kill you."

"We will see, amigo. I *need* that horse. It means life or death to me."

Turner was walking around the edge of the noisy crowd, receiving pats on his back and making jokes.

Felton moved away from the wagon and waited. Suddenly the crowd grew silent.

The sergeant strutted toward Felton and reared back with his right fist. Turner didn't see the lightening fast left jab that cut him over his right eye or the quick right that smashed into his nose. The punches caught him by surprise but his head barely moved.

The men erupted with taunts and yells. Felton backed up quickly. Turner was following closely and tried a left-right combination that Felton deflected. Turner's guard was up now. Felton faked another left then punched an uppercut into the belly. When Turner's hands dropped, Felton cut the left eye.

Both his eyes were bleeding, but Turner seemed unfazed. He lunged, caught Felton by the shirt, and jerked him forward. A rock-hard fist landed on the side of Felton's head and rang his ear. He twisted violently and tore free, Turner still grabbed for his throat. Felton slapped the hand away and spun to Turner's rear. He buried both fists into Turner's kidneys, then backed up just as the sergeant turned and swung wildly.

Turner's eyes were beginning to swell. Enraged, Turner charged Felton. Felton dropped and rolled toward Turner. The big man tripped and landed face down in the sand. Both men were instantly on their feet. Turner charged again but this time came in low. Felton let him come.

Expecting Felton to dodge to the left or right, Turner's arms spread wide as he charged. Felton braced himself and squatted. Swinging an uppercut, Felton used his legs and caught Turner under the point of his chin. The blow lifted him several inches but he was only stunned.

Felton tasted blood. His cheek had been cut by Turner's single blow. The man had taken Felton's best punch and was still on his feet. He would not go down. If he ever got hold of Felton, it would mean the end.

The eyes were Felton's only chance. Felton peppered them wickedly with two left-right combinations. The punches weren't designed for a knockout, only to maim.

Above the fanatic cries of the soldiers, a shot rang out from outside the circle. Soon another was fired from the opposite side.

An instant later there was dead silence. Captain Calloway and Lieutenant Baldwin sat their horses. Their eyes blazed with an unspoken but lethal threat. No orders were given, yet the men immediately disbursed.

Calloway rode through the men and stared down at Turner. The sergeant's eyes were nearly shut. His face was bathed in blood. He panted like a dog.

"My apologies, *Capitan*," said Felton, bowing to Calloway. "We fight over my horse. It is all I have to outrun the Apaches. You have many horses. I have only this one."

"Sergeant Turner," snapped Calloway. "This man's horse is his own. If you attempt to take it, he has my permission to shoot you…if I hear any more talk about you deserting I will put you in front of a firing squad. Is that clear, Sergeant?"

Turner did not answer. He was almost blind from the swelling. His fists were still clinched.

Baldwin rode forward. He glanced at Felton, then smiled with satisfaction down at Turner. Pointing to one of the privates that had initially come with him, he ordered, "Take the sergeant back to his camp. Make sure he stays there or you'll both be slapped in chains and sent to Yuma."

As the private led Turner away, Baldwin spoke softly. "Don't turn your back on him or anyone associated with him, Mr. Fuentes. You have made a life long enemy."

"The sergeant has friends," added Calloway. "You should remain with Mr. Soleil until we reach the Pima village. There we will decide what to do with you."

Soleil watched the officers ride away. He walked to Felton and took a close look at the gash on his cheek.

"You could use a stitch or two there. Come on over and have a seat on the wagon tongue. I'll get my rigging."

Felton's right hand was beginning to swell. If it wasn't broken it was severely bruised. He worked it open and closed as he took a seat on the tongue. The heat of the fight still pulsated through him. It felt good. Feeling the sting of the cut on his face, he smiled.

What would Bricela think of him if she knew such fights were common with him? What if she knew he was not the gentleman she envisioned nor a gallant soldier? He hadn't been honest with her from the beginning and she deserved better. Now she thought she was in love with him. But it was Lieutenant Felton that had captured her heart, not Caleb Felton.

From a small leather pouch, Soleil took a piece of black thread, licked one end, then slipped it through the eye of a curved needle.

Pinching both sides of the inch-long gash, he forced the needle through both pieces of flesh, then drug the thread behind.

"I never heard of any Mexican fighting like you just did. That must have been your Portuguese side."

Soleil tied off the first stitch. The poke of the needle hurt worse than the punch he had taken. Felton did not flinch.

"I have been many places," offered Felton. "I learn many things. Some from one, some from another."

"It appeared to me," said Soleil, starting his second stitch. "That you had a plan from the get-go. You went for his eyes."

"All men, no matter how big, have weaknesses. This, my grandfather taught me."

After tying off the second knot, Soleil stepped back and nodded.

"Just like sewing up a sail. You feel up to gathering wood?"

"No *problema*," answered Felton. He stood and buckled on his pistol belt.

"I'll cook what I have for you. Anyone that can lick Turner deserves a banquet. How does pork belly, beans, and coffee sound?"

Felton stuck his Army revolver in his sash. "Fit for a king."

Wood was scarce near the station and the pieces were small. Cactus skeletons would burn so Felton added them to the pile. Meandering slowly to gather sticks of mesquite and palo verde, he observed the other soldiers in the column. They were a hardy, capable looking lot, well armed and over two hundred strong. They were certainly a match for Hunter's single company. According to Soleil, these soldiers were only a fraction of what was to follow, but Soleil could be wrong or things may have changed. Before Felton returned to Tucson he needed to know more...and he had not been gone long enough.

Soleil lined the fire pit with flat rocks and started a small flame to simmer the beans. The sun was a half hour from the horizon and the day's heat was gone. Felton leaned on one elbow, pulling cactus spines from his jacket sleeve.

Soleil sat down. He took a stick from the fire and lit an ivory pipe. "Before you lit into Turner, you were saying women were a fever to you like gold is a fever to me. I never did get to finish what I was about to say on that subject."

"A story about women? I am always ready for such a thing, amigo."

"Well, I was about to say that I used to be like you. Then I got cured...or maybe I was cursed. Either way, I'm done with chasing."

"Ah. So you got married?"

After a few thoughtful puffs on his pipe, Soleil answered, "No. That will never be."

Felton sat up and crossed his legs.

"What happened to make a sailor forsake women? This I never hear of!"

Soleil folded his arms and blew out a cloud of white smoke. "It was close to twenty years ago. We were whaling off the coast of Africa but were mired in a dead calm sea with fog so thick you couldn't see stem to stern. My watch was the last before sunrise but there was no way to tell when it ended due to the light. We had been drifting for two days when I first saw her…and she saw me.

"Her hair was gold and hung to the sides of the prettiest face you ever saw in your life. Her eyes were green as the sea and her skin…it was nearly white and smooth as silk. Her breasts were full and as naked as the day she was born but she was as innocent about it as a child.

"I fell in love with her at first sight…and her with me. I saw her every day for a week. The wind came up and we sailed away. I never told a soul on ship. I've never needed or wanted anyone else."

Felton suppressed a smile. His grandfather had told stories of mermaids but never with such conviction.

"That surely is a sad story, Soleil…if one can believe such a tale. You speak of mermaids, no?"

Soleil puffed on his pipe. "When I strike it rich, I'm going to set sail on the big water and see my lady again."

For a moment, Felton studied the old man. Amazingly, he seemed to believe what he was saying.

"But, my friend," said Felton skeptically. "Even if you could find what you look for you could never be…together." Felton clasped his hands, locking his fingers. "You know, *together*."

Soleil puffed again on his pipe. "I know what you're driving at, Carlos, but when you get as old as me you realize there's more to this life than meets the carnal eye."

Sliding off his box, Soleil added more wood to the fire and stirred the beans. He opened the top of the box and brought out a small white figure.

"I've been carving these since the day we sailed away," said Soleil, handing the figure to Felton. "This was carved from a walrus tusk. That's what she looks like."

Felton stared at the small ivory mermaid. The face was angelic, the detail intricate, and the artistry near perfection. The old man had captured his fantasy and made it real. "It looks like she is waving," said Felton. "Does she say hello or goodbye?"

"Depends on your point of view I suppose. For me she's a saying 'Hello!' and 'Welcome home!' and I'm saying 'hello' right back at her."

"Muy bonita!" said Felton. "Very, very pretty, Soleil. You are an artist. A very fine artist. She is as you say, beautiful."

"She is my lady of the big water."

Caleb Felton blinked. He raised his eyes and stared at Soleil. Owl Woman had used almost the exact words. She had said something about a lady and big water, or was it a lady that lived in the big water? Despite having long ago dismissing her visions as superstition if not outright fabrication, he tried to remember what she had said.

There were eagles that could not land, and something about medicine. It made no sense at the time. Even Owl Woman laughed when she spoke of the lady he was to meet. If he remembered it right, the meeting was to be some sort of sign.

Looking up from the mermaid, Felton asked, "Have you ever been to the Papago village?"

"Never heard of it."

"This is ivory?" asked Felton, almost forgetting his Mexican accent.

"Yes."

Felton thought of the first time he saw Bricela and how he felt. It was as if they had already met...already cared for each other. Her dog was named Robespierre and the brand of his horse matched the tree grown into a Z. He gave her an ivory pendant and now held an ivory figurine in his hand. The grips on the pistol he took from Cade Mosby were also ivory...with eagles carved into them.

After wiping his face, Felton shook his head. Despite the bizarre string of coincidences, his mind remained unchanged. Bricela was just as unattainable, just as much a fantasy as the mermaid was for Soleil. They were both cursed.

Handing the mermaid back to Soleil, Felton swore.

"What is it?" asked Soleil.

"I don't think I could be happy...if I were you. I still say your story is a sad one."

Soleil put his hand up and gestured with the ivory. "That one's for you, Fuentes, for taking care of Turner. It'll bring you luck."

"*Gracias.* It is fine gift, Soleil."

Curiously studying the figurine, Felton asked wistfully, "Did you ever tell her you loved her? Even though the two of you were so…different, did you speak the words to her?"

"Just before we sailed, I did. I made certain of it."

"Why? Did she not know it already?"

"I suppose she did, but a woman wants to hear the words, words spoken sweet and simple. It's something they'll always remember and cherish…no matter what happens after."

Slowly nodding his head, Felton's eyes narrowed thoughtfully. "I hope you find her again someday."

"There is always hope, my friend. Like the Good Book says, 'faith, hope, and love'. That's all a fella needs to be happy. I got all three."

Felton sighed and leaned back on his blanket. He looked into the fading sky and placed the mermaid in his jacket pocket. "I got none of them, amigo. But I have only been given what I deserve."

CHAPTER 8

Fearing a massive counter attack, Calloway had been digging rifle pits and trenches for more than a week when Colonel West marched into the newly fortified post surrounding White's mill. With his additional four companies of infantry, and one of cavalry, West built more earthen barriers and doubled the number of trenches. To honor the fallen lieutenant and boost moral, he named that part of the Pima village Fort Barrett.

When West first arrived he questioned Felton himself and received the same misleading answers as Calloway. For some unexplainable reason, the Pimas of the village told a similar story about the large number of Confederates and fortifications in Tucson. It was enough to stall West, who was waiting for one last company of infantry before advancing.

There was little for Soleil and Felton to do while the soldiers worked. Felton spent his time circulating among the men. He smoked with them, told stories of beautiful women, and gambled just well enough to arouse no attention. He stayed clear of Turner and the flour mill. If White's cook was still there, she might recognize him as one that captured the mill and Captain McCleave. Other than having a heavier beard, he looked the same as he did that night.

It was after dark on the eleventh day at Fort Barrett when the routine ended. Felton saw the men beginning to pack for a long march and quickly went back to Soleil's wagon. A cook fire was burning. Soleil was busy shoving boxes of supplies into the wagon bed.

"Everyone is busy this evening," said Felton, noticing a stack of boxed medical supplies.

Soleil stepped into the firelight. "Help yourself to the pork and beans. Word's come down we're leaving at three this morning. We're finally headed for Tucson, all five companies of infantry and one cavalry. Carleton's orders. West was just waiting for the last company of infantry to come in and now he thinks he has enough men to do the job. He's taking the jackass battery, the twelve pound howitzers with him, too. He's taking no chances."

Squatting by the fire, Felton dipped into the pot of beans with a cup and filled a tin plate. It was time to warn Hunter of what was coming. If the Confederates had not been reinforced, they would have no choice but to retreat.

"I think I will stay here, amigo. Or if they let me, I go on to Los Angeles. This fighting is not for me."

"What about that pretty señorita you left in Tucson? You could see her again."

"You speak of Juanita. She is beautiful, it is true. But there are others…and where there is less danger. I am a lover not a fighter. You go to face Picacho pass again, my friend. You will face many bullets, I think."

Felton took a spoonful of beans. He could not appear to be interested in what Soleil knew. So far he had aroused no suspicion.

Soleil grabbed another wooden box and slid it into the wagon.

"According to the other muleskinners I talked to, we won't be going by way of Picacho. Carleton's giving orders from Yuma but he fought down here during the Mexican war. He knows the country. He's sending us in from the north. We'll go on up the Gila to the San Pedro and come in through a place called Cañada del Oro. It's a longer trail, but they say the lay of the land will get us close enough to surprise them. Their sentinels will all be looking to the west."

Continuing to eat, Felton poured himself some coffee. He would need a lot of it. As soon as the opportunity presented itself, he would ease out of the fort with his horse and take the stage road back to Tucson. With the route being shorter and with West slowed by five companies of infantry, it would be easy to beat them back and warn Hunter.

West was not impressed with Captain Calloway's handling of Picacho. Soleil said only one company of cavalry was to be in the column going to Tucson. West rode in with his own cavalry and would no doubt leave Calloway and his men at the fort. That could lead to another confrontation with Sergeant Turner and, as in any fight, the outcome could be different. Felton would have to leave tonight.

"Maybe I think about Tucson again," said Felton. "Maybe there is little shooting. I have not seen a woman in many days and Tucson is close. Maybe I change my mind and come along."

"Suit yourself, Carlos. As soon as the Confederates are routed, I'm finished. I'm taking off to look for gold. My contract only goes to Tucson."

Felton ate in silence as the teamster continued balancing his load. It had been almost a month since he had seen Bricela. His mind had been occupied with gathering information and maintaining his disguise as a neutral Mexican. Now he was headed back. She would be waiting for him and he would have to face her one more time.

There was an unmistakable bond between them, an abiding kinship that defied explanation. Would it survive what he must tell her? Was their relationship any stronger than two ordinary people? Would the mystery, the unspoken understanding and sense of previous encounters evaporate like a mirage or was what they had an enduring reality? Was Owl Woman guessing about everything or somehow seeing the future? Was there any such thing as fate, or luck...or God for that matter?

Soleil came to the fire and sat on the box that held his collection of mermaids. He seemed pleased as he poured coffee and inhaled the night air.

"Soleil, my friend," said Felton sincerely. "I must ask you a question."

Old eyes narrowed. A smile creased the corners of the seaman's face. "Heave ho, Carlos."

"Do you...truly... plan to go back, to sail across the ocean to look for a mermaid?"

Soleil's expression did not change. He took a sip of coffee. He swallowed, still smiling at Felton.

"I did see her once, Carlos. At least I saw something...anyway, a man has to have a dream. She is mine. She fills that space in the heart that many a man leaves empty."

"She is not so much of a lover, amigo."

The smile on Soleil's face grew wider. "Son, there are all kinds of love. We only have one puny word for it. There should be a dozen or more to describe what the heart can hold for another. All the different kinds of love are equal in their own way. Not all of them are understood completely. The older you get the more you'll see the truth in what I say. This life is full of mysterious and powerful things. Love is at the top of the list."

"You are a philosopher, Soleil. I am but a rascal. I have to touch the woman I will love. To love a woman and not be with her, that for me would be a curse."

Soleil studied Felton's face. He took another sip of coffee as the amber firelight danced in his eyes. "You ever *been* in love, Carlos? For real?"

Felton struggled to swallow a mouthful of beans. It was a simple question, but the answer hung up in his throat. He coughed and gulped some coffee.

"Once...but it is for me like your mermaid. I must walk away from her. I think it is a lucky hombre that can love a woman and be able to make love to her."

"There is luck, to be sure," agreed Soleil. "A patient man makes his own luck. I will find my gold by-and-by. If you keep at it long enough, Carlos, you will find your woman."

After finishing the last spoonful of beans, Felton went to a nearby dishpan and started washing the utensils he had borrowed for the last few weeks. Soleil had been good to him. Fortunately, he was only a teamster and cared more about gold than the war. He would be in no danger even if Hunter received reinforcements.

Drying his hands on a dishrag, Felton looked up at the star-studded sky and said easily, "I saddle my bay. He has not been ridden so much and will be at the bit if I do not ride him before we leave. He is too hot-blooded to walk behind a dusty column of soldiers. He will want to lead if I do not tire him some."

"Careful you don't go near the sentries. They might take a shot at you."

Picking up his blanket and saddle, Felton started for the picket line.

"I play cards with them. They know me. I will be in no danger from them."

Away from the campfire and in the dim starlight, Felton took a deep breath and let it out slowly. It was time to leave Fort Barrett. If he were caught, he would be sent to prison in Yuma...or shot.

With five companies of men preparing for a long march, nobody paid any attention to him saddling his mount. Before swinging into the saddle, Felton stepped deeper into the shadows and tossed his sombrero into patch of ocotillo. Even in the dark, the broad-brimmed hat would be easy to spot, and if his plan were to work, it would only get in the way.

Felton rode unnoticed past dozens of busy soldiers and blazing campfires to the perimeter of the fort where the earthwork formed its first line of defense. Beyond those walls and pits, the stage road led to Tucson. There were two sentries at the entrance to the fort. A quarter mile further, two more were posted where the road entered the Pima village. He had gambled with most of the men that pulled guard duty and knew them by name.

Riding further into the darkness the camp noise diminished. Straight ahead, the road glistened gray white in the starlight. Felton heard the rustling of cloth and the crunching of sand under leather soles.

"Who goes there?" demanded a voice as two dark figures appeared in front of him to block his way.

"It is only I, amigos. Carlos Fuentes," answered Felton as he dismounted. "I am soon to leave with Soleil and wish to calm my horse. He is restless at all the preparation in camp and paws to be on his way."

The guards relaxed.

"Tucson, eh?" said one. "You goin' back for them señoritas you been harpin' about?"

"*Si*, amigos. You know me too well, I think."

"We can't let you go past us," said the other sentry. "You'll have to go back or they'll have our hide."

"My horse, he needs to run. The camp is too full of soldiers. Just down to the edge of the village and back will lather him. He has been tied for much too long. There are two more soldiers there. I cannot go further. I will be back in a few minutes only. Everyone is too busy to care."

"I still say no," said the second guard.

Recognizing both voices, Felton smiled. He reached into his pocket and took out a gold double eagle. He held it up for the soldiers to see.

"Amigo, you worry too much. You hold this until I come back. If I run away, it is for the both of you. I come back. I no give you my only gold and run away."

"What do ya say, Smitty?" said the first sentry. "Even if he quits the country, we can say he snuck by us. Who cares about a Mexican."

Smitty took the gold coin and looked closely at it. He tested its weight.

"Where'd you get this?"

"I am a gambler, Señor. Are you?"

There was a moment of hesitation as Smitty tossed the coin up and down in his hand.

"Alright. Three minutes. If you ain't back in three minutes the gold is ours. Any more than that and you lose it. That's the deal. Take it or leave it."

Felton mounted. "I will be back in two, Señores."

When the bay felt the spurs it lunged into a full run. In seconds, Felton was out of the guards' sight. There was no watch to check the time. By now Smitty would be busy explaining how they would cheat the Mexican out of the gold. Smitty was greedy and always tried to cheat at poker.

Felton had ridden for thirty seconds when he yelled out in perfect English, "Run away, run away."

Immediately, he looped his elbow into the loop woven into the horse's mane and hooked his boot into the near stirrup. He leaned completely to the side and in the darkness, merged with the speeding gelding.

Two men jumped on the road waving their arms trying to stop the charging horse. It sped by them in a cloud of dust. They choked and swore at the animal as it passed. There were no shots. Without a scratch, Caleb Felton was clear of the Union Army.

After two miles, Felton slowed the bay into a steady gallop. Tucson was ninety miles away and it was unlikely any officers would be aware of his escape for hours. With his head start and a shorter distance to travel, he could afford to pace the horse.

When his absence was finally discovered, West and Calloway would at least suspect he was a spy on his way to warn Hunter of the attack. What would West do if he became aware Carlos Fuentes knew the route they would take, the route ordered by General Carleton?

If they followed orders and marched up the Gila and the San Pedro rivers with all five companies, the infantry would slow them down to twenty miles a day. If Colonel West suspected a spy was already headed for Picacho Pass to warn the Confederates, he would almost certainly move ahead with his company of cavalry. If he did that, it would be a race to Tucson.

The sides of the stage road were lined with intermittent thickets of cactus, brush, and the long eerie shadows of giant saguaros. A band of Apaches could be hidden in a thousand places. Luckily, they did not fight at night. His departure from the Yankees could not have come at a better time of day. If the bay did not bottom out, he would be in the Old Pueblo by noon.

Picacho Peak was silhouetted by a pale yellow sunrise when Felton slowed the bay to a cautious walk. He stopped one hundred yards from the stage station. A wisp of smoke rose from the clay chimney. No horses were in the corral. Hunter surely would have ordered sentries posted somewhere on the mountain.

No Apache would normally make a fire inside the adobe, but Swilling had taught him never to underestimate their cunning. He gently nudged the bay and slid his rifle out of its leather scabbard.

Felton rode another twenty yards and pulled back on the reins. The bay's breaths were hard and heavy, his ears turned toward the stage station.

Looking carefully over his shoulder and to the left and right, Felton studied the road in the increasing light of daybreak. There were tracks near the corrals and at the hitching posts in front of the station. Apaches would have been more careful if they planned an ambush.

"Company A," called Felton, "Texas Mounted Volunteers."

The door to the station opened. A rock rolled from somewhere on the side of the mountain.

"Who might'n you be?" questioned a voice from the darkness of the station.

"I would be Lieutenant Felton, fresh from the biggest camp of Yankees you ever saw."

Three men emerged from the adobe and walked toward Felton. Each had a rifle resting on his shoulder. All were bearded and ragged.

"We about give you up fer dead," said a tall, raw-boned private.

"Did Captain Hunter get his reinforcements?"

"Narry a one."

Felton sighed and took a piece of jerky from his pocket.

"You boys better mount up. There's five hundred Yankees and some artillery headed for Tucson. They're coming in from the north. There's no use guarding this road anymore. We need to warn Captain Hunter to get out of town."

"Cap'n Hunter's done left for Mesilla. Only Lieutenant Tevis and a handful of men stayed in Tucson. Your black stallion is there waitin' for ya. Cap'n Hunter made sure of that."

Felton took a bite of jerky and chewed it for several seconds. His spying had been for nothing. "You boys cooking breakfast?"

"Nope. Got nothin' to eat. We was going to hunt us up a snake or one of them big red lizards if we had to. We ain't 'et too good of late."

"You all may as well get on to Tucson," said Felton, taking out his last piece of jerky and handing it down to the men. "Your horses are fresh. You can get there faster than me. Sooner the better. When you get there you won't have much time before the Yankees show up."

The private bit off a piece of meat and handed it to the man beside him. "You best come along with us, Lieutenant. Never know when ya might come on Injuns."

"Have there been any around Tucson?"

"Naw. But ya can't count on that. When ya don't see them devils is when you best be lookin' fer 'em the most. There ain't been none seen nowhere. Folk in town think we run 'em off but we done no such thing."

"I've already ridden over forty miles. I'll have to save this bay or I'll be afoot. You go on ahead. I'll be fine."

Another man came from behind the station and joined the group. The sun was cresting the mountain peaks to the east. The air was still and cool.

"Is this all of you?"

"Yep. Jed was up on the mountain. We got our horses hid in the brush just in case. There's water in the trough yonder."

Felton dismounted. His legs were stiff and his back had been aching for hours.

"When I've watered my horse and rested up a bit, I'll be along. Tell Lieutenant Tevis to go on east without me. I have some business to attend to before I leave Tucson. It could take a while. If the Yankees get close I'll have the black to get me away in plenty of time."

"If them Yankees is as close as you say, we best have your stallion tied and ready for ya. Wouldn't do to waste time chasin' after him in that plaza corral. How 'bout we tie 'im in front of the Shoo Fly fer ya?"

Felton nodded and glanced at the rising sun. He had made good time to Picacho Pass. The Confederates would be well on their way to Mesilla before West and his cavalry were within miles of Tucson. He would have enough time to properly say goodbye to Bricela. "Good idea. He's a good mount, but can get mighty rank if he hasn't been ridden in a while."

"We'll be seein' ya on the road to Messilla," said the private. "Good luck to ya."

Felton led his sweat-lathered mount to the station. He tied it to a hitching rail and loosened the cinch. The horse would have to cool down before getting water and a twenty-minute rest would hurt nothing. Felton stretched out on the planks of the porch and felt the knots in his back start to unwind. The sun warmed the side of his face as he heard the Confederates ride away. Sliding his hand to the ivory mermaid in his jacket pocket, he rested it there. He closed his eyes and thought of the angelic smile of Bricela Verde.

He would embrace her one last time, look into her innocent eyes and confess his love to her. He would tell her he had to leave...the war was taking him away. There would be no discussion of the years that separated them, no indication he would never return. That would come in a letter, a letter that also explained who Caleb R. Felton really was and why she should forget him. For now, she would hear the truth, plain and simple.

Felton thought of Soleil and his tale of the mermaid. Was there a real woman involved or was it merely the fantasy of a lonely seaman? Was he haunted by some distant memory of a lost love? Whatever it was, the old whaler cherished the memory of her.

A smile spread on Felton's chapped lips. His mind drifted. He and Soleil weren't so different. It was a pleasant thought and he was exhausted.

Felton awoke with a jerk. He sat up, blinked his blood-shot eyes and tried to grasp what had happened. The sun was well above the mountains and the air was hot. He had slept at least an hour. For an instant he panicked. His mind cleared and he remembered the four Confederates. Everything was fine.

Rubbing his face with both hands, he took a deep breath and let it out slowly. He blinked again to moisten his eyes. He focused them on the desert in front of him. During his weeks inside Fort Barrett, he had not noticed the change in seasons. Flowers were blooming everywhere. The endless miles of sand and thorns had transformed into a sea of brilliant colors. Above the horizon, the cloudless sky was deep blue.

"I'll be damned," muttered Felton. "Would you look at that."

Untying his horse, he let it drink at the wooden trough. He filled his canteen. Unlike the first half of his ride, the last forty miles would be under the desert sun. Even in the spring it would get hot.

Felton tightened the cinch and checked the caps on his pistols. He learned enough from Swilling and Tevis to always be prepared. With the Apaches especially, there was no such thing as being too cautious.

Swinging into the saddle, Felton let the bay walk the first mile, then broke into an easy gallop. The road led to the southeast and without his sombrero the glare of the rising sun made it difficult to see ahead. If there were any Apaches waiting for him, it would make no difference. They could hide in almost anything and be invisible at midday.

Continually altering the gait of his horse in order to save its strength, it was noon before Felton had gone thirty miles. Riding easily, he watched the tracks of the four horses ahead of him. They changed from dark to light. He had no real idea of how long ago they had been made. Swilling was a trailer and could read sign better than anyone in the company. He had tried to teach Felton as they rode west but he paid little attention. Tracking skills were of no use at a poker table.

Bringing the bay back to a walk, Felton uncorked his canteen, threw his head back and took a long drink. With only ten miles to go, he could afford to drink as much as he wanted.

When he brought his head down, he squinted at the road. He corked the canteen and wiped his eyes. A band of dark sand had been turned up fifty feet in front of him. Instead of following the road it crossed over it and into the desert.

Pulling his Army Colt, Felton rode to the tracks. Several horses had come down a dry wash from the north and continued following the drainage to the south. None of them were shod. These were Apaches and there had to be at least a dozen of them.

They had crossed the road after the Confederates, but how long ago? Was it a few minutes or an hour or more? Where were they headed? Tucson was more to the east than the south. Perhaps they were bound for Mexico or the mines along the border. Whatever the destination, people were about to die. If Swilling's stories were true, some would die slowly.

Felton's heart raced. If the tracks were fresh he could be the one tortured to death. Had they seen him? Were they waiting for him to ride into a trap? Were the Apaches as cruel as Swilling claimed? If he could not escape should he, could he, fire a bullet into his brain as Swilling suggested?

The rifle was good at long range, but the pistols had six shots and the road was narrow. Felton rode on with the ivory handled Colt in his hand. Now every flowering cactus, every bed of color sprouting from the sand could hide death. The sun beat down on his shoulders. His mouth was already dry. Who would live in such a place? The flowers were merely a cleaver deception, a disarming trick of the heat and thorns.

The more distance Felton put between him and the tracks, the better he felt. Nevertheless, he kept the pistol ready for the next hour. When he saw the dingy white of Tucson's adobes, he tucked the pistol in his sash and took the bay into a fast gallop. He could easily keep that pace for the last mile.

Felton rode into the main plaza and headed toward the saloon. The town looked deserted. The black stallion stood ready just as the private had promised. Most of the Mexicans were at siesta but someone sat in the shade of the Shoo Fly porch. It was James Tevis. "We thought you were on the wrong side of the dirt, Caleb. What took you so long?"

Felton tied the bay and shook hands with Tevis. He glanced inside the saloon and saw Cade Mosby sitting at a table by himself.

"That's where you'll end up if the Yankees get here," warned Felton. "Why are you still here?"

"I sent everyone else down the road. I figured you would need some company."

Untying his cinch, Felton smiled, "I've got to say goodbye to someone first. It won't take long."

Tevis grinned as Felton switched the wet blanket and saddle to the black.

"You'll have to do that some other day. She's not here," said Tevis.

Felton's stomach turned. He kept working at the saddle. "Who's not here?"

"Come on, Caleb. I'm not blind. Miss Verde was looking cow-eyed at you since we got here. She and her Mexican friend got a ride with some of Mosby's miners to the San Xavier Mission. They wanted to see the flowers and visit that Papago medicine woman."

His eyes flaring with panic, Felton turned to Tevis. "When did they leave?"

"About an hour ago, I suppose. They were on a wagon with two armed guards. They had ten more on horseback. Even so, I told the ladies they shouldn't go. Nobody's seen any Indian sign in so long, they wouldn't listen. You know women."

Switching the bridle as fast as he could, Felton said hurriedly, "I saw Indian pony tracks ten miles out, heading south. I'm going to warn them."

Tevis swore. "You could get cut off by the Yankees doing that. Besides, we have orders to go east."

"I know," agreed Felton, swinging onto the black. "If I get trapped I'll go down to Sonora. When it's safe I'll work my way back to Texas and find you. Tell Captain Hunter I had no choice."

Tevis reached up and shook hands. "*Vaya con Dios,* friend."

"If he'll have me," sneered Felton, who then wheeled the stallion and charged across the plaza and down Calle Real.

The mission was nine miles to the south. If they left an hour before with a wagon, they would only be halfway to the church. With the speed and endurance of the stallion, it would only take a quarter hour to overtake them.

Swilling said Apaches never attacked unless certain of victory and twelve armed men was a small army. Felton had no real idea how many Indians crossed the stage road or if they were anywhere nearby. In the desert, from the right vantage point, the dust from Mosby's men would be visible for fifty miles.

The stallion had hardly broken a sweat when the road dipped into a small basin where the sand changed to a faint shade of red. A mile ahead to the right of the road, a red bluff rose a few feet above the saguaros and ended in a flat mesa. From the top of that bluff, it would be easy to see the entire road from Tucson to San Xavier.

Felton's anxiety grew steadily stronger. His eyes watered from racing through the heated air. Bricela was near but something was wrong, terribly wrong. He felt it. The sensation engulfed him. He spurred the stallion again, now fighting off a wave of panic. A moment later he knew he was riding into hell.

Rounding a slight bend he saw the first bodies sprawled in the middle of the road. Three Mexicans lay almost on top of each other, dead where they fell from their horses. The stallion veered sharply to the side but kept his speed as he ran by the pile of corpses. Another body to his left lay face up with a cholla crushed under his back and two more lined the right side of the road.

The wagon tracks suddenly turned off the road toward the red bluff. They were trying for the rocks at its base.

Leaping over a patch of beaver tail cactus, the black followed the ruts at full speed, then slowed to weave around the taller cholla and ocotillo. Another man sat upright with a mesquite at his back. A lance protruded from his chest.

Near the base of the bluff Felton caught a glimpse of the wagon. It was on its side. One mule was down, the other still stood. A few feet from the wagon, a small black dog lay in a pool of blood, riddled with a dozen arrows.

Felton jumped from the horse and let the reins fall. He drew both Colt Navies and dropped into a crouch to listen. The only sound was the heavy breathing of the stallion.

Quietly he moved away from the horse toward the wagon. When he could hear better he stopped. Closer to the bluff near a cluster of red boulders he thought he heard a voice.

Easing his right pistol back into its holster, Felton drew the heavy-bladed Bowie knife. Again he heard the sound. His heart sank. It was a moan and seemed to be coming from a giant saguaro less than fifty feet from the wagon.

Unable to restrain himself, Felton moved quickly. He came to a boulder and slowly eased his head around to see. He froze.

A black-haired woman had been stripped and lashed to the cactus. Her head drooped low. Her bowels lay at her feet. She moaned again.

Felton ducked back behind the rock. He wanted to vomit but somehow did not. Briclea was out there somewhere.

Forcing himself to look again, Felton scanned the desert in front of the woman. Shreds of her dress were scattered in the sand. Some pieces had been thrown into the branches of nearby mesquite and palo verde trees. On the ground by one of the tree trunks, a red ribbon with a touch of white caught his eye.

Trying to look in every direction at once, he went to the ribbon. He picked it up. It was the ivory brooch he had given Bricela. He was numb. His instincts took over.

Drag marks and moccasin tracks pointed the way. He followed the trail walking tall. There was no more fear. His death meant nothing. This day, this moment, he would kill or be killed.

A boulder lay in front of him. He knew she was there before he heard the lustful grunt. He walked closer. He saw the soles of a pair of moccasins and brown legs. Outside them, bare white legs had been spread apart.

Felton took another step. He was at the edge of the boulder when the moccasins suddenly moved. An Apache buck stood suddenly and turned. He saw the blade of the razor-sharp Bowie coming at his neck but there was no time to duck. His head fell from his shoulders before his body collapsed in a fountain of blood.

A second Apache darted for cover but the Colt exploded breaking his spine. A second and third shot punctured his lungs and heart.

Nothing else moved. Not even Bricela. Her eyes were open, staring into some unknown place.

Blood still pumped from the decapitated Apache's neck. Felton jerked him away from Bricela. She was bathed in crimson.

His jacket was too small. He covered her as well as he could with it, then ran back to the stallion. Leading the horse to Bricela, Felton cut a hole in the center of his blanket and knelt beside her. Raising her up, he slipped the crude poncho over her head. After tying his sash around her waist to close the edges of the blanket, he eased her back down.

He began to think again. These two bucks were young. They must have stayed behind to get what they wanted. If they didn't return to the band, soon the others would come back. Bricela would have to be moved quickly but there was one thing he must do first.

Lifting Bricela to her feet, Felton guided her foot into the stirrup, then encouraged her to step up. She made a feeble effort. With help she finally swung her leg over the saddle.

Felton clinched his teeth. Supporting Bricela with one hand, he guided his horse back to the saguaro. The woman tied to it was still breathing. Tevis said Bricela left with her friend. Was this Juanita, the sweetheart of Jesus Elias? Felton did not want to know who it was.

Leaving Bricela a few feet away, he drew one of his Navies. It was a smaller caliber than the Army. Somehow it seemed more kind. He put the barrel to the woman's temple. Before pulling the trigger he turned his head.

Riding behind Bricela and holding her in the saddle with one hand, Felton was in view of the San Xavier Mission in less than an hour. He rode to Owl Woman's home and carried Bricela inside. With the old woman's help, he carefully laid her on a bed.

Felton kneeled down close to her. He stroked her hair as she silently turned away from him and rolled on her side. Covered with dust, blood and dirt, she slowly drew up her legs and wrapped her arms around her knees. Her eyes, still glazed with shock, remained locked straight ahead.

Owl Woman would know how to care for Bricela physically. Somehow he must tell the medicine woman that no one was to know what happened to her, especially no one in Tucson.

Hoping the old Papago understood Spanish, Felton spoke to her softly. He explained that white people were peculiar about such things and Bricela would suffer more than enough in the days and years to come. If she was ever to recover, if she were ever to have a decent life, she would have to put the past behind her. All that she endured would have to be kept secret and, if possible, erased from her memory.

When he was finished speaking he looked down at Bricela. It was the feeling of total helplessness that caused Felton to remove the small mermaid from his pocket and gently place it in her hand. It was all he could do for her before going outside and closing the door behind him.

Unaware that he was also covered in dried blood, Felton sat waiting in the shade of Owl Woman's *ramada*. He did not move for hours. Several Papagos passed by to stare at him. By late afternoon they began gathering in small groups in front of the house.

Felton's mind was blank. He chose not to think but to wait. There was nothing more he could do.

The shadows of the mission were growing long when the sound of pounding hooves finally brought Felton out of his trance.

Looking past the mission, he saw a patrol of blue uniforms galloping his way. He could have mounted the stallion and easily outrun them but he sat where he was. Bricela was all he cared about.

Felton watched them come closer. Cade Mosby was riding next to a captain and pointing at the stallion. Seeing Felton in the shade, his finger shifted to the *ramada*.

Felton sighed. He leaned his head back against the wall and said softly, "I should have killed him."

The Indians moved out of the way as the soldiers surrounded the adobe.

Mosby pointed again but took a second look at Felton's bloody face and shirt before bellowing, "That's him. He's one of them. He's a lieutenant."

The captain dismounted and looked closely at Felton. Mosby started to step down but the captain held his hand up. "Stay where you are!" he ordered. "No one dismounts."

Stepping under the *ramada,* the officer asked, "Are you a Confederate officer?"

Felton hesitated. He glared at Mosby. "I am."

"I am Captain Fritz, sir. I will have your weapons."

Felton reached for the Army in his waistband but it was not there. He looked down but realized he must have dropped it while helping Bricela onto the horse. Easing the Navies out of their holsters, he handed them butt first to Fritz.

Fritz checked the cylinders and faced his men. "Sergeant, take your patrol to the mission and stay there until I return."

When the soldiers were out of hearing distance, Fritz asked politely, "May I see your knife, sir."

Felton lifted his arm and Fritz removed the Bowie. The blade was bloody.

Fritz thoughtfully glanced at the closed door but did not go inside.

"We came upon a massacre today, Lieutenant. We found two Apaches among the dead. Mosby, our informant, tells me there were two women. We found the Mexican."

There was a long silence.

"Should I assume," Fritz said finally. "That the white woman escaped unharmed?"

Coming to his feet, Felton looked into the captain's eyes. Fritz had read the sign left at the bluff and seen the empty cylinders. He saw the blade of the Bowie knife. He knew.

"Yes. Completely unharmed, sir. Somehow she managed to get to the Papago village."

"I can be assured there are no Confederates inside this adobe?"

"You have my word, sir."

Fritz nodded. "Consider yourself a prisoner of the Union Army...with my compliments."

The Tucson adobe Hunter had used for his headquarters had its windows covered and now served as a dingy jailhouse. For two days, Felton ate well and got some much needed rest. On the third morning the door to the adobe flew open. Captain Calloway and Sergeant Turner eagerly stepped inside to see the prisoner.

"So it *is* you," sneered Calloway. "You are the prisoner."

"He's no prisoner," said Turner. "He's a spy. Aren't you Fuentes...or whatever your name is."

"Thought you'd make a fool of me didn't you, Fuentes?" jeered Calloway. "You were part of that bunch at Picacho Pass that killed Barrett and his men. You snuck past our lines wearing no uniform. You'll face a firing squad for that. I'll have Lieutenant Barrett's men make up that squad."

Felton was sitting on the only chair in the adobe. He squinted at the sunlight coming through the door. They still did not know his name. For Bricela's, sake that was for the best. "You should talk to General Carleton first," advised Felton.

"You will be dead long before he arrives," said Calloway. "And why would we do that?"

"Because if you kill me, Captain Hunter will kill Captain McCleave. That was decided before I left Tucson."

Calloway hesitated but Turner was a quick thinker. "How's General Carleton going to know anything about that if you're dead?"

"Because I told Captain Fritz three days ago. He sent a courier to Yuma to offer a prisoner exchange."

Turner's jaw muscles rippled with hatred and Calloway fumed. Both had been humiliated and both wanted revenge. Calloway was about to storm out of the room when Turner stopped him. "Captain Fritz is still up at old Fort Brechenridge," said Turner. "We could at least brand him a spy, brand him like we do deserters. With an S instead of a D. Brand him down to the bone, I say."

A smile brightened Calloway's sour expression. He paced back and forth for a full minute before stopping to glare at Felton. "Excellent suggestion, Sergeant. Under the circumstances, I am sure Colonel West will agree with the punishment. We will do it in the plaza at the whipping post. A public branding will do nicely.

"Have the brand made at once. I want this done today, before Captain Fritz returns."

"Request permission, sir," said Turner with a smile. "To do the branding myself."

"Permission granted, Sergeant. Personally, I detest the smell of burning flesh."

Felton started to wince as he thought of what the hot iron would feel like but he kept a poker face. They would not get the satisfaction of seeing him sweat. Whatever the pain, it would be nothing compared to what Bricela was experiencing. He would think of that when the time came.

Calloway left. Turner waited until Calloway was out of earshot. The red-blue scars around his eyes had not healed completely. "Ever seen what a red-hot iron can do, Fuentes? I'm going to burn you to the bone."

Something deep within Caleb Felton stirred. A part of him he had never known reared its head. He smiled wickedly. A flame danced in his eyes, his skin seemed on fire. "You better kill me while you're at it."

"Maybe I will," returned Turner defiantly, but now there was a hint of uncertainty in his tone. "Let's see how brave you talk when you're tied to that post."

Felton said nothing. He thought only of what a Bowie knife would do to the big man's gut.

After Turner shut and locked the door, Felton stared at it like a caged animal. When his blood cooled, he marveled at the changes going on inside him. Until three days ago he had never taken another man's life or even considered it a possibility. Turner was evil. The thought of killing him now came naturally. It was more than a fantasy or fleeting thought. It was a palpable desire.

Taunts outside the adobe broke into his thoughts. Turner was spreading the word of what was to happen at the whipping post. The capture of McCleave and his men, and the deaths of four comrades had demoralized the entire army. When the Union cavalry rode out of Oro Canyon and finally made its heroic charge into Tucson, there was no one to fight. The Confederates had bested them at every turn. The branding of one of their officers would go a long way to even the score.

A blacksmith's hammer could be heard above the voices. They were wasting no time but it did not matter. Carlos Fuentes, the Confederate spy, was preparing to defeat them one more time.

The metallic pings continued for a half hour before they stopped. Felton could smell smoke. Most of it was coming from the smith's fire but now some was drifting in from the whipping post. They were ready and so was he.

A cheer went up from the crowd outside the adobe. Three men burst through the door. One of them was Turner. He carried the hastily made brand. Two of the men tore off Felton's shirt. Turner pointed the iron at his face. "Take a good look, Fuentes. You're going to carry this mark the rest of your life."

Felton sighed and shook his head in disbelief at what he saw. He thought of Bricela's tree by the Santa Cruz River and the brand on his horse. She believed the similarity of two figures was some sort of sign. Maybe she was right.

One man held Felton's hands together as the other tied them with leather strips.

"We cut them strips of leather from your stallion's reins," jeered Turner. "We're givin' him to the general when he gets here."

A rope was tied to the straps. Turner jerked Felton to his feet, then pulled him out the door as he would an animal to the slaughter. At the sight of the prisoner another cheer went up. He was surrounded by hundreds of soldiers as they made their way to the corner of the plaza where the post and fire were waiting.

One man appeared above the mob following at a distance on horseback. He caught Felton's eye. It was Jesus Elias. His face was drawn and sympathetic but there was nothing he could do.

Parading his prisoner to the pole, Turner yanked the rope several times, trying to make Felton fall. He managed to keep his balance. He was tied to the post as one to be burned at the stake. His hands were held down while a rope was wound tightly around his body, spanning from his neck to his ankles. He could barely breathe.

Turner stuck the brand in the blazing fire a few feet away. The crowd grew wild with excitement. What liquor they could find was being passed from mouth to mouth. Some men started to dance, others were laughing and pointing fingers.

When the brand was red hot, Turner grabbed the handle of the iron and triumphantly held it high over his head. He walked in a circle, soaking up the cheers but the iron was losing its glow. He stepped close to Felton and brought the brand up. Slowly he inched it closer to Felton's left breast. He jammed it into his skin.

Smoke rose from the burning flesh. More howls and cheers drowned out the sound of white skin sizzling under the crooked ribbon of hot iron. Felton jerked violently. He clinched his teeth and managed not to cry out. Instead, a low growl nearly ruptured his vocal chords.

Turner pressed harder with the brand, trying to reach the rib cage but the iron had cooled too much to go more than a half inch deep. He burned into the muscle but no deeper.

When the prisoner refused to scream, the frenzied crowd grew quiet. A man enduring that much pain without crying out in agony was enough to sober them.

Turner was too frustrated to notice the eyes of the man tied to the post or the mistake he made with the brand. He shoved the iron back into the fire. Some noticed the eerie stare of the Confederate. Others noticed the mark on his chest. The eyes of the prisoner held a promise of death and the carelessly made brand was backwards. Instead of a crude S, the scar on his chest would be that of a Z.

The subdued mood of the soldiers caught the attention of Turner. He mistook the reason for it.

"Somebody get more wood," he roared. He shoved the brand deeper into the glowing coals of a dying fire. "We're not done with him yet!"

A voice from the crowd rang out, "You done enough, Serg. Let him alone."

"Any man with that much sand," said another. "Don't deserve no more."

A hush settled over the spectators. The sergeant glared back at them, looking to his left then to his right. "This rebel killed Lieutenant Barrett," bellowed Turner. "Maybe you forgot that. I ain't about to."

Grabbing the handle of the brand, Turner again started for Felton. A pistol blast from the opposite corner of the plaza stopped him.

Colonel West and Captain Fritz galloped across the square. West held a pistol in his hand.

"What's the meaning of this, Sergeant?" he demanded.

"Captain Calloway's orders, sir," answered Turner, with eyes full of disrespect. "This man is a Confederate spy so we branded him."

West rode through the men to take a closer look at Felton. The Yankee's face twisted with contempt. "Isn't that the Mexican, Fuentes?"

"Yes, sir. He's a Rebel in Hunter's command."

"Why wasn't he shot? Or hung?"

"On account of Captain McCleave. Fuentes is to be exchanged for McCleave."

After holstering his pistol, West arrogantly brushed the trail dust from his jacket with the palm of his hand. "Captain McCleave is worth fifty Rebels," said West, glancing at the brand still held by Turner. "Very well, Sergeant. It appears you have already carried out your orders. Take him back to the guardhouse...and give him a blouse. We mustn't behave like barbarians."

As West and Fritz rode away, Turner reluctantly barked out some orders, then went into the Shoo Fly. Two privates went to the whipping post, untied the ropes and helped Felton walk back to the adobe. By the time they finished untying the leather straps around his wrists, Felton was able to stand on his own. When the adobe door closed he fell to his knees and vomited. Fighting excruciating pain, he crawled to a wall and leaned back. The cool adobe bricks felt good.

To block the pain from his mind, Felton thought of Bricela. His ordeal was nothing in comparison. She saw her friend slammed against the trunk of a cactus, tied to it, and gutted alive. Bricela, a young and innocent woman, full of wonder and hope...perhaps even in love...had been raped by a band of savages.

The brand was nothing. It was what he deserved. Not for spying, not for a misspent life, not even for allowing Bricela to fall in love with him...it was for falling asleep at Picacho Pass.

Tevis said she had left for San Xavier only an hour before he rode in. An hour. He would have at least delayed her departure. More likely he would have talked her out of going. Certainly he would have...if he had only been there.

The poor Mexican woman the Apaches had murdered had to be Juanita. The two of them were going to see Owl Woman. If the old Papago could see the future, why hadn't she seen this?

An hour. Why that hour? Why that day?

Felton's head was spinning when the door opened again. The sun was low now and the light that entered softer. The guards were allowing a civilian inside. It was Jesus.

Felton said nothing.

The guards kept the door open but stayed outside.

"I brought you a shirt and a poultice for your wound. It is made from the glondrina weed."

Felton did not answer nor make eye contact. He sat motionless, fighting the pain.

Jesus knelt beside him and gently placed the poultice over the seeping brand. He laid a Mexican style white shirt beside his friend, then leaned against the wall next to him. Neither man spoke for several minutes.

"I should not have gone to work at the mine," said Jesus finally. "She would be alive if I had not."

Felton slowly turned his head and looked at Jesus. He knew about Juanita.

"It's my fault, Jesus…I went to sleep at Picacho Station…for an hour…the same hour I needed to get here before they left."

Turning his eyes from Jesus, Felton stared at nothing. "It will be my fault as long as I live."

"We will both live with it," said Jesus. "There is no escape. Not ever." For several more minutes the two men sat together. Hearing nothing, a guard looked in. "You got one more minute," he said, stepping back outside.

"Miss Verde," said Jesus. "She is not well. Owl Woman cares for her. You were right to take her there."

"No one must know anything, Jesus," said Felton. There was a sudden urgency in his voice.

"Juanita was my sweetheart. That is the only reason I was told by the Papagos. No one else will know."

Felton relaxed. For a few seconds he had felt no pain.

"She asks for you. She does not remember it was you who brought her to Owl Woman. No one has told her."

Closing his eyes, Felton leaned his head back against the wall. "If she asks…tell her it was a man named Carlos Fuentes. It's best she never knows the truth. She would look at me differently if she thought I knew…If she were to ever see me again."

"You love her, Caleb?"

"Yes…before I knew better, it was too late."

"Will you see her again?"

"I was going to say goodbye before…she needs to forget. She needs to forget everything…including me. I will only remind her of the past. She has to forget and start her life again.

"I was leaving for good anyway. It wasn't right. I didn't know how young she was, Jesus. I just didn't know."

"She will stay with Owl Woman for now," said Jesus. "Miss Verde has much healing to do."

"Do her relatives know, her aunt and uncle?"

Jesus shook his head.

"The new army took them away. They take the Robinsons, Ourys, and even Mr. Mosby to the Yuma fort because they are for the Southern *Americanos*. I don't think they know nothing about Miss Verde.

"I think, maybe, they take you to the prison at Yuma, too. It is a bad place."

"What will you do, Jesus?"

There was a long silence. Jesus stood slowly. "I will kill Apaches. All I can." Jesus walked somberly to the door. He stopped and looked back. "For what you did for my Juanita, you will always be welcome at my house. *Vaya con Dios*."

Chapter 9

May 24, 1866

Jesus Elias sat on his heels in front of the post office smoking a cigarette. An oil-stained bundle of muslin lay at his feet. Across the dusty Calle del Correo, a dozen Tucson citizens waited at the Butterfield Station. The stage was late, which was not unusual but still there was uneasiness. The Apaches were a constant threat to any traveler.

Most of the people that came now were white. Most spoke no Spanish and complained about the street names. Some of the ones that were forced to leave like Estevan Ochoa and William Oury had returned. There were others but mostly the residents were new *Americanos*.

Two weeks earlier a letter addressed to Jesus Elias had arrived. A friend was coming on today's stage. He was ill and came for the dry climate. Near the end of the Civil War, a pistol ball hit his friend's lung and the healing was slow. The doctors told him if he stayed where he was, the humid air would kill him.

Fate had brought Elias and his friend together once again. This was no ordinary day nor was Caleb Felton an ordinary man. Some thought Owl Woman had made a mistake about him. She had not. This day was no coincidence. It was part of destiny and Elias believed in such things. He had seen too much to doubt.

His brown eyes shifted under the shade of his sombrero. The stage was turning onto Calle Real. He stood and crossed the street with the bundle tucked under his left arm. His friend would not use the name of Felton. He was no longer Carlos Fuentes. Elias was to ask for Mr. Conway Fargo.

The stage pulled to a halt in front of the station and the bystanders excitedly greeted the ones they had waited so long to see. One by one, the passengers stepped down to hug or shake hands. They were dressed in nice traveling clothes but all were covered with a fine layer of yellow dust.

The last to exit the crowded stage wore a cheap suit that years before had fit someone smaller. His hat brim was tattered on one side and his shoes worn down at the heel. He was clean shaven. His cheeks were sunken and his skin was more pale than Elias remembered.

Elias stepped forward and shook hands with Felton. His illness had not weakened his grip.

"Welcome to Tucson, Mr. Fargo. I am Jesus Elias."

"A pleasure to meet you, sir," said Felton with a faint smile.

The stage driver tossed a small handbag down to Felton. He caught it but the quick movement of his hands caused him to cough.

Elias formally extended his arm and said, "This way, Mr. Fargo." When they were away from the station, Elias grinned broadly. "It is good to see you, Caleb. I am very happy you have come."

"I can't pay much, Elias. I'll do what I can for my upkeep."

"De nada, amigo. De nada. You are my guest. Your money is no good to me. Speak of it no more."

Felton nodded and looked around. "The town hasn't changed much."

"We have more people every week. Stores are open…cantinas. The Apaches still keep the town small."

"Are there…many people that will know me?"

"Si," answered Elias. "Some of the whites you knew have returned. Many of the California soldiers have stayed to live here. With them, you will have to be careful. Without the beard you wore as Carlos Fuentes, it will be more hard to know you, I think."

"I'll stay out of sight as much as I can. Do you live in the same place?"

"No. Too much there reminds me of Juanita. Now I live on the edge of the Pueblo. We go there. First we see some other thing…at the Church of San Augustine."

It was a short walk down Calle Real to Calle de Mesilla. When they turned the corner, Jesus paused. "You are not armed?" asked Elias.

"I sold everything I owned to pay my way out. All I have to my name is in this handbag.

Elias took the bundle from under his arm and handed it to Felton.

"This belongs to you. I have kept it for you."

Accepting the gift, Felton asked, "What is it?"

"It was given to me by a man called Fritz, a captain. He found it. It was near Juanita.

"The captain could read sign, Caleb. He asks many questions in Tucson. He knows that we are friends. He knows Juanita was my woman. He gives me this and tells me what you did. He says if I see you again, it is yours."

Felton lifted an edge of the muslin. He saw the ivory grips and part of the eagles carved on the Army Colt he had lost. It was the pistol he had taken from Cade Mosby.

"It is loaded and capped. I will give you more powder and lead when we go to my casa."

Opening his handbag, Felton carefully placed the pistol inside. His eyes looked hollow. "Thank you, Elias. I am sorry you should have to be reminded. It still plagues me. A day never passes that I don't think of it."

"Come," said Elias. "There is more."

The two men walked side by side up Calle de Mesilla. Neither spoke. As they neared the church plaza Elias became uneasy. "Today you come to Tucson, Caleb. It has been four years and each year has many days. It is this day you come. I know it is the day you were *meant* to come."

Felton looked at Elias, then at the adobes they were passing. "Something is happening today isn't it. What is it Jesus?"

"Soon you will see," answered Elias. He pointed to the corner of an adobe. One side faced the church and the other the street. "We stand here in the shade. When you see what comes, hide your face."

Several horses and three buggies were waiting outside the church. It was the plaza where the Confederates had kept their horses. Now flowers grew along the walls of the church and a few of the adobes near it.

Felton asked no more questions. He stared at the church doors two hundred feet away.

Elias glanced up at him. Even though he was sick, Caleb was a strong man. He would have to be. This was fate...or God. It would be over soon, or at least this part of it would be.

The church doors swung open and men and women filed out. A moment later a man in a black suit and a woman in white came out. Rice was thrown at them. They both got into a buggy. The men mounted their horses and followed the bride and groom as the small entourage trotted toward the two men.

Felton swore. As Bricela Verde and her new husband approached them, he lowered his head and turned away. The buggy passed.

Elias waved and smiled at Bricela. She returned the smile. He kept watching her as the buggy went down Calle del Mesilla. Suddenly she turned and looked back. Elias smiled again. This time it was not meant for Bricela, it was for Felton. She could not have recognized him. Nevertheless, she had felt something just coming near Caleb Felton. Years had passed, but as Owl Woman had once said, there was medicine between them. They were twins. Somehow, in some way, they were meant to be together.

"She thought you were dead," said Elias. "We all thought you were killed. It is fate that brought you here today. Do you remember what Owl Woman said to you? It is the medicine. You share it with her."

"I can't stay here," muttered Felton. He coughed again, this time repeatedly. "I can't do it, Jesus. Medicine's supposed to make you well. I feel like I'm drowning."

"I have a cousin in Tubac. You will stay with him, my friend. It is God's will you have come. I am certain of it."

"I thought you put your faith in Owl Woman," said Felton, too ill to hide his sarcasm.

"Owl Woman prays to Tei-as, to God. She goes to the Holy Mother Church. She still sees what she has always seen."

"What's the point, Jesus?"

Elias thought for a moment. There had to be a reason for such a day as this day. "Did you come back to marry Miss. Verde?"

Clinching the bag he carried with both hands, Felton's eyes hardened. "I may not live out the winter, Jesus. I don't have a dime to my name."

"You wished to see her, no?"

It was Felton's turn to think. He took a moment to answer.

"I did want to see her. At least once more. That was all."

"How can it be that you feel so bad?"

"I don't know, Jesus. Damned if I ever understood any of it. I do know I can't be near her. At least not now."

Elias grinned with satisfaction.

"My good friend...for now...it is Tubac. Someday you will meet her once more."

Chapter 10

AUGUST, 1882

Caleb Felton was a mile south of Yselta, Texas when he saw the stand of cotton wood trees and whitewall tents of the Texas Rangers. Several tough-looking men were lounging in the camp. This was Company A of the Frontier Battalion. Captain Baylor was in charge. He was a by-the-book Episcopal. Liquor never touched his lips nor did an oath of any sort get past them. Until a few years ago, he was an Indian fighter. Now his main concern was border ruffians and murderers.

Felton rode into camp with a Winchester .45-75 across his saddle. He wore a Mexican style hat and buckskin jacket. His pants were tucked into knee-high boots. Around his waist hung two .44 caliber pistols and a Bowie knife. One of the pistols, with ivory grips, was set in a crossdraw. The grips were worn from heavy use.

All of the rangers stopped what they were doing. Each had the eyes of a hunter. They locked onto Felton and followed him until he stopped by a hitch rail.

"Howdy stranger," said a young ranger. "What can we do you for?"

Felton glanced around, and said easily, "I'm Con Fargo, sergeant in Captain McNelly's ranger battalion out of San Antonio. I'm looking for Captain Baylor."

The ranger stepped forward. As he extended his hand, the other half-dozen rangers gathered around. Shaking hands with Felton, he said respectfully, "I'm James Gillett. Captain Baylor's out on a scout. Don't expect he'll be back for a day or two."

After dismounting and stowing his rifle, Felton shook hands with the rest of his fellow rangers. He was taller than most of them and his shoulders were broader. "You boys got any coffee?" he asked.

The ranger that had introduced himself as George Lloyd answered eagerly, "Shore do Sergeant. Set right there on that stump and I'll fetch you a cup. You et yet?"

"No."

"I'll fry you some bacon. We got bread from breakfast and the fire's still hot."

Felton smiled and took off his hat. His shoulder-length black hair was streaked with gray, as was his mustache. There were wrinkles at the corners of his eyes but still he looked younger than fifty-three. "You boys eat no better than the rest of us, I see."

Taking a stump next to Felton, Gillette asked, "What brings you so far west, Sergeant?"

Felton accepted a steaming cup of coffee from Lloyd. He lifted it to his lips. Blowing across the rim, his eyes narrowed. "Is Captain Baylor any relation to Colonel John Baylor that fought under Sibley?"

"A cousin, I think," said Gillette. "Did you fight under the colonel?"

Felton ignored the question and asked another. "You all recollect two men by the name of Morton and Brown?"

"You bet we do," said Gillett. "They were murdered just south of here last year. They were found at a sheep ranch outside of San Elizario. In fact, me and two other men trailed the murderers to Guadalupe. That's fifty miles from here."

Felton took a sip of coffee and nodded, "I read the report."

"You know I had the alcalde arrest the murderers," said Gillett.

"I do. I am aware that while you were arranging extradition papers, that same acalde let them go."

"It happens all the time," said Lloyd, returning with a plate of bacon and bread. "Why, just last winter me and James took after a murderer named Baca. We had to kidnap him out of Saragosa to get him to trial. He was over there clerking in a store pretty as you please. They knowed he had murdered a man up at Soccoro but there he was. On top of that, when we brung him back, his uncle, a judge in El Paso, tried to bribe us to let him go. Them Mexicans is crooked as snakes when it come to protecting one of their own.

"They're all time, murderin' and robbin' and then hightailin' across the Rio Grande. Captain Baylor won't allow us to go after 'em without papers. By the time we get the paper's writ up, them damned alcaldes let 'em go. Sometimes, it don't even take no bribe money. They's practically all related, anyhow."

"That's right as rain," agreed Gillette. "Captain Baylor about had a conniption fit when we showed up with Baca and no proper papers. He said the governor might disband all of Company A on account of us. Said it was going to cause a 'breach of international comity', whatever that is."

Felton chewed on a piece of bacon, then bit off a piece of bread. He washed it down with coffee, studying Gillette and Lloyd. "The names of the men that murdered Morton and Brown were Esquibel and Molina?"

"Yep."

"Any question as to their guilt?"

"None," said Gillette disgustedly. "They were the herders at the sheep ranch where the murders took place, and they had a pearl-handled pistol that belonged to Morton. I saw it in Esquibel's belt myself. We tracked them from the sight of the murders right to Guadalupe. They are guilty as the gates of hell are hot."

"You after them two?" asked Lloyd.

"Could be," smiled Felton.

"You got the papers?"

There was a silence as Felton continued to eat. The rangers looked from one to the other. The name of Conway Fargo was known to most of them. "Morton and Brown have family in San Antonio…and some influence," offered Felton. "They put up some reward money, too. Sometimes it's better not to ask too many questions. Let's just say that Captain McNelly and the governor are likely to be looking the other way about now."

Felton handed the plate and cup to Lloyd and mounted his horse.

"Much obliged, boys," he said, then galloped toward San Elizario.

Watching Felton ride away, Lloyd said, "Hell's gonna be a poppin' now."

"What do you mean?" asked Gillette.

"You see that black stallion he's a ridin' and that brand? I could see he had two more pistols under his buckskin jacket and another'n in his left boot top. There ain't no doubt about it. That's the one they call The Parson. Some call him Judge n' Jury Fargo, Jury Fargo for short."

Gillette swore. "That's The Parson?"

"In the flesh. Nobody knows how he does it. Some say he's part Mexican. Some say he ain't. If he ever brings a prisoner back alive, hell will freeze over."

"I can figure the Judge n' Jury part," said Gillette. "But why The Parson?"

Lloyd shook his head. "They say Fargo got religion some years back. Somethin' happened to him out in Arizona long before he become a ranger. After that he hunted Injuns with the Army up in New Mexico and around Prescott. They say he was a Pinkerton for a while too, but he was too mean fer 'em so they fired him. Then he come to be a ranger for McNelly.

"He gives his condemned men time to say a prayer before they meet their maker. Then he kills 'em...or least wise they all seem to die while tryin' to escape or drown or some such notion. Anyhow, that's what I hear told. That's how he come to be called The Parson.

"Somebody once told me he even give a redskin time to sing his death song. But I don't much favor he done that."

"Kind of interesting," said Gillette, "that Captain Baylor was sent out on a scout just before Fargo got here. The captain might have tried to stop him."

"Now that you mention it...I'd say it was good luck. Good luck for the folks of Texas and bad luck fer them two murderin' Mescans. Morton and Brown were good men. They deserved better'n to have their brains beat out with a piece of mesquite."

It was past sundown when Felton rode into Guadalupe. He needed daylight to capture Esquibel and Molina. He spent the night in the livery. The next morning he breakfasted in a cantina and watched the village wake up.

Guadalupe was no different than any other Mexican town. *Rastras* of red chili peppers hung on the outer walls of flat-roofed adobes. Dogs and chickens roamed the streets. Here and there a donkey pulled a *carreta* full of vegetables to market. In the center of town there was a church and a plaza. As the morning sun rose, men appeared with their sombreros and *serapes*. The women wrapped themselves in colorful *rebosos*.

Somewhere near the plaza, the president of the town, the acalde, would have an office. He would arrive late today, if at all, but he would have one or two deputies on duty.

When the sun was above the rooftops, Felton finished his last cup of coffee and went to a nearby saloon. The bartender pointed out a deputy. He was leaning against the wall of the church and smoking a cigarette. Con Fargo went to him and spoke in Spanish. "Good morning, Señor. I wish to speak with the acalde."

The Mexican's eyes moved up and down, studying Felton and his weapons.

"What do you want so early?"

"I am a Texas Ranger. I believe there are two men in Guadalupe that are wanted for murder in El Paso. I wish for the acalde to arrest them and hold them until all the papers are completed."

"Who are these men?"

"Their names are Manuel Molina and Santiago Esquibel."

For a moment the deputy stopped smoking. His eyes flashed with recognition. He knew at least one of the men. It would be enough.

"The acalde is not in so early. I will tell him of these men when he arrives."

"Are they here in Guadalupe?" asked Felton.

"They are. But you have no authority here. You can do nothing. Do you have any papers to give the acalde?"

"No. If the acalde will hold them, I will go to Captain Baylor and tell him they are here in jail. He will go to Paso del Norte as soon he can with the extradition papers."

A crooked smile betrayed the Mexican's intentions.

"I will tell the acalde as soon as he is in. We cannot hold these men long. You will need to have the papers very soon."

"Good. I will leave immediately. I should be back in two days."

"Sure. We will hold them."

"Two days," agreed Felton as he turned to leave. "Three at the most."

When Felton passed by the cantina where he had eaten, he glanced back at the church. The deputy was still watching him. The Mexican would want to make certain the Texan was leaving before he made his move. He would either go directly to the bandits or to the acalde. Either way, the murderers would be warned to leave town. They would not go north to Paso del Norte. They would take the road to the south.

Crossing the Rio Grande, Felton started north but then swung the stallion in a wide half circle and re-crossed the river five miles below Guadalupe. After checking the road for sign, he made a small camp alongside it and tied the black in plain view. He built a small fire ring and a few feet from it, laid out his saddle. Before unrolling his blanket, he slid a sawed-off double-barreled shotgun from its center. He removed his pistol belt and hung it over his saddle horn. The fire had been burning less than an hour when two men rounded a bend a mile to the north.

When the riders were within two hundred yards, Felton grabbed the shotgun. Squatting by the fire, he held the scattergun concealed behind his back with his right hand. With his left hand he smoked a cigarette. As the two bandits approached, Felton smiled and stood.

"Buenos dias amigos."

The descriptions of the Mexicans were good ones. Molina was short and stocky with pockmarked skin. Esquibel was average height and weight but had a distinctly angular jaw line. Both were armed but it was Molina that wore the pearl-handled pistol.

Molina eyed the stallion and then the saddle and pistols. Esquibel stared at Felton.

Molina said in Spanish, "Yes, it is a fine day, Señor. What is it you are doing out here? It is not safe to be alone on this road."

"Oh, I am never alone. I travel with God, my friends. Would you like to have coffee with me?"

Esquiblel grinned and added, "We are in a hurry. You can have your coffee but I think we will take your horse. We will take your guns, too. You can better travel with God. God does not need your guns or your horse."

Molina laughed but sat his horse without making a move for his pistol.

Felton took a puff on his cigarette and casually blew the smoke into the air. "To steal a man's horse is the same as to steal his life. We hang horse thieves in Texas."

"You are not in Texas," sneered Molina.

"Yes, this is true. So you will not hang. Do you intend to beat out my brains or shoot me with a stolen pistol...Manuel Molina?"

Molina's eyes flared. He reached for his pistol as Felton jerked the double-barrel from behind his back and fired it with one hand.

Molina flew backwards off his saddle. Esquibel wheeled his horse around but before it took its first leap, Felton shouldered the scattergun and emptied the second barrel.

Esquibel screamed, the impact of the buckshot knocked him sideways. The horse lunged, flipping him over backwards. He landed face down. He moaned and rolled onto his back.

Breaking the action of the shotgun as he walked forward, Felton flipped out the smoking shells and dropped in two more. Molina was dead. Esquibel was coughing up blood.

Felton spoke once again in Spanish. "You should have stayed in Guadalupe, Esquibel. Now you will die without a priest. If you know any prayers you should say them."

The Mexican's lips moved but there was no sound. A moment later his eyes glazed and his breathing stopped.

Gillette bent over and held a candle close to the dead mens' faces.

"That's them alright. And that's the pistol stolen from Morton."

Marshal Stoudenmire threw the blanket back over the faces of the bandits. They were laid out behind his El Paso office after dark. The Ranger that brought them in was taking no chances.

"That's good enough for me," said the Marshal. "I'll wire San Antonio to that effect Mr. Fargo. You've done us a service."

"Much obliged, Marshal. If it's all the same to the both of you, I would like to keep this on the dead quiet. I don't need their friends and relatives on my trail."

"Understood. What do you want to do with their outfits?"

"Sell the horses for what you can get. One of them took some buckshot in the neck and the other is just a cayuse. They should cover burial expenses and a decent marker for the both of them.

"The pistols should be returned to the families in San Antonio. That pearl-handled one, especially, will be a keepsake."

"They don't deserve burying," said Gillette. "They left Morton and Brown stripped of their clothes with their skulls caved in. By the time we found them the coyotes had been at work for three days."

"I have no sympathy for murderers. But a good burial can sometimes put an end to it. The less I have to look over my shoulder for vengeful brothers or cousins, the better I like it."

The three men walked into the well-lit office. Marshal Stoudenmire went to his desk and picked up a letter.

"Almost forgot this," he said, handing it to Felton. "This came in from San Antonio. Captain McNelly figured you would show up in El Paso so he sent it out by train."

Felton glanced at the writing on the envelope, then took a closer look. The handwriting was elegant. It was addressed for general delivery in San Antonio, Texas. It was written to Mr. Conway R. Fargo. It was the R that jolted him.

Since re-christening himself Con Fargo, he had never used a middle name or initial. Whoever had sent the letter knew his true identity and his general whereabouts.

Stuffing the envelope into a pocket, Felton hid his surprise. A quick glance at the marshal told him the middle initial meant nothing to him. It was just a letter.

"I saw a new hotel when I rode in," said Felton. "Think I'll sleep in a bed tonight."

"They got tubs," offered Gillette. "The Southern Pacific Railroad just came to El Paso this year. Now the town's going to grow."

"Saw the rails. Where do they go from here?"

"The northern line makes its first stop thirty miles north of here at Mesilla. From there it goes to Rincon and up to Sante Fe. The western one goes to Tucson and then all the way to California. It only takes about twenty-six hours to get to Tucson from here.

"There's nothing but desert from here to there, but Tucson'll boom now, too. All they got to do around those parts is keep the Apaches under control. There's lots of talk they might jump the reservation again."

Felton recalled the Confederate's long cold ride from Mesilla to Tucson twenty years earlier. It took three miserable weeks of hard riding. Since that time, no one but the bravest souls dared take wagons or the stage to Tucson. It was more than three hundred arduous miles through Indian country. Now any fool could make it in a day.

"I'm going to the hotel," said Felton. "I'll be leaving before sunup."

It was after nine o'clock when Felton crossed the dirt street to the new two-story hotel. The wood to build it was shipped out from an eastern mill and still had the look and smell of fresh-cut lumber. The owner boasted of having the best floor in all of West Texas. As most of the inhabitants had never seen one, he got no arguments about his claim.

The heat of the summer day faded with the red sunset. The saloons and gaming houses were just now warming up. It was late for an honest man to be out and about, but the streets of El Paso were coming alive with activity. The railroad injected the village with new life and there was money to be made twenty-four hours a day.

Felton rented a room and ordered a bath. When it was filled, he eased himself into the steaming water. As the initial sting passed, he slid down to his chin and closed his eyes. For a moment he thought of nothing but the simple luxury of soaking his aching muscles in a hot tub. He had been on the trail for weeks.

His pants hung next to the tub along with his pistols. Before he undressed, the letter the marshal gave him was like having a tarantula in his pocket. It couldn't be ignored but he hated to reach in and pull it out. The time in his life when he used his middle initial was best forgotten and left alone.

His past molded him into who and what he was, but it took half a lifetime to leave those memories behind. Occasionally the ugly scar on his chest chaffed and he would briefly be reminded how it came to be there. He still rode the same breed of stallion as he did at the start of the war, and the pistol he took from Cade Mosby was converted to use cartridges. He had grown accustomed to using them both. His weapons and mount were merely tools of his trade. He rarely considered the small piece of ivory that constantly hung around his neck.

Felton slowly submerged his head for several seconds. He raised up and ran his fingers through his long hair. He grabbed a muslin towel and dried his face and hands. Stretching for his pants, he fingered the letter out of the pocket and stared at the handwriting.

Few people west of the Mississippi knew he had a middle name, much less that it began with an R. Even if the letter were from a long lost brother or sister, what could they want after so many years? Mama died long ago and he was the black sheep no one talked about except in whispers.

When taken to the Yankee prison at Yuma he went as Carlos Fuentes. He used that name until he was released to fight Apaches. Since that time he was known only as Conway Fargo.

Carefully and with growing curiosity, Felton tore open the letter. Inside was a single sheet of paper and a second sealed envelope with no writing on it. The second envelope was yellow with age.

He unfolded the letter.

Dear Mr. Fargo,

I received information of late that suggests you are an old acquaintance.

If you are the C.R. F. of years passed, you will know the meaning of a black Z and a tree of the same letter.

Felton's stomach knotted. He sat up in the tub and swore. The letter was from Bricela Verde. His heart pounded. He blinked his bloodshot eyes and read on.

I understand that, for reasons known only to yourself, you prefer to remain C.F. of present. However, I wish for you to know that, years ago, I   was wrongly informed you had been killed in the early years of the late war.

I am in desperate need of help. You have been highly recommended by Mr. Pinkerton. According to that fine gentleman you possess skills, though not suited for his agency, that are in perfect harmony with my present needs and the grave dilemma I face.
Financial arrangements can be negotiated upon your arrival. Secrecy is, however, of utmost importance as witnessed by the care taken in this letter. Therefore, I will pass by above mentioned tree at noon each day for one month hence. Should you graciously accept my request for aid, it is there that once again we shall meet.
August 14, 1882
Sincerely
B.V.

Felton shook his head and rubbed the back of his neck. It could not be. She should have forgotten him years ago. She was only fifteen when they met...yet she even remembered his middle initial. Had she discovered her dog, Robespierre, bore the same ridiculous name as he, recalling the R would be understandable. He hadn't told her of that strange coincidence.
A smile grew on Felton's face. Years of suppressed memories rose from the dead and played in his mind like scenes on a stage. A sense of joy and expectation engulfed him. He stared at the letter and sank deep into the tub.
She had not forgotten him after all. Not only had she not forgotten, she was asking him to return.
Felton opened the second envelope. It was a poem. He read it slowly.

Tears of a Wandering Angel
    By B.V.

Sunrises, skies soft and blue
Twisted into knots, no one to untangle

Soaring together, one spirit and mind
Dashed to earth, crippled for life

Days serene, full of wonder
Horribly torn, scars forever lasting

Hope eternal, love avowed
Alone to suffer, only comes a stranger

Patiently waiting, love enduring
A cold steel dagger thrust twice through my heart

    Goodbye my dearest
    March 26, 1865

After finishing the poem, Felton squinted dumbfounded at the date on bottom of the paper. The elation he felt moments before sank into a sea of ominous uncertainty.

The lines had been written seventeen years before and almost three years after her terrible ordeal. The poem was obviously meant for him but why send it now? What did it mean? Why was she saying goodbye to him and yet asking him to come back?

Felton rubbed his eyes and read the poem but this time out loud. The pattern of the verses was more powerful with the second reading, and the rhythm more dramatic. He listened carefully to the words, trying to decipher any hidden message.

On the third reading, "Soaring together, one spirit and mind", triggered the recollection of a similar expression. The thought of those words sent him back to the Papago village he and Bricela visited so long ago. Most of the details of the trip had faded. Those that remained were cherished memories. Felton smiled once more. Bricela was so beautiful...and so trusting. She was a vision of perfection.

Old Owl Woman talked a lot about the two of them that day. She had said he and Bricela were twins, that they would soar together like eagles. Bricela liked that part.

Felton shook his head and laughed softly. Bricela was upset when Owl Woman said they would not be together. She was so innocent, so radiant. She wanted everything to be perfect.

The smile vanished suddenly as darker memories broke through. Whatever the medicine woman might have been, she had not seen what was in store for Bricela and Juanita. How could a person predict something as trivial as a mermaid in the future of a total stranger and not see the grisly death of her own granddaughter and rape of Bricela? That question had haunted Felton for twenty years.

Looking back at the paper in his hand, Felton frowned. The poem, at least in part, described what Bricela suffered on the road to San Xavier. If the poem were solely about that tragic day, the last verse, "thrust twice through my heart" did not fit. Why "twice" and why did it say "Goodbye my dearest?"

Carefully replacing the letters and envelope, Felton got out of the tub and dressed. He took a candle to his bed and sat down. Once again he took out the poem. For the first time he noticed the ink in two of the words was slightly smeared.

Holding the letter closer to the light, Felton swore and felt his stomach roll with nausea. The paper had been stained with two drops. Tears shed by Bricela seventeen years ago had fallen on the paper he now held in his hand...but the tears that had fallen so long ago were not for Con Fargo. They had been shed for Lieutenant Caleb R. Felton.

Felton closed his eyes for a moment. The present vanished and time seemed to bend backwards. It was as if the stains on the poem were still damp. He sensed her closeness, smelled her perfume. He could feel the warmth of her hand through his arm as they walked in the moonlight. The air was cool. He could see her eyes, hear her voice. Holding her one last time, he kissed her gently. She was so happy...and so very impossible to embrace. Like the old teamster Soleil, Felton knew what it was like to be in love with a myth.

Taking a deep breath, Felton opened his eyes. Whatever the true meaning of the poem, one thing was clear. She said goodbye to Caleb Felton in March 1865, almost two decades ago. She married the following year. She wanted no misunderstanding and wisely included the poem as a warning. This was not meant to be a romantic reunion. This was business.

She was a woman now. Likely, there were children in her house. She would be thirty-four or thirty-five years old, almost the same age he was when they met. It was another coincidence but their lives were intertwined with them. Many were extraordinary and unexplainable but all turned out to be meaningless…or so it seemed most of the time. At other more wistful moments, such as now, he was not so certain. He would see her again. They would meet by the same tree outside of the same town. Were they completing a foreordained circle, a path determined twenty years before? Was the journey to end in Tucson or would fate send him back around?

If the last two decades had taught him anything, it was that life had more questions than answers. Whatever he might face the next day or over the next horizon was totally out of his hands.

As Conway Fargo, he hunted hostile Apaches for the Army, been a Pinkerton agent, and was now a Texas Ranger. Despite his reputation as a killer, he fought on the side of law and order. What he did, no matter how brutal, was for the good of others. Though time had eased the pain and faded some of the memories, it was because of that day…because of what happened to Bricela Verde, that he became Con Fargo.

If the two of them never met, had he not interfered in her life, she would never have suffered so terribly. If he had not fallen asleep at Picacho Station, not failed her when she needed him most, she could have moved back east and lived her life without hidden scars.

It was his fault. It had always been his fault and that bitter knowledge overshadowed every aspect of his life. Twenty years before, he swore her loss would not be just another pointless tragedy. He vowed a flame of redemption would rise from the ashes of that terrible day and so it had. His life of reprisal was one of atonement, and what he did with a gun, he did for her. For her sake there was at least some justice in the world, some reckoning for the defenseless. Because of her, many evil men no longer plagued the earth.

For years he had not looked back or questioned the hard life to which he had grown accustomed. Those years were now erased by a letter. Everything was circling back to the beginning. Again, she was in Tucson and needed his help. She asked for Con Fargo and Fargo she would get. This time, however, he would not fail her.

Felton loaded the stallion into the freight car and carried his saddle on his shoulder. Walking over the newly built loading platform to the passenger cars, his boot heals hammered the rough-sawn planks. His large rowled spurs jingled rythmically as several pairs of eyes peered at him from the dimly lit windows of the train. It was an hour before sunrise. The air was still and cool.

Under a broad-brimmed hat, streaks of gray highlighted his shoulder-length hair. His eyebrows were jet black. His eyes were those of a hunter and held the threat of death. Women found him handsome but men said he looked like the devil himself.

Before leaving the hotel he decided against a haircut and only trimmed his chin beard and mustache. Bricela would see him as he was, not as she remembered him. What did it matter? She was married. It was his help she wanted.

For the passengers' sake, Felton placed his pistols and cartridge belt in his saddlebags. His rifle was in the leather boot and the sawed-off shotgun was hidden in the Navajo blanket tied behind the cantle. Under his gray vest was a shoulder holster and sheriff's model Colt.

Stepping up into the car, Felton passed by several empty seats and went to the rear. Dropping his saddle next to the window, he took the seat next to it. He wanted no company, no casual conversation. The double seat opposite him was empty and he hoped it stayed that way.

More passengers arrived and the car began to fill. One look at Felton's face kept most of them at a distance. The train was about to pull out when a young woman and boy started down the isle. The only space left open in the coach car was across from him.

When the woman focused on Felton her eyes flared and she quickly looked away. She wore a neat traveling dress and matching bonnet. The style seemed eastern and out of place in El Paso.

The boy looked to be ten years old and wore knickers. He held a dime novel in his hand. His eyes were wide as well but unlike the fear reflected in his mother's expression, his were full of awe.

"May we sit here, sir?" asked the woman. "Are you expecting anyone to join you?"

Felton glanced at her and shrugged. "You got no choice, lady. Coach is full. I hear they have room in the sleeper."

The woman smiled feebly. "Too expensive," she said and quickly slid in to take the window seat.

The boy sat across the aisle from Felton. "I'm Tommy," said the boy, offering his hand.

Turning toward the boy, Felton looked into his eyes. They were blue like Bricela's…and full of innocence as hers once were. She could have children this age by now. Would they have her eyes?

"My name is Fargo, son," replied Felton and shook the small pale hand.

Tommy stared at Felton for several seconds. He glanced down at the dashing figure on the cover of the Beadle's Dime Novel he held in his hand. He studied it for a moment then looked back at Felton. "We're from Chicago," said Tommy.

"That so?"

"We're going to California to see my father. Can I call you Fargo?"

"Tommy!" scolded the woman. "That is improper."

Felton laughed, something he rarely did. The boy was brash. That too reminded him of Bricela. "It's alright, ma'am. Things are different in the West. Fargo is just fine. You may address me as Mr. Fargo if you wish. However, Tommy is a young man and I'm taking a liking to him. He can call me Fargo if his fine mother will allow it."

The woman relaxed. Felton could still be charming if he chose.

"I am Mrs. Wilson," said the woman as the train started with a lunge.

"A pleasure, ma'am."

Tommy held up the dime novel and pointed to the drawing on the cover.

"You look like him, Fargo. Are you Buffalo Bill?"

Felton shook his head. The train was picking up speed. "No, Tommy. Bill's a good man though."

Tommy seemed disappointed. He hung his head and ran his finger over the cheap paper cover of the novel. Suddenly he looked up again. "You know Buffalo Bill Cody?"

"Met him a time or two up north."

"Wild Bill Hickcock? I've read all about him…and all about Buffalo Bill. I read a lot."

"Him too. Cody and Hickcock were both Army scouts years ago. Hickcock was the best pistol shot I ever saw. Until the day he died he never swore a lick."

Leaning forward, Tommy looked Felton over carefully. He studied the worn saddle and rifle butt protruding from the scabbard.

"Don't ask too many questions, Tommy," said Mrs. Wilson. "I have been told that is not considered polite in the West."

"Your mother is right, Tommy. I don't mind you asking a few questions. But she is right."

"How come?"

Felton chuckled. The boy was pluky. "Some men have things they want to hide…or to forget. Everyone gets a new start out west. The past is forgotten. Nobody asks questions about it. Some men start over and go straight, some don't. But it's best not to ask things like, where are you from, or what side of the war did you fight on. Things of that nature."

"What about Indians," asked Tommy. "Can I ask about them?"

Felton's eyes hardened. Easterners had no concept of what desert Indians were like. Their ideas were formed by romantic authors that never met a warrior much less witnessed what they did for a living.

"There are all types of Indians, Tommy. There're good ones and bad ones. I think you're a little too young to be asking folks about the Indians out west. You should leave that alone for now."

"Can I ask you about them?"

For several seconds Felton stared straight ahead. The first image that flashed through his mind was that of Juanita tied to a cactus and disemboweled. If he wanted he could recall dozens of similar scenes.

"No."

Again Tommy was disappointed. He frowned and opened his dime novel.

"Have you ever seen a real gun fight like this one?" asked Tommy pointing to another illustration.

"Tommy, that is enough for now," said Mrs. Wilson firmly. "Leave Mr. Fargo alone for awhile. We have a long ride in front of us."

Tommy was a good boy. His young mind was full of dime novel adventures. He was frail and needed to be out in the sun. His mother was a pure Easterner. Without the train, neither would ever have ventured west of the Mississippi. Now they were gliding over the same rugged country that claimed the lives of countless men, women, and children that had pointed their wagons west in search of a better life. Their toil and sacrifice, even their graves would soon be forgotten.

Felton leaned his head back and slid his hat down over his eyes. Thinking of Bricela's letter and poem kept Felton awake much of the previous night. One after the other, suppressed memories crept out of the darkness. He constantly shifted the ivory keepsake around his neck, and questions about Bricela swarmed in his mind like angry hornets. Only the break of day brought a semblance of order to his thoughts and now he was tired. Hopefully, he would sleep for a while…and the nightmares of years past would not return.

Bricela Wetham stood in the shade on the porch of her home. It was almost twelve and Jesus Elias was late bringing the buggy from the ranch. He was breaking a rank bay gelding this morning. Jesus was the best in the territory at his work, but even he said it would take a long time to make a good Christian out of that one.

The ranch was only three miles from Tucson and spread along the Santa Cruz River. Until recently, the Apaches had not come near it or stolen any of the stock. But lately there was unrest on the San Carlos reservation. Rumors were everywhere. Another large war party could jump at any moment if something wasn't done to stop them. If they made a break for it, a trail of blood would follow. It always did.

Jesus had two men working with him and all three were Indian fighters. They felt safe enough but when the cows began to disappear, Jesus sent his wife back to town. He took no chances when it came to Apaches. Like all Mexicans for the last two hundred years, he hated them.

Raising her hand, Bricela extended it into the sunlight. The rays were intense at this time of day. The desert was as harsh as it was beautiful. It was no place for someone like her husband. Mark had tried running a store before they bought the ranch. He was a good man but his heart was not into raising horses or anything to do with ranching. The trip he took back east would be good for him. He could escape the summer heat and visit his family and friends in Boston.

If he could find enough financial backing there, he hoped to start his own power company and bring electricity to Tucson. Then again, he was fascinated with the invention of the telephone as well. Either business would keep him out of the sun and his hands clean. It was a chance for him to do the kind of work he dreamed about.

Bricela gazed at the calluses on her fingers. Caleb Felton would not recognize her. She was almost thirty-five years old and a woman that ran a ranch. And except for her Anglo shoes, she routinely dressed more like a Mexican or Papago than an American. She wore a medicine bag around her neck and preferred a muslin skirt and white blouse. Caleb would remember a well-dressed, dainty fifteen year old with soft feminine hands ...if he remembered her at all.

She waited three years for him to return to her but he never came back. She waited until the devastating news of his death reached her. Only then did she abandon her dreams and move on. But damn him...he was not dead. At least Jesus said so. He knew something. He had always known *something*.

A flash of sunlight reflecting off a black leather canopy caught Bricela's attention. A buggy turned the corner and trotted toward the Robinson house. Bricela walked down the stone steps and stood under the shade tree next to the street. It was where Caleb had tied his black stallion the first night she met him. It was a wonderful night...damn him.

Jesus pulled up next to her and stepped down. He was still sweating when he handed her the reins.

"Did you get that gelding broken?" asked Bricela flatly.

Jesus replied with a good-natured smirk, "Yes, Mrs. Wetham. He is ready for you to finish. It took longer than I thought. He was very stubborn. The two of you should get along very well, I think."

Snatching the reins, Bricela stepped up into the buggy and slid into the seat.

"If you weren't the best horseman in the territory, I'd fire you, Jesus Elias!"

Elias grinned.

"Maybe he will be there today, Bricela. He will come soon."

Bricela's eyes rested on the brand on the flank of the mare in front of her. It was the Double Eagle. She selected the brand herself and told the black smith what she wanted. Only Jesus suspected what it meant.

"You have more faith in him than you should, Jesus," snapped Bricela. "I don't understand why you are so confident he'll show. Or that he is even alive."

Jesus shrugged. His eyes narrowed.

"He is alive. Unlike so many women...a man never stops loving. He always thinks about the special ones in his heart. He will come. I know him."

Turning slowly, Bricela glared at Elias.

"If half the things I've heard about this Con Fargo are true, he is as much a rogue as I ever thought. No, a scoundrel! That's what he is, a low-down scoundrel."

"No, Briclea," said Elias. His smile reflected admiration. "He was a scoundrel when you knew him. Now...now he is what you thought he was."

Bricela sighed and asked, "Did you fall on your head this morning? That makes absolutely no sense."

"Maybe I make a riddle, eh? Like the Double Eagle you put on your horses and your cows."

"It's just a brand," snipped Bricela. Her face flushed with color and she snapped the reins. "I should have fired you years ago."

Elias laughed and watched the dirt fly from the wheels of the buggy as it swung around and headed for the river.

"You will see, Mrs. Wetham," he called out. "You will see!"

Bricela swore and urged the mare into a trot. Her troubles had started six months ago when she took the stage to Globe. The milk cows she sold to an agent of the San Carlos Reservation somehow ended up in that neighboring mining town. The cows were supposed to go to the Indians so she reported what she saw to Agent Tiffany. He was clearly disturbed by the news and said he would investigate the matter.

A few days later, the rest of her cows were stolen from her ranch along with two of her horses. She told the sheriff and he said he would look into it. The general store stopped offering her credit. The bank manager talked of foreclosure, something he promised he would never do.

She desperately needed to replace her livestock. No cows were available so she bought steers with what little money she had left. The ones she purchased turned out to be stolen. The bill of sale she had was no good and the sheriff hinted that criminal charges might have to be filed against her.

Her suspicions grew over the months. She stopped believing in coincidences long ago and too many things were stacking up against her. Neither Agent Tiffany nor the sheriff solved either case of the missing cattle and everyone she went to for help seemed to turn against her. There was no one left to go to, no one to trust. Jesus reported hearing rumors from the Papagos that her cattle had been stolen by San Carlos

178

Apaches. It was then she told him of her attempt to secretly employ the Pinkertons. She told him they recommended a man called Conway Fargo.

Bricela turned the mare down Main Street remembering better times when it was called Calle Real. She turned on Alameda, once Calle de las Milpas, and headed for the Santa Cruz River. The newcomers were changing everything.

She shook her head. Could it be it was only two months ago that Jesus told her Caleb Felton was alive? Jesus claimed he used an alias…Con Fargo. She screamed at him for saying such a thing. She cried and even called him a liar.

The next day Jesus assured her he was not lying. Since then her mind had not stopped. She was not convinced…yet painfully hoped his story was true.

Years before, Owl Woman taught her everything happened for a reason, that life was a journey. The medicine woman was her guide in the darkness and helped her heal…over time. Old wounds, though, were starting to open. She thought she was over the prolonged episodes of sadness and the waves of unidentifiable guilt. But they had returned. The thought that Caleb Felton was alive resurrected confusion and fear. Now, however, those old emotions were mixed with a seething anger.

She always felt such a connection with him. Their souls seemed to intermingle, to commune with one another. Then he was gone. If he was not killed in the war, he had deliberately chosen not to come back. Caleb Felton had left her alone when she needed him most. He had abandoned her.

Bricela pulled to the side of the road. She got out of the buggy. As the days before, her heart raced. The tree was there, still alive, still bent into the mysterious Z. She walked to the tree and looked in every direction. Caleb R. Felton was nowhere.

CHAPTER 11

Felton awoke with a jerk. He instinctively reached for his pistol. He grabbed for the familiar ivory grips of the Colt but there was nothing. His mind cleared. He was on a train. There was no danger. He was leaving Texas and on his way to Tucson. He remembered now.

After adjusting his hat, Felton rubbed his eyes. A gentle, hot breeze was coming through the windows. The *clackty-clack* of the moving train was soothing. It had helped him sleep.

Tommy had his head in his mother's lap and she was nodding. Everyone on the train seemed to be dozing. It was midafternoon and even with all the windows down, the temperature in the wooden train car was over ninety.

Outside, there was nothing but endless miles of desert. They would have to stop soon to take on water. How far had they come? Felton never carried a watch. He tried to calculate the time.

As near as he could tell, the train had been traveling for at least eight hours. The man that sold him the ticket to Tucson said the train was slower than a horse over a short distance but it could cover twenty miles an hour all day and all night. They would be nearing the Arizona border in an hour or two. It was hard to believe. There was something unfair about the whole thing. It was *too* easy. It wasn't real. The desert was harsh and unforgiving. It would not yield so easily as tenderfeet might think.

Opening his vest, Felton took out the poem and the letter. Both were nearly memorized but he read them again. The letter was formal. It asked for his help but was devoid of any emotion, any hint of what they once meant to each other. Had she changed so much? Was there nothing left of what they once shared? Would she at least have a few fond memories to share with him? What, in fact, did she remember?

Bricela was almost unconscious the day he found her at the red bluff. She never spoke a word, not even his name. He took her to Owl Woman. That was the last she saw of him...if she even saw him at all. Some women didn't remember what happened to them...some did, then went insane.

The more Felton read the poem the more it made him cringe. It was written with anguish and a pitiful tone of loss. He hoped to God he had nothing to do with it...yet she sent the verses to him. Was there a message of blame hidden in the wording? He felt it in El Paso and the sensation was growing stronger. The blame, if it was that, appeared more and more to be aimed at Caleb R. Felton.

Felton glanced down in the isle. Tommy had dropped his Dime Novel. Tucking the letters back inside his vest pocket, he picked up the novel. The title read "Wild Bill, The Wild West Duelist, or The Girl Mascot of Moonlight Mine."

The drawing on the cover resembled Cody but it showed a man much too tall. Bill was hell on wheels but he was short.

After reading the first page, Felton thumbed through the story. Someone discovered gold. A bad man and Cody had a gunfight. There was Cody saving the beautiful young woman. In the end he gallantly rode off into the sunset.

It was pure fiction, especially the part about the sunset. That just marked the end of a long, hard day. Too often, you thanked God for merely living through another one. Women that lived in the West weren't that helpless. That kind never lasted long.

The train slowed. Felton laid the novel next to Tommy and signaled for the porter.

"What are we stopping for?" asked Felton softly.

"Watering station. We need it to get up the grade. Won't take but five minutes."

Slowly the train coasted to a complete stop. When it did Tommy sat up and yawned.

"Watering stop," announced the porter. "You can stretch your legs if you want. We leave in five minutes. There's nothing but a water tank out here for miles, so don't go far off. If you..."

Before the porter finished, two men entered from the front door of the car. Both wore flour sacks over their heads with holes cut out for their eyes. Each held a cocked pistol in his hand. The first man on board was small and wiry, the second taller and heavier set.

"Everybody just stay where you're at, now," said the first man, his voice shrill with excitement. "Our business won't take long."

Keeping his hands low, Felton immediately untied his blanket from the saddle and draped it over his legs. With his left hand he grasped the shotgun and put it under the blanket. He kept his hand on the shotgun and cocked both hammers. His right hand rested on top of the blanket.

"Don't nobody get no ideas," bellowed the larger man. His words betrayed a Southern upbringing. "We don't want to shoot nobody. But we will. Now hand over your purses and money belts."

The small man started down the isle with a flour sack in his hand demanding money while the second watched over the stunned passengers. The other cars were likely being robbed as well. There were four coach cars. It would take at least eight men to do the job right.

As the little man drew near, Tommy's mother fainted. Tommy clinched his Dime Novel and tried not to cry. Felton could see the eyes through the holes cut in the sack. This man was young.

"Hand it over, old man," demanded the robber. "Let me see what you have for us."

As Felton opened his vest with his right hand, he said, "I have no money. I spent what I had on the ticket."

"I see you got a hideout gun, Mister. And some papers in that inside pocket. Hand 'em both over. Don't finger that pistol none too much."

"You can have the pistol, sir. The papers are worthless to you."

"You don't say," mocked the bandit pointing with his pistol. "Now hand 'em over, papers first."

Felton shook his head and frowned.

"You would rob a cripple?"

A wicked laugh, slightly muffled by the sack, filled the train car.

"I'd rob Christ on a crutch," he howled. "Now hand it over."

"That is blasphemy, boy. They say there's no hope for a blasphemer. But I'll give you a chance to say a prayer, anyway."

"The hell you say," sneered the gunman. "What are you? Some kind of preacher?"

"Far from it. About as far from it as you'll ever see. I've been killing men like you since you were a titty baby."

The second gunman suddenly walked halfway to the rear of the car. He took a look at Felton and stopped suddenly.

"Back off, Johnny," he demanded. "Leave him be and back up."

"Why? He ain't nothin'."

"You the one they call The Parson?" asked the big man.

"Some call me that."

Johnny's eyes flared wide and he involuntarily took a step back.

"You give us your word you won't shoot and we'll be on our way," offered the big man. "Nobody gets hurt."

Felton's eyes were locked on Johnny. If the robber flinched, he would get a belly full of buckshot.

"No need to get innocent folks shot up," replied Felton smoothly. "You have my word."

The two men slowly backed up. When they were near the front door they darted out. A moment later several horses galloped south across the desert toward Mexico.

As the hoof beats and dust faded the passengers turned to stare at Felton. Their faces were pale. Some showed fear, some shock.

Only the porter came to the back of the car. He watched Felton take the shotgun from under the blanket and ease the hammers down.

"Who's The Parson?" he asked. "Why'd you let them get away?"

Ignoring the first question, Felton said, "I could have killed one of them easy enough. Killing the second one could have cost some of your passengers their lives. As you could see, there were other men in the other cars. Money is not worth dying over. You can always make more of it."

"You didn't give them your money. They could have killed you."

"No, sir. In fact I have no money. I am on my way to Tucson but could only pay up to Benson."

The porter was skeptical.

"What about those papers. They could be bank notes. You didn't give them up. Were *they* worth dying over?"

Felton looked into the eyes of the porter.

"You ask too many questions, Mister. That can get unhealthy."

Grumbling under his breath, the porter walked away. The passengers spoke among themselves. Some men, now suddenly brave, swore and made threats. Those that lost little in the robbery laughed. They had been in a Wild West hold up. For an Easterner it would be the story of a lifetime.

Tommy's mother was fanning herself and trying not to faint again. Tommy dejectedly looked down at the cover of his novel. He slowly raised his head and glanced at Felton's legs.

"Are you crippled?"

"Nope. Didn't say I was, now did I?"

"I suppose not," admitted Tommy. "You let them take everyone's money."

Starting to roll his blanket, Felton said evenly, "Didn't turn out like you thought, did it? Well, things generally don't.

"You remember one thing. Money is not worth your life. Not the losing of money or the earning of it."

"Wild Bill would have stopped them," muttered Tommy.

Felton tied the blanket to his saddle but did not make eye contact with Tommy.

"Could be. But not me. Not today."

"Why not," insisted Tommy. "They were afraid of you. I could tell."

Shaking his head, Felton said, "No, Tommy. They weren't afraid. It's what we call a 'draw'. There was nothing to gain for anyone, that's all. As you get older you're going to have to decide what's worth fighting over."

"So, what do you think is worth fighting for?"

Felton turned and looked at Tommy. He *was* like Bricela.

"Turn to the last page in your book, there, Tommy. I'll show you."

Tommy found the page. A man and a woman sat on horses watching the sun sink behind a distant mountain range. Felton pointed at the sketch of Wild Bill and the heroine.

"Like I said, things usually don't work out like you hope they will, but if you're lucky, you may get to watch the sun go down with your true sweetheart by your side. Now that…that is important. It's worth all the money you'll ever make."

Felton leaned back in his seat. He sighed and looked straight ahead at nothing. "But then, things have a way of going south when you thought they'd go north."

It was five o'clock in the morning when Felton unloaded his horse from the stock car at Benson Station. The sky was pale yellow along the eastern horizon and blue gray in the west. Smoke billowed from a black funnel atop the steam engine as the train pulled out of the station and on toward Tucson. It would arrive there in less than three hours but Felton preferred to ride horseback into town.

The stage road that Captain Hunter's Confederates had followed was still the main road to Tucson from the east. Felton's train ticket only took him to Benson but he welcomed the chance to retrace his steps of 1862. There was something wrong about returning to Tucson in a wooden box rolling in on steel wheels. There was no freedom in it…or romance.

Giant saguaros he had not seen in years rose thirty feet high on both sides of the road and far out into the desert. Their silhouettes triggered an array of memories, of sights and sounds he had not visited for years. Even the gentle breeze and the familiar smells drifting in the air sent him backwards in time. It was a morning to remember.

Felton mounted the black and let him stretch his legs on the stage road. He calculated the distance to Tucson and the time he would have to arrive. He wanted to be there by twelve and it was close to fifty miles. When he finished planning how to pace the stallion, he reached for his collar to make certain the ivory from Bricela's choker was tucked under his shirt. Feeling the brooch, he swore.

Picacho Peak was exactly the same distance west of Tucson as Benson was east. It was at the Picacho stage station where he fell asleep instead of continuing on with the other Confederates. If he had gone on to Tucson with them instead of taking a rest, Bricela would not have left for San Xavier. He had ruined her life…in more ways than one.

Easing the stallion into a gallop, Felton again calculated the time. He would get to the tree by eleven and be waiting when she got there. He had been late once but not this time. Whatever trouble she was in, he would not fail her. The debt he owed was impossible to repay and the past gone forever. She had asked for his help. Regardless of the circumstances, she at least wanted to see him.

It was difficult to grasp the fact that he was actually on his way to see Bricela Verde. She had long been a sacred memory, an oasis in a barren emotional desert. Now, each step he took brought him closer to a life he had left behind, yet a life he could never have lived. He held her once for a few seconds but she was as an angel, just as unreachable and untouchable.

Felton thought of the last time he looked in a mirror. There were wrinkles between his eyes and crows feet at their corners. Would she even recognize him? Would she be shocked by what the years of strain had done to him? She was young and no doubt still beautiful. She remembered him when he was thirty-three. Of course she would be shocked.

As the stallion continued its easy gallop, Felton wondered how he would react when he saw the disappointment in her eyes. He would surely see it. No one can hide their unguarded emotions. How could she possibly imagine what he looked like now? He was over fifty and there was gray in his hair.

What of Bricela? She was a revered memory. That hallowed vision would now be displaced with a more sober one. It would be a loss of one of his most cherished possessions…and perhaps one of hers.

Felton gritted his teeth as haunting images crossed and re-crossed his mind like actors on a darkened stage. He swore at himself. A man could think too damn much. No matter what happened, no matter how she reacted when she saw him, he would smile. He would be strong. She would expect it of him.

Sheriff Cade Mosby walked up the back stairs to the Congress Hall Saloon and knocked on the door. As he waited, he turned and looked over the town of Tucson. Wooden structures were starting to show above the flat-roofed adobes. Now that the Southern Pacific railroad had come, more than two thousand people lived in town. The initial boom in population dwindled to nothing when rumors of Indian unrest spread. Something had to be done with the Apaches…one way or the other.

A short man wearing a black suit opened the door. He took a cigar out of his mouth and nodded to the sheriff. "It's about time."

Mosby snorted derisively at the man holding the cigar. He stepped past him into a room clouded with smoke. Six more men sat around a large oak table. All wore black vests and ties. Most of the ties were pierced with gold nugget stick pins. The biggest man at the table had a pistol strapped to a shoulder holster. Big Ben Turner was the worst of the lot. He had been a sergeant under the command of Calloway. He was not as good with a gun as Mosby, but could whip anyone in Tucson with his fists.

All but two of the businessmen came to Arizona with the California Column during the war. By the time many of the soldiers were mustered out, most had staked mining claims or taken over ranch land confiscated from secessionists. This tightly knit group owned most of the businesses in town. They were influential men in the Territory and in Washington.

"Have a seat," said Turner. "What's the report from San Carlos? We haven't had much activity since the fight at Big Dry Wash."

After picking a cigar from a box on the table, Mosby took off his hat and sat down. "I talked to our man Tribolett this morning. He says Agent Tiffany has everything under control. A few more broncos have left to join the renegades and he expects more will jump. Right now Nachez and Geronimo are in Mexico. He doesn't have a clue when they might raid across the border again."

Turner smiled and puffed on his cigar. "Fort Lowell is full again and that means hundreds of soldiers just east of town. This last round of breakouts will keep us busy for at least another year. Our saloons better stock up. We have a corner on most of the banking, the women, liquor, and even the forage for the Army horses.

"What would it take, sheriff, to get this to bust wide open? What would make the whole lot of them jump the reservation?"

"We could cut their rations again," offered the short man that opened the door. It's worked before."

Mosby shook his head and said, "They've been putting up with that for a long while. All they do is grumble. Tribolett says the Apaches get mighty itchy when soldiers show up on the reservation. We could ask for more troopers. That'll be sure to do it."

Blowing smoke out his nostrils, Turner looked to his left. "Well, Mr. Mayor, how's your pull with the Departmental Commander? You think you can stir up enough trouble to get Wilcox to send us more troops?"

"I'll send a telegram today," said the mayor. "I'll have the *Citizen* do another editorial about the unrest on the reservation. We'll write up the latest murders in more detail. That'll stir the pot here in Tucson. Word will spread to Tombstone and Globe. Give it a day or two to simmer and Wilcox will do anything Agent Tiffany wants."

Another man sitting at the table asked, "How many do you think will make a break for it, sheriff?"

Striking a match, Mosby lit his cigar. "The usual, I suppose. Seventy to a hundred warriors. They'll take their squaws along too. Not as many as Victorio had, but plenty enough to do the job."

Turner looked down the table with expectant eyes. "Henry, what do you calculate our profits to be if they make another raid?"

Henry shuffled through his notes until he found what he was looking for. He peered at a sheet of paper through a pair of wire-rimmed glasses. "Beef sales will remain unchanged for the reservation. Sales should, however, double for Fort Lowell. With forage, liquor sales, so on and so forth, our profits should triple within the first six months.

"If the campaign goes on longer, profit margins will continue to rise. If it is short and decisive and the Apaches are subjugated once and for all, Tucson's population will double within a year's time. That will lead to an estimated increase in profits of forty percent compared to present day."

"Sheriff Mosby," grinned Turner with his cigar between his teeth. "How soon can you get word to Tiffany?"

"I'm seeing Tribolett in town today. He's picking up some more liquor for his whiskey shacks. He's going back to San Carlos as soon as he loads up. He'll get word to Tiffany."

Henry looked up from his pile of accounting papers and took off his glasses. His eyes were cold as they focused on Mosby. "Have you had any more complaints from your friend…Mrs. Wetham? She could be trouble if she's not silenced."

"Running off her stock shut her up," answered Mosby. "She's too worried about losing the ranch to cause us anymore trouble. I got her all in a knot about buying those stolen cows. She don't want to go jail."

"Do you think the people of Tucson would accept the idea of a woman, especially a longtime resident like her, being placed in jail?" asked Henry.

Mosby shrugged and answered, "Jailing most women, especially a pretty one, would cause a flap. Bricela Wetham is a handsome woman, but she's known to be a little loco. She don't eat no meat at all and you see how she dresses. Everybody talks about how much time she spends with them Mexicans and Papagos. Some say she's not respectable.

"No. Most folks would just shake their heads and go about their business. You got nothing to worry about from the town folk. She won't make any more trouble for us."

"What if you're wrong?" asked Turner.

Leaning back in his chair, Mosby blew smoke up toward the ceiling. In all the years he had known Bricela she had never responded to his advances. Even when he became sheriff, that wasn't good enough for her. She still turned her nose up at him. To make things worse, the prettiest woman in the Territory married a sickly looking Easterner.

"If I'm wrong she'll have another visit from the Apaches. This time she won't get off so easy. It's Jesus Elias we got to worry about more than her. He's a tough man to deal with. If he takes up for her, we'll have to kill him to stop him."

Turner nodded, his head barely moving on his short bull neck. "Alright. Let's all keep an eye on Elias. He can't do much by himself. If he tries anything I want to know about it."

Caleb Felton stopped on the same rise where Captain Hunter had waited for him two decades before. That day, it was bitter cold and cloudy. Now the desert heat lay over him like a smothering blanket.

The mountains stood where he remembered, the desert was as cruel as ever but Tucson had changed. The limits of the town had grown little but the density of houses was stunning. He could see wooden frames everywhere and many were two stories high. It was no longer a village. The Old Presidio was now a town.

Felton looked at the sun. It was close to noon but he would still arrive early. Moments before, he felt pangs of hunger. Now his stomach churned with anxiety. His pulse quickened.

For the last hour the weariness of the long ride numbed his mind. The memories and questions faded until they were finally quiet. Now, his imagination was taking over once again.

Would she recognize him? What would she be like? What would he say to her when they met? More importantly, what would she say to him?

Hoping to catch a glimpse of Bricela before she could see him, Felton nudged the stallion into a gallop. If he could get to the tree or somewhere near it before she arrived, he might be successful. Seeing her at a distance would help steady his nerves. He could prepare himself and think of what to say after so many years. Perhaps then, he would not make a fool of himself. He looked forward to their meeting, but dreaded it as well. He wished for time to pass quickly yet wanted to savor every remaining second. Such a reunion occurred but once in a lifetime. It would be over soon enough.

He had hunted Apaches and bandits, killed men and been shot at more times than he could remember, but that was nothing compared to what lay ahead. How could a woman have such an effect on a man? Why was it that some wells never ran dry?

Bricela sat on the steps of her home with a basket in her lap. She wore a full-length dress for the first time in years. Jesus would be surprised. He would likely make a joke about it but she did not care. The feeling within her was strong, stronger than it had been since the day of her wedding fifteen years before.

At midmorning, the sensation washed over her just as it had the day she rode away from the San Augustine Church with her new husband. She had thought it was merely a dream, a passing sentiment. Today she was determined to get an answer from Jesus. There was no reason not to tell her the truth about that day, not now.

The buggy rolled down the dusty street as before but this time Jesus turned it back toward the Santa Cruz River before he stepped down. When he walked around the rear wheels he looked up at Bricela and stopped.

"Madre de Dios," he said wide-eyed. "You look beautiful today."

Bricela's eyes were steady as she walked to Jesus. She halted a half step in front of him.

"Jesus, I want a straight answer from you."

Glancing down at the basket, Jesus asked, "Answer for what?"

"There is no longer any reason to dodge my question."

"What question," asked Jesus defensively.

"When did you last see Caleb Felton?"

Jesus sighed and looked down at his feet.

"Was it my wedding day? Was it him standing next to you in the plaza that day?"

Raising his head just enough to peer at Bricela from under the brim of his sombrero, Jesus answered, "Yes. It was the same day he came on the stage. He made me promise I would never tell you."

There was a long silence before Bricela spoke again.

"Damn him," she said softly. More forcefully she added, "Damn the both of you."

"You remember now?" asked Jesus. "You saw him then?"

"No, Jesus," said Bricela. She hesitated. "I saw only a man next to you. His head was down. He was thin. That's all I saw. But I…I remember looking back at the two of you. Then at him."

Lifting his head higher, Jesus looked into the eyes of Bricela for a moment, then back down at the basket.

"You believe he comes today," said Jesus. "You take a lunch this time."

"Was he ill, Jesus? Was he ill that day?"

"Very much. He came for the desert air to heal him."

"Where did he go?"

"To Tubac. To live with my cousins."

"What happened after that?"

Jesus shook his head and muttered, "No *se*. He rode north."

"I think I liked it better," said Bricela, as she stepped around Jesus and into the buggy. "When I thought he was dead."

Bricela started the mare toward the river but this time she kept it at a slow walk. When she first discovered Caleb might be alive she tried to hate him. Mark was a good husband. He was solid and dependable but there had always been a place in her heart for the dashing lieutenant. He was her first love and there could be but one.

Mail service was slow during the war but it did arrive. He could have written. He had more than three years to write a letter. It was the worst time of her life and he knew nothing about it. He left her and never looked back. There could be no excuses. He was nothing like she once thought.

How old was he now? She knew men in their forties and they looked old. She was thirty-five. Was he in his fifties? How could a man of those years be recommended so highly by the Pinkertons and why did Jesus speak of him as if he were a known man, a man to be reckoned with in the state of Texas?

Bees seemed to be buzzing midway between Bricela's heart and stomach. Her hands were trembling and it angered her. Why should *she* be so nervous? He was the guilty one. While he was out doing who knows what, she was fighting for her life and her sanity. The Yankees sent her family to Yuma and only Owl Woman remained to guide her through the impenetrable darkness that swallowed her.

Even Jack Swilling came back a time or two. The stories he told about Lieutenant Caleb Felton shocked her but she was willing to overlook the past. It all happened before they met and didn't matter. She had no reason to be nervous. If he came at all, he should be ashamed to even show up. So why was he coming? Maybe it was just for the money.

Bricela felt like screaming. She glared at the lunch basket. He didn't deserve to be fed, not by her. In fact, if half the things Swilling said were true, no woman on earth should feed him.

When Bricela looked up she saw a black horse tied to a tree on the side of the road. Recognizing the Z branded on its flank her stomach knotted. Her head was spinning when she pulled in front of the horse and stopped.

Trying to act at ease, she took several deep breaths and the nausea subsided. She took the basket and stepped down. The tree was fifty feet up the river. She started for it. She could have walked to it blindfolded but pretended to watch her step. Her heart was pounding, her palms were sweating but she would be damned before showing Caleb Felton how she truly felt.

At the tree she stopped and laid the basket down in the shade. She leaned against the tree where it turned upward. When she raised her eyes, he was standing a few feet away. She had no doubt he would be there but the sight of him startled her. Only the eyes looked familiar.

Bricela could think of none of the words she had planned to say. Her thoughts were lost in a fog of shock.

"How was your trip?" she asked mundanely.

Felton took off his hat and answered flatly, "Fine."

Barely making eye contact, they took a few steps toward each other. There was an awkward hug. Both quickly stepped back.

"I hope you are hungry," said Bricela. She forced herself to look directly at him. He had not changed as much as she had first thought. The hair made him look half wild and there were a few wrinkles at the eyes, but essentially he looked the same as she remembered. His shoulders, though, looked broader. "I brought lunch but I'm afraid I forgot a blanket."

Felton smiled faintly. His eyes now looked into hers for the first time. Bricela was surprised to see sadness in them. She had seen him look that way once before. It was in the moonlight before he left…and never came back.

"I'll get mine," said Felton. "It's been on the trail awhile though."

"I'm sure it will do," said Bricela. She wanted to say, "I'm sure it will do, *Caleb*," but didn't have the courage. It was too soon.

As Felton turned she noticed he wore two pistols. One had carved white grips. Most men in Tucson carried only one gun. Jesus said he had become a known gunman.

Bricela fumbled with the basket and tried to remember what Jesus had said to her the day before. It was a kind of riddle. He remarked that

Caleb Felton was a scoundrel when she knew him, but had become…what she once thought he was.

What did she think he was when she was fifteen years old? Certainly not a saint. Even then, she knew better. But she did think of him as gallant and chivalrous. What was Jesus trying to tell her about the man she once loved?

"I have to warn you," said Felton, returning to the shade with his blanket still rolled. "That I keep a weapon hidden in here."

"Another gun?"

Felton unrolled the blanket on the sand revealing the sawed-off shotgun. At the sight of it, Felton saw Bricela shudder. If she knew how many men he had killed with it she would have nothing to do with him. Women generally didn't understand.

"That is an evil looking thing," she said. "What is it for?"

Felton looked at the shotgun. It was a weapon like any other. What did she think it was for? Leaning it to one side, he shoved the butt of the gun into the sand and secured the barrels in the fork of a small shrub. "Protection," he said, continuing to spread the blanket. "And keeping the peace. Nobody argues with a scattergun."

Bricela sat and arranged the tin containers from the basket and removed their lids. She laid a loaf of bread on a large napkin and handed Felton a fork. She placed a cup near him and filled it with milk.

"Milk?" questioned Felton as he took a seat across from her.

"Yes. That is part of what I do now. I raise milk cows."

Felton raised an eyebrow in surprise but said nothing.

"You may as well know that I eat no meat."

"No meat?" Sticking a fork into a tin, Felton brought out a piece of melon and looked it over. "I've never heard of that. Why no meat?"

Bricela was beginning to relax but the question made her uneasy. She would tell him as little as possible.

"Do you remember the little dog I used to have?"

Felton laughed softly. For a moment his eyes grew distant. "Sure. Robespierre."

"You remember his name?" exclaimed Bricela. "How could you remember a thing like that?"

"Oh it wasn't hard, Bricela," answered Felton. "I guess I never told you my secret."

Hearing Felton speak her name resurrected a wave of pleasant sensations and forgotten memories. Bricela smiled as they drifted through her mind. "What secret, Caleb. You don't mean to tell me...you have secrets?"

"Just one. Well, I'll admit to just one."

"Go on."

"First of all, do you remember anything about my name? You asked me about it once and I refused to answer. It was when we first met."

Bricela looked at Caleb. She was enjoying herself and he was smiling at her like he used to. For a moment at least, the past twenty years had no meaning.

"Let's see. When we met...we were in the parlor." She could see him standing with a drink in his hand and the revolvers on his hips. He was handsome and dashing. There was something else about him that had intrigued her. She remembered feeling it for the first time. It was immediate but profoundly indefinable. What ever it was had no name and seemed suspended somewhere between dream and reality. "We were introduced and...and I recall asking what the R stood for. Aunt Charlotte was appalled that I was so forward. You refused to answer. You said...you said..." Bricela's eyes flashed with revelation. "No! It can't be!"

Felton grinned halfheartedly.

"I'm afraid so."

"Caleb R. Felton," said Bricela. Her eyes narrowed. "Caleb *Robespierre* Felton?"

"Remember how you used to point out all the coincidences that we shared?" asked Felton. "Now you know they started the moment we met. I have to admit there were quite a few of them back then. I didn't believe in such things so I never told you about my name."

"*Were* quite a few?" questioned Bricela. "We're sitting under a tree grown into a Z and you still ride a horse with a Z on it. I don't see that too much has changed."

Felton became strangely quiet. He forked out another piece of melon. After nearly two decades they were meeting for a second time. For the second time he concealed another coincidence. This one, however, testified to a deeper more twisted irony. The Z branded on his chest left an ugly scar. He could never forget how he got it or what it meant...to both of them.

"That's my third horse with that brand," said Felton, trying to forget the smell of his own flesh as it burned under heated iron. "What about your dog and the meat eating? What's the connection?"

Taking a knife, Bricela cut slices of bread from the loaf and handed one to Felton. She tried to talk while blocking the picture of the dying pet from her mind. She hadn't counted on an explanation. She should have known he would ask.

"The poor animal gave his life trying to protect me. It was horrible. I decided that nothing else would die for my sake. I haven't eaten meat since Robespierre was killed."

Quickly changing the subject, Bricela asked a question. "What have you been doing with your life?"

Felton took a bite of bread. He felt like swearing as he chewed. How could he have been so stupid? He knew how the dog died and where. He should have left it alone. He forced her to go back there, to remember. What, in fact, did she remember? She spoke as if he didn't know about her dog. Did she think he hadn't seen the animal? Was it possible she didn't even know he was there? Could it be all these years she never discovered he was the one that had found her?

"Law enforcement, mostly," said Felton. After chewing longer than necessary, he added, "Most of what I've done isn't fit to repeat."

Bricela took a drink of milk. She looked over the rim of her cup and studied the man that answered her letter. Did he understand the poem she included? Would he ask about it? Did he care how much it meant to her? She deserved some answers.

"I know you came back to Tucson, Caleb. You came back once before. I guessed it on my own but I made Jesus admit he knew about it. It was May twenty-fourth, wasn't it? The day I got married."

Felton dropped his head. He fingered the cup of milk but did not pick it up. Years had gone by. What did it matter now that she knew? "When did you figure that out?"

"Just today. Jesus kept it to himself all this time."

"Today? How?"

"Well, that is my secret. I have a few of my own."

"So Jesus kept it to himself all these years. He's a good man."

"Why didn't you come see me? You were in Tucson the day of my wedding and didn't even say hello."

Felton sighed. He shifted his weight and rubbed his forehead. He wanted to tell her what a terrible day that was for him. He wanted her to know that seeing her with another man tore at his insides and made him wish he had never come back. There was no point explaining his feelings. Nor was there any point in telling her he still loved her. "You had just been married. I would have ruined it."

"Jesus said you went to Tubac. You must have stayed there a while. You could have come later. You were so close...Caleb, I thought you were dead. I was told...I was told you were killed before the war ended. I was told that more than a year before I was married."

"I almost died. Maybe that's how the story got started."

"What happened to you, Caleb?" Bricela's voice was soft, almost pleading.

Felton took a drink of warm milk. He would have to be careful with his answer. Bricela seemed to know nothing of his presence at the red bluff.

"Shortly after Captain Hunter left Tucson, I was captured along with some others. I spent two years in Yuma Prison. I was supposed to be exchanged for Captain McCleave, if you remember him, but the glorious Confederacy forgot about that and left me in Yuma. I swore an allegiance to the Union so I could go up to the Tonto basin and fight Apaches. I became what they called a 'Galvanized Yankee'. Jack Swilling wasn't in Yuma but he did the same. It was Jack that arranged to have me released from prison. During the Apache fighting I was wounded and got malaria from the Gila River. That's when I came here for my health. After that, I became a Pinkerton, then a Texas Ranger. That, dear Bricela, is the sum total of my life."

Bricela took some scrambled eggs from a tin and made a sandwich for herself. Caleb had not completely understood her question or had chosen not to answer it fully. His answer was not good enough. She waited three years for him. At best, he only accounted for two years that he might have been unable to contact her.

"Wouldn't they allow you to write letters in Yuma?"

Felton looked at her for a moment. He obviously understood what she was asking but would he answer? He owed her that much at least. Not one letter, not then, not in all the years since.

"No."

Bricela waited for more but there was only silence. She wanted to slap him...or to kiss him. Yuma was a terrible place. Two years could seem like an eternity. Was he telling her the truth? Swilling had said he was a natural born spy, a natural liar.

"What about you, Bricela? Have any kids?"

"No," answered Bricela. She would have other chances to get an answer to her question. Didn't he know he had broken her heart? How could he not?

"Not yet, anyway. Mark…my husband…it has been very hard on him. He came from a large family and always counted on having lots of children. He especially wanted sons. After so many years, I fear he has lost hope. Mark's back east on business but has family and friends to visit as well. I'm taking care of the ranch while he's away."

"You're a rancher?" asked Felton, his eyes filled with disbelief. "It's hard to believe Bricela Verde became a rancher!"

"You still think of me as a girl, don't you?" snapped Bricela. "Well, I grew up!"

Felton raised his eyebrows, startled by her sharp response. "You've grown into a beautiful woman, Bricela. I apologize if I offended you. It is hard…I'm trying to blend the Bricela Verde I knew with the rancher Mrs. Wetham."

Bricela cooled down while she chewed some of her sandwich. Why was she suddenly so angry? He was merely surprised at what she did for a living. Anyone that knew her years ago would be.

"You thought I would go back east?"

Shrugging and glancing away, Felton answered, "Yes, Bricela. I never thought this was the place for you."

Taking a few deep breaths, Bricela eyed Caleb closely. Was it possible he did not understand she had waited for him…waited until there was no hope he would return?

"You didn't know me that well. I feel…I've always felt at home here"

"May I ask you why?"

Fighting the impulse to call him a fool, Bricela answered calmly, "There are several reasons I stayed, Caleb. One being that I discovered my strength here, my soul if you want to call it that. I learned to do things, to routinely accomplish what I would not have even dreamed of if I lived in the east. I was never one to attend gossipy tea parties or quibble about the latest French fashions. My life…my life was destined to change the moment I entered Tucson. I doubt you will understand but I know it is here where I belong."

Felton nodded and smiled. "Fair enough. You're right. I don't understand. What is it exactly that you do?"

"I raise horses and milk cows. I sell mainly to the reservations at San Carlos and Fort Apache."

"You sell *milk cows* to Apaches?" questioned Felton. "They're just going to eat them."

"The squaws have come a long way since you were here, Caleb. Some are learning to feed their children with a rubber tube and glass bottle just like the whites."

Felton nodded and muttered, "They *are* quick to learn. I'll say that for them."

"I also spend a lot of my time with the Papagos. I am a midwife for them and Owl Woman has taught me much of their remedies and how to use them. I guess I am sort of a doctor, too."

Felton had noticed a small beaded pouch hanging around Bricela's neck. He assumed it was a mere trinket. Now he was curious.

"Owl Woman?" questioned Felton.

Bricela hesitated. "Do you remember her? We…met her once."

"The name sounds familiar," said Felton. If not an out and out lie, his answer was deliberately misleading. He was suddenly uncomfortable. Owl Woman was too close to the ugly reality that seemed to be hidden from Bricela.

"She is a medicine woman for the reservation. She has…been sort of my teacher and guide."

"Is that little bag you're wearing from the Papagos?"

A wisp of a smile brightened Bricela's face. She touched the pouch with her finger tips. "Owl Woman made it for me. It's a medicine bag. I wear it like some people carry good luck charms. The Papagos believe strongly in such things. They like to see me wear it when I treat them or deliver babies for them."

"Can I ask what's inside?"

"If I told you, it would weaken the power of the medicine. Owl Woman says it is very powerful. The Papagos claim they can feel it when I come near."

"What do you say? Do you believe in Owl Woman and her medicine?"

Bricela thought for a moment. She looked at the bent trunk of the tree and then at the brand on Felton's horse. "I believe we are surrounded by things we don't understand. I have seen things, heard of things out on the reservation that I could never explain."

"Do you always wear the bag?"

"Whenever I go to the reservation I do. And…when I'm nervous or uneasy about something."

It was Felton's turn to smile. He was finally close to Bricela Verde. If he wanted, he could reach out and touch her. She smiled and so did he. For now, after being so long apart, they were sitting together in the shade of their tree on the banks of the Santa Cruz River.

For a few moments they ate in silence. A gentle breeze rustled the leaves overhead and stirred the heavy air. It was peaceful.

The knot in Felton's stomach began to loosen but was far from unwinding. There was so much he wanted to say but knew he must be careful. For years, he ached to tell Bricela how he felt on the day of the massacre and how desperately he wanted to comfort her. He wanted her to know how sorry he was for failing her, for what she endured…and how he was taken from her by the Yankees. His confession was all he had to give but he *had* to offer it. His desire to express his grief and guilt was unquenchable. Now it burned within him trying to find a way out. How could he tell her without resurrecting the worst day of her life, a day she no doubt wanted to forget?

He was here to help her. That would come first. Before he was finished, the opportunity to make his confession would present itself. First, they needed time to adjust. More than enough had been said for one day.

"There's a lot I want to catch up on, Bricela, but can we do that another time? I'd like to get started on why you sent for me. I came as soon as I got the letter…and the poem."

Bricela put down her sandwich. She had eaten only half. "Did you read the poem?"

"Many times. I have to say I don't understand it."

"You saw the date on it?"

"March twenty-sixth, eighteen sixty-five."

For several seconds, Bricela gazed into Felton's eyes.

"I wrote that…the day I was told of your death."

Felton swallowed hard. His eyes were fixed on Bricela's. At least part of the bittersweet poem had indeed been about him. He felt a rush of flattery collide with a wave of nausea. As both emotions entangled themselves, he thought of the mysterious last verse: A cold steel dagger thrust twice through my heart. Had he hurt her twice or was one thrust his death and the other her own unspeakable ordeal?

"I'm sorry, Bricela. I know how I would have felt if the tables were turned."

"Do you, Caleb? Do you *really* know how I felt?"

"Yes, Bricela," said Felton. Before he thought better of it, he added, "We are twins. Remember?"

For several seconds Bricela and Caleb looked at each other. Slowly they began to smile. It was there. Living, breathing and totally unexplainable, the bond only they understood had survived.

"Who told you I was dead?"

Bricela shook her head. "Cade Mosby."

Felton still smiled as did Bricela.

"Seems like old times," said Felton.

"It does. Almost like a circle."

"He's part of the reason you sent for me, isn't he?"

"He is," said Bricela. "He's sheriff of Tucson."

"That scrawny scarecrow?"

"He's not scrawny any more. He's a big man and he likes to use his size to push men around…and his gun. Tucson is full of roughs but sometimes he goes too far. He enjoys it."

"He's a born coward," sneered Felton. "I saw it in him. His kind may learn to act tough but deep inside Mosby's still yellow. Remember that night after the dance when someone took a shot at me?"

"I remember. You said it was just some drunk, a wild shot."

"Well, it was Mosby."

"How can you be sure."

Felton pulled the ivory-handled Colt from its holster. "Because I took this off of him that night. It was him alright. The pistol had just been fired and I recognized his tracks. In those days, no one in Tucson but Mosby had a stride that long."

"You still use a cap and ball pistol?" asked Bricela.

"No. I had it converted to cartridges years ago. It's a reminder of sorts."

Touching the polished grips with her fingers, Bricela asked, "Is that ivory?"

"Yes." Felton watched Bricela closely, wondering if she would think of the ivory choker he once gave her, the same piece he wore hidden just above his heart.

"There is an eagle carved on it?"

Felton turned the pistol over. "There's one on each side."

"Two eagles," said Bricela. Her tone was uneasy. "Double eagles."

It was happening again. Unlike twenty years earlier, Felton now accepted the uncanny coincidences and took them in stride. Perhaps as Bricela once believed, they were part of some grand scheme, a scheme that was yet to unfold. Eagles seemed to play a part in the drama, mermaids another. How they fit together was anyone's guess. Years ago he stopped trying figure it out. He merely observed the presence of the unexplainable and withheld judgment on beliefs he used to reject as nonsense.

"You said Mosby was part of the problem. You sent for me. I assume you can't rely on him."

Bricela flicked a red ant off the blanket. "I hate to do that. They work so hard."

Thinking of a man he once found buried up to his neck in an anthill, Felton said nothing. Bricela always had a soft heart.

"Anyway, it started when I sold some horses to the buyers contracted by the San Carlos agency. They were to go to the Indians there. I also sold them five cows. All of my stock are branded. What I saw in Globe was no mistake."

"What did you see?"

"While I was there on business, I passed by a corral. My cows and horses were there. There was no attempt to alter the brand. I asked what they were doing there and someone told me they were to be sold the next day to the miners.

"I rented a hack and went to see the agent at the reservation, Mr. Tiffany. I told him what I saw and Mr. Tiffany seemed quite shocked. He said he would look into the matter but was certain there was some explanation.

"Two days later the rest of my cows were rustled. I went to see the sheriff. Cade said renegade Apaches or bandits had done it.

"Then my husband left for Boston. Since I hadn't heard from the reservation, I wired Tiffany and asked what had been done about the stock I sold. I got no response. The next day the dry goods store refused me anymore credit. So did the feed store."

"I hate to ask, Bricela, but why credit?"

Bricela flushed a faint pink. "Mark is a bit of a dreamer. He's invested all our money in trying to get electricity to Tucson. He even borrowed on our ranch. We're almost broke. That's why he's back East. He's looking for investors."

"I understand."

"To make matters worse, I did something stupid. Two men came by with some cattle to sell and I bought them cheap. I asked about the bill of sale and they said it was good in Arizona but not so good in Mexico. I knew what they meant, but I was desperate. I thought I could make a quick profit.

"Cade came out a few days later and said I had stolen cows in my corral, that they were stolen from Tombstone. He claimed he might have to take legal action against me, but he would do what he could to keep the owners from filing charges."

"Then what?"

"The bank…the bank that told Mark they trusted him for the repayment said they might have to foreclose on the ranch. They are no longer going to extend credit unless we begin to pay down the loan."

"That's a string of bad luck, Bricela, but what does it have to do with me?"

"At first, nothing. Jesus started asking questions of the Mexicans in town. After that he went to the Papagos. We had heard rumors before but everything started to fit."

"Like how?"

"There had been stories for quite sometime about San Carlos. The agent that Tiffany replaced was said to have sold tons of Indian rations outside the agency. They say he made off with fifty thousand dollars. We hoped Tiffany would be different. The same rumors are back. Not only about him but others in town. A dozen or more men are thought to be in on it. In whispers, they are called the "Ring" or "The Boys.""

"The Papagos and the Apaches are hated enemies, but even the Papagos say the Apaches are being cheated. Soon, more will leave the reservation and go to war again. Victorio has only been dead two years and Juh, Nachez, and Geronimo are raiding both sides of the border. If the rumors floating around town are true, much of the blame rests with the whites that are getting rich off the Indians' rations. They don't care how many die in the meantime."

"All I know," sighed Bricela. "Is my trouble started the moment I spoke with Agent Tiffany."

Shaking his head in disgust, Felton muttered, "Not one agent Washington sends out here is worth his salt."

"Well, Tiffany may be no different. He controls the stock buyers, the grain buyers, all the financial records and distributes the government rations. Everything is under his control. A few men in Tucson own most of the stores, the saloons, and the bank. They have large land holdings along the Santa Cruz where tons of grain and hay are grown. You can guess where they sell most of their forage."

"You believe Mosby is owned by them, too? It would make sense."

"I don't know anything for sure. I don't believe all that happened to me is...well...coincidence. It's as if someone is trying to keep me quiet. I don't know who it is so I don't trust anyone."

"Well," said Felton. "Now I know why I'm here. But I'm not sure what I can do."

"I wired the Pinkertons first," said Bricela. "They recommended you. They said you were the best man they knew of for my situation."

"That's high praise," chuckled Felton. "Coming from those that fired me."

"Will you help me, Caleb?"

Felton came to one knee, put on his hat and tugged it down tight. He looked curiously at Bricela. "Of course I will. I hoped you would know that."

Bricela started gathering the tins together. Why would he say such a thing? Him of all people? Didn't he understand how much he had disappointed her twenty years ago? Why on earth should she *know* he would help her? Why was he leaving so soon? They hadn't seen each other in two decades and he was already excusing himself!

"You do agree we should not be seen together?" asked Bricela. "You could be in danger if they discover you are...well...working for me."

"If they think you hired an investigator, Bricela, you could be in more danger than me."

"We can send word by Jesus or some of his friends. He's agreed to do it."

"Does Jesus work for you, too?"

"He has for years. He breaks and helps train my horses."

Bricela closed the basket while Felton rolled the shotgun back into the blanket.

They both came to their feet. There was no hug goodbye. Felton put his hat back on and Bricela clasped the basket handle with both hands.

"Where will you start?"

"The saloons. Is the Shoo Fly still here?"

"No. There's Congress Hall and The Palace. They're much nicer than the Shoo Fly."

"Where's Congress Hall?"

"It's on...Do you remember where you played Pull-the-chicken?"

"It's on Calle del Alegria?"

"They changed all the street names from Spanish to English ten years ago. Alegria is Congress Street now. All the old names are gone. You can't even buy a Mexican meal anymore. It's all American food now."

Felton's brow wrinkled with disbelief. "Why did they change the names of the streets?"

"I was about the only American that resisted it. The whites moved in with money and with money comes power. They called it 'progress'."

"I heard Tucson is as wide open as Tombstone. That doesn't sound like progress to me."

"You will have to be careful, Caleb. It is a rough town but it always has been. That part hasn't changed. The Palace is around the corner on what was Calle Real. Now it's Main Street."

Bricela started for the buggy. Felton remained by the tree, watching her go.

After a few steps, Bricela turned and looked back. "I'll send Jesus to Congress Hall. He is waiting at home."

"Is it the same house you used to live in?" asked Felton.

"Yes. Uncle Palatine died. Aunt Charlotte went back to Virginia. She left me the house."

"I have to say," said Felton tentatively. "I'm surprised you stayed."

Bricela's lips tightened and paled. Several seconds passed. "Don't be," she said, icily. Her eyes were hard. "I had my reasons."

Felton swore at his own impatience as Bricela turned the buggy back toward Tucson. He was starting to pry. She had revealed a few details of her life since the massacre, yet too many haunting questions remained unanswered. He knew he was not entitled to any answers, but the lack of them left a hole inside him that begged to be filled. Now he was back where it began. Once more he stood on the sandy bank of the Santa Cruz. He had seen her, sat by her and, for a moment, touched her. Finally, he could reach out to her and she would not vanish. This time, it was not a dream.

After waiting five minutes, Felton stepped into his saddle and started for the saloon. He didn't have the courage to ask Bricela if she thought he had changed much. The moment her eyes first met his, they merely voiced recognition. There was a formal smile. She seemed on guard, almost emotionless. Her anger, something he had not seen before, slipped through once or twice but that was all.

Cade Mosby was barely dry behind the ears twenty years ago. He would remember a clean-shaven and well-groomed Caleb Felton. If the sheriff recognized him, it changed nothing. If those left over from the California Column discovered he was Carlos Fuentes, there could be trouble. They still blamed the Mexican spy for the death of Lieutenant Barrett, and soldiers on both sides of the war still simmered with hatred.

It was the hottest part of the day and the streets of Tucson were almost deserted. A few Mexicans squatted in the shade watching him ride by. When he neared Congress Street he could hear two pianos playing. One from the Congress Hall and the other from the nearby Palace.

Taking extra precautions, Felton decided to ride past the Congress Hall. Instead of stopping, he followed the wooden signs and went to the end of the street where he left his horse and saddle at Lexington Stables. Stallions were less common than they once were, and the Z brand might trigger someone's memory. It was best to keep the horse out of sight and some walking would feel good.

Most of the buildings along Congress were made of adobe. The new ones were made of lumber. Some of the stores had false fronts and glass windows. He passed a post office on his left, then a photographic studio on his right. Across from the studio was the newspaper office of the *Arizona Star*. Between the buildings he could see the painted white walls of San Augustine's Church. When he came to the next corner, Felton stopped.

A few steps in front of him was the spot he had tried to pull the chicken buried in the middle of Calle Alegria. Ninety feet to his left was the adobe wall he had leaned against on the day of Bricela's wedding.

She said she had guessed he was there that day and that Jesus had always kept that secret to himself. He distinctly remembered hiding his face as she went by. Word must have come to her from Tubac. How else could she have pieced it together?

Jesus pulled the chicken where Mosby had fallen in the dirt. How many in Tucson knew what had happened here or even cared?

Felton continued on. The saloon was just ahead to his left. It had four large-paned glass windows and a long shaded entrance. Several horses were tied to hitch rails out front. The piano playing paused and the sound of tinkling whiskey glasses mixed with the clattering of porcelain plates and men's voices. He could smell the liquor and smoke, the sweat and the horses.

He adjusted his pistols just before he stepped from the dirt street onto the wooden boardwalk. He paused briefly, then went through the batwing doors.

Waiting for his eyes to adjust to the light, Felton stepped to one side. Most of the tables were full. Some men were eating, a few played cards but most had come to drink. A few heads raised and gave him a quick glance. There were no stares that he could detect.

What gentlemen called a "hostess" made her way through the crowded room. "Hello, handsome. Are you new to Tucson?"

"Just in today."

"Well, welcome," she said, putting her arm through his. "Let's have a drink and I'll introduce you to everyone. I'm Libby."

"Why not?" smiled Felton and escorted Libby to the bar. "Two whiskeys."

"You here on business or pleasure?"

"Just sizing up the town."

The bartender filled two shot glasses. Libby took hers and slid Felton's closer to him. "What should we drink to?"

Felton picked up the glass and thought for a moment. Libby was average looking with crooked front teeth. If she were lucky, she might be still in her twenties. "To the tears of wandering angels," he said, then tossed back the whiskey.

Libby hesitated. She looked curiously at Felton. "Now that is down right purty."

"It's from a poem I once read."

Swallowing the straight whiskey as if it were water, Libby set the glass down and pointed to it. "How 'bout another?"

Before he could decline, a familiar voice spoke behind him. It carried the faintest hint of a German accent. "Is that you Conway? Con Fargo?"

Shaking his head, Felton smiled and turned. "Al Sieber. They haven't hung you yet?"

Both men shook hands. Sieber was at least ten years younger than Felton. He had brown hair and a thick, sandy colored mustache. At one hundred and seventy pounds, he was lighter than Felton, but on foot could cross the desert and keep pace with the best Apaches. He spoke their language and, as chief of Indian scouts for the Army, understood how to control them. Years before near Prescott, he and Felton worked together chasing hostile Apaches for the government. Since then, Sieber had become the most famous Indian fighter in the territory.

"There's still time, yet. You still chasin' banditos in Texas?"

"Mostly."

Sieber put his hand on Felton's shoulder. His breath smelled as if he'd had more than his share of whiskey. "Bring your glass and come on over to my table. I want to introduce you to coupl'a good men."

Felton tipped his hat to Libby and went with Sieber. They stopped at a round table where two tough-looking men sat. Like everyone in Tucson, both were well armed.

"Boys, this here is *Tats-ah-das-aygo*," smiled Sieber. Least that's what the Apaches called him when we scouted together up near Prescott. Whites label him Con Fargo. Him bein' a Texas Ranger these days, would make him your cousin.

"Con, these are Arizona Rangers. That ornery lookin' cuss under the beard is Captain Tom Ross. The other no-account is Sergeant Bill Todd."

Felton shook hands with the two Rangers. He took a seat at the table. Like him, they were dressed in ordinary trail clothes. Neither wore a badge that could be seen.

"What brings you to Tucson?" asked Ross.

Al Sieber had been drinking, which was not unusual when he was in town, but he was still an excellent judge of character. He had vouched for these men. They could be trusted.

"A friend," said Felton just above the barroom clatter. "A friend that believes there's something in Tucson called The Ring and that it may be causing my friend some trouble. I need to keep everything on the dead quiet. My friend tells me there's no one to trust here in town."

Sergeant Todd was listening carefully. He leaned forward. "What's that Apache name of yours mean?"

Felton hesitated. "Quick Killer."

"You that Ranger they call The Parson, the one that used to be a Pinkerton?" continued Todd.

"In Texas, we ran out of Apaches to kill. All we had there was bandits, so I tried the Pinkertons for a while."

Todd leaned back in his chair. "Damnation," he muttered, and shoved his glass toward Sieber. "Pour me some more of that tarantula juice."

After glancing at Felton and thoughtfully scratching his beard, Ross' eyes narrowed. "There's talk of such a ring as your friend believes. But there's no proof anything illegal's going on. My gut tells me your friend is on the money."

"I hear the local law around here is as much use as tits on a boar hog," said Felton. "Have any ideas where to start?"

The three men looked one to another. A mutual frown of disdain lined their faces.

"Tribolett," grunted Sieber. "That son-of-a-bitch would know somethin' if anybody would."

"Who's he?"

"He's a government beef contractor," offered Todd. "And a whiskey peddler. Whiskey, guns, ammunition…anything the Apaches want."

"Why don't you arrest him?" asked Felton. "Or kill him?"

"Hell, Fargo," snickered Ross. "I thought Sieber was bad."

Felton shrugged. "Selling guns to Apaches. And whiskey. Why not kill him?"

"Because," replied Ross. "He sells just outside the reservation or just over the line in Mexico. He hasn't done anything illegal we can catch him on."

Casually pouring himself another drink, Felton asked, "Any idea where I can find this Tribolett?"

"Right now he's got a tent shack between Globe and the San Carlos reservation. He sells bad whiskey to anybody that shows up. Mostly he does business with the Indians that sneak off the reservation. Even the Apache Army scouts show up and get drunk."

"What's the best way to get to Globe from here?" asked Felton.

"Stage," said Sieber. "You can make it in a day. With the Apaches out, it's safer than going alone. You can rent a horse in Globe."

Todd glanced skeptically at Felton. "You think you can get Tribolett to talk?"

"I know a trick or two."

Sieber laughed. "Hell, boys. Con will have him singing the Battle Hymn of the Republic. Ain't no Apache around can best Con in that department."

"If you're going after The Ring," said Ross. "I best swear you in. As it is, you got no jurisdiction in the territory and you'll need the law on your side every step of the way."

"Suits me," agreed Felton.

Ross nodded. "Raise your right hand."

Felton raised his hand.

"Do you so swear to uphold the laws of the Arizona Territory as a duly sworn Ranger thereof?"

"I do."

"I'll clear it with the governor. Now it's all legal. Pay is forty a month."

"When does the next stage leave for Globe?"

"Don't know," said Todd. "Maybe tonight. It's the best time considering the Apaches don't fight at night. The passengers can beat the heat. You can check at the station over on Pearl Street."

Felton turned the whiskey glass between his thumb and fingers. "The Texas Rangers along with some Pueblo Indian scouts finished off the last of Victorio's Apaches up in the Diablo Mountains last year. Since then, we've had no trouble with them in Texas. What's the situation here in Arizona?"

"Same as it was ten years ago," sneered Sieber. "General Crook come here back in the seventies and cleaned it all up. He was sent up north to fight the Sioux. Now it's just as bad as it was before.

"They crowded all the Apaches onto the San Carlos reservation even though some of the bands was deadly enemies. The crooked agents cheated them out of their rations while the Department of Indian Affairs looked the other way.

"The Army couldn't do nothing 'cause the War Department didn't have no say in what was goin' on. So the wild Apaches jumped. Don't take much to have them break out. They can't go six months without murdering somebody. They don't care who. Could be peaceful Apaches, Mexicans, or whites. They don't give a damn who they murder just so's they can make a raid.

"We stopped a bunch of them last year at Big Dry Wash. That didn't stop the Chiricahuas. They're still out murderin', stealin', and rapin'.

"When General Crook was here as head of the reservation, he controlled 'em. He was tough but fair minded. They respected the old 'Gray Fox' as they called him."

"I hear," said Felton. "You command the attention of your Apaches like no other chief of scouts ever has. How do you do it?"

Sieber waved a disregarding hand. "Oh, that's nothing. When I tell them I'm goin' to kill 'em, I do it. When I tell 'em I'm their friend, they know I mean it. It's the same with the general."

"Have any Apaches been near Tucson lately?"

"Just broncos that are on their way to join with Geronimo and Nachez," said Ross. "No one knows where they're hold up right now. Likely, the Sierra Madres in Mexico. The whole bunch will cross back over the line. You can be damned sure of that. It's just a matter of time."

"Well, hell," blurted Sieber. "If this ain't homecoming week. There's Jesus Elias comin' in."

Sieber stood and waved his arm. "Elias! Come on over here you damned goat herder. How long has it been?"

Jesus grinned and shook hands with Sieber. "Seven years, maybe eight," he said. He nodded to the Rangers. "Captain, Sergeant."

After a quick glance at Felton, Elias looked back at Sieber.

"Jesus, this here is Conway Fargo. Just signed up with the Rangers. He's a hell of a Injun fighter from way back. Me and him fit the Apaches up in the Tontos."

Elias and Felton shook hands as if they were strangers. Elias grabbed an empty chair and sat down at the table. "So you know this no-account gringo?"

"Yep," said Felton. "The two of us learned the trade of Indian fighting back in the late sixties."

"Now you are a Ranger. It is good. We need all we can get."

"That we do, Jesus," agreed Ross. "So why don't you re-enlist?"

"You know why, Captain. Nothing has changed. Mrs. Wetham's ranch still needs protection...now more than ever."

Sieber slid his glass to Elias. "Put some hair on the dog, Jesus."

"Maybe later. It is too early and too hot for me."

"Suit yourself," said Sieber retrieving his glass. "I got to drink while I can. Won't be long and I'll be hired out again and won't be able to touch a drop. I seen this all before."

Felton slid his chair back. He needed to get away so he and Elias could talk in private. He was about to excuse himself when the daylight coming in over his shoulder was blocked out. Someone was standing behind him.

"Hello Captain Ross. Recruiting more Rangers I hope."

Ross looked up at the speaker. "We got us one more."

"Did you sign up again, Elias?" asked the speaker.

Felton noticed Elias hesitate. He seemed uncertain and tense. "No, Mr. Turner. Not this time. It is Mr. Fargo here. I have only just met him today."

Turner stepped around to the side of Felton's chair and extended his hand. Felton looked up and immediately knew what was wrong with Elias. Felton came to his feet to shake hands with the Yankee sergeant.

Watching Turner's every move, Felton said graciously, "A pleasure to meet you, Sir."

Turner's eyes flickered with curiosity as they measured Felton. "Fargo. Is that Spanish?"

The sergeant was dressed in a fine black suit. There was a slight bulge near his left shoulder where he carried a hidden pistol. A gold tiepin and matching chain hanging from his silk vest pocket indicated he had done well since the war. His eyes beamed with arrogance, the kind of arrogance that wealth and power bring to the foolish.

"It is French," countered Felton. "Or what is left of it. My grandfather was the victim of illiterate immigration officials. It used to be spelled quite differently though pronounced the same."

"Oh," said Turner, the suspicion vanishing from his face. "For a minute there, you reminded me of a Mexican I once knew. My mistake. Welcome to the Rangers. We need all we can get."

Turner walked to another table and joined their conversation. Felton continued to stand. "I need to check on that stage to Globe. Did you say the station was on Pearl?"

Elias did not hesitate. "I must go that way. I will show you where it is."

"I'll be here all afternoon," said Sieber. "You two come back if you've a mind."

"We'll be in touch," said Ross.

Felton and Elias casually walked outside and turned left on Congress Street. They took several steps before either spoke.

"Welcome back…Señor Fargo."

"That was quite a welcome back there," said Felton. "Do you know who that was?"

"*Si*, amigo. Do you think he recognized you?"

"No. If I spoke with a Spanish accent he might have put it together. That's all he ever heard from Fuentes. It's been twenty years. I've changed."

"Will you kill him?" asked Elias.

Felton thought for a moment. "Not unless he gives me a reason. But I wouldn't pass up the chance."

"The stage you want that goes to Globe leaves at six o'clock," said Elias. "We need to talk. Can you meet me in the church of San Augustine in five minutes? It will be safe there."

"Five minutes," agreed Felton. He walked to the opposite side of the street and paused in front of the Pima County Bank.

When Elias disappeared down Meyer Street, Felton went another block and headed east on Main. A few minutes later, he crossed the dusty plaza that once served as the Confederate's corral. Seconds beyond the plaza, Felton stopped in front of the church where Bricela Verde emerged as Bricela Wetham. Until she rode past him with her husband, he had no idea what was happening. The memory of that day, like too many others, had not faded enough.

Taking off his hat, Felton grasped the cast iron ring bolted onto the heavy wooden door of the church. Pulling it open, he stepped into the dim light. Elias sat in the back pew of the empty sanctuary. Sunlight filtered through stained glass windows. The air inside was surprisingly cool. The melodic sounds of Felton's boot heels and spurs echoed off the stone floor and up into the vaulted ceiling. He took a seat next to Elias.

"How have you been, Jesus?"

"I have been well, my friend."

Felton slowly looked around the church and at the plaster statues of the saints. "It has been quite a life hasn't it, Jesus?"

Jesus leaned forward, turning his sombrero with both hands. He sighed heavily, thoughtfully. "It has."

"Did you marry?" asked Felton. There was a reverence in his tone. "Did you find someone after Juanita?"

"Yes."

After a long silence, Felton said sincerely, "Good. Good for you, Jesus."

"You are alone? Have you not found someone for yourself?"

"I thought so a couple of times...but no. Too busy I guess."

Elias nodded halfheartedly. "Sometimes...life itself can be a curse."

"Beats the alternative, I imagine."

There was another silence before Jesus spoke again. "Bricela holds much anger for you. There is much she does not know."

"I could see she wasn't all that happy to see me. I don't remember her like that."

"My friend, she wanted very much to see you once more. That she could not hide from me. She is angry you are not dead. She has not forgiven you for never coming back. It was better...in her heart, to believe you would have if you had not been killed."

"Does she know," asked Felton softly. "What happened at the red bluff?"

Jesus shook his head. "It took many months before I was certain...but she has no memory that you rescued her from the desert...and from the Apaches."

Felton stared at a statue of the Crucifixion. "Does she remember...the two Apaches?"

Jesus answered reverently. "Yes. She knows what they did to my Juanita. Of you, she remembers just a man. She knows him only by the name others told her. She believes a passing Mexican saved her...by the name of Carlos Fuentes."

Taking his eyes off the cross, Felton looked down at his hands. That day, they were covered in Apache blood. He was baptized in blood from head to toe. It was no wonder she did not know it was Caleb Felton that covered her with his blanket, or that he held her as they rode, gently reassuring her.

"Maybe you should tell her," continued Jesus. "It is time she knew."

"If she believes it was Fuentes that saved her, then she also believes I know nothing about what happened to her."

"This is true."

Felton thought for a moment. "Let her keep thinking that. It's better that way. There'll be no reason for her to be ashamed when she talks to me. She won't have to wonder what I'm thinking about her being violated...and she won't have cause to remember what happened under that bluff."

"She is a strong woman, now," asserted Elias. "She should know."

"It's over, Jesus. She's married. It's best she hates me."

"She will never hate you, amigo. She still loves you, I think."

Looking up, Felton glared at Elias. "How could she? You said she liked it better when she thought I had gone under."

Elias shrugged but said nothing.

"Once...maybe," conceded Felton. "She didn't know any better. I think she's got the right idea about me now. If she doesn't, she soon will."

"No, *amigo*. You do not understand. The ranch...she started it only three years ago. Before that, her husband had a general store. He is not much for ranching so Bricela makes most of the decisions. She chose the brand for the stock and had it made herself."

"And?"

"It is called the Double Eagle. It is to show two eagles...soaring together. Do you remember this? Do you remember the day with Owl Woman? I have not forgotten. Neither has she."

Felton dropped his eyes. It was how the old medicine woman described the two of them so long ago. For twenty years the two ivory eagles on his pistol and those carved on the brooch around his neck were a constant reminder. Of course he remembered. The Double Eagle brand, though, was not a sign of affection. It was simply a sentimental choice, a remnant of shattered innocence.

"Well, even so," disagreed Felton. "That was before she knew I was still on this side of the dirt. She won't think so fondly of me now."

"When she brought the buggy back to me this day," smiled Jesus. "Her words were angry but her eyes...they told a different story."

"Angry about what?"

"She still asks why you did not write even once. If she did not care for you, she would not ask. She looks at me when she speaks but she is talking to herself. Her face gets very red.

"She thinks you rejected her. This makes all women angry. If she knew this was not so, it would be good for both of you. Tell her about the years in Yuma Prison and the years fighting the Apaches with the Yankees. Tell her they still treated you as a spy and allowed you no letters. Then of your illness, that you almost died. All this she should know."

"I can't do that, Jesus. I like it the way it is. Besides, all that's only partly true."

"How so?"

"Sure I was held in Yuma the better part of two years. Then I went out with the Yankees to fight Indians. After a while I could have gotten a letter off if I wanted."

"Why didn't you?"

Felton hesitated. "We fought the Apaches everywhere we could find them. Most of the time we got where we were needed too late. What I saw...I don't have to tell you, Jesus.

"Every time I saw what they did to a woman, I thought of Bricela at that red bluff. If I had been honest with her from the beginning, none of it would have happened. It was my vanity that caused it all. I started to write her once or twice but finally gave up. It was no use opening old wounds, hers or mine. Nothing has changed."

Jesus shook his head. "Juanita is gone. I love my wife and she is a good woman. I still love Juanita. You and Bricela are not together, but surely you can still love each other. What exists between a man and a woman does not change. It is no sin."

"Maybe people change," muttered Felton, "I've committed enough sins to last three lifetimes. The way I see it, I've got a long way to go before me and the Lord come anywhere close to breaking even. So let's get to it.

"Now, what kind of trouble is she in, anyway? How bad is it?"

Slowly leaning back in the pew, Elias said, "Very bad trouble, I think. More than she understands."

"How so?"

"Her livestock were stolen by Apaches. This she knows because I followed the tracks. She does not know that the Apaches met with white men afterwards. They were together for a while far out in the desert. All her problems come after she saw her stock in Globe and then reported it to the Indian Agent. It looks like someone at the agency...sent the Apaches to steal. If they can do that...if they can send them to steal her cows, they can send them to do much worse. Nobody would think anything of it…just another Indian massacre. There would be no investigation and soon it would be forgotten.

"I tell her it is maybe better to say nothing more about what she saw. She knows what an Apache outbreak means…what it can mean to others…like what happened to her. This, I cannot argue against. She is a strong woman."

"Have you heard of a man named Tribolett?" asked Felton.

"Yes, many times. He is no good."

"Captain Ross said he could know something. The captain said I should start with him. Have any idea what he looks like?"

Elias pointed. "He is missing this tooth. He is tall, skinny, and always dirty. He has pits in the skin of his face. He smells always of sweat and bad whiskey. You will know him if you see him."

"Captain Ross said he was last seen up around Globe. He sells whiskey and guns to the Apaches from San Carlos."

"This is why you go to Globe?"

"Yes. I want information. If I find Tribolett, I'll get what I'm after."

"You do not need to go to Globe. I see him ride into Tucson this morning with his wagon. He must be out of whiskey and needs more to sell."

"Did you see which road he came in on?"

"He comes from the north on the road through Cañada del Oro. With the Apaches out, it is a dangerous place. Many broncos ride through the canyon to join Geronimo and Nachez in Mexico. There are cattle and horse thieves, too. Los hombres son muy malos."

Felton thought for a moment. "Is there anything else you know about Tribolett?"

"He comes and goes. He says little to anyone. He has a beef contract with the reservation. This I know. He is one of the agents that buys from ranchers and sells to the reservation for profit. Some say he buys from rustlers."

"He's a busy man," said Felton. "Did he buy Bricela's stock?"

"No. It was another. I did not know him."

Coming to his feet, Felton asked, "How do I contact you when I'm in town?"

"Go to the end of Meyer Street. Find any Mexican child and tell them to go to my home with your message. We will meet in the adobe where the Shoo Fly once was. It is empty now."

"Tell Bricela I need to borrow what cows she has left. How many does she have?"

"Twelve only. They are the ones the sheriff says were stolen cattle. He says for her to keep them until the owner comes for them or there is a trial."

"I can handle a dozen if they're trail broke."

"They are all two-year-old long horns but they are broken to trail. Why do you need them?"

"I'm turning rustler, Elias. Mexican rustler. Where is the ranch?"

"Three miles up the Santa Cruz on the road to Yuma. The cows are along the edge of the river."

"How much did they pay Bricela when they bought her milk cows that were supposed to go to the reservation?"

"Ten dollars a head. The buyers always pay the same. They sell them for twenty to San Carlos."

"Why don't the ranchers sell them to the Indians themselves?" They could double their money."

"Only an agent with a contract from the agency can sell to San Carlos. Only Agent Tiffany says who gets the contracts. He gives very few so the ranchers have to sell to agents."

Felton considered the contracts for a moment. It was something to remember. "Tell men at the ranch not to shoot me when I drive the cows off. When I see which way Tribolett is headed, I'll drive the cows to him and offer to sell them. If he's smart, he'll know they're stolen. If he buys them from me, he'll believe I'm a rustler. If he does, it will give me an edge."

"Anything else, amigo?"

"Yes. Tell Bricela to report the cattle stolen. Don't tell the sheriff until tomorrow morning. I want to see if Mosby will do anything."

Elias stood and extended his hand. "Vaya con Dios, amigo."

Felton shook hands with Elias. Twenty years before, James Tevis spoke the same words to him just before he galloped out of Tucson toward San Xavier. It was the day he found Bricela. It was also the day he found himself. Nothing in either of their lives was ever the same.

"Always," said Felton.

With only a half-dozen saloons in Tucson, it was easy to find Tribolett. He was at the bar when Felton entered The Palace. Immediately recognizing the whiskey peddler, Felton casually took a seat at a table along the far wall and waited. When Tribolett left an hour later and walked into an alley, Felton followed at a distance.

Halfway down the alley, two men were lifting an oak keg into a wagon where several smaller kegs had already been loaded. Tribolett climbed onto the bed. He jerked a canvas over the load and halfheartedly tied it down. He mumbled something to the men and started the team of horses. They were pointed north.

The men loading the whiskey went through the back door of an adobe as the wagon made its way to the end of the alley and turned left. Felton waited a few seconds. He followed the tracks until he located a clear print. There was a small nick in the right rear steel rim. Even on a busy road, it would be easy to follow the wagon.

At the corner where the wagon turned, Felton stopped. He eased his head around a wall. Tribolett was leaving Tucson on the only road that went due north. He was taking the long trail that led through Cañada del Oro, going back the same way Elias had seen him come in.

Before going to the stables, Felton stopped at a barbershop for a quick shave and haircut. He left only the mustache. Leaving there, he bought a battered sombrero and *serape* from an old Mexican and thanked him in perfect Spanish. It was a role he had played many times since the appearance of Carlos Fuentes. Along with his dark complexion and sordid past, assuming the identity of a dangerous *bandito* came easily.

It took an hour to find Bricela's small herd of cattle. With the sun low in the sky, the steers were easy to drive out of the cottonwood thickets lining the river's edge. Once they were pointed north and the leader established, Felton fell in behind with his stallion. Only then did he notice the fresh brand carried on each hip.

Two V's, open wide across the top and with their tips curled upward, were branded an inch apart, one on top of the other. The brand resembled two soaring birds and the design would be almost impossible to alter with a running iron. The Double Eagle was a good mark regardless of why Bricela had chosen it.

Even if Jesus was right about the meaning of the brand, it was based on the hopes and romantic notions of a fifteen-year-old girl. No one could have lived up to them, certainly not Caleb R. Felton. Not on his best day.

Felton glanced at the brand again and swore at his misfortune. Bricela was different from other women. He knew it from the start. If he were half the man she thought he was, he should have walked away from her the day they met and not looked back. Like an entranced fool, he had stayed. He remained near her knowing there was no future in any of it. He also knew he was being inexcusably selfish.

Thankfully, providence kept him away from her until the day she was married. Providence or maybe coincidence. Or perhaps coincidence was merely the tool of providence. At least believing in providence helped a person sleep at night. If everything was merely coincidence, life was nothing more than a curiosity.

Was there ever any significance to the name of Robespierre? Was any meaning to be found in soaring eagles, ivory figures, or even the Z branded on his chest? Did Owl Woman actually *see* anything?

Felton spit the dust out of his mouth and cleared his head. Once he saw a man in a saloon rolling dice. Eight times in a row he came up with seven or eleven and won over two thousand dollars. The same night he was robbed and killed. There was no meaning to be found there. Just luck. Good and bad. Sometimes, one or the other just happened.

CHAPTER 12

When the sun set behind the Sierra Tucsons, it was over one hundred and ten degrees. A quarter moon was rising over the Santa Catrina Mountains. The sand still radiated the day's heat. As the steers lumbered up Cañada del Oro, a gust of wind stirred the evening air. The feeble breeze, far from being refreshing, reminded Felton of someone opening an oven door.

The canyon, if it could be called that, was miles wide and almost level. As far as the eye could see, palo verde and stunted mesquite trees dotted the desert floor with large dark clumps. The needles of the ocotillo, cholla, and towering saguaro absorbed the silver blue light of the moon and shrouded each cactus with a deceptive soft glow. Even the tangled gray thorn and crucifixion thorn looked white and delicate. Except for the muffled sound of plodding hooves, it was quiet. For a few hours the desert would rest peacefully under the stars.

Felton glanced down at the road. Tribolett was the only wagon that had been in Oro Canyon in weeks. For the last six miles he had been heading due north. Now the tracks were veering off the road toward the mountains to the northeast. They followed the edge of a wide dry wash. It was a dead end for a man with a wagon.

Turning the cattle, Felton followed the wagon tracks. They would have to stop in three or four miles. After that, only a man on horseback or on foot could continue on into the mountains. Where the wash narrowed there was said to be a spring. Near there, before the Apaches ran him out, a Mexican named Romero built a ranch beside an ancient Indian village. It was the only water for miles and a favorite rendezvous for the Indians.

Tribolett would likely have a camp set up near the spring to sell his whiskey and somehow the Apaches would know he was there. Hopefully, the camp would be neutral ground for those wanting to do business. Anyone selling guns or stolen cattle was usually accepted by such renegades and scallywags. If there was trouble however, Felton would have no choice but to shoot his way out.

Following the trail and pushing the cattle ahead of him, Felton thought of what little he knew about Bricela's problem. Bricela had seen Double Eagle cows that were bought for the San Carlos reservation taken to the town of Globe. The agent at the reservation was told of the possible theft of the cows, but it was after that meeting with Agent Tiffany that all hell broke loose for Bricela. She was convinced there was a secret plot to destroy her because of what she had discovered. It was a strategy designed to silence her.

Other than the cows, there was nothing to support her fears. There were simple explanations as to why her cows ended up in the mining town. Maybe there weren't enough squaws that wanted to try bottle feeding. Or perhaps the reservation already had enough milk cows. It's possible that her problem was no more than a string of bad luck.

Whatever the case, the Arizona Rangers fingered Tribolett as a scoundrel that sold whiskey to Apaches. If it wasn't illegal, it should be. The letter of the law was not always right. Any man that dealt with Apaches was no better than them and deserved the same fate. The only good Apache was a fully reconstructed Apache.

Thinking of Indians, especially renegade Apaches, began to heat Felton's blood. The red bluff where he found Bricela was less than twenty miles to the south. Being in Tucson and seeing her once more had peeled twenty years off his worst memories and was rapidly rekindling his hatred of Apaches.

What they did to her and others like her, he had seen too many times. While fighting Apaches with Jack Swilling and Al Sieber, he witnessed more suffering and death than any ten men should ever see.

Sieber taught him a great deal about the Apaches, but the chief of scouts always appeared unmoved by the endless scenes of torture and slaughter. He killed more Apaches than any one man but strangely held no grudge against them. Killing for Sieber was merely a job to be done and he was a master craftsman.

It was different with Felton. Unlike Sieber, it was never about fighting for peace on the frontier or forcing the Apaches onto a reservation. It was about a friend being tied to a cactus and disemboweled. It was about a fifteen-year-old girl being repeatedly raped. Peace had nothing to do with his war with Apaches. Con Fargo campaigned for one reason. He fought for justice, justice for the helpless and innocent.

The trail turned slightly. A mile ahead two campfires could be seen on top of a small mesa. If those at the fires didn't know he was coming up the trail they soon would. Sound traveled in a canyon, especially at night.

Felton began to sing, not too loud, not too soft. "No me mires con esos tus osos, Mas hermosos que el sol en el cielo, Que me mires de dicha y consuelo, Que me mata! que me mata! tu mira!"

The Mexicans used to sing that song in Tucson during the war. It had come in handy working along the border in Texas and it would serve its purpose tonight.

Trailing cattle around the ocotillo and saguaro at night was slow work. It took a full half-hour to reach the camp. Felton sang the entire time. Riding up the edge of the mesa he saw the wagon next to a canvas wall tent. A second wagon with a larger box and wider wheels was a few feet beyond it. A small campfire burned between the wagons and a lantern illuminated the tent. Two barrels held up a single plank that served as a crude bar. A stoop-shouldered man, his elbows resting on the plank, watched Felton ride in. His cheeks were sunken, his face pockmarked.

Fifty feet from the wagons, a second fire was burning. Three saddles lay nearby. No one was in sight but Felton could smell the Indians. They lurked somewhere in the darkness, no doubt watching his every move.

Felton stopped in front of the tent as the cows lazily started browsing the scant tufts of dry grass that grew between the cacti. Tribolett came out of the tent. He glanced at the cows. In the fire light, he could not miss seeing the fresh Double Eagle brand.

"What do you want?" demanded Tribolett.

"Whiskey, Señor. And some money for the cattle I bring. It is said to me you will buy."

"You got any money for the whiskey?"

"No, Señor. I am but a poor Mexican. I have only my cows."

Tribolett's eyes went over Felton's pistols. "You got a bill of sale for them cows. I know that brand."

Felton acted uneasy and surprised. He felt for his vest pocket and patted it. "I think I lose the paper," he said with a smile. "My friends tell me to bring these here. They tell me you will understand these cows."

Squinting suspiciously, Tribolett asked, "What friends would that be?"

Leaning forward and lowering his voice, Felton said, "The friends that don't want that woman to make no more troubles. They don't want her to have no cows no more. I do what I am told, Señor. I lose the money they pay me at the saloon already."

Tribolett relaxed. "I thought we took all she had."

Felton dismounted. "She buys more. Now there are no more. How much you give me for them?"

"Two dollars a head. That's my goin' rate for rustled cows."

"Two dollars is not so much. I think ten dollars. You sell them for twenty to San Carlos. We both make money."

"Two dollars is good money considerin' you can't sell 'em nowhere else," said Tribolett, sauntering back inside the tent. "I'll throw in a free drink to boot."

Shoving back his sombrero, Felton scratched his forehead and looked at the cows. "Is good enough then, I think maybe."

Stepping up to the bar, Felton kept an eye on the saddles. "You are not alone, Señor."

Tribolett poured whiskey into a dusty shot glass. "Three Apaches come in at sundown. I'd stay clear of 'em seein' how you're Mexican."

"Comanchero. Not Mexican."

"Well, all the same, keep your distance. They been drinking already. You know how they can be."

Felton studied Tribolett for a moment. Judging a man's character was as important as knowing the pattern of a snake's skin. This man was treacherous but not brave. If anything, he was a backshooter. "They are far from the reservation, these three."

"Broncos, I reckon. None of my business who they are...or who you are neither. I'm a business man."

Throwing back his drink, Felton winced. The whiskey was bad. "You pay me twenty-four dollars for the cows. How much for another drink?"

"One dollar."

"One dollar? Do the Apaches pay one dollar?"

"Sometimes I trade. These here got silver dollars from somewhere. They pay the same as you."

Placing his glass down, Felton pointed to it. "One more."

223

As Tribolett poured, three Apaches appeared out of the night and stood around their fire. Each wore a pistol and a knife belted around a long muslin breech clout. They laughed as they passed a bottle around."

"How much for a bottle?"

"Twenty dollars."

Felton nodded, picked up his glass and went outside. If the Apaches had twenty dollars in silver, they must have stolen it. Stealing twenty dollars would require killing someone.

After stretching and looking up at the stars, Felton casually strolled to the second wagon. A mule, still in its harness, was down. Its throat had been slit. A large piece of meat was cut from its hindquarter. The Apaches had eaten before they started on the whiskey.

Blood covered the wagon seat. It was sticky to the touch. The wagon bed was carelessly piled with household belongings and a small cedar chest with its lid broken off lay on top of a woman's coat. Pinned on the collar of the coat was an agate cameo with the head of Medusa carved in relief. A handful of letters were scattered on the ground.

The Apaches were thirty paces from the tent. Felton took a few steps toward them. He stopped and pretended to take a drink from his whiskey glass. The Apaches glared at him for a moment. In the poor light there was little they could see. When they turned their attention back to the bottle, Felton continued walking slowly. He meandered on an indirect path but kept edging closer to the fire.

Singing softly, Felton pretended to look at the stars but kept an eye on the Indians. One threw more wood on the fire sending sparks up into the black night. Flames blazed brightly. Their faces glowed with amber light but their deep-set eyes remained hidden in dark holes.

They were overconfident and getting drunk. Normally, no Apache would stand so close to a large fire and expose himself in the bright light. They were celebrating and they were careless.

Felton took a few more steps. He was within twenty feet of the fire when the older of the three Apaches noticed him. The buck stared at Felton. He moved his head side to side as if trying to see something in Felton's face. His eyelids narrowed into slits.

Felton stared back. He made no effort to hide what was on his mind.

Suddenly the Apache's face stiffened. His eyes ignited with unmasked hatred. "*Tats-ah-das-aygo!*" he sneered.

The other Apaches turned to face the man called Quick Killer. One held the bottle. The hands of the other two were empty, stained with dried blood.

"That'd be me," returned Felton. "*Dee-dah tats-an.*"

Understanding the words of death, the older Apache reached for his pistol. He was half drunk. Even stone-cold sober, he would never have been fast enough. Felton drew his Colts and fired. Both barrels thundered at the same instant. Two Apaches fell backwards and the third turned to run. Felton fired one pistol then another. The last Indian crumpled and landed face down in the sand.

Without hesitation, Felton moved in and emptied two more rounds into the bodies of the first two Apaches. He kicked their guns away and stepped back. Tribolett ran out of the tent but stopped suddenly. He was unarmed.

"What the hell did you do that for?" he roared.

Felton lowered one pistol and holstered the ivory-handled one. Tribolett would have a hard head and the frame of the converted percussion pistol was no good as a club.

"Lo siento mucho, amigo. These three were old enemies. They recognize me from many years ago, I think maybe...so we have some troubles."

"Damn," grumbled Tribolett as he started forward. "Any money on 'em is mine. Everything they had is mine, including the horses. This is my camp."

Felton stood next to the older Apache and waited for Tribolett to come closer.

"No *problemo*, amigo. I will be happy with my twenty-four dollars. I think maybe I take three scalps."

"Suit yourself," said Tribolette. He kneeled beside the Apache for a closer look. "I used to sell scalps down in Mexico after the war. Nobody's buying 'em anymore. Not that I know of, anyhow."

"We will see," answered Felton, then smashed the gun barrel of his Colt across the side of Tribolett's skull.

When Tribolett half opened his eyes, the eastern sky was turning pale blue and a steady breeze was blowing from the south. He tried to rub his eyes. His hands would not move. He blinked and tried again. He turned his head to the left and saw his wrist tied to a wagon spoke. He jerked his head to the right and saw the same. He was sitting on the ground. His feet were covered with a pile of dead branches. He tried to kick them off but his ankles had been tied and staked down. "What the hell?" he said. His voice filled with panic. "What the hell!"

Felton came from behind the wagon and squatted at the feet of Tribolett. "Ah. You wake up, my friend."

Tribolett was incredulous. "You! You told the Apaches it was me that murdered those three, didn't you? Damn you for a lying Mexican! You won't get away with it. They know me. I'll tell 'em. When I do it'll be you they'll tie to this wheel and burn, not me. They know me. They know I'd never kill one of their own. You'll see, damn you!"

"The only Apaches here, Señor Tribolett, are dead ones. I see many times how they kill my people. The gringos, too. I learn very good. I do not have so much time today. So I kill you pretty quick…still you die the Apache way."

Sweat beads formed on Tribolett's forehead. "What do you want? You can have all the money. The horses too. Take it all."

Felton smiled. "I have these things already. But…two dollars for a cow. That is not so much you offer me. You make a big mistake when I know you pay ten to others. To this poor Mexican you give two dollars."

"I only pay ten to men I know…and to the ranchers. I don't know you and don't give a damn you're Mexican. That's just how it works."

Glancing over at the bodies of the Indians, Felton frowned. "I don't think I like how it works. No, I want your business. I make more money that way."

"What? You want to sell whiskey? You don't need to kill me to do that. Anybody can do that."

"You sell more than whiskey. You sell what is in the second wagon, what the Apaches bring you. You sell guns and ammunition to the Apaches. You sell cows…stolen cows to the agency. You no work alone. You no smart enough. You work for someone, my friend. I think, maybe, you work for many men. I want to know these men, too. Then I get rich. Not the one who offers me two dollars. You make a ver' big mistake, hombre."

"What are you talkin' 'bout? I don't work for nobody but me."

Felton took a match from his vest pocket and struck it on the seat of his pants. "No. You are not so smart. Hombres like you…they work for someone that is much smarter."

Tribolett tried desperately to free his legs as Felton touched the match to the cluster of dried grass and small twigs. The flame caught immediately and Felton withdrew the match. He blew it out and watched smoke rise from the blackened tip. Hungry flames began to spread.

"Tiffany!" yelled Tribolett. He struggled violently to free himself. "He tells me what I can do with the cows. He gave me the contract. He tells me what he wants done!"

Slowly coming to his feet, Felton shook his head. "I see you in town today. Tiffany is far away at San Carlos. I think maybe you lie to this poor Mexican. First you cheat, then you lie."

The sticks crackled as the flames spread. The heat was growing intense. Tribolett screamed and swore. "Turner! That's all I know! He'll kill me, dammit! That's all I know. I swear!"

"What does he do?"

"He tells me who to buy from and who to steal from. I tell the cowboys or Apaches... and I get my whiskey from him. That's all I know!"

Felton looked at the flames and then at Tribolett's sweat streaked face. How many times had he come upon the charred remains of men slowly burned to death? How many ways had he seen men, women, and children tortured by the noble red man? Tribolett deserved to die Apache style...but not today.

Kicking the burning sticks off of Tribolett, Felton said casually, "I think maybe you tell the truth. So today I let you live a little longer."

Tribolett's boots were smoldering. His pock-marked face dripped with sweat and his fists were clinched white. He gasped for air."

"Who else is there? Besides Señor Turner?"

Tribolett hesitated. "I don't know nobody else. There's more of 'em...but...but I ain't privy to who they are."

"The sheriff? He does not catch your rustlers?"

"He don't bother me and I don't bother him none."

"What is in the wagon? Where do you sell it?"

"Globe mostly. The miners don't ask no questions."

Felton stared down at Tribolett. He was an accessory to one murder and likely dozens of others. He was a cattle rustler and thief. Ordinarily, the man would get a bullet in the head and be thrown over a saddle. But he could still be useful and Bricela was in serious trouble. The Ring, or something like it, was real.

227

Felton swung into the stallion's saddle. "It will be very hot today, amigo. I think maybe I don't untie you for a while. Some more of your friends will come. I will be gone by then."

"What if they don't come?" protested Tribolett. "You can't leave me like this. I'll die!"

"You will live long enough, Señor. You can talk to God while you wait. Maybe you will not wake up in hell someday soon."

Tribolett spit. "To hell with you, greaser!"

Tipping his hat and wheeling his horse, Felton said, "Vaya con dios, amigo. Vaya con dios."

Bricela rose early. She had not written a poem or recorded her thoughts in years. Except for a few unremarkable entries about her husband, her diary was blank. Taking a pencil, she gazed at the rising sun through an open window. A breeze stirred the lace curtains.

Caleb Felton was back. She liked it better when he was dead. Like other tragedies in her life, she had accepted his being gone and moved beyond the pain. Owl Woman taught her that much. The medicine woman had not prepared her for a resurrection. Nor had she prepared her for a rebirth of buried emotions.

Bricela looked at the hand that held the pencil. It was thick with muscle and calloused from hard work. How delicate she once was. So much in love and so certain of the future. They were meant to be together. Their souls knew each other the instant they met, perhaps even before. But he had died and nothing made sense anymore. Even Owl Woman, her guide through the darkness, did not understand his passing.

Everything was dismissed. It was the dream of a young girl, a fantasy that abruptly ended. Her hope was entombed along with the last remnant of her innocence.

The medicine woman was over ninety now and almost blind. When Bricela told her Caleb Felton was alive, the old woman smiled. Tears started running down her cheeks. She refused to answer any questions. All she would offer was, "You will find your way."

Bricela started to write.

He is different than I remember…and yet he is unchanged.
I could not prepare myself for what twenty years had done

to him…but after a moment I could see him. It all came back. The force, the power of the attraction…yet through the eyes of a woman now, not a girl. Something was lost because of it, yet something gained.

He showed no emotion for me. I admitted none to him. How could I? He did not deserve to know. He had abandoned me. He was in prison…but only for a while. I will always be in mine. No one can free me completely. Caleb could have helped me. He did not.

I will confront him. I must. If I am to be free of him…if I want to be free of him…I must know…I deserve answers.

The words flowed easily. Bricela continued to write.

Untitled

In all life's beauty, there she remained
Chased by laughter in the wind

Tears lost in lonely darkness
Ease the broken pain

Parting words were softy spoken
In an air of silent love

My life is not in vain
For the warmth of that moment is safely tucked away

I surrendered to his gentle touch
And for a few precious heartbeats, rode the River of Joy

Closing the leather cover, Bricela locked the diary. She opened her dresser drawer and carefully concealed the book with her underclothes. Mark would never look there. He would have no reason. She would never give him one. It was a private matter that did not concern him.

Throwing a multicolored *rebozo* over her shoulders, Bricela went downstairs and out the door. Unlike yesterday, she dressed in the loose fitting muslin blouse and skirt she normally wore. Many in Tucson thought she was part Mexican or even Papago. She did not care what they said about her. She lived her life the way she chose. On several occasions she had told her critics what they could do with their opinions. Those that knew her best gave her a wide berth.

Bricela started across the plaza as the rising sun cleared the flat roofs of old adobes. Only the Mexicans still referred to it as the Plaza de las Armas. The Americans called it Court Plaza. It was no longer the center of Tucson. Most of the stores, saloons, and hotels were now blocks away. The Shoo Fly had been empty for years.

Walking past the abandoned saloon, Bricela reverently paused by the whipping post. With all the changes in Tucson, it had stubbornly survived. Buried deep in the sand, the weathered beam was a symbol of cruelty, but also of bravery and compassion. The poor Mexican that had rescued her from the Apaches and shielded her from public disgrace had been falsely accused of a crime. For punishment, the American soldiers branded his chest while he was tied to the post. When she heard what they had done to him, she wept for hours.

It was said he did not make a sound when the hot iron seared his flesh. His bravery was legend among the few whites that knew the story. Among Papagos and Mexicans, he was still spoken of as the handsome and mysterious Don Fuentes. He was a stranger that had appeared from nowhere, then rode off into the sunset never to return. Some claimed he came back to see his lover only to suffer a broken heart. Others say he became a captain in the Mexican Army and killed one hundred evil Apaches.

Bricela thought of the stories and smiled. As she had done so many times before, she kissed the palm of her hand and pressed it against the post. She whispered a prayer for Carlos Fuentes and continued on.

Walking two blocks from the plaza, Bricela crossed the dusty street and entered the sheriff's office. Cade Mosby sat lazily behind his desk with his boots propped on top of it. He held a porcelain coffee cup in one hand and a newspaper in the other.

Bricela stopped just inside the door. She stared at Mosby as he continued to read the paper. A young deputy entered from the back room. There was a swagger to his step, two pistols on his hips, and an impudent smile on his lips. Lony Drake was no more than a hired gunman.

"Miss Wetham," said the deputy tipping his hat. "What brings you here so early this morning? You having more rustling at your ranch?"

Watching Drake closely, Bricela answered smoothly, "Yes, I am. All of my cattle were stolen last night or this morning."

The smile vanished from the deputy. Mosby slowly took his feet down and sat up in his chair. Mosby motioned for the deputy to leave. When the door closed behind him, Mosby tossed his copy of the *Citizen* on his desk. "Are you sure about that?" asked Mosby.

"Come out and see for yourself."

"Were the horses shod? Did you see any tracks around your ranch?"

"I saw tracks of twelve steers being pushed to the northeast. The rest of it is your job, sheriff."

Mosby came to his feet and set the coffee down. "Now don't get your ears layed back, Bricela. I'll go out and have a look. They weren't your cows, anyway."

"I paid for them."

"They were stolen. You shouldn't have bought stolen cattle, Bricela. Now you may have to pay full price for them to the rightful owner. You could be paying twice for cows and not own a single one...That's if you don't go to jail.

"You know half the people in town think you're a little loco. They may think jail is the best place for you."

Bricela thought of Caleb Felton...or did she *sense* him. For the first time in over a month, she felt a surge of confidence and optimism. "I won't be the one going to jail."

"I wouldn't be so cocksure if I was you," said Mosby, walking from behind his desk and standing in front of Bricela. "Maybe we could work something out...now that your husband's not around."

Mosby put his hand on Bricela's shoulder. When she slapped it away, he only laughed. "I always wondered how you got away from those Apaches at the bluff...and what you did for that Carlos Fuentes fool. Everybody knows you go out to your ranch by yourself with those Mexican men. You and them there all alone...while your poor excuse for a husband is way back east."

"You're disgusting!" snapped Bricela. "You always have been."

Bricela spun and reached for the doorknob. Mosby grabbed her by the shoulders and turned her toward him. He pushed her against the door, pinning her arms down.

"He'll kill you for this," threatened Bricela. There was no fear in her voice. Her eyes blazed with rage.

"Who? Your lily-livered husband? Let him try. You'll make a pretty widow."

Bricela sneered. "I'm not talking about Mark. I'm talking about…Lieutenant Caleb Felton. The man you told me was dead."

Mosby's face paled. His grasp on Bricela weakened but he did not let go.

"What are you talking about?"

Now it was Bricela's turn to smile. "You remember, Cade. The man you took a shot at outside the Shoo Fly. The man you tried to murder. He's coming back to Tucson. In fact he may be here already. He still has your pistol, Cade. They say he's a gunman now…a cold blooded killer."

"You're lying."

"You should know, Cade. You're the one that told everyone he was killed in the war. You were lying then and that's why you know I'm not now. You know he's coming…you can imagine what he'll do to you if he finds out what happened here today."

Mosby released her and stood back. His cockiness vanished. He tried to hide his fear but his eyes betrayed him. "Let him come. What do I care?"

"He was right about you," said Bricela. "He was right from the beginning."

Bricela opened the door. Another man blocked her exit. His large frame filled the doorway. It was Turner.

"Excuse me, Mrs. Wetham," said Turner. He stepped back to allow her to pass. "I was just coming over to have a word with Sheriff Mosby. I just heard your last cows were stolen. Is that true?"

Turner was once a sergeant with the California Column. After the war, he was one of many that stayed. Bricela cared for none of them but she especially disliked the big sergeant. It was rumored that he was the Yankee that had branded Carlos Fuentes.

"Yes. They took all twelve."

"Your horses?"

"They were not stolen."

The sergeant blinked thoughtfully. "That's unusual wouldn't you say?"

"Perhaps. I'll take any good luck I can get."

Nodding his head sympathetically, Turner replied, "Yes, Mrs. Wetham. You have had more than your share of hard times. I wish there was something I could do."

Bricela looked up at the large square head. There were scars over both eyes where someone had gotten the better of him in a fight.

"You could allow me to buy on credit again at your store."

"Oh, I would, Mrs. Wetham. If it were up to me I would but I have to answer to my silent partners. Business, you know."

"Yankee business," muttered Bricela, then angrily stormed out of the sheriff's office.

Swearing to herself, she walked across the boardwalk and out into the street. She shouldn't have mentioned the name of Caleb Felton, but who knew what Mosby may have done? She wanted to wipe the smirk off his face. He would discover Caleb was in town sooner or later and she was desperate.

Bricela started for home. She had only taken a few steps before her anger disappeared. In its place was a feeling of intense exhilaration. She was no longer fighting her battle alone. Once again, Lieutenant Caleb R. Felton was standing by her side!

Turner watched Bricela for a moment. He shut the door and looked quizzically at Mosby. "Was it you that ordered those cows stolen?"

"No. Didn't you?"

"Why would I do that? They're our only evidence she bought stolen cattle. Without them we can't prove nothing."

"You want me to go after them?"

"Hell, yes! Find out who took them. If they're not working for us, kill them. We can't have other rustlers horning in on our territory."

"There's something else," said Mosby. "She says an old friend of hers is coming to town…maybe to lend her a hand."

"Do you know him?"

"He was here during the war. He was a lieutenant with the Rebels that took over Tucson. He was sweet on Bricela…or so I heard."

"What kind of man is he?"

Mosby thought of the shot he had taken at Felton outside the Shoo Fly twenty years before. He missed him and headed for home. Someone standing in the shadows slugged him and took his father's ivory-handled pistol. It could have been Felton. Nothing was ever said about it. "Back then he was a sporting man. The other Confederates said he was a lady's man and not too handy with a gun. Some said he was running from the law and he joined up just to get away from a jealous sheriff."

Turner chuckled derisively. "He doesn't sound like much to worry about. Maybe she asked him to come because her husband's back east. Maybe the rumors we been spreading about her aren't too far off."

"She seemed to think he was a dangerous man," said Mosby uneasily. "He could have changed some...with the war and all."

"One man," sneered Turner. "If he starts to get in the way, I'll take care of him myself. It's been too long since I limbered up my fists on a no-account Rebel. Our Mrs. Do-gooder will get a lesson in what happens to her friends if they come here to cause trouble."

Mosby frowned. Bricela spurned his advances even as a teenager. In Old Tucson, it was no secret she had fallen in love with the Confederate. They walked together and danced together in front of everyone. She should have been his. If it were not for the damned lieutenant, she *would* have been his. "If he tries anything, I say we kill him outright," said Mosby.

Turner shook his head and reached for the door. He smiled conceitedly. "How dangerous can one man be?"

A mile from the whiskey camp, Felton sat in the meager shade of a palo verde that clung to the side of a mountain. Several hundred feet below, two riders rode up the desolate canyon following the trail left by the cows. They had come from the south and were most likely rustlers or residents of Tucson.

Felton took out his field glasses. Bracing his elbows on his knees, he focused on the riders as they entered the whiskey camp. The men immediately went to Tribolett, cut him loose and gave him a canteen. After a long drink, Tribolett waved his arms and pointed to the dead Apaches.

Tribolett was close to five-foot-ten. When he came to his feet it was easy to see one of the riders was at least six-two. The other was much shorter. If the riders returned to Tucson, the tall man would tower over most of the townspeople. He would be easy to spot.

The trio went to the dead Apaches, then looked up into the surrounding mountains. Something flashed on the tall man's chest. A watch chain, a button...maybe a badge.

Felton sharpened the focus of the field glasses. He steadied his hands to see through the rippling heat waves. The man wore a black hat. His pants were tucked into knee-high boots and he rode a bay horse.

Turning his attention to the shorter man, Felton looked him over closely. He wore two pistols, something only gun fighters or greenhorns tended to do. His movements were quick, almost careless. Chances were good that he was young.

The men went to the wagon the Apaches had brought in. Ignoring the letters on the ground, they quickly rifled through the belongings and shoved several items into their pockets. Most of the time the smaller man used his left hand. It was something to remember.

Another minute passed in conversation. The two riders mounted and began gathering the cattle. They turned the steers back from the spring and started them down the canyon. If the riders were rustlers, they would take the cows to some remote holding pen or drive them to another buyer. Either way, they would be worth following. Tribolett was part of an organization and had given up Turner's name. But two men did not make a ring. Perhaps the rustlers or buyers would give him more to go on.

From where Felton sat, Tucson was at least fifteen miles across the desert. Even without field glasses, the white walls of the clustered adobes were visible. When the rustlers reached the entrance to the canyon, they would turn northwest to Oro Canyon or southeast to hide the cattle deeper in the Santa Catalinas. When they were out of sight, he would follow at a safe distance.

While the cattle moved slowly down the canyon, Felton continued watching Tribolett. He mulled over what little he knew.

Sieber and the Rangers suspected Tribolett of dealing with Apaches and they had been right. Tribolett claimed Turner was giving him orders and supplying him with whiskey. The Yankee sergeant that had branded him at the whipping post was now a respected business man in Tucson.

Bricela said her milk cows, sold to the reservation, somehow ended up in Globe. She reported her cows stolen and that the sheriff had done little if anything to investigate. Previous Indian agents were known to have been crooked and her information would have at least aroused some suspicion as to the honesty of Agent Tiffany. Mosby should have checked with the agency at San Carlos to see if any of her cows were sold to the reservation. If they had been, there would be a record of the brand. Had Mosby even done so much as check? If for some reason he had not questioned Tiffany, why hadn't he?

If Turner ordered Bricela's cattle rustled, what reason did he have? Did he merely think she was a woman alone and it would be easy? Did he know Mosby would not investigate? Was Mosby incompetent or on Turner's payroll? Was Turner just after the money he got from cattle rustling or was he, as Bricela claimed, trying to silence her?

What if Bricela's stolen cows had been sold to San Carlos? There would have been no legal bill of sale. Did the agent care about such records? Did he get the cattle cheaper if they were stolen, cheaper than what he reported to the government? It would not be the first time Indian agents were dishonest. Most took their ill-gotten money and moved to a big city. None were ever successfully prosecuted.

If the agent was knowingly buying stolen cattle, he would have to cover it up somehow...or be assured the law from Tombstone, or Tucson would not interfere. The Earp brothers in Tombstone were battling rustlers on a personal level and had their hands full. It was likely they had no time for San Carlos. Mosby appeared to be no threat.

If the law was ignorant or looking the other way, the door would be wide open to rustlers and embezzlers. It would take more than one person to keep that door open. The cattle were the key. If they in deed went to San Carlos, Bricela could be in grave danger.

Felton thought for a half hour but as the cows neared the entrance to Pima canyon, he had come up with more questions than answers. He came to his feet and shoved his hat back. He wiped the sweat from his eyes and raised his field glasses. It was time for them to make their move.

"Come on," muttered Felton. "It's hot. Make up your mind."

He took down the glasses. They had not turned. The cows were still headed south toward the road to Tucson.

Felton waited then looked again. There was no question they were headed back to Tucson, but that made no sense. Two men appeared to be returning Bricela's cattle to her, the same two men that had freed Tribolett, and walked past three dead Apaches to a stolen wagon full of personal belongings. They took what they wanted leaving Tribolett to do as he pleased.

Whoever they were, there was no need to follow them now. It was more important to get to San Carlos. He would be riding onto a reservation set aside for Apaches of several different bands. Most bands hated each other but the Indians that knew Felton hated him even more. One of the Apaches at Tribolett's camp recognized him. There could be others. They too would try to kill him if they got the chance.

CHAPTER 13

Riding easily through the heat of day and then harder after sunset, Felton followed Cañada del Oro until midnight. He camped above Old Camp Grant where the Aravaypa River ran into the San Pedro. A few of the buildings still stood. The military had abandoned the post years before. Now the only inhabitants were scorpions and snakes.

After making coffee the next morning, Felton mounted his stallion and ate a breakfast of jerked beef as he rode north along the San Pedro. Two hours later, he crossed the San Pedro River just before the Gila River joined it. He followed the Gila northeast through a rough canyon and eventually started down a range of barren mountains toward the San Carlos River.

The land opened up. The mountains eased into gentle hills with miles of flat desert between the ranges. There were no palo verde or giant saguaro. There were no organ pipe cactus, no cholla, or ocotillo. Mesquite trees, which the Apaches relied on for food, were nowhere in sight. Of the scarce plants that grew in this barren waste, none seemed to grow more than waist high.

Leaving the Gila near noon, Felton took the dusty road that led to the agency. He had been on the reservation for the last several miles but had seen no Apaches. He had seen no sign of life at all. As deserts went, this was the most desolate he had ever seen.

After riding another three miles, he began to parallel a narrow arroyo that ran through a flat plain no more than a mile wide. Shriveled trees, less than ten feet high and barely clinging to life, lined the dry banks. Several brush wickiups had been erected in their meager shade. A handful of children and a few squaws sat in the dirt watching him ride by.

Rounding a bend in the road, several buildings came into view. Most were low-lying adobe. Some were gabled and made of lumber. Empty corrals were off to one side.

With the renegade Chiracauhas in Mexico, only minor trouble had been reported on the reservation. But with Apaches, nothing could be taken for granted. Felton loosened his pistols and kept an eye on his backtrail.

Nearing the buildings, Felton made out a long line of men and women standing in front of an adobe. There were hundreds of them. They seemed to be waiting for something.

A rider emerged from the crowd and started his way at a gallop. Felton drew up and waited. He felt a trickle of sweat run down his back. He dried his palms and narrowed his eyes under the shade of his large-brimmed sombrero.

The man approaching appeared in every way to be an Apache. He rode like an Apache and wore a breech clout and moccasins. His hair was thick and wild. Instead of black, it was a dirty red. The man's left eye was half closed and his cheek was scarred. When he stopped an arms length away, Felton could see his eyes were not brown but green.

"Who you?" grunted the redheaded Apache. "What you do here?"

"The name is Fargo. I am a Ranger. I am here to see Agent Tiffany."

"You stay by me," said the Apache. "I police. You safe. You not by me, you no safe."

Wheeling his horse, the Apache galloped off. Felton spurred his black and came alongside the Indian policeman. He was obviously a captive that had been raised as an Apache.

"Who are you?" asked Felton.

"Me Mickey Free. Scout. Now Apache Police."

"You are an Army scout?"

"Sometime. Sometime not. Sometime speak for Apache to white mans."

Felton played a hunch. "You know Al Sieber? Sieber is a friend of mine."

Free glanced at Felton. "Me, Al Sieber *mucho* good friend. You his friend, you my friend. Why you come?"

"I'm looking for stolen cattle. They may have come here and been bought by Agent Tiffany. I need to know this."

Slowing his horse to a walk, Free waved his hand across his chest. "Fat agent no help you. Fat agent no good no more. Agent get fatter, Apaches all skin now."

The pair passed alongside the long line of Apaches. "They wait for food. They wait long time but no much food as promise. They no like fat agent."

Felton looked at the faces of the Apaches as he passed by. It was hard to read an Apache, yet these faces were filled with an unmasked mixture of hopelessness and hatred. It was a deadly combination.

Free dismounted in front of the adobe and walked past the waiting Apaches and opened the door. He kept an eye on the Indians as Felton entered the large room.

A short man with delicate features sat at a desk writing in a book. He wore wire-rimmed glasses over a beaked nose and sunken cheeks. His hair was greased down close to his skull. He finished what he was writing before he looked up.

"What is it?" he demanded.

"This man want talk to agent. He Ranger."

The man sighed and put down his pencil. "Tiffany is not here. He's at his house eating his dinner."

"I'm investigating stolen cattle," said Felton. He thought he saw a flicker in the clerk's eyes. "Who are you?"

"Dodge. Charles Dodge. We don't have any cattle now. As you could see on the way in, our corrals are empty."

"Who's in charge of recording which cattle come in?"

Dodge stiffened. "I am."

"Then you would have a record of the brands. I'd like to take a look at them."

Adjusting his glasses with a pair of bony fingers, Dodge leaned back in his chair. An arrogant smile parted his lips. "You'll have to ask Mr. Tiffany about that."

Felton wanted to knock the grin off the clerk's face but instead he nodded. "I understand. Mind if I have a look around in the meantime?"

This time Dodge definitely hesitated. He cast a disgusting look at the policeman. "Take Mickey Free with you. He's half Irish, half Mexican and all son-of-a-bitch, but he'll protect you from these savages."

"He looks Apache to me," returned Felton.

Dodge sneered. "Raised by them. Speaks their language. He might as well be one of them. They don't like him but they will follow his orders.

"Now if you don't mind, I have work to do. This is ration day."

Felton glanced at Free. He went outside and untied his horse. He waited for Free to join him. The two started for the corrals. When they

240

were beyond hearing range of the Apaches, Felton took a closer look at Free. "What happened to your eye?"

"Bear. Claw face when boy. Me kill bear."

"You lived with the Apaches?"

"With people of Cochise. They take me."

Coming to a sturdy line of heavy wooden rails, Felton stopped. The stock corrals were impressive.

"White mans build. Fat agent pay big money to white mans."

"Where are the scales? Where do they weigh the cattle when they come in?"

Saying nothing, Free started for a large open-ended shed at the far end of the fence. It was constructed of new lumber. The scales were set under a shaded roof and appeared to be in good condition.

"Do you know how to work the scales," asked Felton, studying the brass sliding weights and iron counterweights.

"Only Dodge do scale. No Apache."

"How about Tiffany?"

"Fat agent no do work. Sometime ride around in buggy. Mostly stay in big house and eat food of Apache."

Felton walked his horse onto the scale and dropped his reins. He went to the balance and slid the weights. He checked the number and returned the weights to their original position.

Picking up the reins, Felton looked back toward the rationing building. A storage shed blocked it from view. The clerk would not know he had weighed his horse.

Walking back to the corrals, Felton thought of what Free had said about the agent eating Apache food. The statement could be taken many ways.

"What did you mean when you said the agent eats Apache food? You mean he eats mesquite bread or mescal?"

Free grunted. "Him eat all time. Apache get little. We hungry much. Him fat. Our food leave on wagons. We no see no more."

"This is ration day. The Apaches are here for their food. I see them waiting."

"They wait long. Get little to eat. Many Apache angry. Some in jail for no reason. Some bad Apaches, no in jail. Blankets come for Apache. We get old blankets. New blankets leave on wagons. Fat agent eat fresh meat. Apache get rotten meat. Flour with bugs. Fat agent no get bugs."

Felton turned and took another look at the long line of Apaches. If he did not hate them so much he would almost feel pity for them.

"Why are you telling me this?"

Without pausing, Free said, "You friend Al Sieber. I know you, *Tats-ah-das-aygo*. Quick Killer. Apache hate Al Sieber. Hate Quick Killer. But Apache trust Al Sieber. Trust friend of Al Sieber. Al Sieber no lie Apache. I no lie you."

Looking squarely at Mickey Free, Felton spoke evenly. "Quick Killer also hates the Apache. I hate bad white men almost as much."

"Someday, you kill Apache," said Free. "Someday Apache kill you. We all got to die sometime. Better to die in fight, than starve on reservation."

The wild Chiracauhas under Geronimo and Naiche had likely jumped the reservation because of blood lust, but most of the Apaches bands had remained at San Carlos. If conditions became intolerable even blanket Apaches would hit the war path.

According to the reservation scales, Felton's twelve hundred pound stallion weighed over a ton. The way the weights were set, a five hundred pound yearling would register as much as a two-year-old steer. On each cow, the United States government would pay for hundreds of pounds of beef that did not exist.

If the scales had been altered on purpose, much of what Free was saying could be true.

Felton used the toe of his boot and scratched the Double Eagle brand into the sand. "You ever see that brand in these corrals?"

"First time," said Free. "Those cows too skinny. They taken away by white mans. Next time, those good cows. We eat all."

"So two herds came in?"

"Two time, cows come that brand."

"Did you see who brought the second cows?"

"White mans. One called Tribolett. Sell whiskey, guns to bad Apache. No good."

Sliding the sole of his boot over the brand, Felton smoothed the sand. Bricela's first herd of milk cows had at least made it to the corrals. Her stolen cows had definitely been purchased by the agency and the meat distributed to the Indians. The branded hides were likely long gone.

Dodge had just been informed stolen cattle may have been brought to the reservation. When asked for his record of the brands, the clerk smiled. He would not have done so unless he knew something, something he found amusing. Was he confident no brand of the Double Eagle, nor brands of any stolen cattle would show up in the books? He was the bookkeeper. If he had purchased rustled cattle and falsified the records it would make him an accessory.

If the brands weren't recorded and the hides destroyed, there was no proof. An Indian was not to be believed and their testimony was not allowed in any court in the Territory. So far, there was nothing to go on but the word of a redheaded half-breed, a man even the Apaches didn't like.

"I want to talk to agent Tiffany."

Free made no reply. He started walking for a newly built frame structure with several windows along each side. It had a small porch in the front and was rectangular in shape.

"Is this a church?" asked Felton.

"Schoolhouse," replied Free as he stepped onto the porch. "Apache no like. Fat agent make his house. He no like adobe."

Free knocked on the door and stepped back. His face was unreadable.

A man of medium height opened the door. His hair was thinning above a short forehead. His mustache was thick and long. He wore a buttoned suit vest stretched to the breaking point over a white shirt. A napkin was tucked into a starched collar. His skin was pale, eyes sickly. He would tip the scales at three hundred pounds.

"Good day," said Tiffany. He pulled the napkin from his shirt collar. Around it was a black bow tie. "What can I do for you?"

"My name is Fargo. Your clerk sent me over."

"Yes. Mr. Dodge."

"I want to take a look at your brand book. I'm an Arizona Ranger."

Tiffany opened the door wider. "Come in. Come in Mr. Fargo. It is cooler inside. Mickey, tell Mr. Dodge to bring the brand records."

Felton stepped inside the schoolhouse. A large woven rug covered half the wooden floor. All the furniture was arranged around the edge of the single room. The furnishings were modest.

"How long have you been an Indian Agent?" asked Felton, noticing a large Bible on top of a dresser.

"I was appointed by the Dutch Reformed Church two years ago. I'm a Methodist myself, but I felt it was my Christian duty to offer my services."

"My father was a preacher," said Felton dryly.

"You must be a good Christian," smiled Tiffany.

"I suppose I'm Christian but I sure as hell am not a good one. I tend to fall more in the category of reformed heretic."

Tiffany's eyes widened at the comment. He blinked several times as if trying to digest the apparent contradiction.

"So you were here," continued Felton. "When Geronimo jumped last year?"

"Yes. It was perfectly dreadful. There was a troublemaking rascal, a medicine man that caused all the unrest. He's gone now and we've had no outbreaks since. These are good Indians."

"Are you missing any?"

"Missing? Missing any Apaches? Why of course not. They stay on the reservation."

Felton looked round the room. There was no sign of extravagance. If the agent was embezzling money, he was hiding it well. "If you come up missing three bucks, don't leave a candle in the window. They won't be coming back."

"Oh?"

"I killed them."

Before the agent could respond, the door opened and Dodge came inside. There had been no knock. He walked over to Felton. Poorly concealing his smugness, Dodge handed over the brand book.

"The brands are listed by the date they came in. I'm sure you'll find nothing out of order."

Felton took the book and smiled. "I heard that some Double Eagle cows were seen in Globe a month or so back. Cows that were sold to the agency for milk."

Dodge was unmoved. Tiffany reacted quickly. "A month ago, you say? It sounds familiar. You will have to excuse me. I have been absent most of the time since June. I've been ill. I've just returned this week and am leaving shortly. Mr. Dodge has had to run the agency in my stead.

"Mr. Dodge can you shed some light on this?"

Pointing to the book, Dodge said, "If you check the records you will see the cows came in and were recorded. We purchased the stock thinking some squaws could be enticed to try feeding their babies with cows milk as white women are starting to do. They would have nothing to do with it so I sold them to Globe. We made a handsome profit and the funds were used to buy more flour from farms in Tucson."

Felton held onto the record book but did not open it. He glanced at Tiffany then at Dodge. His gut told him Dodge was guilty of something. Tiffany was another matter. He was either a good liar or very stupid.

Handing the book back to Dodge, Felton said, "Sorry to have wasted your time, gentlemen. I have what I came for."

Dodge took the book. "Make sure Free rides off the reservation with you. You seem to be a known man to some of the bucks out there…we wouldn't want anything to happen to you."

Looking down at the little man, Felton's eyes hardened at what sounded like a veiled threat. "I'll do that…him I trust."

Felton walked to the front door and opened it. Before stepping out, he turned back and looked at the agent. "Mr. Tiffany."

"Yes?"

"Are you familiar with Proverbs 11:1?"

Tiffany's brow wrinkled for a moment. "A false balance is an abomination to the Lord."

The smirk on Dodge's face disappeared. Felton smiled but said nothing. He shut the door behind him. The clerk was lying about the milk cows and the brand book. Tiffany's Bible wasn't just for show but he could still be a willing participant. Most likely he was a pawn.

Now there were at least three names. Tribolett, Turner, and Dodge would have allies, but for now they were enough to form the framework of a ring. Bricela was right.

Free was squatting on his heals in the shade of a storehouse when Felton came back outside. He stood and waited for Felton to approach. He held a melon-size stone in one hand. When Felton came along side, Free offered him the rock.

"What's that for?" asked Felton.

"To eat. It is white man's flour."

"Flour?"

"These come in sacks with flour. Must be flour. White man no give rock to Apache. Must be flour."

Taking the stone from Free, Felton estimated the weight at eight to ten pounds. Almost a fifth of a fifty-pound allotment was being stolen. "How many of these come in the sacks."

"Many come, each wagon load. They take to scale, then give to Apaches."

"Where does the flour come from?"

"Tucson. Everything come from Tucson."

"Do you know any names of the men that bring the flour?"

"No names. Just white mans. Always same mans bring wagon."

"Is one of them a big man, a strong man? Is he bigger than me?"

"No. No big man come with wagon. Sometime big man come on horse. Big like bear."

"Have you seen him up close?"

"I see."

Felton pointed just above his eye. "Does he have a scar here?"

"Has scars. You know this mans?"

"I gave him the scars."

Free looked Felton over for several seconds. "You no have *mucho* scars. You hit Bearman with war club?"

"No," said Felton, dropping the stone. "Agent Tiffany wants you to ride with me until I am off the reservation. I'm ready to go."

Mounting his horse, Felton followed Free back to the line of waiting Apaches. Looking at them now, it was hard to believe they were among the toughest and most brutal fighters the world had ever known. Looks, like so many things, were deceiving. If the conditions were right and the opportunity arose, these same men and women would terrorize every human being living in New Mexico, Arizona, and Northern Mexico. No ranch, village, or traveler in thousands of square miles would be safe. Cheating an Apache was the surest way known to cause an outbreak.

The cruelty of the Apaches was unimaginable. Felton had witnessed firsthand scenes the human mind could not invoke in its worst nightmares. Anyone intentionally fomenting the rage of Apaches was guilty of inciting torture and murder. The law might not see it that way but law was never perfect. It was a tool, not a religion. Useful for the most part, but not to be worshiped.

Free rode up beside Felton. "*Tats-ah-das-aygo* help Apache?"

A jolt went through Felton. Help an Apache? The thought was revolting. For twenty years he wished they were all dead. Evil undoubtedly roamed the earth but in Arizona it walked on two legs and wore turned up moccasins.

Felton swallowed hard. These Apaches were on the reservation. At least this time they remained when they could have jumped. Some, no doubt, wished they had gone on the raid to share in the gore and plunder...but they had stayed. Now they were being rewarded with a bitter taste of the white man's greed.

"Some white men are almost as bad as Apaches," said Felton. "I'm going to kill a few of them to keep your people on this reservation. That's all there is to it."

The two men started riding slowly past the destitute Indians. Felton could not help but notice several adults pointing him out to their small children as they rode by.

"They tell the little ones," offered Free. "You are killer of many Apache. A great warrior. You have big medicine. It an honor to see you...and to kill you some day maybe."

"Nits turn to lice," muttered Felton.

Free snorted. "Maybe they get big, take white man road. Learn to cheat heap good. Maybe nits turn to whites."

Turning to Free, Felton glared at him for several seconds. "Not all white men cheat."

"Not all Apache bad," returned Free.

Felton started to speak but his mind drew a blank. Could an Apache, any Apache, ever be anything *but* bad?

Sheriff Mosby pushed his way through the batwing doors of the Palace Saloon. It was long past noon and he was hungry. Lony Drake was a good man to have as deputy but was cocky and too sure of himself. He was supposed to come back to the office after he had his lunch. Instead of relieving him as he was told, Drake was leaning against the bar talking to his sweetheart. How the deputy could court a whore was something Mosby never understood.

The sheriff walked over to Drake. Mosby was good with a gun but the kid was faster and deadlier. It was best to go easy on him.

"Time for you to head back, Lony. I got to eat."

"Sure, sheriff," said Drake. He smiled but there was no humor in it. "I was just sayin' goodbye to Liz."

Noticing the cameo around her neck, Mosby tipped his hat. "Liz. How are you today?"

The young woman was round faced and thick waisted. She tipped her chin back, exposing the cameo of the Medusa. "See what Lony brung me? It's so purty."

"Looks real nice, Liz," said Mosby. He noticed Turner coming into the saloon along with his accountant. "Excuse me. I've got to talk to Mr. Turner. I'll see you back at the office, Lony."

Turner and his assistant were taking a seat at a table when Mosby pulled up a chair next to them.

"When did you get in?" asked Turner.

"Last night. We got the cattle back to Bricela late last night."

"Where'd you find them?"

"We trailed them to Tribolett's whiskey camp up at Romero Springs. Some Mexican stole them and was trying to sell them."

"One Mexican...alone?"

"Yep. A greedy one from what Tribolett tells me."

"What do you mean, greedy?"

Mosby shook his head and leaned back in his chair. He grinned. "The damned greaser killed three Apaches then slugged Tribolett. When Tribolett woke up he was tied to a wagon wheel and his feet set on fire. Well almost anyway. He claims he talked his way out of being burned. He was swearing like a teamster when we cut him loose."

Turner glared at Mosby. "And?"

"The Mexican thinks he can horn in on the rustling. Tribolett gave him your name to keep from being burned. I expect you'll be hearing from him. He told Tribolett he was taking over and for Tribolett to get out of the Territory."

For a moment Turner said nothing. "What'd he look like?"

"Mustache, hair cut short. Six feet tall, maybe one-eighty. He spoke pretty good American and rode a black horse. He wore two pistols. One had ivory or bone grips."

"Anything else?"

"Let's see," muttered Mosby as he scratched is jaw. "Well, Tribolett said the Apaches knew him. That's why he killed all three of them. Said it was an old grudge or some such."

"If he shows up," said the accountant. "I say we kill him. We don't know him and we can't trust outsiders. There's too much at stake."

"Nobody will miss a greaser," agreed Turner. "I don't want my name being tossed around by strangers."

Mosby nodded agreeably. "As soon as you figure out who he is, point him out to me."

"Not you," said Turner. "Not unless you can do it outside of Tucson. If it comes to a shootout here in town, have your deputy do it. No man wears two pistols unless he's a gunman. No use for you to take any chances. Tell that fool kid to make it look legal. That's what keeps us in the money."

Avoiding Oro Canyon, Felton returned to Tucson by taking the stage road to Globe and then to Florence. The trip took an extra day but following the same trail twice in wild country was a good way to end up dead.

Instead of riding into Tucson after midnight, Felton stopped at Nine Mile Water Hole just east of town. He would sleep there until it was light enough to see. For what lay ahead he wanted to be well rested.

After watering and picketing his horse, Felton made a small fire and sat down on his blanket. Taking his last piece of jerky from his saddlebags, he stared into the flames.

It was only a matter of time before someone discovered his true identity. Either Turner or Mosby would figure it out. When they did, all hell would break loose. So far, the only one in Tucson connected with the ring and the threats made on Bricela was Turner. Before Turner was killed, he would have to name the others in the ring. If he could be enticed out of Tucson, getting him to talk would be easy...and satisfying.

For several minutes Felton chewed on his last bite of jerky. He uncorked his canteen and washed it down with warm water. Using the tip of his boot, he shoveled sand over the fire and watched the smoke rise into the night air. Tomorrow men were going to die.

CHAPTER 14

At first light, Felton rolled out of his blanket and started gathering pieces of ocotillo skeleton to build another fire. Lifting a large piece of wood, he uncovered a three-inch scorpion. When it opened its pincers and threateningly raised its venemous tail, Felton suddenly remembered something Mickey Free had said the day before. Riding away from the Indians at the reservation, Free claimed the Apaches thought he possessed big medicine. The words echoed in his mind as he walked away from the *escorpion* and knelt down to start his fire. Just before he dropped a palm full of coffee into his battered tin cup, the words of Owl Woman resurfaced from his buried memories.

She had said he had medicine. She said the same of Bricela. Though no white man could understand what an Indian meant by "medicine," it was supposedly there nonetheless. Was this the same medicine the Apaches referred to? If it was, what was it?

Felton placed the cup on a flat rock next to the fire to heat. As the water simmered, he thought of the whiskey camp, the agate brooch on the woman's coat and the ivory brooch he wore around his neck. His brooch had two eagles scrimshawed on it. The pistol he used to kill the Apaches had two eagles carved on ivory grips. There was a Double Eagle brand on Bricela's cattle. If old Soleil's mermaid was the same as "a woman that lives in the big water," everything that Owl Woman predicted, in some respect, had come to pass.

The old woman had said they would be like two eagles soaring together but never landing. If he and Bricela were those eagles and if they ever had soared together, it was in Old Tucson and then only briefly. One thing rang true. They had never been together for long nor did it look as if they ever would be.

Felton pushed the foolish sentiments from his mind and rolled his blanket. He needed coffee. It was no time to be daydreaming about the past.

As usual, the loaded shotgun was concealed in the blanket. He would have to keep his horse near him in case it was needed. Besides

Turner, there were at least two other men he had to worry about. One was tall. The other wore two guns and favored using his left hand.

Going to the fire, Felton took the boiling cup and set it on the sand to settle. The smell of coffee and camp smoke was one of the few pleasures he enjoyed. He was nothing like the carousing Confederate lieutenant that once rode into Tucson. What he had become since that regretful day wasn't much better. But what he did, what he did so well, was for Bricela Verde.

In the shadows of the San Xavier Mission he swore her suffering would count for something. The last twenty years were spent fulfilling that oath. This day, however, Bricela would discover once and for all, who and what he was.

Caleb Felton killed the Apaches that ravaged the woman he loved. Carlos Fuentes protected her from disgrace. But it was Conway Fargo that Bricela had sent for and Conway Fargo that trailed The Ring. Revenge was a sin but the law was ordained. And as far as Texans were concerned, a Ranger was the fiery hand of God Almighty.

Felton glanced eastward toward Tucson. He would face at least two dangerous men and should have more of a plan. But this morning was different than others. For the first time he wondered how much of his survival over the years was due to planning and how much to fate. If Owl Woman actually saw something that day at San Xavier, she would only have been a bystander, an unexplainable witness to a plot yet to unfold.

There were times in the solitude of a desert night that Felton thought he sensed something stirring in the darkness, a presence that slowly surrounded him, then silently moved on. Was it merely imagination induced by extended periods of loneliness or were there forces at work just beyond the sight of man? Was there such a thing as fate?

Was it only coincidence that he was returning to Tucson on the same road, from the same direction to see the same woman he had two decades before? Were the circumstances that had brought him back to Bricela beyond his control? If they were, if there was a grand design to his life, his planning was of little consequence.

If fate was a reality, no bullet could kill him before his time. Geronimo and Custer had said as much. Others he knew had come to the same conclusion. Had those men felt the same forces stealing through the night? Had they also heard the whispering that haunts a tortured mind?

Felton went to his coffee and took a careful sip from the steaming cup. The sun would be up in an hour. He would go to the sheriff's office first. It would set things in motion. From there he would play it by ear.

Most of the detailed plans he made over the years changed within a few seconds anyway. It was the ability to think on one's feet, the instinct to react that set most gunfighters and lawmen apart. It was a talent that few men had.

After the sheriff's office, he would go to the Palace and have breakfast. Jesus Elias should be told what was happening. If there were any Arizona Rangers in town, they would come in handy in case of backshooters. Al Sieber would likely have a hangover, but even then, he was one of the toughest men in the Territory. They all could help. If a ring did exist, Turner would have plenty of men to protect it.

As he took another drink of coffee, Felton rubbed his chest. The scar left by the branding felt raw to the touch. Turner had enjoyed burning him and would have killed him if the rest of the Union cavalry had not arrived.

Turner was a member of the Indian Ring. He wore a business suit instead of Yankee sergeant stripes, but he was as treacherous as he ever was. He carried at least one hidden gun and likely a knife or two. He had to be watched.

Bricela was suspicious of Cade Mosby. If he was in The Ring or paid by it, he would have to be dealt with sooner or later. Unlike Turner, however, he was a born coward. He had been twenty years ago and his kind never changed. Mosby tried to murder him outside the Shoo Fly as a teenager and would try the same thing again if given the chance.

For a moment Felton watched the fire die and enjoyed his coffee. A warm gust of wind lifted a wisp of smoke and carried it away. This could be his last day alive and then he too could vanish. If he died for Bricela, his death would count for something. He had lived over fifty years. He had wasted ten of them. Then he met Bricela. He owed her for the wrong he had done to her and for turning his useless life around. She had saved his soul from hell.

Felton smiled and drank the last of his coffee. If he died today, it would be an honor. But deep inside, he knew this was not to be that day.

The sun was still behind the Santa Catarina Mountains when Felton rode into Tucson and back to the stables. Getting rid of the sombrero and *serape*, he retrieved his hat and remounted. The streets he rode down were busy with whites and Mexicans. It was the first of September and everyone was trying to get their chores done before the heat of midday arrived. It would be well over one hundred degrees before noon.

Felton tied his horse in front of the sheriff's office and went inside. A young man sat at the desk. His hair was tangled from sleeping on it. He cupped a mug of coffee with both hands. His eyes were bloodshot. They narrowed with irritation as Felton entered. "What is it?" grumbled the deputy.

"I'm looking for Sheriff Mosby."

"He ain't up this early. Won't be in 'til after sunup."

"Are you a deputy?"

"Yeah. The name is Drake."

"Well, do me a favor, Deputy," said Felton. He watched Drake closely. "Tell the sheriff Caleb Felton is in town and would like to ask him a few questions. I'll be down at the Palace having breakfast."

Drake's eyes flickered with recognition. It was obvious he had heard the name before. "I'll tell him."

A thought occurred to Felton. "When I knew Cade he was just a kid. I suppose he grew up some since then. How big is he nowadays?"

"The sheriff's six-three in his stocking feet."

"That tall, eh?" Felton nodded and reached for the door. "Much obliged, Deputy."

Drake spoke up quickly. "Don't see many men wearing two pistols." Drake's tone held a challenge. "I hope you're not looking for no trouble."

Opening the door, Felton paused and turned. "I never look for more than I can handle, Deputy but today I'm feeling kind of lucky."

After mounting the stallion, Felton glanced at the office window. Drake was standing next to it watching him. The deputy wore no pistols and was scarcely more than five foot seven. He held his coffee cup with his left hand.

Reining the black out into the street, Felton thought of the two men he had seen at Tribolett's camp. One was tall, the other short and very likely left handed. Bricela had suspected Mosby was involved with The Ring. However, considering what lay ahead, he had to be sure.

Felton dismounted in front of the Palace. The smell of fried ham hung in the still morning air. After looking over his shoulder he tied his horse. He should get word to Jesus that he was back in town but that could wait until after breakfast.

The saloon was nearly empty. Felton walked to the far corner before taking a table. He wanted his back to the wall and a view of anyone that came through the batwing doors.

The cook came out of the back room carrying a pot of coffee and a cup. Felton ordered steak with eggs and was blowing on the rim of his tin cup when Al Sieber pushed his way through the swinging doors.

Sieber stepped inside the saloon and stopped. He yawned and stretched before recognizing Felton. He nodded and started walking to the rear table. "Howdy, Conway. Mind if I join you?"

"Have a seat. I just ordered breakfast."

Sieber sat down and yelled to the cook for more coffee.

"Hangover?" asked Felton.

"No. I been sober for three days. I'll be going to work directly."

"Scouting?"

"Sure enough. I hear the Army's going down to Mexico after Geronimo."

"When do you go?"

"Don't know," said Sieber. He waited for the cook to pour his coffee and leave. "I ain't been hired yet but I will be. An old friend of ours is coming to Fort Lowell."

"Who would that be?"

Sieber grinned and sipped his coffee. "Wilcox is being replaced on account of last year's outbreak. General Crook is coming back. He'll be Departmental Commander again."

"He's the best Indian fighter the Army's got," agreed Felton. "When he left Arizona ten years ago everything was quiet. All the Apaches were behaving."

"You know how he is, Conway. The first thing he'll do is want to hear the Apache's side of it. He always gives 'em a fair shake before he sets out to kill 'em."

Felton drank his coffee and thought for a moment. Crook was a fair man but ruthless when necessary. His only interest was peace. Justice was of no concern to him. No matter what the Apaches did, no matter how atrocious, Crook considered it an act of war. He was too forgiving. At least he understood the Apache mind.

"You know as well as I do," said Felton. "An Apache doesn't need much of an excuse to go off the reservation and raid. I don't know what caused Geronimo to leave. I do know others are about to join him if things don't change."

"You learn something from that Tribolett character?" asked Sieber.

"He gave me a name. I went to San Carlos to see what I could find out about some stolen cattle. I may not be able to prove it, but I know the Indians are being cheated. Any fool could see it if they made half an effort to investigate."

"Damn those agents to hell. How bad is it this time?"

"The cattle scales are doctored. There are rocks in the wheat bags. Some of the meat they're issued is almost rotten and the best beef goes to the agent and his men. You can bet the agency is buying stolen cows at dirt-cheap prices and reporting top dollar cost to the government. I'm sure there's more going on. Somebody out there is getting rich. They don't care that whites and Mexicans are being slaughtered by renegades in the meantime."

Sieber sourly shook his head. "I seen it before. As long as the government keeps on sendin' thieves to run the reservations, we ain't never goin' to have no peace."

"The whites doing the cheating are no better than the renegades. They all need to be hung."

"You thinkin' Tiffany is the ring leader?" asked Sieber.

Felton leaned back in his chair. His brow wrinkled. "I don't know. He could be. I'd bet my bottom dollar his clerk is in on it. His name is Dodge. He keeps the books. That's what makes everything so hard to prove. I'm sure the books will add up right."

"Is Dodge the name Tribolett give you?"

"No." Felton leaned forward and spoke softly. "The name he gave me was Turner."

Sieber leaned in close. "Turner!" he said in a half whisper.

"I saw two others through my field glasses but I haven't identified either one of them yet. They're here in Tucson. They work together. One tall, one short."

"You goin' after Turner?"

"I am."

"He's a big man in Tucson. Lot's of friends. That includes the local law."

"Figured it that way."

"You beat all, Conway. You best wait 'til there's some Rangers in town. They's all out right now."

"Can't. I already opened the ball. It started this morning."

Sieber drank some more coffee as the cook set a plate of food down in front of Felton. When the cook had gone, Sieber looked casually around the saloon. A few more customers had come in but the room was mostly empty.

"You be careful with Turner. He carries a pistol in his pants pocket. He's been known to put his hand inside and shoot without even bringin' the gun out. It's a dirty trick if you ask me but he gets away with it.

"A year ago he beat a man with his fists so bad that he went off and died. Turner likes to brawl no holds barred. You see how big he is. He's forty-odd years old but he's still tough as boot leather. He'll go two hundred and forty pounds if he's an ounce."

Felton chewed on his steak and said nothing. He beat Turner in a fight once before but the sergeant had been caught off guard by some skillfully placed jabs. He would not be so easy to beat a second time.

"You'd be best to just shoot him first chance you get. Whatever you do, don't let him get too close to you. Stay out of his reach. Watch that hand goin' into his pocket."

Swallowing his mouthful, Felton pointed at his plate with his fork. "You going to eat anything?"

"No," said Sieber setting his cup down. He slapped a dime down on the table. "That's all I got. I done run out of money. I'm ridin' out to Fort Lowell to eat for free. Crook'll be along any time. When he hears what you just told me he'll be askin' for you."

"I'll be in town."

"He'll want to sign you up for six months. There ain't many of us scouts that can do the job like he wants. The general will remember you from the Tonto Campaign."

"How far is Fort Lowell from Tucson?" asked Felton as Sieber stood.

"Four or five miles, I reckon."

"Tell the general...tell him I might be interested if I'm assigned to Fort Lowell. I kind of like Tucson."

"I favor Fort Apache, myself," said Sieber. "I'll tell him for you. You be careful."

"Always am."

Watching Sieber go, Felton wondered how Bricela would react if he were to stay in Arizona. It would be good to see her from time to time. More importantly, he could be nearby if she needed his help. Until The Ring was dissolved and the Apaches brought in, no one would be safe. Tucson was where he could do the most good.

On the other hand, she had not been especially friendly when they met. He was hoping their reunion would be more sentimental. It bordered on the impersonal. She had hired him because he had been recommended by the Pinkertons. She might have done that strictly out of desperation. Maybe that was all it was. She had no other choice but to see him again.

If she hated him, no one would blame her. Perhaps it was best to do what he could, then leave. She had a husband and a ranch now. She was protecting her home and business by hiring Conway Fargo. Fargo was nothing like the man she once knew.

A hostess came down the stairs and made her way around the occupied tables. Her powdered cheeks looked sickly white. Her lips were painted bright red. "Hello, stranger," she said smiling. "After that big breakfast you'll need a drink...or if it's too early for whiskey, maybe you'd be interested in something else?"

"Ham and eggs will do me. And I'll stick with coffee."

"I'll bet you like it strong and black."

Felton looked up at her for the first time. His eyes came to focus on the jewelry hanging from her neck. "You're right. Strong enough to float a horseshoe."

"My name is Liz. If there's anything else you want...anything at all...just ask."

Gazing at the brooch she wore, Felton asked casually, "What's that you have around your neck? It sure is a pretty piece."

Liz put her hand to the brooch. "I just got it last night. The pin on the back was busted. Lony made it into a necklace for me so I could wear it."

"Lony?"

"Lony Drake. He's a deputy sheriff here in Tucson. I think he's sweet on me. He said the woman's face that's carved on this necklace reminded him of me."

"It's a Medusa."

"A what?"

Studying the innocent eyes of the saloon girl, Felton smiled. She had no idea the brooch belonged to a murdered woman. "A Greek goddess."

"Oh, that Lony," sighed Liz, turning for the kitchen. "He's so romantic."

Felton watched her go. Lony Drake had to have taken that Medusa from the wagon at Tribolett's camp. Mosby could have been the man with him. The flash seen coming off the tall man's chest might have been a sheriff's badge.

Two men trailed the stolen cattle to Tribolett. If they were Drake and Mosby, releasing Tribolett from the wagon wheel was simply part of their duty as lawmen. The three dead Apaches would be of no particular concern to a Tucson sheriff, either. But after talking to Tribolett, the pair went to the wagon stolen by the Apaches. Fresh blood covered the wagon seat and personal letters lay in plane sight. With those letters in hand, it would have been easy to determine who had been murdered.

However, instead of gathering the letters and confiscating the stolen wagon, the two riders took what they wanted from the wagon and left. Why Drake and another man came for the cows was a mystery but both were as dirty as Tribolett.

Cade Mosby yawned and opened the door of his office. Drake was pacing the floor with both pistols strapped on and tied down.

"What's got you all fired up?" asked Mosby. He yawned again as he shut the door behind him. "The day hasn't even started yet."

"The man you been waiting for is here. He come in here a half hour ago. He don't look a damn thing like a sporting man to me. He's a gunfighter if ever I saw one."

Mosby blinked and stood more erect. He was suddenly awake. "You mean Caleb Felton?"

Drake stopped pacing. "That's the name. He's wearing two smoke wagons. One has ivory grips. He looks like he's hell on wheels."

"You sure he said Caleb Felton? What'd he look like?"

"Black hair with some gray in it. Black eyes. Around six foot. I suppose the women would say he was good lookin'. He rode a black stallion with a Z brand."

The skin on Mosby's face tightened and paled. "One of the pistols...did you see anything else about those ivory grips?"

"I could see the head of an eagle carved on one side."

Mosby rubbed the back of his neck. "He's going to be more trouble than I thought."

"Let me handle him," sneered Drake. "That old man won't stand a chance."

Still rubbing his neck but more vigorously, Mosby asked, "What did he say?"

"Said he would be at the Palace and he wanted to see you."

"What for?"

"Didn't say."

Mosby went to a gun rack and took down a Winchester rifle. "You go to the saloon and keep an eye on him. I'm going to talk to Turner and see how he wants to handle this."

Drake watched Mosby fumble with a box of cartridges. "You scared of this Felton?"

"I'm afraid of nobody!" snapped Mosby. "You know who runs this town. I've got to find Turner. He has to be told, that's all. I'll kill Felton if I have to."

"All the same," muttered Drake as he went for the door. "If he crosses me, I'm goin' to plug him."

Liz picked up the empty plate from Felton's table. "Want any more coffee?"

"No thanks. One cup is all I want this morning."

"Somethin' special about this mornin'?"

Felton took in a deep breath and let it out slowly. "It's a day that's taken twenty years to get here. I'd say that makes it the most special day of my life."

For a moment the words confused Liz. Before she spoke again the batwing doors swung open. Lony Drake stepped into the saloon. This time he had a pistol on each hip.

"There he is now," said Felton.

Liz turned. Felton placed a silver dollar on the table and stood. He stepped clear of the chair and picked up his hat as if he was about to leave.

Drake stopped fifteen feet in front of Felton. Liz went to his side and put her arm in his.

"You are so romantic, Lony."

The deputy's eyes locked on Felton. They were full of eagerness. "Why's that, Liz?"

"Cause this necklace has a Greek goddess on it and you said it reminded you of me."

"A what?"

Pointing to Felton, Liz said, "He said it was a...a..."

"Medusa," offered Felton. He put on his hat and tugged it down tight.

"What the hell is a Medusa?" demanded Lony.

"For one thing...it's something you never paid for."

Drake eased away from Liz. "What does that mean?"

"It means...Deputy...that you stole it."

Drake's eyes ignited with fury. "You callin' me a thief?"

The few men seated in the saloon jumped from their chairs and hurried outside. Some could be heard yelling as they ran down the street. Others stopped and peered in from the front windows.

"Both you and your partner are thieves. I saw you at Tribolett's whiskey camp...where I had left him tied up."

"Me and the sheriff had business to attend to," blustered Drake. "Besides, Tribolett said it was a damned Mexican that got the drop on him."

"So it was you and the sheriff in that canyon."

Drake glanced at Felton's pistols, then at his brown eyes.

Felton's stare grew cold. "El jornada del muerte es para usted, amigo. Vaya con Dios."

Drake's left hand flinched and Felton palmed his Colt. Both guns came up and exploded at the same instant. Drake's lead splintered the wall just to the right of Felton's ear. Without thinking, Felton thumbed back the hammer of his Colt and fired a second time.

Drake looked down at his chest. He put his palm over two holes in the center of his shirt. Without raising his head, he fell backwards onto the hardwood floor.

Liz backed away. She held her hand over her mouth but did not scream. Nor did she cry.

Felton turned to the bartender who had rushed out of the kitchen into the saloon.

"When the sheriff gets here tell him I'm waiting for him in the old plaza. I'll be at the same place where he tried to get me once before."

From the second story of Turner's Dry Goods, Sheriff Mosby heard two shots. He was half a block from the Palace Hotel. "Did you hear that?"

Turner wiped shaving cream from his bull neck. "Hear what?"

"It sounded like shooting."

"That's nothing new in Tucson," said Turner. "We have a man for breakfast almost every day."

Mosby went to the open window and looked out. He suddenly ducked back in. "He's coming down the street."

"Who is?"

"Felton. The man I was just talking about."

Tossing his towel on a dresser, Turner walked to the window and drew the curtains back. "Which one is he?"

Pointing at Felton as he drew nearer, Mosby said, "That one. The one with the two pistols. That's Caleb Felton. He's older now, but I'd recognize him anywhere."

Turner pulled the curtains open for a better look. "That's not Felton. That's Conway Fargo. He got a hair cut since I met him but I'm sure that's Fargo."

"The one with the pistols!" demanded Mosby. "Look again. He's wearing two pistols. That one."

"That's who I *am* looking at, dammit. That's Conway Fargo. He's a Texas Ranger."

"If he told you that," said Mosby. "He was lying. I've known him since the war. He was one of the Confederates that took over Tucson before you got here. He was a lieutenant and a friend of Bricela Wetham. Only then she was Bricela Verde."

Turner rested both his massive hands on the window sill and stared at Felton until he was out of sight. Pulling his head back inside the room, he glared at Mosby for several seconds. "You say he was here in Tucson with the Rebels, Hunter's men?"

"He rode in with Captain Hunter. That was February of sixty-two."

Turner scratched at his jaw. His eyes narrowed for several seconds. "Now I remember who he reminds me of."

"Who?"

"A damned Mexican spy we captured during the war. We ran him down at the San Xavier Mission. I branded the son of a bitch over at the whipping post. This Felton or Fargo, who ever he is, looks a lot like him."

"No!" blurted Mosby. "You caught a *spy*...at the Papago mission?"

"Yeah. So what?"

"It can't be...It just can't," muttered Mosby. "They can't be the same."

"What are you dribbling about now?"

"The Mexicans and Papagos have told a story around Tucson for twenty years. I thought it was just something they used for their kids. According to the story, a man taken from their mission and branded was some kind of hero. The way they tell it, after he was branded, he went into the mountains and killed a hundred Apaches. That couldn't have been Felton you took. The story says he was a Mexican, a Mexican they called...Carlos Fuentes."

"Fuentes!" boomed Turner. "Hell, that's it. Fuentes. That was the spy's name."

Mosby sat down on the bed. He shook his head. "*You* were the one that branded Carlos Fuentes. I thought the branding was only part of their story."

"Who cares about Fuentes anyway? We sent him to Yuma Prison. No one ever heard of him after that."

"The Mexicans and Papagos sure as hell did. He became a legend."

"That's just a lot of bull and you know it."

Mosby's shoulders slumped. "They say Fuentes rescued a beautiful señorita from the Apaches. He killed them by cutting their heads off with his knife."

Turner laughed. "Cut off their heads with a knife? That's crazy."

"You know who it was that Fuentes was supposed to have saved?"

"Suppose you tell me," mocked Turner.

Mosby slowly raised his head. "The rumor is that it was Bricela Verde. She's now Bricela Wetham."

Bricela's name sobered the Yankee sergeant. His cockiness was gone. He rubbed a scar above his eye and tried to think.

"Bricela was only a kid," said Mosby. "She liked Felton. Felton liked her. It all fits."

"Caleb Felton...Carlos Fuentes...Conway Fargo...Damn! You could be right. CF, CF, and CF. They could all be the same man."

"If he *is* Fargo as well as Fuentes," said Mosby. "We have to kill him as fast as we can. Fargo has a reputation as a cold-blooded killer. He doesn't take you to jail. Nobody knows how many men he's buried and I don't intend to be one of them."

"He's got no reason to come after you. Besides, you're the sheriff of Tucson and a respectable citizen. Don't worry. We can get him before he even gets suspicious."

A knock came at the door and Turner answered it. It was the bartender from the Palace.

"What is it?"

"Somebody just shot Drake. He's dead. Beat him to the draw in a fair fight and shot him twice before he hit the floor."

"Who? Who shot him?"

"Don't know his name. He said to tell the sheriff he'd be waiting in the old plaza. He said something about being where the sheriff tried something one time. I don't know what he meant by it. He didn't say."

Turner looked over his shoulder and stared at Mosby. "Well?"

"It's Felton," admitted Mosby. "I took a shot at him one night after a dance."

"Now he killed Drake...in a fair fight?"

"He has my pistol. He took it off me the night I tried to kill him."

"If that's why he's after you," mused Turner. "I've got nothing to do with it. He's got nothing against me."

"You branded him."

Turner hesitated. "That was war. He's a sworn Texas Ranger now. The war is over. He won't come after me. We don't even know if he's after you. Maybe he just wants to tell his side of the shooting. We don't even know what the fight was about."

The bartender spoke up. "It was on account of a necklace Lony gave Liz. That's what she told me, anyhow."

"They were fighting over a woman?" asked Turner.

"Not exactly. Liz said the man that shot Lony first called him a thief. Claimed he saw him steal the necklace from a wagon...then it was, the name of Tribolett come up."

Mosby came to his feet. "Tribolett? What did he say about him?"

The bartender frowned. "The man said he seen Lony take the necklace when he was at Tribolett's whiskey camp."

"Anything else," asked Turner.

"That's all I know. Said he saw him take it."

For a moment Turner said nothing as his mind worked quickly. "Who all saw the shooting?"

"Liz was the closest. Everybody else that saw was outside looking through the windows. Liz was maybe ten feet away."

"Good. You tell Liz to say Fargo drew first."

"Fargo?"

"Yeah. Use the name Fargo. He's known as a gunman. Work the people up about it. Say it was murder. Tell them we're forming a posse to hang Fargo."

Turner closed the door and went back to the window. He looked down on the street. "What happened out at Tribolett's camp?"

"Me and Lony trailed Bricela's cattle out there. We found three dead Apaches in the sand and Tribolett tied to a wagon wheel. Somebody had started a fire around his feet and was going to burn him...it had to be Felton who did that. After we untied Tribolett, we went to see what the Apaches had brought in. That's when Lony took the brooch. Felton must have been watching."

"Felton made it look like the steers were stolen, then drove them to Tribolett?"

Mosby nodded. "Tribolett thought he was a Mexican just like you did. He said it was the Mexican that killed the Apaches."

"Why did Felton burn Tribolett?"

"To get him to talk...to talk about stolen cattle maybe."

Turner's face flushed red. "What did he tell Felton?"

"He thought he was dealing with a no-account Mexican, someone we would kill when he came to you to ask for a cut."

"Come to me?"

"Tribolett said you were in charge of the rustling. Conway Fargo is after you, too."

CHAPTER 15

Felton ran his finger across the old adobe wall where Mosby's pistol ball had left its mark. The deep chip was head high. That night his aim was only a few inches wide of its target. The pistols were cap and ball then, but just as deadly as brass cartridges. In the dark and at more than fifty feet, it was an excellent shot. But nobody was shooting back.

Most men lost their nerve in a head-to-head battle. Their shots went wild. Mosby was more of a backshooter. If he came to the plaza now he would not come alone. His type was only courageous with a crowd behind him.

A horse's hooves broke the silence. Someone was riding hard. They were coming into Tucson from the east. Felton levered a round into his Winchester and leaned it against the adobe.

A rider on a lathered bay horse turned sharply off Main Street and on to Alameda. Dirt flew from the hooves as the horse plunged across the Plaza de las Armas. It was Jesus Elias.

Elias leaned back and the snorting stallion slid to a stop ten feet in front of Felton. "I see you're still riding those crowbait horses," said Felton.

Pulling a rifle from the saddle scabbard, Elias grinned and dismounted. "When this is over, amigo, I will show you and your cayuse what my stallion's backside looks like."

After taking a box of shells and a canteen from his horse, Elias slapped its rump and sent in galloping away.

"I just heard," said Elias. "Word is spreading fast. I sent a vaquero to San Xavier for help."

"What have you heard?"

Elias looked at the abandoned Shoo Fly. The walls were thick, bulletproof. "The sheriff is asking for a posse to come after you. They say there will be no trial for killing the deputy."

"What's Turner doing? Is he involved in it?"

"Yes. They are both at the Palace. Turner is buying drinks to give his men courage. Some of them have heard of you. It will take some time before they are brave enough."

"What are you shooting?" asked Felton.

".44's. Both pistol and rifle. I have only my cartridge belt and this box."

Looking off toward town, Felton said, "I have a scattergun inside the saloon. My pistols are .45's. This rifle is a .45-75. We won't be trading any cartridges."

Elias shrugged. "We can hold out until we get help."

"I was told the Rangers are out on a scout. I'm not sure who you think will help us."

"The Papagos will come. They will help Bricela. She is a woman they respect. I told the vaquero to tell them also that Carlos Fuentes needed their help. They will come to see the man they have heard of for so many years."

"That's eighteen miles round trip," said Felton. "That'll take some time."

"You asked if Turner was with the sheriff. Is he part of The Ring?"

"He is. So is Mosby. Drake was in it with the sheriff. There are some more out at San Carlos. I don't know who else in town is part of The Ring. I ran out of time before I could find out.

"Mosby and Turner will put all the pieces together. They'll know who I am and who I was years ago. They'll figure out that I know they're both guilty of cheating the Indians and accomplices to murder. It won't be long until they know Bricela sent for me. The only way to protect her now is to blow the lid off The Ring."

Elias held up his hand, signaling Felton to listen.

Another horse was thundering down Alameda. It suddenly appeared and tore across the plaza at full speed. It jerked to a stop in front of the two men. The rider straddled the saddle but wore a dress. A small leather pouch hung around her neck.

"Good morning, Bricela," smiled Felton.

Bricela glared red faced at Felton. Her horse pawed the dirt and fought the reins. "Caleb! Caleb!...don't smile at me, Caleb Felton!"

Elias dropped his head to hide a smile of his own.

"Yes, ma'am," said Felton. She was even more beautiful when she was angry.

"Sometimes...sometimes Caleb you make me so mad!"

"I have that effect on lots of folks."

Bricela clinched her teeth. "I'm going to Fort Lowell. The military can't let this go on."

Felton shook his head. "They didn't help Billy the Kid last year up in New Mexico. I doubt the Army will interfere in civilian matters here."

"You're not Billy the Kid," snapped Bricela. "You're a Texas Ranger. They have to come. You two will be killed."

"Just in case," said Felton as his smile faded. "Mosby is in The Ring. So is Turner and a man named Dodge at the reservation. That information may get an investigation started. If I don't get a chance, tell that to General Crook. He will be here sooner or later."

"Caleb," pleaded Bricela. "Leave while you still have time. Just go."

Felton looked deeply into Bricela's eyes. "I did that once. I'll never do it again."

There was a long silence as three people shared a communion of memories, unspoken tragedies, and mutual understanding. They looked from one to the other. Words were unnecessary.

Finally, Bricela spoke, her voice soft, "I'll be back as soon as I can."

Kicking her heals into the horse's flank, Bricela took off on a dead run. Riding west out of the plaza, she passed by the whipping post and soon disappeared down Church Street.

Felton watched the dust settle behind her. For the first time he noticed the post at the edge of the plaza. A vision of red-hot steel flashed through his mind. He again felt the searing pain of the brand as it burned his skin. He smelled the stench of his charred flesh.

A wave of suppressed rage slammed into him. "Some things never seem to change," muttered Felton, still staring at the whipping post.

Elias followed Felton's eyes. "It is evil, amigo. Evil is always with us."

"Yeah. But it's time to whittle it down a notch."

Elias looked past the post, then took several steps to his left. "Men are gathering on Congress Street near the saloon. Soon they will have drunk enough courage to come for you."

"Let them have their fill. I've never known a drunk to shoot very straight."

"Do we make a stand in the old Shoo Fly?"

"It'll make as good a fort as any. We have windows on two sides and a door in the back. They can't burn us out and I doubt they'll make a charge. We can hole up until dark if we have to."

Across the square, a family of Mexicans hurried from their flat-roofed adobe and headed for Main Street. The Plaza de las Armas, once the heart of the Mexican presidio, was empty now, a ghost town surrounded by a crumbling wall of mud bricks.

The midday sun bore down on the rooftops and began to scorch the sand in the streets. In an hour, Tucson would be an oven. If the mob was coming, it had to be soon. If they delayed much longer, it would be late afternoon before they made their move.

Walking back to the Shoo Fly, Felton and Elias stood under the sagging *ramada* that shaded the entrance. Elias studied the hole where flying lead once chipped the plaster and exposed the adobe brick beneath.

"Did you ever discover the shooter that left this mark?"

Cradling his rifle, Felton crossed his arms and leaned against the wall. "It was Mosby. I followed his tracks that night. I caught him before he got back to his house. I took the pistol from him."

Elias smiled. "Took it?"

"He was just a scrawny kid then. He's grown some."

"What did you do with it?"

Felton smiled back at Elias. "I put it to good use."

"So I have heard. It was the pistol with eagles, no? The one you still carry?"

"I had it converted to cartridges in seventy-four."

Shaking his head, Elias took out the makings to roll a smoke. "Now you wait here for the sheriff. You wait for him where he tried to kill you, and you will use his own gun to kill him. I think you have the heart of a poet, just like Bricela. You think like her."

"Down deep, maybe," frowned Felton. "But up on top...she's like an angel. I'm pure hell. If it hadn't of been for me, she would have had the life she deserved."

Elias lit his cigarette and took a puff. "You still blame yourself, my friend. It is time to stop. She would want you to stop, I think...if she knew everything."

"No. It's better to leave well enough alone. I don't want her to remember. I don't want to give her any reason to think of that day...ever. No good can come from it. Let her forget as much as she can."

Voices rose and fell in the distance. A cheer went up. Voices grew louder.

"Sounds like they're ready," said Felton, wiping the dust from the front bead of his rifle.

For a moment the two men listened as the mob grew closer. Elias levered a round into the chamber of his Winchester and casually took another puff from his smoke. Felton continued to lean against the wall.

"I think maybe, there are a dozen," offered Elias. "Fifteen or twenty maybe."

"We'll let them see us first. We can duck inside if we have to. I want to see who's in the lead. It's best to kill them first."

"I will follow you, amigo. And cover your back if it comes to that."

"How good a shot are you, Elias?"

"Mucho bueno, amigo. Mucho bueno."

"Most likely, they're coming down Main Street. If they are, they'll be about a hundred yards away when they turn into the plaza. When they see us they'll likely split up. Some will try to come in the back door."

"I will take the back," said Elias. "And some of the side windows too."

The voices grew steadily louder until a solid mass of two dozen men rounded the corner of a distant adobe wall and suddenly came to halt. They stood shoulder to shoulder. In the center and slightly in the lead were Mosby and Turner.

Recognizing Felton, Mosby called out across the plaza. "You're under arrest, Fargo."

"Is that you, Cade?" returned Felton. "It's been a long time since you tried something like this. At least you came in the daylight this time."

For several seconds there was silence. Turner's voice boomed across the old parade grounds.

"You murdered Deputy Drake, Fargo. You tell who ever is with you to get out of the way. We're coming after you!"

"*Hola* amigos," called Elias. "It is me, Jesus Elias. You all know me very well, I think. You know I work for Señora Wetham. The Señora and Con Fargo are friends. The Señora and the Papagos are friends, too. We have sent for them and soon they will come. Maybe we wait for our friends before we come with you."

"Get out of there, Jesus," said Mosby. "Nobody wants to see you get hurt."

269

Before Elias answered, Turner started forward. He took a pistol from his pocket and raised it over his head. "Come on boys, let's get 'em."

Mosby hesitated, then started forward. The mob followed behind but began to spread out. Some ducked inside the nearest adobes. They had taken only a few steps before Turner fired.

Felton and Elias dove inside the Shoo Fly just as lead peppered the walls where they had stood. Elias crawled to a front window and fired four shots rapid fire without taking aim. Felton rolled over onto his stomach and with his rifle barrel only inches from the dirt, fired twice at a man running for cover. When the smoke cleared, the plaza was empty.

Keeping low, Elias went to the open back door. Taking position behind a heavy wood beam, he waited in the shadows. From the darkness he could easily see out the door and one of the windows.

Felton rolled behind the wall. A half-dozen slugs chipped the door jam and drilled the dirt floor next to him. For several seconds a constant barrage of lead smashed harmlessly against the walls of the saloon. A few rounds flew through the windows and exploded clouds of dust as they buried themselves into the soft brick of the back walls.

After the initial volley there was a lull in the gunfire. The men excitedly yelled back and forth. Some were in buildings to the right of the saloon and some to the left, but everyone seemed content to stay where they were. To get closer to the entrance of the saloon, they would have to expose themselves. Even with the liquor inside them, no one was ready to risk death.

Easing back into the shadows, Felton peered out into the blazing sunlight. He rested his rifle barrel across a broken chair and aimed it at a window where blue white gun smoke still hung in the air. He eased back the hammer and rested his finger on the trigger.

He took in a deep breath and let it out slowly. He blinked his right eye to clear it, then looked down the barrel and centered the front bead in the rear sight. A flicker of light appeared just inside the window and Felton squeezed.

The .45-75 roared bellowing flame and smoke. Someone screamed and the firing erupted once again.

Felton scrambled to the safety of the inner walls as the room again filled with lead and dust. Elias fired twice in rapid succession out the door. He ducked behind the beam and rose to his feet. He fired once more out the window and dropped back down again. The firing suddenly ceased.

"You alright?" asked Felton.

"Much better than two of them, I think. And one hombre for you?"

"I at least winged him. One of yours wasn't Mosby was it?"

"No. They were too small. The sheriff will make a big target."

"I doubt he'll show himself. Mosby's yellow. Turner is the one we need to get. I have a feeling he's at the bottom of all of this. Him or men like him. Mosby doesn't have sand enough to run an outfit full of thieves and murderers."

Elias shoved cartridges into his Winchester. "You think Bricela can bring the Army?"

Felton leaned against the wall and replaced the three rounds he had fired. "You recall that Billy the Kid was holed up like this two or three years ago in that Lincoln County War?"

"Yes. Most of those with him died, including old man McSween."

"Well, they were trapped like we are in the McSween house there in Lincoln. Mrs. McSween went to the Army for help just like Briclea. The colonel didn't help her. He could have, but he just let them die on account it was not a military concern."

"So then we must hope the Papagos come to save us."

"What do you think the odds are," asked Felton skeptically. "That Indians are going to come to save a *white* man?"

"They will come, my friend. You forget how Bricela helps them. She is almost one of them. You kill their hated enemy more than any white or Mexican. You are to them Carlos Fuentes, remember? The great killer of the Apache. The Papagos, Caleb…have as many terrible memories about the Apaches as you. They know the legend of Fuentes and they believe Bricela has powerful medicine. You will see."

A voice from outside the saloon broke into their conversation. "Jesus," called the sheriff. "This is Cade Mosby. We've been friends a long time. I got nothing against you. None of us do. Nobody wants to see you dead.

"You come on out with your hands up, and I'll see to it no harm comes to you. You can go on home to your wife, a wife that don't want to be a widow. She's too young to be a widow."

Several seconds passed. Another voiced bellowed across the plaza. "Elias, this is Turner. You know I don't condone lawlessness and bad behavior, but I can only do so much to help you."

Elias grinned and wiped some dust from the barrel of his rifle. "I think," called out Elias. "That you have done enough for me already, today."

Turner responded without hesitation. "Lony was a good friend to some of these men. They don't take kindly to you siding with the man that murdered him.

"I hate to say this Elias, but there's been some vile threats made against your woman. I won't repeat what those men said they would do to her when you're dead…It's too indecent to speak of…you don't want that do you, Elias?

"Come on out. Go home to your wife where you belong."

Felton looked into the shadows where Elias was crouched. He no longer wore a smile. "That's a good speech, Jesus. Something to think about."

Elias snorted. "Turner thinks I am a fool. He believes Mexicans are cowards. If my wife is harmed, many gringo throats will be cut. I have friends too, more than he knows. He forgets, this was once our town. My people survived here fighting the Apache long before any white man saw this land…we know how to kill, too."

"Well, one thing is for certain," said Felton. "They can't let me escape. I know too much…and they'll assume I told you what I know.

"The Ring is making big money. It's far more than just Mosby and Turner. The Indian agency is involved, the grain growers, the teamsters, the rustlers, the store owners in Globe and Soloman. It could go even higher. Maybe all the way back to Washington.

"You, me, and Briclea stand to ruin a lot of powerful folks. Our only hope is to expose them before they can silence us. When the people of the Territory find out who it was that made the Apaches jump the reservation and start another murdering rampage, they'll take the law into their own hands. They won't care who it is."

"So, amigo, it is as you gringos say, we 'root hog or die'."

"That's about the size of it."

Elias slowly stood up behind the beam. "Sheriff Mosby," he called out through the window. "I have an answer for you."

"What is it?"

Guessing which adobe the sheriff's voice had come from, Elias aimed at a window and fired.

Mosby swore as rifles erupted from a dozen windows and doorways on both sides of the plaza. Felton and Elias held their fire and ducked behind the safety of the front wall.

Elias grinned and yelled over the barrage of bullets, "I stirred up the nest."

Felton nodded and traded his rifle for the sawed-off shotgun. "I'll give them something to think about."

Cocking both hammers, Felton scooted underneath a window. Seated with his back against the wall, he raised the shotgun backwards over his head and fired both barrels through the opening. A scream mixed with the roaring of gunfire. The commotion gradually slowed to a stop.

"You brought a canon with you," said Elias.

"This belches eighteen balls at once," replied Felton, dropping two more shells into the shotgun. "They'll think twice about charging us now."

Reaching for the canteen, Elias took a drink. He offered it to Felton. "What do you think they will try next?"

"They'll be wishing they had some dynamite. Do you know if there's any in town?"

"Maybe. Nobody sells it. There is not much mining since the Apaches left the reservation. By tomorrow they could send for some by train."

"We'll get out tonight…one way or the other. We can't hold out any longer than that."

For several minutes Felton and Elias sat listening for a hint of what might come next. Hearing nothing, Felton reached into his saddlebags and took out a round shaving mirror.

Elias looked at him with an unspoken question in his eyes.

"I was a Pinkerton detective for a while. They taught me a few things."

Raising the mirror high enough to clear the window sill, Felton looked into the reflection.

"What do you see?" asked Elias.

Felton turned the mirror from side to side. "Nothing. Nothing at all." Handing the mirror to an impressed Elias, Felton offered, "Have a look for yourself."

Holding up the glass as Felton had done, Elias eagerly scanned the plaza. "I think I like these Pinkertons."

"See anything?"

Elias started to answer, then hesitated. He took the mirror down. "No. But I hear something."

There was a long silence before the Mexican spoke again. "Horses. Many horses. They come slowly now."

"Sounds like there going around the outer walls of the plaza," whispered Felton, reaching for the mirror.

Handing the shotgun to Elias, Felton crawled to the doorway for a better view of the street beyond the adobe houses. Holding out the mirror, he swore softly.

"What is it?" asked Elias.

"Papagos!"

Elias carefully raised his head and peaked out the corner of a window. "They are warriors! Papago warriors!"

Felton rolled onto his side and looked back at Elias. "You can have the honor of telling the sheriff and his gang what they're here for."

"I think by now, Sheriff," called out Elias. "That you see my friends. It is better for you that you stop trying to kill us. They have come for me and they have come for Señor Felton, too. If you shoot us, they kill you for sure."

More than fifty Papagos lined the walls on three sides of the plaza. Each held a rifle as they sat their horses facing the parade ground.

Elias stood. With the shotgun in hand and Felton covering him from the doorway he walked to the edge of an open window. "It is time for you to leave, Sheriff. Caleb and I will go with the Papagos. It is over for today."

"The hell you will," hollered Mosby. "We're not afraid of a bunch of blanket Indians."

"No?" returned Elias. "That is because you have always stayed near town where it is safe. I have seen what they can do. Even the Apaches fear them when they go on the warpath. They are merciless to their enemies."

"You're bluffing, Elias," hollered Turner. "If they harm a white man, the Army will teach them a lesson they'll never forget. They know it as well as I do. Why don't you come out? We got nothing against you."

"Even if I did," said Elias, "It would do no good. They are also here for Caleb Felton. They know him as Fuentes, Sheriff. You know the legend…as do you Señor Turner. The Papagos believe Caleb Felton is Fuentes. They will not permit him to be murdered."

"Felton's the murderer," countered Mosby. "The men with me are all sworn deputies. It's you that's on the wrong side of the law."

Felton caught movement out of the corner of his eye. The Indians at the northwest corner of the plaza were separating.

"Somebody's coming through the Papago lines," said Felton, as he shifted his rifle toward the jostling horses.

First to appear was a mule. On its back rode a man dressed in brown canvas pants and a jacket. On his head was a pith helmet. His face was framed by a stiff gray beard. The butt of a double-barreled shotgun protruded from his saddle scabbard.

Behind the rider came two more. One was Al Sieber, the other Bricela. Following them was a troop of soldiers with carbines slung over their shoulders and dangling by their side.

The column rode to the front of the Shoo Fly and halted. Felton came to his feet and went outside. He walked to the front of the column. Elias grabbed the scattergun and came out of the saloon, but stood in the shade of the *ramada*.

"Good afternoon, General," said Felton.

"Is it?" questioned the man in the pith helmet. "It does not appear so to me, Mr. Fargo. Or should I say, Felton?"

"Fargo will do, sir."

"Mr. Sieber informs me you may wish to be employed once again as a scout. Is this true, Mr. Fargo?"

Felton smiled. "Seems like a good idea. Yes, sir."

"I am also told by Mrs. Wetham, you may have some insight as to why Geronimo and his renegades left the reservation."

"Correct, sir."

The officer straightened in his saddle and raised his voice. "I am General Crook. I am now in command of the Department of Arizona. The man known as Fargo or Felton is now in the employ of the United States Army. I will look with displeasure upon any infringement of his freedom without due process of law."

Turner emerged from an adobe followed by Mosby. As they approached Crook, two dozen others came from scattered buildings around the plaza.

Turner and Mosby stopped a few feet from Felton. They looked up into the steely eyes of an expressionless face.

"This is a civilian matter, General," said Turner forcefully. "You got no jurisdiction here."

Crook glared at Turner for a moment, then glanced at the badge on Mosby's vest. "You would be…Mr. Turner?"

Turner seemed surprised at the mention of his name. "Yea. I'm Turner."

"Mr. Turner…and sheriff, you listen as well…I see close to fifty Indians ready to go to war. If a single shot is fired between these Indians and a white man it will become the concern of the Army and thus within my jurisdiction. I will declare martial law in Tucson and hang whomever I find guilty of instigating trouble."

Crook turned his attention to Felton. "Mr. Fargo, do you wish to accompany the column back to Fort Lowell?"

Felton looked at Turner and Mosby. "No, sir."

"Very well. Report tomorrow morning."

Sieber nudged his mount and came alongside Crook. "If it's all the same to you, General, I'll be staying here a while along with Mrs. Wetham."

Crook nodded and raised his hand. Without a word, the column of men rode to the south. The line of Papagos opened as they neared, then closed behind them as they passed. A cluster of two dozen armed men now occupied the center of the plaza. None of them moved.

Bricela and Sieber dismounted. After tying their horses to the hitch rails in front of the Shoo Fly, they joined Elias and Felton.

"You heard the General," said Mosby. "He said 'due process of law' and I'm the law. You're under arrest."

With the rifle in his hands, Felton stepped away from Bricela. Mosby's pistol was holstered but he too held a rifle.

"Not today, Cade. Not any day by a crooked snake like you."

Mosby's face flushed red.

Felton slowly eased his left hand down to his side. He let the rifle fall into the dirt. Both his hands were near his pistols.

"I got something of yours, Cade. I've been carrying it around for twenty years. How about I give it back to you?"

Turner stepped away from Mosby. "Take him, Sheriff. Do your duty."

Sweat formed on Mosby's forehead. He remembered Caleb Felton. This was Conway Fargo. The killer they called "The Parson" stood less than twenty feet away.

Holding the shotgun, Elias said, "Anybody tries to butt in gets a belly full of lead."

Mosby licked his lips but his tongue was dry. "You'll get a fair trial."

"When was the last time you were in church, Cade?"

The sheriff flinched. "Now wait a minute," he stammered. "I'm no gunman."

"No you're not," said Felton. "You're not a lot of things. If you know any prayers, I'd dig them up and dust them off."

Mosby took a step back. "I'm not fighting you," he said. He took another step backwards. "Everybody knows I don't stand a chance."

"You coward!" snapped Turner. "You got a rifle. Shoot the son-of-a-bitch!"

"If I see you in town after this, Cade," said Felton flatly. "I'll shoot you on sight. If I hear you're anywhere in the Territory, I'll hunt you down and kill you."

Mosby stiffened. He turned his back to Felton. With all eyes on him, he started walking out of the plaza.

"You're finished, Mosby," bellowed Turner. "Do you hear me? You're finished in Tucson!"

Mosby said nothing and soon turned to disappear behind an adobe.

"That leaves you, Turner," said Felton. "You called Mosby a coward. How about you?"

"I don't carry a gun," snipped Turner.

Felton glared at Turner. He was still built like a bull and barely in his forties. His pistol was hidden in his pocket but he was no pistolero. He only used it when he had the drop on his man.

"Al," said Felton. "See if Mr. Turner has a pistol hiding in his trousers. Jesus, you keep your scattergun limbered up in case anyone gets meddlesome."

Making certain not to step between Felton and Turner, Sieber went to Turner and reached into his right pocket.

Taking out a short-barreled revolver, Sieber sneered, "Any fool could see you was heeled, Turner."

Felton unbuckled his gunbelt. "Do you remember the last time we were here, Sergeant? The cavalry rode in just like they did today. In fact they came in from the same direction."

Turner's face was blank for a moment. He watched Felton hand his pistols to Sieber. The big man looked to the northwest corner of the plaza. His eyes narrowed and filled with hatred.

"I remember, Rebel. You was saved by the Army that day, too. If they hadn't a come, I'd of killed you then and there."

Bricela suddenly stepped forward and grabbed Felton's arm. "What do you think you're doing?"

Felton looked at her and smiled. "Don't you see, Bricela. It's all coming back around. It's the end of the circle."

"What are you talking about, Caleb? What's come back around?"

Taking off his hat, Felton handed it to Bricela. "Would you hold this for me?"

Bricela let go of his arm and took the brim of the hat. "You're not...you can't...Caleb, he's too big. He's a beast."

"You ain't changed none, Conway," chided Sieber. "Ain't you gettin' a might old for this?"

"Some," replied Felton. "This started a long time ago. It needs to be finished and there's no better time or place."

Turner's men gathered around him as he grinned hungrily and removed his black suit coat and hat. Some patted him on the back while others laughed at the foolishness of a man that would stand toe-to-toe with the best fighter in Tucson.

Felton removed his Spanish-style jacket and handed it to Elias.

"I think maybe Bricela is right, *amigo*," said Elias. "Turner is too big. He's a brawler. If he gets hold of you, he can break your ribs. I have seen him do it."

Bricela's face flushed red with anger. "You could have gone with General Crook. You still can."

"I owe this man, Bricela," Felton said. "Trust me."

"You'll get hurt. Is it worth getting maimed?"

Only Sieber smiled. Felton squatted and removed his spurs. The sun was directly overhead with the temperature close to one hundred. The air was still and heavy but to a man that lived in the elements it was nothing unusual. Turner was already sweating.

When Felton rose, Sieber took the spurs. He said, "Turner's good with his fists but if he can't get the best of you that way, he'll go to wrastlin'. Don't let him get you down."

"For the last time, Caleb," begged Bricela. "Please. For me."

"Sorry, Bricela. Perhaps you should go. This won't be pretty."

"Maybe I will," snapped Bricela. "Whatever you have against Turner, this isn't the way to deal with it. Violence is not the answer."

Once again, Felton turned and smiled. "My dear Bricela, that depends on the question."

"Now don't be frettin' too much ma'am," said Sieber. "Conway's no tenderfoot."

Felton took two steps toward Turner. The men formed a circle. Several of the Papagos dismounted and came closer. Voices began to rise as Turner started forward.

Felton took another step and planted his feet and raised his fists. Turner would remember their first fight and the cuts over his eyes. He might try to land a few blows but would soon try to use his weight advantage and brute strength. He would be more cautious than he was twenty years ago, but the core of the man remained the same. If Turner got the chance, he would not hesitate to kill.

As soon as Turner was in striking distance, he started swinging with both fists as fast as he could. Felton blocked most of the punches but stumbled and fell backwards several steps. One punch landed and cut the corner of his mouth. He tasted blood but felt no pain.

Felton regained his balance and sidestepped. Turner threw and missed a left jab and a right cross as Felton continued to retreat. The crowd roared. To Felton, the voices sounded muffled and distant. Felton waited for his chance.

For a big man, Turner recovered his feet quickly. He tried an uppercut that narrowly missed Felton's chin. A follow-up hook caught Felton in the ribs and sent him sideways.

Advancing and swinging furiously, Turner pummeled Felton's head and body but could not get past Felton's guard. Felton tripped and fell but was back on his feet before Turner could move in and land a kick to the body or head.

Again Turner charged in but this time Felton ducked, planted his back leg, and buried a right uppercut into Turner's stomach. The thud of his fist sounded as if it had landed in thick mud. Turner hunched over.

Involuntarily, Turner dropped his guard and Felton landed a left cross on the side of Turner's nose. Blood sprayed out of his nostrils.

Turner hesitated but raised his guard. The punch to the gut took some of his wind. Sweat dripped from his face. He needed more air.

Felton faked a left jab. He landed another right under Turner's elbows. Turner flinched and dropped his arm to protect his side. A left hook opened a gash under his eye.

Turner roared and reached for Felton's neck. Felton dodged but Turner's thumb hooked the leather strap around Felton's neck. Something white flew into the air and landed in front of Bricela.

For an instant Bricela took her eyes off the brawling men and glanced down at the object that caught her eye. It was an inch in diameter with a hook on the back. It lay face down in the dirt with the broken leather still threaded through the hook.

Reaching down, she grasped the brooch in the palm of her hand. She stood quickly and focused her attention on the fight. In the time it took to stoop down and stand again the crowd had moved away from her. The circle was steadily moving toward the edge of the plaza.

Bricela opened her hand. Seeing the two eagles scrimshawed into the ivory pendant, she gasped. The ivory Felton wore was identical to the brooch he gave her twenty years ago. At the time, Old Solomon said the brooch was one of a kind but somehow Felton had found another like it or had one made from memory. He wore it around his neck, concealed under his shirt.

Unable to take her eyes from the ivory, Bricela looked at it more closely. It was yellow with age and the scrimshaw had faded. She started to wipe sand from the eagles but a vicious roar from the mob broke her attention. She closed her fist around the brooch and frantically ran toward Caleb.

A huge left fist glanced off Felton's elbow and slammed into his ribs. He felt one crack and spun away from a wide right that would have broken his jaw. Turner's right eye was swelling shut. Felton feigned a left then a right and viciously hooked back with his left.

Turner staggered to the side. No blood appeared over the open eye. Breathing in gasps, he spread his arms wide and suddenly lunged. This time he caught Felton backing up. He buried his shoulder into Felton's stomach and locked his thick arms behind his back.

Felton was lifted into the air. Before Turner could throw him to the ground Felton opened his hands and slapped both palms against Turner's ears. Turner screamed but his grip did not loosen. He raised Felton high and threw him onto his back.

Rolling away immediately, Felton narrowly escaped a boot heel that could have crushed his skull. Turner was trying to kill him.

Pivoting on his elbow, Felton sprang to his feet and backpedaled quickly as Turner charged again. Felton hit something hard. He stumbled around the wiping post.

For a split second both men glanced at the post. Turner's single eye flared. Felton's eyes narrowed. He took two steps backward allowing Turner to advance.

Turner took one step, then another. It was far enough.

Turning quickly, Felton side-kicked the big sergeant just under the heart with the heel of his boot. Turner doubled over with both arms clutching his stomach. His mouth hung open trying to suck air.

Felton planted his feet and put all his weight into an uppercut that caught Turner on the point of his chin.

Turner raised straight up and stiffened. His eyes rolled to the top of his forehead. He seemed to fall slowly at first. He picked up speed as he neared the ground. The back of his skull crashed into the base of the whipping post. The bones in his neck popped. Turner's feet twitched. A gurgle hissed from his lungs.

The jeers and cheers of the spectators slowly died. A lone onlooker went to Turner and bent down next to him. "Why, he's dead. His neck is broke. Turner's dead!"

Still holding the sawed-off shotgun, Elias shoved his way into the stunned circle of men and stood next to Felton. "It's over. You all saw what happened. It was a fair fight."

Sieber joined Elias. His hand rested on the grips of his pistol. "It's hot boys, too hot. Why don't you all go back to the saloon and have a cold glass of beer? There ain't nothin' more to do here today. Like the man said, it's over and done with."

While the men of Tucson stood speechless, the Papagos solemnly filed out of the plaza. Several turned in their saddles and stared admiringly back at Felton. Bricela went to an elderly Indian that remained in the center of the plaza and spoke to him.

Before the warriors were out of sight, a few of the posse turned and walked away. Those that remained huddled in small groups. They swore amongst themselves, muttering vague threats of revenge but soon joined the others. In a matter of minutes the plaza was empty.

Bricela shook hands with the last Papago to leave. She joined the three men at the whipping post. She avoided looking at the body.

"I need to speak to you, Caleb."

"That better wait ma'am," said Sieber. "We best get back to Fort Lowell and let those men cool off. Some of 'em are pretty sore."

"I agree," said Elias. "We are not safe here. Bricela, you should go home and wait. I will come for you when it is safe. You and Caleb can talk then."

Felton glared at the sergeant sprawled at the base of the whipping post. He put a hand on his broken rib. "They're right, Bricela."

Looking grimly down the street toward town, Bricela nodded, "Alright. Don't be too long. It is important...to both of us."

CHAPTER 16

When Jesus Elias left Fort Lowell, he laid his Winchester across the front of his saddle. Turner had a town full of friends and they would want revenge, at least until the whisky wore off. A glance at the cloudless sky told him less than an hour remained before the sun set behind the peaks of the Sierra Tucsons. General Crook was still talking to Felton when he rode from the post. Felton had promised to be along before dark.

Avoiding the center of Tucson for the time being, Elias galloped west until he hit the Santa Cruz River, then followed it north and entered town by Pearl Street. Riding to the Mexican part of town, he stopped at a cousin's house, then went into one of the few remaining Mexican cantinas and ordered mescal.

Sitting in the dim light, he waved off the occasional fly and stared thoughtfully out into the street. His cousin would go the Palace and then the Congress Hall Saloon. He would listen to what was being said of the shootout and the fight. If tempers were still hot, Felton would have to stay at the fort.

Sheriff Mosby had been faced down and called a coward. He likely had left town. Turner was dead. He was well liked in Tucson and had many friends that might want revenge. Turner was also part of a ring of thieves and murderers that would want Felton silenced.

Elias shook his head and scratched his jaw. This was a day like no other. Caleb Felton had returned for this moment. It was his destiny. Perhaps he was also fulfilling the destiny of others. A man could live his whole life and never see a miracle. But today, with the death of Turner at the foot of the whipping post, surely the hand of God was passing over Tucson.

Elias took a sip of mescal and felt the burn go down his throat. What was to become of Caleb Felton? Would he continue his life as Conway Fargo? Had he changed so much over the years that he *was* Conway Fargo?

283

What of Bricela? The secret pain she carried had forever altered the path of her life. Did she love Caleb Felton as she once did? Did he still love her? Was there never to be peace for the two of them?

The doorway of the cantina darkened. A young man hurried to the side of Elias. He spoke in whispered Spanish. "The gringos do not speak of revenge, Jesus. They are too drunk now to be of trouble to you. It is to them, just another killing in Tucson. They speak of the skill of Señor Fargo with his fists and of the death of Turner. Some say it was luck that Fargo won, some say no. Some say if not for the Papagos they would have killed you, but now you and Fargo are protected by the Army. I think you are safe for now."

"What of the sheriff?"

"Gone. They laugh at him. Some say they will kill him themselves. They are drunk and brave because of it."

Elias thanked his cousin and finished his drink. It was time to give Caleb's message to Bricela. Felton would be leaving soon and be gone for days if not weeks. It would be his last chance to speak with her before he left.

Outside the cantina, Elias untied his stallion and swung into the saddle. Before he reined the horse around, he heard a voice from a second story window across the street.

"Hold on, Jesus," said a man leaning out of a room above the post office. "I have a letter for Mrs. Wetham. It's been here for a week. It's come all the way from back east. Could be important. With all that's going on in town, you might want to take it to her."

Elias rode across the street as the postmaster went downstairs. A moment later a short bald man appeared with a letter in his hand. "Don't normally do this, but seeing how you work for Mrs. Wetham, I figure it's alright. Personally, me and my Mrs. are of the opinion that Turner got what was coming to him."

Taking the letter, Elias looked curiously at it. "You say this has been here a week?"

"Yep. I thought it was mighty peculiar Mrs. Wetham didn't come by. Not like her at all. She ain't been sick I hope."

Elias shook his head. Felton had also arrived one week ago. "No. She is not sick. I will give it to her. *Gracias.*"

Nudging the horse up Pearl Street and past the western wall of the old plaza, Elias studied the envelope carefully. He held it up to the sun and was able to see some of the writing. Letting his reins drop, he pressed the paper tightly between his thumbs and fingers and held it up again. The signature of Marcus Wetham was unmistakable.

Tucking the letter behind his belt, Elias swore. It was not a good time for Bricela to get a letter from her husband. A few more hours and Felton and Bricela would meet along the Santa Cruz River. After that, Felton would leave on a scout with the Army. Whatever was destined to happen at sundown would then be over. She could read the letter afterwards.

Elias frowned and shifted uncomfortably in his saddle. But the letter *had* been given to him. Now it was on its way to Bricela and unless he interfered, she would have it in minutes. If only he had not stopped at that cantina or come out at that precise moment, there would be no letter. Was it fate that he was given the letter? Was it his place to hand her the letter or was it fate that he should keep it from her?

Turning off of Pearl and crossing Main, Elias came to Bricela's house. After dismounting and tying his horse, he removed the letter with one hand and made the sign of the cross with the other.

"Madre de Dios," he said, knocking on the front door.

The heavy door opened quickly. "Elias, is everything alright? How is Caleb?"

"All is well," answered Elias. He did not notice the American style dress she wore or the ivory brooch around her neck. "They wrapped his ribs. He will recover. He says he will meet you at the tree at sundown. He tells me you will know what that means."

"Oh, I do," said Bricela anxiously. "Anything else?"

"He must leave this night. General Crook has been speaking to Caleb for a long while. The general asks many questions about The Ring of Tucson and what Caleb discovered at the reservation. Crook wishes to go to San Carlos and speak to the agent and to the Apaches. They will leave for a night march shortly after sundown. You will not have much time."

"Very well," said Bricela. She looked at the letter Elias held. "Did he write me a letter?"

Elias shrugged. "No. The postmaster gave this to me. He said it has been here for a week. He was surprised you had not been by so he gave it to me." Elias sighed and held out the letter. "It is for me...to give to you."

Bricela took the letter and immediately recognized the handwriting. Her heart jumped and her stomach twinged. "It's from my husband...I...I have been so busy."

"I know you have had much to think about, Bricela. I also knew the letter came from Mr. Wetham. I did not want to give it to you. Not today. But...but it is not for me to interfere. The path of this day must be followed to the end."

With her heart pounding, Bricela's eyes filled with uncertainty. "You are right, Elias. You are so very right."

"Will you need the buckboard to go to the place of the tree?" asked Elias.

"No, I have my horse. It's not far. It is a tree we found years ago. The trunk is shaped like a Z."

Elias' head jerked up. "Did you say a Z? The tree is like a Z?"

Bricela looked up from the letter. "What is it?"

"Madre de Dios," whispered Elias. "Madre de Dios."

"Elias, what's wrong?"

"You will see soon enough," said Elias as he turned and went to his horse. Swinging into the saddle he looked back. "This day, it is time for you to see. Vaya con Dios, Bricela."

Bricela slowly closed the door. Elias had always known *something*. No matter how often she asked, he would never tell her what it was. He guarded his secret closely. Now she knew it had to do with Caleb Felton. The ivory brooch with eagles scrimshawed into it had to somehow fit into the mystery.

Had Caleb carved the brooch himself? When he returned to Tucson on the day of her wedding, had he gone back to Soloman and asked him to make another? However it was done, the brooch she once owned had been meticulously reproduced and apparently worn for years. Caleb Felton may have become Conway Fargo, but a man would not have kept such a keepsake unless it meant a great deal to him.

Caleb had seemed cool toward her when they met a week ago. He had made no mention of the intimate poem she had sent with her letter. His cavalier attitude about their reunion angered her, yet she had behaved no differently. Perhaps neither of them knew what to expect of the other or how to act. It had been twenty years and even then they had only known each other a short time.

Walking into the parlor, Bricela remembered where he stood when she first saw him. There was something between them the moment they saw each other. Was he now keeping his distance because she was married? Or had she changed so much he suddenly lost interest? She was hardly the girl he fell in love with so long ago. Did he wear the brooch from habit or merely as a good luck charm?

Bricela clutched the small buckskin medicine bag that hung around her neck. There were undeniable similarities between it and the brooch Caleb wore but the gift from Owl Woman was more than a charm. The medicine in it was real. At least at times it was.

She was only fifteen when Caleb was a Confederate lieutenant but they *were* in love. That was not imaginary. From the beginning, without a word being spoken, both of them knew. It was a young and tender relationship but he must have understood as she did, it was to be an endless one. The attraction was immediate and the bond between them seemed unbreakable. It was a love shrouded in a mist of timeless familiarity. It defied all explanation.

If she had only known of the brooch he was wearing, their second meeting would have been so different. There was but one chance in a lifetime for such a meeting and, for the most part, it had been a disappointment. Instead of a long-anticipated embrace between dear friends, the two of them might as well have been total strangers.

Feeling a twinge of guilt, Bricela studied the letter in her hand. She turned it over in her hand. Her brow furrowed. A sense of dread enveloped her. She did not want to open the letter, at least not until she talked to Caleb. What she had to say did not concern her husband…Or did it?

Bricela paced back and forth. Marcus was a good man. He had been a good husband and she would do her best to honor her marriage to him. Besides the brooch, there were other matters she needed to discuss with Caleb Felton. She could not spend the rest of her life wondering why he never wrote, why he refused to contact her. He was back in her life and she could finally get answers to questions that had haunted her thoughts and plagued her dreams for two decades.

Folding the letter, Bricela tucked it under her blouse and inside the waistband of her skirt. Whatever Marcus Wetham had to say could wait a few more minutes. She owed herself that much.

Straddling her horse, Bricela pulled her skirt down to cover her legs. Women in town gossiped about how she rode a horse. She didn't care what they thought. Most of them were tenderfeet and knew nothing of the Territory or of its cruelty. She was a veteran. She had endured the harsh years before the railroad ushered newcomers into Tucson on slick steel rails. They could go to hell.

Nudging her mount toward the Santa Cruz River, Bricela turned on Main and into the setting sun. The air was heavy but the intensity of the heat was beginning to subside. It would be cooler by the river's edge where Caleb would meet her.

She thought of his face when Turner was pronounced dead at the foot of the whipping post. Caleb was more than shocked. He seemed awestruck.

Seeing men dead on the streets of Tucson was nothing unusual but none had died like Turner. Some were hung, but none had broken their necks in a fall. The whipping post was a monument to man's cruelty. It should have been removed years ago but it was also a reminder that some good remained in the world.

Carlos Fuentes had saved her life and her honor. To protect her, he had been falsely accused of a crime and horribly branded while lashed at the post. It was a terrible story yet a beautiful one.

Turner was a vile man and deserved his fate. Caleb had risked his life to defend her and there in the midst of it all, stood the despised post. It was becoming a symbol of her life's story, a pattern of tragedy and triumph that continually repeated itself.

Fuentes was a fragmented memory, a hand that held her, a shoulder to lean on and a kind voice. Even Owl Woman could not describe him. Caleb was a clear memory that never faded. Now he was back.

Riding past the long adobe that used to be Soloman's store, Bricela thought of the ivory brooch she was wearing. Caleb had purchased the original one there and surprised her with it before he left.

What had happened to him? What had happened to the both of them? At fifteen, she had been certain they were destined to be together. Nothing could have been further from the truth.

What would Caleb say about the brooch? How would he explain it? Would he say he wore it to remind himself of the young woman he once loved? Would he admit it? If he still had feelings for her, would he confess them? Would she confess hers?

Even in the heat, Bricela felt her face flush as she reined in her horse and dismounted by the side of the road. Leading her horse, she followed a short path and tied her mare to a nearby cottonwood. Her heart raced when she saw the bent tree. He would be there soon and they would face another goodbye. It should be different. They both deserved more out of life than what they had been given.

Bricela unbuttoned the top button of her dress and wiped her forehead. It seemed to be getting hotter. To cool off she paced back and forth. The sun would set in a few minutes bringing the evening breeze to stir the air. She would soon be alone with her first love. They would stand under their special tree along the banks of Santa Cruz to say goodbye for who knew how long. Perhaps, if it seemed appropriate, they should kiss.

"Get a hold of yourself," muttered Bricela, then suddenly remembered her husband's letter.

Reaching for the letter in her waistband, Bricela once again felt a sensation of foreboding. Her fingers ran across the edge of the envelope. She took her hand away. Something was wrong. It could wait. She would read the letter after Caleb had gone. It had been twenty years. They deserved a few moments alone, at least one sunset together.

Bricela gazed at the western horizon and waited anxiously. The lower rim of the sun dipped behind the mountain peaks. A twig snapped behind her. She did not turn.

"Caleb?"

"Yes."

"Thank you for coming."

Felton stood beside her, watching the sunset. "It's a beautiful evening."

Bricela turned and glanced at Felton. He was wearing an Army hat and a new jacket with lieutenant's bars. "Yes, it is," she said.

Felton shrugged. "General Crook thought the uniform might turn a bullet or two when I rode back through town."

Bricela cocked her head to one side. She smiled. "Why, you look perfectly handsome...Lieutenant Felton."

Looking at Bricela, Felton grinned. "I haven't been called that in quiet a while."

"Lieutenant or Felton?"

"Either one. Hardly anyone knows who I used to be.

"I suppose not," said Bricela. "I have not forgotten."

"Neither did I."

"I have something of yours, something I need to return."

"What would that be?"

Watching Felton closely, Bricela said softly, "I…I'm wearing it."

Felton blinked. His eyes first went to the medicine bag, then up to the brooch. His face paled. He took a step back. His eyes flared with shock, then narrowed into slits.

"It came off during the fight. I picked it up."

Felton stared at the brooch. He said nothing.

"I'm sorry to say that I lost the one you gave me," continued Bricela. "You remembered what it looked like. How did you do it?"

Unable to take his eyes off the brooch, Felton managed, "Do what?"

"Did you have Soloman make a second one…a duplicate?"

Wiping his dry lips with the back of his hand, Felton looked questioningly at Bricela. He waited for her to speak again.

"Before I give it back to you," said Bricela sincerely. "I wish you would tell me why you wore it…please."

Felton's face twisted with concern. "Bricela…that brooch…that brooch… doesn't belong to me. It's not mine."

"Of course it is, Caleb." Bricela took hold of the brooch and lifted it with her fingertips. "Take a closer look. "It came off during…during the fight."

"Bricela, please."

"Well, didn't it?"

Felton hesitated. "Yes, Bricela. Yes it did."

"Well if it's not yours," asked Bricela, her voice weakening with doubt. "Whose is it?"

Felton swallowed hard. He said nothing.

Bricela lowered her head and began untying the ribbon that held the brooch. "It looks just like the one you gave me. I remember it looking like this one. The same shape…with the same two eagles."

Felton put his hand on Bricela's to stop her. "Bricela, the brooch is yours."

"No. I can't accept it. I was foolish to think…"

"Bricela," interrupted Felton. "It has *always* been yours."

Bricela's hands stopped working at the knot. She slowly raised her head. The last of the sun's rays illuminated the blue in her eyes. At first they framed a question, then suddenly reflected the awakening of a terrible nightmare. "Oh, my God," she whispered. "Oh, dear God, no. No! It can't be."

Facing Felton, Bricela stared incomprehensibly into his eyes. After several heartbeats and with her voice quivering, she managed to say, "Caleb Felton?" She shook her head. "Conway Fargo...Carlos Fuentes?" She closed her eyes tightly, then slowly opened them. "Conway...Carlos...Caleb?"

Taking a step closer, she raised her trembling fingers to the top button of Felton's shirt and unbuttoned it. "Please don't be there," she whimpered. Her hands stopped and rested on Felton's chest. "Please." Tears rolled down her cheeks.

"Please...don't be there," she sobbed. She opened the second button and slid her hands to the third. "Could I... how could I... have been such a fool?"

"Bricela," said Felton, once again placing his hands on hers. "Don't."

"I have to know," pleaded Bricela. She pulled the third button free.

He let go of her hands. She carefully spread the shirt apart. She saw the edge of the ugly scar and gasped. Taking an involuntary step back she placed both hands over her mouth and stared in horror.

Pulling his shirt together, Felton took Bricela by the shoulders. "It's alright, Bricela. It's alright."

Bricela shook her head and sobbed. She could not take her eyes off Felton's chest.

Shaking Bricela gently, Felton said again, "It's alright. It's over."

"It was you. All these years. All those long years it was you."

"Yes, Bricela."

"For so long I...I wished...how I *wished* it would have been you that had saved me...and now...Oh my God. What have I done?"

"You've done nothing, Bricela. You've done nothing at all."

"Oh but I have. I have. Sometimes...sometimes I hated you for not being there for me. I hated you, Caleb. You left me...you left me alone and never came back. But you didn't. Oh, Caleb. How could you? How could you not tell me?"

Still holding Bricela's shoulders, Felton answered, "Two reasons. I wasn't good enough for you. Not back then."

"Don't say that, Caleb. Yes you were."

"The second reason was more selfish. When I left you with Owl Woman that awful day, I had hopes that in time...we might meet again.

If we did, I wanted you to be able to look at me and not wonder what I was thinking. As far as you and I were concerned, I wanted you to be free of it, as if it never happened.

"It was the best I could do for you, Bricela. It was my fault."

"Your fault?"

"You were on your way to see Owl Woman that day. You had questions about us. If it hadn't been for me you would never have gone."

"How do you know that, Caleb?"

"I just know, Bricela. If that were not enough, I fell asleep at Picacho Pass on my way back from spying on the Yankees. If I hadn't, I would have caught you before you left for the mission."

"It was nobody's fault, Caleb. Nobody's. It just happened."

Felton let go of Bricela. "I've always wanted to say...dearly wanted to tell you how sorry I was. To tell you how much I felt your pain...and your loss. I've carried it with me every day."

There was a moment of silence. The breeze caressed Bricela's hair and rustled the leaves in the trees along the banks of the Santa Cruz.

"How do you see me now, Caleb? Now that we both know."

"Nothing has changed. Not for me. I feel the same as the first day I saw you."

"I have changed, Caleb. I had to. I'm not the girl you fell in love with."

Felton smiled faintly. "You can change how you dress. You can change how you live but you...you have not changed."

Bricela looked down. "I wish I could believe that. Since that day...I've never felt the same. Never."

Felton reached out and raised her chin. When her eyes met his he smiled. "You will always be Bricela Verde to me. Always. Only now you are also Bricela Wetham. You've grown up some. That's all."

Forcing a smile of her own, Bricela asked weakly, "What now, Caleb? What do we do now?"

Glancing at the sunset, Felton saw that only a sliver of the sun remained above the mountain peaks.

"I'm not sure. Right now I'm going to do something I've been waiting twenty years to do."

Knowingly, Bricela tilted her head back. "What would that be...Lieutenant Felton?'

Taking Bricela by the shoulders, Felton pulled her against him. "This, Miss Verde." He gently kissed her as the last sunrays vanished from the day.

Their lips parted slowly. Bricela wrapped her arms around Caleb. For several heartbeats they shared an evening that was long overdue.

Behind them, Felton's stallion blew and pawed the ground. Bricela brushed a strand of hair from her face.

"I should be going," said Felton. "I have to catch up with General Crook."

"When will you be back?"

"I don't know. I'm assigned to Fort Lowell. I'll only be four miles away if you should need me for anything."

"Before you go, I have something for you. It…it is something of yours."

"Mine? Did I lose something else?"

Bricela untied the medicine bag from around her neck. "It's nothing you lost."

"Didn't you tell me that if I know what's in that bag, your medicine will lose its power?"

"I have my brooch back and you are here in Tucson. This medicine has served its purpose."

Reaching into the pouch with her fingers, Bricela brought out two eagle talons tied together with sinew. "Hold these, please," she said, handing the claws to Felton.

"Is this it?"

"No," replied Bricela, gazing intently at Felton. "Those…those have yet to work."

Reaching deeper, Bricela slid out a small object and hid it in her hand. She took the talons and replaced them in the bag.

"Keep your hand out, Caleb, and open it."

Felton hesitated.

"Please."

Felton extended his palm and waited as Bricela carefully laid her closed fist on his. Her eyes brightened expectantly. "I always wondered why it gave me such comfort," she said as she withdrew her hand revealing an ivory figurine. "Now I know."

The sight of the tiny mermaid caused Felton to wince. The memory of a scratched, bruised, and bloody young woman flashed across his mind.

"I believed Carlos Fuentes gave that to me. I knew it had a meaning but I could never figure it out. Until today...the message escaped me."

Felton looked up. "What does the lady that lives in the big water tell you?"

"You remember? You remembered what Owl Woman said?"

"I remembered that part of it. It seemed to fit into what she had said. A man named Soleil carved it from...well, it's ivory like your brooch. That seemed to fit somehow, too.

"I quit trying to explain all the little things years ago...you know, the coincidences...I don't deny they exist. They're just there."

"Don't you believe in signs, Caleb? In destiny?"

"Signs? No. I don't put much stock in them. Not like the Indians do anyway. Destiny...I think life is what you make of it."

Slowly shaking her head Bricela smiled.

Felton shrugged half-heartedly and looked out into the desert. "What was it about the mermaid you were going to tell me?"

"You gave it to me," sighed Bricela. "As a symbol of an impossible relationship, of an unfulfilled love. You gave it to me to say we could never be together. That is what you would have told me when you came back from spying, isn't it?"

Felton frowned. "I was hellbent back then. If not for you I still would be. Then I met you. For the first time in a long while I wanted to do what was best for someone besides myself...I wanted what was best for you. I wanted to protect you. I made up my mind to finally do something honorable and decent for a change.

"Yes. That is what I was going to tell you. You're right about the meaning of the mermaid. And of course, you see how it turned out."

Bricela looked over Felton's shoulder to the eastern horizon. The evening star was bright and rising. "You were spying for the Confederacy. Did you use the name Carlos Fuentes then?"

"Yes. I looked the part and spoke Spanish. It was a good disguise."

"They branded you at the whipping post. Was it for being a spy?"

"It was that or be hung."

"May I see the scar again?"

Felton's eyes narrowed. "Why?"

"Please, Caleb."

Reluctantly, Felton pulled his shirt open.

Bricela starred at the brand for several seconds. She looked into Felton's eyes and waited for an explanation.

"They were in a hurry to make the brand. They got it backwards."

"You don't believe in signs, Caleb? You were marked for life with a Z!"

Felton closed his shirt and started buttoning it closed. "I used to wonder about that too. It doesn't mean a thing, Bricela, unless it proves God has a sense of humor."

Bricela suppressed another smile. "It's getting late. The sooner you leave the sooner you can return. We have a lot to catch up on."

With Bricela close by his side, Felton walked to his horse and untied the reins. "I suppose I'll have to wait another twenty years to kiss you again."

Bricela smiled as Felton swung into his saddle. The sky was crimson. A warm wind blew across the desert from the south.

"Come back soon, Caleb."

"I will," said Felton, breaking into a gallop. "This time I will."

Still smiling, Bricela watched Caleb Felton ride into the sunset and saw him vanish into the twilight. Her eyes lingered until the last dust from the stallion's hooves was swept away by the wind.

Taking the letter from her waist, she tore open the envelope. Before she read the first line she knew what it said.

My Dearest Bricela,

You have always been such a dutiful wife, I can scarcely conceive how to write you such a letter.

Bricela stopped reading. She let the wind pluck the letter from her fingers and carry it away.

Turning back to the Santa Cruz River, Bricela gazed across the water and into the desert. As Owl Woman taught her, she waited for the medicine to come. A gentle breeze ushered in the starlight. She listened to the evening stillness. The moment embraced her and then she heard it. Placing her hand on the ivory brooch, she smiled and whispered a name.

"Robespierre."

www.ingramcontent.com/pod-product-compliance
Lightning Source LLC
Chambersburg PA
CBHW020558260626
47157CB00003B/762